LEAH BEACH

To Those Who Wait

This book was professionally typeset on Reedsy.
Find out more at reedsy.com

Contents

Acknowledgement

This book would never have made it out of my brain and onto the page without the incredible outpouring of love and support that I received from so many people throughout this process. First off, thank you so much to Angela, my best friend, my rock and every good thing about my characters. When you can walk up to a friend at work one night and say, "Hey I think I'm going to write a book," and they literally start crying, you know you're going to be supported. Angela, you kept me on task and kept me pushing through even when I thought I might quit. Thank you.

Second, thank you to my reader/picky editor, Kirstan. You found all of my little mistakes that would have driven me crazy on yet another re-read. You saw me through this process with so much love and your excitement kept me going through the hard times.

Nick, you got the dedication, but I would hate to miss an opportunity to thank you one more time. You are the best cheerleader and even though you'll probably never make it through this book, you supported me through the writing. And everyone thanks you for that.

To my parents, Jeff and Vicki, thank you for letting me kill the parents of the protagonist and not taking it personally. Thank you for reading the first two chapters and then being patient for the rest of it. Thank you for encouraging my creativity and not letting me quit things when they got hard.

Without my hospital work crew, I would have never finished this book. Every time I came to work, I was asked "Are you done with your book yet?", and look guys, I finally am! Thank you all.

Chapter 1

Lexa

Sunday

And......there, I exhale. I turn back and forth, checking my reflection in my water-spotted mirror. I make a mental note to clean that when I get off shift tomorrow. I sigh, but decide if I can't see my new mountain of a zit under this concealer then no one else can either.

Tonight's my last shift for a week because it's wedding week! Yay! Not mine of course. Ansley's. But as maid of honor, it honestly feels more hectic than I imagine my own wedding would. I'm running a bit late, as usual. My hair thrown up in a scrunchie bun on my head, my only makeup the concealer over Mount Pimple. But it'll have to do. If I have any chance of stopping for coffee on the way, I have to leave now. And without coffee, I'd be better off calling out sick.

Luckily for me, my favorite coffee shop is on my street. I always wonder if the coffee is really the best in the city or if it's just the convenience that makes it taste that way.

I wave hi to Mrs. Reynolds as I walk out of my building, she's always coming in from work as I'm leaving.

"You just look cute as a button in those scrubs, Lexa baby. It's a wonder one of those handsome doctors hasn't snatched you up yet," Mrs. Reynolds says as I show off my new navy set.

"You know I'm too good for them anyway, Mrs. R," I respond quickly. False confidence is my go-to defense mechanism in these never-ending conversations. Every dinner with friends. All of my well-meaning and very nosy elderly neighbors. Even my charge nurse and best friend, Ansley. I know they all mean it as a compliment, but continually being asked why I'm still single feels a lot like asking me to list my worst qualities and what specifically makes me unattractive for a long-term relationship to the opposite sex.

Now don't get me wrong, I've had plenty of relationships. Well, like, a healthy amount of relationships. I dated a few guys in high school, none of them really ever seemed interested in what I wanted. I dated a guy for a while in college, who was too interested in what I didn't want.

Now here I am, twenty-seven years old, living with a handsome, black-haired beast that loves a good cuddle. His only problem being that he will not learn to feed himself and I'm constantly having to clean up after him. All in all though, Sneakers *is* a pretty great cat.

I'm self-aware enough to see that maybe the problem all along has been that I don't even know what I want. Ask me today and I want to settle down with a nice guy and raise a sweet family–of cats and dogs. But ask me next week and

I'll say that I can't ever see myself leaving my night shift job at the hospital and can only really entertain fun, simple relationships right now.

As Ansley always reminds me, "How is a guy going to know what you want from your relationship when you don't even know for yourself?" Yes, of course she's right. She's always right. But how am I supposed to just *know*? It's different for her. She and Landon met so early on in college, they were able to have fun and still have the serious conversations that an adult relationship requires. I feel like now, with online dating and quick meets and, let's face it, a total apathy towards "finding your soulmate," it's next-to-impossible to have both.

Just last week, I met up with a CupidSays match that seemed like my perfect date. His profile said he also plays pick-up soccer in Forsyth Park, we have the same taste in books and he even has a cat. Perfection. However, in reality, we had *literally nothing* to talk about. Sure, we hit the high points of where ya from, whaddya do...then *BAM!* Proverbial brick wall.

I mean, yeah, he was nice to look at. At least the pictures weren't a lie. However, I would bet my last ten dollars that that man has not read a book over 25 pages in the last three years. This man had the audacity to say his favorite book was *To Kill A Mockingbird* and then ask if I was talking about a dog when I brought up Scout. It just simply would not do. We didn't meet up for a second date.

I've tried—too many times to count—to explain the intricacies of dating as an adult to someone who hasn't been on a first date since she was 19. Things have changed on the dating landscape in the last decade. We're no longer living in the era of *The Notebook* and *Titanic*. Nowadays, it's more like *Naked and Afraid*.

Wow, this wedding sure is bringing up some doomed thoughts for me. That's enough of the pity party for one day.

Don't get me wrong, I am over-the-moon excited for Ansley and Landon and this is going to be a very fun week. We get to see a bunch of our friends from college. I definitely can't wait to see Claire and Weston from nursing school. I haven't seen them since our class got together for a mini-reunion a couple of years ago. Last I heard, Claire had left the ICU to start CRNA school. Weston is an OR nurse and absolutely loves it. I don't know that I'd like to see that many internal organs a day, but to each their own. As an ER nurse, if something is outside of your body that is supposed to be inside your body–intestines, bones or babies–you're leaving our unit to go somewhere else.

Claire, Weston, Kristen and Grace should all be getting in tomorrow with everyone else arriving either Tuesday or Wednesday. With the rehearsal dinner on Friday night and the wedding Saturday, that still gives us plenty of time for catching up. The best man flies in on Tuesday night from Chicago. As part of my maid of honor duties, I have graciously agreed to pick him up from Hilton Head International. It wouldn't feel like such a chore if the best man weren't also my college ex. Luckily, we ended on good terms and we can be friends now. Ansley likes to point out that relationships that end amicably never contained any true passion to begin with. In college, I might have argued against that, but looking back I can see what she means. We never really fought about anything because I never saw a future with us worth fighting for. As harsh as that sounds, it's the truth and that's all I'm really interested in right now.

I'm so far into this train of thought, I walk right past the door of the coffee shop. I whirl around and head back toward the smell of heavenly bean water. Hopefully, this brew will bring me back to the land of the living so I can keep others from leaving it.

Outstretched hand on the door to head in, I notice a flyer on the glass for a music festival in Atlanta a couple months from now. Skimming the lineup, I see several names I would pay good money to see play live. With my other hand I whip out my phone to check my work schedule for that month, maybe I'm already off that weekend. If not, I could probably find coverage this far out. Phone in hand, I stride to the counter, ready to place my usual order. There's a new barista behind the counter. Just my luck, when I need my guy Mike to already be whipping up my large cowboy coffee with an extra espresso shot and a dash of caramel, I have to explain my order and give my name. I watch as the new girl–whose name tag shows Cindy with a little curlicue off the "y"–slowly writes my order in barista shorthand on the side of the cup. I try to discreetly check my watch. By the exasperated look on her face, I fail to be sneaky. She then asks for my name. "Lexa," I say and try to smile politely so she knows that I am, in fact, a nice person underneath my chronic RBF. She timidly returns the smile and writes on the cup again.

After paying and tipping, I move to a deserted corner to continue planning my weekend in September. It looks like I am off that weekend. *Sweet,* I think and then cringe at my own unspoken word choice. We've been seeing too many drunk teenagers in the ER recently and their vernacular is rubbing off on me. Mentally rolling my eyes at myself, I continue to scroll the list of performers, checking off the ones I'm unfamiliar with. As with every music festival, they'll probably create an online playlist so you can listen to songs from the bands and singers you haven't heard before. There's only a few I can't name at least one song for and I'm becoming more and more convinced I need to buy tickets for this. I would love to bring a friend but I know Ansley is not a fan of festivals. Maybe Amanda would be interested. I'll have to check with her and I'm pretty sure she'll be at work tonight.

"Alexa?" I hear my often used misnomer called across the room. I make my way to the counter. As I'm reaching out for my cup, a polite smile again stretching my lips, I say, "It's just Lexa."

"Sorry, I'm new here," Cindy apologizes.

"It's oka-"

"Don't worry, she's used to it," a deep and familiar voice cuts in from behind me. I spin around to face him with a quick reply on my tongue. But as my eyes take in his face, my mouth stops working except to work against me. Unfortunately, I think it even gapes open a bit. I gather myself, wet my dry mouth and say, "Oh, hey Drew."

God, why does he have to look so good?

Chapter 2

Drew

It's honestly amazing how someone can look so startlingly sexy just by turning towards you with their mouth slightly open. I drink her in, from her deep auburn hair and bright green eyes down to her cute little feet in their pink tennis shoes. God, those scrubs were made for her fit little body. At 6'2", I'm more on the average side of height, but looking down at all 5'3" of Lexa, I feel like a giant.

I quirk up my mouth at the corner and give her my most charming half-smile.

"Fancy meetin' you here," I drawl.

"My God, you even have the Texas twang down now," she replies.

"Well after living there for the past eight years, it has finally started to sink in."

I smile again, knowing my charms are affecting her some- what at least, if that bright blush creeping down her neckline is any indication. It's always a shock, realizing I'm attracted to my little sister's best friend. She's been in my life for a decade now and I still harbor a school boy's crush on this girl. Woman, I mean. Definitely woman. These past 10 years have been good to her. Deepening that luscious red hair while brightening those very disarming eyes. Back in college, her eyes seemed to be more of a mossy color, but when she would laugh or cry, they would always brighten to this color almost akin to jade. Now they seem to stay the lighter color all the time. I don't know if that means she's happier more often or cries a lot more. Deep in my gut, I'm hoping it's the former.

"I would ask what you're doing in town, but seeing as how I'm squeezing myself into a bright pink frilly dress this weekend, I guess I know you already have some plans," she jokes.

God, now I can't get the image of her in a tight dress out of my mind. I'm praying her bridesmaid dress isn't nearly as fitted as she's letting on, or I won't be able to focus on Ansley and Landon at all.

I chuckle while shaking my head to clear the arresting image. I manage to get out, "Well it ain't a small Southern summer wedding without those awful frilly messes."

We both laugh, although it's somewhat choked on my end. Lexa, however, seems at ease as usual. Even caught off guard like this, she still seems totally in control of the situation. That is something I have always loved about her. When Lexa walks into a room, she owns it immediately. Whether in scrubs or a formal gown, it's her runway. Without even looking, I can feel everyone's eyes in the cafe on her. Not that she'd ever notice of course. Another thing I love about Lexa, she's a thinker. She lives in her own head, sometimes to the detriment of the rest of us mere mortals. While we're all admiring her goddess qualities, she's planning next week's lunch with a friend she has a text written out to and scheduled to send when it's "normal people hours." That's what she and Ansley call daytime. Working the night shift apparently comes with its own lingo.

As if reading my mind, Lexa chirps, "Well off to save lives!" and turns to strut away.

I can't help myself as I call after her, "Don't be a stranger this week! I know you and Ans are both off after tonight!"

Whoops, did that come off a little bit stalkery? I chuckle under my breath and turn back towards the counter. I came in to grab myself a coffee before going to meet up with Landon. I'm staying at a short term rental apartment just down the street and the internet said this was the best coffee in town. Now that I think about it, I'm pretty sure Lexa lives in this neighborhood as well. Now my parting comment to her does feel a bit creepy. I shake it off, asking myself if I really need caffeine now that my heart is beating out of my chest.

It's not like I'm obsessed with Lexa, I hardly ever seem to think about her when I'm at home in Texas. That's not to say she never crosses my mind. We end up running into each other often for living 1,000 miles away from one another. She's at a lot of our family events and over 10 years, there's been a bunch of holidays spent together. Our family kind of adopted her once she and Ansley met at freshman orientation. Lexa doesn't have a lot of family. Her dad raised her on his own and he passed away just after she graduated nursing school. Mine and Ansley's mom loved having another girl around the house and Lexa relished having our mom adore her.

In the spirit of complete honesty with myself, I have had feelings for Lexa for a long time. But when I was confident enough to make my move after we first met in college, she went on a first date with Jackson, who she ended up dating for a couple of years. God I was so jealous of Jackson. I knew him of course, because we were on the baseball team together, along with Landon. That's how Landon and Ansley met and consequently how Lexa met Jackson. Even then, I knew Lexa and Jackson weren't end-game, but they dated long enough for me to graduate and move away before breaking up. Selfish.

Ansley actually called me the day Lexa and Jackson officially called time of death. From what I've heard, it wasn't a nasty split and I'm fairly certain they still maintain contact. Ansley is fond of pointing out that they're only able to stay friends because there was no other future for them. I was so happy getting that call. I wanted to immediately call Lexa to just, you know, check and make sure she was okay. But a scared—and admittedly immature—part of me told me to hold off. I waited a week, then called. When she answered the phone, she sounded like she was at a frat party. And that's when I remembered that she was a junior in college, just starting nursing school and I was an *adult*. I quickly thought of a lie and asked if she knew where Ansley was because I couldn't get a hold of her. Her answer was garbled by the music thrumming from the nearby speakers. So I told her I would text her if I still wasn't able to reach my sister and then hung up. Sitting in my bedroom, staring at the ceiling, my heart broke all over again. There was no way. I wasn't going to ask her to put her college life on hold so that

I could selfishly *have her*. Not that I would ever phrase it that way to her. She's too strong of a woman for my proprietary thoughts.

So I set a new action plan. I would wait until she was ready to give us a try. There's plenty of other women. Half the world's population, right? I was 1,000 miles from where I grew up and over 500 miles from where we all went to school. *I live in a city of over 1 million people*, I thought to myself, *there's bound to be someone that enraptures me the way she does.* So I waited and I dated. I've been with a few incredible women that I thought I might see happily ever after with. But inevitably, it would end. Time after time, relationship after relationship. They say lightning never strikes twice in the same spot, but I could only hope to be so unlucky.

Holy crap, what is it about weddings that makes our world view so fatalistic?

I decide after swimming through those memories, I deserve an energy boost. I browse the menu behind the counter while the little brunette barista stares at me expectantly. I glance behind me to ensure there's no line. As I turn back to the barista, I hesitantly ask, "Do you remember what that woman in front of me ordered?"

✿

Coffee in hand, I stroll across the park and settle onto a bench. I still have an hour before I have to meet up with Landon and after the plane ride from Dallas and that chance encounter with Lexa, I need some alone time. I watch as a tidy stroller bounces across the pavement with the cutest little baby inside. I glance up at the mom—who predictably has a phone in her hand with her eyes glued to the screen—and see someone who cares more about how her baby's appearance reflects on her rather than developing a socially mature child. Poor baby.

I'm not always so cynical, these past couple of months at work have been really trying. I loved my job when I first started, fresh out of college. I thought if I worked hard enough and was a team player, promotions would come quickly. Turns out, life is not a baseball diamond. Contrary to what Coach always said, you don't lose as a team. In real life, if your team loses, the loss can be analyzed and blame can be placed. Often on the wrong person. Especially when everyone you work with knows you would never throw someone else under the bus. How does that saying go? Nice guys finish last.

I take another sip of my coffee, and man this stuff is strong. I didn't realize the caramel I smelled in Lexa's cup was only to cover the bitterness of the 5 shots of espresso mixed with drip coffee. This is too much caffeine. Does she have the heart rate of a hummingbird? I'll have to investigate this later.

For now, though, I will be sipping this sparingly, trying not to have a heart attack at the ripe age of 30.

As I'm lifting my cup to take another sip, I catch a blur of movement out of the corner of my left eye. I snap my head around–my reflexes making me pull away from the rapid movement–and see a soccer ball flying towards me. I almost spill my coffee trying to block the ball from hitting me in the face. I bat the ball away just before it hits me and manage to save the rest of my drink as well. *Close call. Maybe I need to get back to the batting cages,* I think sharply.

I look to my left, thinking I'll see a bunch of kids kicking around. Instead I see a small field full of grown men. One of them is holding their arm up in the universal sign of, "Over here!" Keeping a firm grip on my cup, I lob the ball back towards the field. Some of the guys give me an impressed look after my lengthy toss, but I just wave them down and turn back to my bench. Playing center field has some uses later in life, apparently.

I look at my watch and realize I'm supposed to be meeting Landon downtown for dinner in 10 minutes. I pull up the map on my phone and see that it's an 8 minute walk. I head in that direction while I let my thoughts wander back to seeing Lexa again. While I don't understand her choice in coffee, I am feeling slightly hopeful about the prospect of several days together in the same town.

Chapter 3

Lexa

Due to the unforeseen meeting at the coffee house, I am now running really late. I hustle through the doors and clock in without a minute to spare. I try to nonchalantly slide into my station for patient report, hoping that Ansley hasn't seen how flustered I look. Keeping with best friend tradition, we don't have secrets. But how am I supposed to tell Ansley that I'm looking all hot and bothered because of her older brother? Her *extremely hot* older brother. With his tousled light brown hair and deep blue eyes that seem to see too much of me. Nope. Not going there. Not right now. I've got patients to see and I've got things to do. *Lord help me.*

I see Ansley heading towards me with a suspicious look on her face. I jump up, almost toppling my chair in the process, and screech out, "Thanks Sam, I'm going to go check on those fluids for room 2." Right…not suspect at all.

As I walk towards my rooms at the end of the hallway, I try to slow my breathing. Maybe that extra shot of espresso wasn't the best idea. I can feel my heart trying to escape through my rib cage. Question is, do I attribute that to the coffee or to seeing Drew again? I swore to myself in December, when we were all at their house for Christmas, that this silly little crush I have on my best friend's older brother has to stop. I am not some ditsy little school girl. I can't have a crush on someone I barely ever see. We live 4 states away from each other and I will not be leaving Savannah anytime soon, especially to move to Texas. I've found a home here. I have my work family as well as Ansley's family who now claim me as their own.

After Daddy died, I felt so alone. I don't have an extensive family tree. I have a great-uncle on my mom's side, whom I've never met, that lives in Wyoming. I think my second cousin on Daddy's side is in California, but I haven't heard from Patricia in years.

I grew up in Tennessee, but this is home now. I love living near the coast, being able to drive to Tybee Island whenever I want. The weather is so much nicer here. I do not miss the occasional snow. But deeper than that, I feel a sense of belonging here that I never felt before meeting Ansley. I have "a usual" at the coffee shop on the corner. The secondhand book store owner calls me when they get new shipments with Agatha Christie novels. And my best friend lives 5 blocks away.

I never had a best friend growing up. Being raised by a single dad made me into a tomboy that the other girls didn't really care to associate with. I was too sporty to bond with the girls and I dressed too much like a girl to hang out with the boys. So I was always left out of the crowds. I was usually picked first in gym class, only because everyone knew

I would win whatever we were playing that day. But then no one talked to me after class.

That all changed in college. I met Ansley at freshman orientation a week before classes started. I was sitting in the back of the auditorium, minding my own business. I was paying attention but not trying to actively engage in the conversation. That was my sweet spot. Well this gorgeous, long-legged goddess with perfectly curled chestnut hair down to her waist, walks in and sits right next to me. I ignored her, obviously. Next thing I know, I'm taking an elbow to the ribs. I hear a snorted laugh and turn to see the brunette next to me cracking up about a joke on a popsicle stick. She's still laughing as she holds the stick out for me to read. *Why do cows have hooves? Because they lack-toes.* I look up from the stick in time to see a new wave of laughter pass over this girl's face. That's when I lose it too. Watching this girl who could be walking a runway, laugh *and snort* at a dad joke is the funniest thing I've seen in a long time.

"I'm Ansley," she says.

"I'm Lexa," I reply, *and I want to be your friend.*

We spent the whole week leading up to the start of classes together after that. We quickly learned that although she had 5 inches on me, we could still wear all the same clothes except for jeans. I had never met someone who looked so cool but acted so goofy. And I loved her for it. We went for runs on the quad, tried out all of the campus dining halls and watched too many movies. We bonded over our love for *Clueless* and *13 Going on 30*. "As if" became our catch phrase for at least a semester.

When my dad got sick our senior year, her family rallied around me. Her mom came to campus and stayed in our apartment for a week, cooking us meals, making sure I was getting to classes and helping me to stay focused. We were nearing finals of nursing school, which meant we had to take our boards soon. Mrs. Parker would tell me, "You've worked too hard to not see this through." I knew she was right, but it was so hard to listen to my lectures when my dad was in a hospital alone and dying.

Daddy passed away about a month after I graduated. The week after I passed my nursing boards. I miss him every day. Before I met Ansley, I would've told you that he was my best friend.

After finishing my rounds and starting a new drip in room 2, I head back towards my station. Ansley's smiling face pops around the corner and startles me out of my reverie. I will never get tired of having her megawatt smile aimed at me. It instantly brightens my day. Like now, I'm already forgetting that I was thinking sad thoughts. I rearrange my features into the best smile I can manage. But like always, she can tell something is bothering me.

"It's about that time of year, huh?" she asks, referencing the nearing anniversary of my dad's death. I nod and try to change the subject to something happier, like her upcoming wedding. She's having none of it. "You know he loves you. And he's proud of the amazing woman you've become."

"You say that like he's still here," I reply, looking down at my hands.

Ansley grabs my hand, urging me to look up at her. "He is here. With you all the time. Beside you as you're living out your passion of taking care of others. Sitting beside you in your car, watching over you. He's here because you're here and you have all of his best qualities."

Tears well up, despite the fact that we're in the middle of a crowded nurse's station. Thankfully, no one turns to look at us. Ansley continues to smile down at me, knowing full well how much I hate crying in public places. I didn't even cry at my dad's funeral for fear of someone seeing my ugly, streaming tears. I can trace this specific neurosis to a singular event in my childhood.

I was playing in the courtyard at recess one day when I fell and scraped my knee. I began crying when I saw blood staining the leg of my jeans. An imposing shadow fell over me and I looked up to see Mrs. Hayward glaring down at me. "Stand up little girl," she hissed through her teeth. "And do not let me catch you wailing and carrying on like that again. Ladies do not display such violent emotions. You would know that if you had a mama at home to raise you."

I sucked in a breath and attempted to stifle my tears. Her comment cut deeper than she could imagine. Daddy did the best he could with me but he would never be a mother. I decided then and there that I would act like a lady—according to Mrs. Hayward's standards at least—and never cry in public. Becoming friends with Ansley has changed several things about me since that childhood oath. She's one of the strongest women I know but wears her emotions like a badge of honor. Her willingness to be vulnerable has begun to wear off on me. Like now, crying at the nurse's station. I realize that to some, this may seem weak, but I know now that it takes strength to let your guard down for the people that you love. And it is something that I continue to work on daily. I want the people in my life to know the real me.

In that vein of emotional honesty, I decide Ansley deserves to know how I really feel about her brother. But it can wait until after the wedding. She has a lot on her plate this week.

I squeeze her hand back, "How are you feeling, love? Excited, nervous, ready to run?"

Ansley laughs, shaking her head. "I have never been more sure about anything in my life," she says, a dreamlike quality entering her voice.

I'm still holding her hand I notice then. I give it another quick squeeze and let it drop. She gives me another sweet smile and I know she's about to ask about my rushed entrance into work tonight.

Before Ansley can start digging where I don't want her just yet, I return her smile and spin back towards my computer. I begin scrolling through my patient list to check for new orders. I can feel Ansley's eyes scanning the side of my face, looking for the tiniest clue as to my mental state. I revert to an old habit and let my face turn to stone. Out of my peripheral vision, I see her gently shake her head and turn away. She has far too much to do to be staring at my face all night anyway. Luckily for me, we're pretty busy tonight. She'll be too distracted for most of the shift to turn on the third degree.

✿

The remainder of our night seems to fly by, in the way it does when you're too busy to even eat a full lunch. Before I know it, it's 6:30 and the day shift will be walking in soon. Although I did see Ansley glance my way several more times throughout the night, she never tried to question me again. We usually walk to our cars together when we're both able to leave at the same time. I look around for her and Audrey informs me that she got pulled into a room by another nurse. I pop my head into that room to make sure they don't need anything and motion to Ansley that I'm heading out when they say they're all set.

Walking back through the sliding glass doors, I remember my emotional state of the night before while running through these doors. I don't know what's changed in the last few years, but seeing Drew unexpectedly last night definitely made my stomach do some weird flips. Most people would probably describe this feeling as butterflies. It feels like so much more of a nuisance though, like a bee sting. Painful but only in the spot where the venom has been injected. In this case, my heart.

Chapter 4

Drew

Monday

Going out with Landon last night was definitely a mistake. It started with a meal and a cocktail at this trendy new downtown restaurant that he said he's been wanting to try. One cocktail quickly turned into two which then turned into a bar crawl of some of our favorite downtown haunts. We ended up getting back to his and Ansley's apartment around 2 a.m., completely hammered. My 30 year old body does not handle a hangover like it did when I was 21.

As I lay on the couch and nurse a bottle of Gatorade, I am thankful that I at least don't have plans today.

Shit. I suddenly remember that I told Ansley I'd meet up with her for lunch and to run to the shop to pick up my tux. Apparently she didn't trust me to complete that chore on my own. I consider myself a decently responsible person. I pay my bills on time, I never miss work and I'm the person that schedules any maintenance needed on the house that I can't fix myself. Joe and Turner are completely useless when it comes to getting those jobs accomplished. Having roommates as an adult is not something I would have foreseen for my life. But honestly, it is nice having someone to come home to and spend time with after work. Even if that time ends up being spent playing Xbox and trash talking. The majority of our free time is spent fishing and visiting the local breweries.

Another major perk of having roommates is the divided rent on a house. Dallas isn't necessarily a cheap place to leave as a single person. Splitting rent and utilities definitely helps. I probably make enough at work now to get my own place, but it would be tight and I've really grown accustomed to those assholes I call friends.

I met Joe at preseason training for baseball our freshman year. We ended up rooming together with Landon for the rest of college. We met Turner our senior year at a party and immediately hit it off. We integrated him into our friend group without much effort and when we found out he was wanting to move to Dallas as well, Joe and I recruited him to be our third roomie. We live in a little 3 bedroom, 2 bath rental house with a decent sized backyard that we can play catch in when we need a little stress relief. I've been needing more than throwing a ball around can give me though lately.

Thinking about lunch with Ansley reminds me of my encounter with Lexa yesterday. I wish I knew when she might be heading back to the cafe. I might could get her to at least recommend me a different coffee than the liquid death she was drinking last night.

I need to get this girl out of my head. I don't even think she sees me that way. All I need is another round of heartbreak. It would all be worth it though, for a chance to see where we could go. I know she feels settled here, but her job could be done anywhere. We don't have to end up in Dallas, but I don't know that I'm ready to move back to where my entire family lives either.

It's not that I don't love and miss my family. We still get together for every single holiday. I just don't think I'm ready to be within *drop-in* distance of my mother. Ansley complains to me all the time about the amount of times a week our mother "just stops by" or "just happened to be running an errand in the area." Sometimes she doesn't even make the flimsy excuse, Ansley says, she just knocks and lets herself in with her key. Ansley had to have a talk with her about letting herself in after she and Landon moved in together. Ansley had to break it to our mother that she might find them in a compromising position should she barge in without knocking at least. I honestly don't know that I could have that same discussion with our mom.

Ansley said lunch at noon downtown and it's only 10 a.m. now. I realize at this point that I am on Ansley's couch and remember that I never made it back to my place. Luckily it's just about 6 blocks away. I sit up, looking around to find my shoes. I slept in the rest of my clothes. I wouldn't even worry about leaving except that I am in desperate need of a shower after a day of flights and a night of intoxication.

I spot my shoes by the end table and my keys, wallet and phone are on the coffee table near me. I stand up to start gathering my things but have to immediately sit back down. My head is absolutely killing me and I think I almost just passed out. I sit still for another minute before slowly standing up again. This time I make it to a full standing position. I gently reach down to grab my stuff and stagger to Ansley's medicine cabinet in the kitchen. I need some Advil now or I might not make it home. I fill a glass to the brim with water and gulp it down along with the pills.

I take a few more breaths and turn to head to the door. As I pass the fridge, something catches my eye. I pivot to face the fridge door. I study the picture for a second longer than necessary. Ansley has a picture of me and Lexa from my senior year of college on her fridge. Not a picture of the three of us. Right beside a magnet copy of her save the date, Ansley has pinned a picture of Lexa and I, cheek to cheek, huge grins stretching our faces. I remember when this picture was taken. Our baseball team had just won regionals and we were headed to the national championship playoffs. I was standing with my parents when Ansley and Lexa ran up to us. Before Ansley could reach me, Lexa jumped up to hug me, squealing in delight. I grabbed her up and spun her around. My mom, sensing the perfect photo op, told us to smile and we complied. I never noticed just how happy we both looked in this picture until now. I'm still confused as to why this picture is the only one on the fridge. I'll have to ask about it at lunch.

I make my way to the door, still somewhat in a daze. I have two hours to get back to my apartment, shower and change. That might even leave time for a nap. I didn't see Landon before he left for work and I didn't see Ansley before she went to sleep. It's not worth waking her up now to ask about the picture. Hopefully I don't forget about it, I want a copy. It's a sweet picture.

Walking down the stairs, I'm thinking so hard that I almost

run straight into the person walking up the stairs.

"Whoa, excuse me," I say, trying to avoid the near collision.

"It's okay, you looked pretty deep in your head. Hey, don't I know you?" she asks.

"I'm not sure, who do you think I am?"

"Ansley Parker's brother, possibly?"

"Oh, then yes. That's me. Who are you, may I ask?"

"I'm Claire! I'm your sister's friend from nursing school. I just got in today and Ansley told me to come over whenever I landed. Is she home?"

I think I remember her now. Probably from Ansley's graduation. "Yeah she's home, but she worked last night so she's not awake," I answer.

"Oh, well I can come back later in the day," she mutters as she tries to look past me up the stairs.

"I'm going to lunch with her downtown at noon. You're welcome to join us. I know she's excited to see you."

Her eyes light up and she replies, "I would love that, thank you. Let me give you my number so you can text me the address and in case you need to update me on any change in plans."

I hand her my phone and watch as she keys in her name and number. She hands the phone back and smiles up at me. We stand and awkwardly stare at each other for another moment before we realize that we're now going the same way and she turns to head back down the stairs. I follow behind her towards the exit. As we walk out of the building, I turn left to walk home while half-twisting to say bye to Claire. I get a small shock seeing that she's still walking beside me. I look down at her and ask, "Where are you staying while you're in town?"

"Over on East Bolton, in a short-term rental," she answers.

"That's over near where I'm staying, I'll walk you home."

"Oh you don't have to do that," she replies, in typical female fashion. She's blushing now though so I think she's pleased by the idea.

"I insist, madam," I tease. More blushing.

She ducks her head and keeps walking for several paces before speaking again. "You live in Texas right?" she asks.

"I do. I live in Dallas. I moved there right after graduation about 8 years ago."

"I thought so, I remember Ansley being so sad when you moved so far away."

Now it's my turn to look down and not speak for a minute. I know it was hard on Ansley when I moved away but I needed to get away for a little while. I didn't think it would become such a permanent move. I still think about moving back home here to be around our family again, but I've made such good friends in Dallas that it feels just as hard to leave them as it did to leave my family the first time. I'd have to have a great reason to uproot myself like that again right now.

As I'm contemplating this major life decision once again, I realize I haven't said anything out loud in a while. I look down at Claire, to gauge where her head is at, and notice that she also looks lost in thought. We're a block away from her street at this point, so I ask, "Are you leaving Sunday or are you thinking about sticking around a few days after the wedding?"

"I had planned on leaving Sunday, but I didn't buy my return ticket yet. I don't work again until Wednesday," she replies.

"Okay well I'll be around until next Thursday, we could go grab coffee or something if you're still in town," I offer.

Her eyes light up and she says, "That sounds great, I'll let you know now that I have your number."

I smile at her, slightly confused as to why her mood seems to have changed so drastically.

"Alright well, see you at lunch," I say as she stops in front of the stairs for an older apartment building.

"Great, see you soon!" she chirps and bounces up the stairs. She pauses before pulling open the door to turn and throw another smile my way.

I give her a smile and turn to head to my place. My thoughts return to lunch with Ansley and now with Claire as well. I'm excited for this food, it's one of my favorite lunch spots in Savannah. It specializes in greasy comfort food, perfect for this intense hangover I gave myself. I need to watch my nights out with Landon so I don't feel like shit all week. Now that Ansley is off work, I don't anticipate too many other wild bro nights. Which is honestly for the best. I'm too old to be acting like a kid.

As I'm walking through my front door, I suddenly remember that I need shoes for the wedding too. My brown dress shoes bit the dust last week and I didn't get a chance to replace them yet. I pull my phone out of my pocket to type a quick reminder. I realized a long time ago that I am not the type of person to keep "mental sticky notes." I push my phone back into my front pocket as I toe my sneakers off by the front door.

I head towards the bathroom, shedding my shirt and jeans and tossing them on the bed. I slip my briefs off as I reach the bathroom, turning on the water. I glance at myself in the mirror as I wait for the shower to warm up. I should probably try to squeeze in a few gym days while I'm here. Maybe I'll go after lunch today. *If this hangover headache goes away*, my brain snarks at me. Right, can't really push my body while my head feels like it's going to explode. I'm glad I went ahead and took meds, but this shower and a tall glass of ice water sound like heaven right now.

I thrust my hand under the water stream to test the temperature. It feels amazing. I step in and let the water run down my body. I turn to face the shower head and let it hit my neck and look down to see as the droplets skim across my chest, down to my abs and follow a drop as it makes its way down my inner thigh. I take a deep breath and reach around to find my shampoo. I scrub it through my hair and gently massage my scalp, trying to ease some of the tension in my head.

My mind wanders to thoughts I shouldn't be having. *I wonder what Lexa looks like in the shower, water running down her chest, eyes closed with face turned up towards me.* Shit. I need to stop. It's going to be a long week.

I finish up my shower, turn the water off and step out onto the rug. I reach for my towel and catch my reflection again. Great, I'm aroused just from a thought. Maybe I should've had a cold shower instead.

I shake off the thoughts, toweling off and heading back towards the bedroom. I check the time, only 10:30. I can take an hour nap and still make it to lunch.

I lay down naked–I honestly don't feel like finding clothes right now–and throw some sheets over me. I stay conscious long enough to set an alarm and quickly fall into a dreamless sleep.

✿

My alarm shocks me awake and I don't immediately know where I am. I throw the sheets back and realize I'm naked. *Oh yeah,* I think, *nap before lunch.* I gotta get up and get dressed if I want to be there on time.

I jump up, a little too quickly, and my head starts pounding again. *Shit.* I walk out to the kitchen, grab some water and gulp down a glass. I amble back to the room, deciding it's another jeans and t-shirt day. I grab my jeans from the floor where they fell during my nap. I go to the closet to check out my shirt options. I knew that I was going to be here for almost 2 weeks, so I tried to pack accordingly. I had to check a bag for my flight for the first time in years. I am much more of a cram everything into a small carry-on and stroll off of the plane uninhibited type of person. Having to wait for my bag after the flight took too much time for my liking.

I grab my go-to gray shirt that makes me look like I put some effort into my appearance. I pull on my jeans and a belt. I walk to the bathroom, hoping my hair isn't beyond saving since I fell asleep directly after my shower. My reflection shows my worst fears. My hair is everywhere. I grab a brush and some styling gel and get to work. Two minutes later and I'm somewhat happy with the result. I head to the kitchen area to grab some more water, grab my keys and wallet and slip into my tennis shoes. I pat my pockets to check their contents once before opening the door, a habit I've never been able to break. It's not so bad of a habit to have anyway, checking to make sure I have my life together.

Closing and locking the door behind me, I pull up my phone to make sure I remember where this place is located. I should've eaten something when I got home because now my stomach is roaring from hunger. I really didn't think I would be able to handle very much this morning, however. I was a little queasy. Thankfully, most of my hangover passed with all of the water and my short little nap. I open my messages app to check that Claire has the right address.

Hey, I'm on my way to lunch. You got the address I sent? I quickly type out.

I get a reply within a minute. *Hey, yeah I'm on my way there now. I'm so excited to see Ansley!*

I push my phone back into my front pocket and head down the stairs of the building. I'm so glad I'm only on the third floor. It's just the right amount of stairs to not want to take the elevator and to force myself to get some steps in. I sit way too much at my job so I've been really focusing on moving when I can.

I do love the scenery in Savannah. And everywhere I like to go is any easy walk or bus ride. I had a bike when I lived here that I loved to ride. Maybe I'll get another one for Dallas. I look around at all of the greenery, the tree branches dripping with Spanish moss. I can't deny the beauty of this city. I turn onto the street that houses the restaurant and see Claire walking up as well.

"Right on time," I say with a smile.

"I didn't want to be the first one here, but couldn't be the last either," she replies.

I hold the door open for her to walk into the restaurant in front of me. I spot Ansley sitting at a corner table, talking to a redhead.

Oh shit shit shit. Why did I not realize that Lexa was going to be here? Why would she not be here?

At the same moment I notice them, Ansley sees us and her

eyes fly open in recognition, shock and glee. She squeals and runs towards us, throwing herself at Claire.

"When did you get in? How did you know I'd be here? What are you doing with him?" She releases rapid-fire questions at Claire who tries and fails to answer each one before the next can come out.

"I got in this morning, you were still asleep. I ran into Drew here at your place and he told me about lunch," Claire lays out for Ansley. Ansley seems to accept this timeline of events and turns her questioning gaze towards me.

"Had a little bit of fun last night, I heard," she says to me.

"A little, yeah," I laugh out. "How was Landon feeling this morning?"

"He looked like death warmed over when I passed him on his way out."

"Nothing that a long day of work can't cure," I say, laughing again.

She looks at me like she has more questions, but I decide I would rather have food for this interrogation she has planned. I move towards the table, noting Lexa's gaze on me before it flickers to Claire. Lexa stands up, edging around the table to envelope Claire in another bone-crushing hug.

"I am so glad you're here!" she squeals. "Now the party can really get started."

This is something I had forgotten about Claire from the few times we hung out while they were all in nursing school, she was the resident party animal. She could always be counted on for wanting to go out after classes and was never one to shy away from a night of drinking and dancing.

Claire blushes and looks up at me, obviously reading my thoughts from my face.

I smile and say, "Let's have a seat and order some grub. I'm starving."

I look back at Lexa, again meeting her gaze. Her eyes are unreadable but definitely darker than they were at the coffee shop yesterday.

Chapter 5

Lexa

Did he just wake up? His hair looks so damn sexy when it's this messy, I realize.

I shake my head to clear my thoughts and turn back towards Claire. I can't say that I wasn't shocked to see her walking in here with Drew. I wonder if he knows she used to have the biggest crush on him. From that smile on her face and their proximity at the door, I would bet that she still does. Claire barely knew him, only met him a few times when he would come to visit Ansley. That didn't stop her from falling head over heels for him. Claire has had a lot of bad luck with guys recently, but I don't know that going after Drew now is a good idea.

Not because I'm jealous or anything. God no. I just want to see her end up with someone who matches her energy and lifestyle. Although they do look good together. Her bright blonde, brown-eyed beauty matches up well with just about anyone and she looks so happy right now. Maybe I am a little jealous. *I'm the worst,* I think. It's not like I have any kind of relationship with Drew to claim. He's just my best friend's older brother that I happen to like to look at and talk to and dream about. No big deal.

That dream I was having earlier was something else though. I don't know if it was the mimosa I drank with breakfast when I got home or if it was just seeing him again unexpectedly, but I had the most beautiful dream about the man sitting across from me at lunch. I can still vividly recall the feel of his hands on my thighs and the taste of his lips on mine. I look up to see those same lips as his tongue runs over the bottom one, way too slowly to be accidental. I meet his eyes again and feel the rush of heat spread across my face and down my neck. The heat courses even lower as his eyes turn to a darker shade of blue, scanning my face and the blush searing it. My mouth opens just slightly, but enough that I notice my bottom lip is quivering. I immediately slam my lips together and tear my gaze away before something even worse happens.

I turn towards Ansley sitting beside me to realize that she was staring at me, mouth gaping open. *Shit.* By the look on her face, she just saw the entire show.

"Bathroom, be right back," I half-shout as I scramble out of my chair, almost overturning it in my haste to get out of Drew's sight.

Once in the bathroom, I stare at myself in the mirror, willing the blush to fade. I take several deep breaths, trying to steady myself. *What the hell just happened?* I have to go back out there and sit at a table with people who saw me coming undone. Maybe I can play it off as oncoming nausea. *Yeah right like anyone will buy that one.*

A few more deep breaths, a splash of cold water, and I

head to the door to face the inevitable. By the time I reach the table again, everyone has ordered drinks. I see someone ordered me a diet soda, probably Ansley. *Bless her,* I think. I need some caffeine.

I sit down, aware of more than one person's eyes on me. *Here goes nothing.*

"Sorry, I had some weird nausea there that caught me off guard. Probably the mimosa I had with breakfast after shift," I throw out my best smile, hoping against hope that they'll at least act like they believe me.

"No worries girl! We've all been there," Claire replies, bubbly smile in place.

I look at Ansley who is shaking her head with a grin on her face and then at Drew who is staring at me in what can only be described as fascination. I don't know what to do with that so I turn away again. This lunch was supposed to be fun. I didn't even know that Drew was coming until Ansley texted me about it this morning. I was definitely excited to see him again, but I didn't foresee this type of visceral reaction.

I reach for my drink and take a deep gulp. *Please talk about something, talk about anything*, I think at the group, willing them to hear my thoughts and act quickly.

Ansley—that asshole—says, "You got really red there before you ran off. The last time I saw that happen, you had just been thrown into that cute new doctor while trying to put a hip back in." She guffaws as I again start to blush. *Dammit, is that going to keep happening?*

"Well if you must know, I was just remembering a scene from that particularly filthy novel you lent me last week, Ans," I retort as I stare her down. I tally up my win as she now flares crimson. I smile as we come to the silent but mutual agreement to let this go for now.

Looking to Claire, I ask, "When do you have to go back?"

"I don't have to work again until next Wednesday so I was thinking about hanging around for a few extra days after the wedding," she answers, turning to throw a shy smile at Drew. *What is that about?*

Drew picks up the thread of the conversation, asking Ansley, "When do you leave for the honeymoon? Not until Sunday morning, right?"

"Well," Ansley starts, "I think we're actually pushing the flights back to the afternoon. We were thinking about having a little breakfast with the wedding party and some family before we left. Just for whoever is still in town."

"Oh, that sounds wonderful Ansley!" Claire bubbles out. She really is just so happy to be here, huh? God I sound so mean right now. I either need more caffeine or more sleep. Probably both.

I smile and turn to Ansley as well, saying, "Well whatever our sweet bride wants, she shall have." I take my well-deserved slap on the arm and scowl back before we both start laughing. One thing Ansley and I have been loving recently are wedding shows and movies featuring the dreaded *bridezilla.* I like to joke with Ansley that I'm the only one besides Landon that can handle her fire breath. In reality, she has been so easy-going about everything so far. She keeps saying, "I don't care what happens, as long as I end up married to my best friend." Which yes, cute, but also gross.

"Where are you wanting to have this Sunday breakfast?" I ask, pulling my phone out to start an internet search.

"Hmm, maybe that cute little cafe on Bay Street?"

"I'm on it." I navigate to my messages app, opening the

wedding party group. I type out a quick text asking who all will be in town for a breakfast on Sunday morning. I also shoot a quick text to Ansley's parents, knowing she will want them there. I set my phone back down on the table and look up to see Drew staring at me again. "What?" I demand.

He startles a bit and quickly says, "Oh nothing, you just type so fast on your phone."

I laugh and he reddens a bit. Looks like it's the day for blushes galore. I roll my eyes a bit and grab the menu. I still haven't decided what I want to eat and I know they're going to be coming back around soon to take our order. I do love their French fries here, but those are kind of tough to screw up. I note that everyone else has stopped talking and is now looking at their menus, too. *What were they doing while I was in the bathroom? Talking about me?* God I sound paranoid. I quickly shake those thoughts and refocus on the menu.

Chapter 6

Drew

Okay, so…what was *that*?

I just keep staring at her, I know it's making her more uncomfortable but I can't stop. She went from looking very strange and flushed, to rushing to the bathroom to planning a breakfast on Sunday within 15 minutes.

I'm also still not sure what I saw when I first sat down. If this was some other woman, I would swear to you that she was thinking *improper thoughts.* But about me? There's no way. Sure, we flirt every once in a while, but like friends do. Single friends flirt with each other right?

I glance at Ansley to see if she knows what's going on. She's looking at Lexa with this knowing and slightly smug look on her face. Okay, so she does know. I'll ask her at the tux shop.

And now that she's so focused on her menu again, I can't take my eyes off of Lexa. Her auburn hair is piled on top of her head again and her eyes are a deep, dark green as they skim the words. *Hmm, that's a new color.* What does green like a pine forest mean? As I'm thinking over the changes in her eyes, I notice that they're on me again. I shrink from the intensity of her gaze.

"Take a picture, it'll last longer. God, you're being creepy," Lexa snarks.

"Sorry, just lost in thought," I say.

She snorts a laugh and says, "Don't hurt yourself."

I glare at her, but she just looks back down at the menu. "All those books you've read and it's taking you this long to read a menu?" I ask, making her look up again. Her eyes are returning to their normal mossy green now.

"I don't like to settle, so sometimes it takes me a minute to make a decision," she replies, with a grimace on her face.

I feel like that was directed at me somehow, but I don't quite catch the meaning. I look at Ansley and then Claire, who are both pretending to be busy reading their menus as well. I know they're faking it, because I haven't seen either of their eyes move yet. They're just boring a hole through the menu.

"What are you looking to get, Ansley?" I ask, hoping to cut through some of this weird tension.

"Out of this conversation," mumbles Ansley, before looking up to see if I heard her. I did, of course, and she knows that. "Um, I think the Swiss burger and sweet potato fries. What about you Claire?"

"The chef's salad looks good. And I think I'll get an order of the jalapeno poppers as an appetizer, if anyone wants some," Claire replies, looking sheepish.

Lexa looks up from her menu again and says, "That sounds good Claire, I'll split them with you. I think I'm going to go with the All-American special. Burger, fries and wings."

They all turn and look at me then, waiting for my answer. "I think I'm going to try the wings for an appetizer and have a burger and sweet potato fries as well." And now that we've all answered the safe question, no one seems to know what to say next. Luckily, we're saved by the arrival of the waiter, asking for our lunch order.

I watch as each of the ladies order, then I place mine, making sure to order extra ranch for my wings.

As soon as the waiter is gone, I notice the tension start to ease back in. *Come on, something's gotta give.* "So Ans, have you decided on a cake topper yet? I know you were between two last time we talked."

"Yeah, actually. We decided to go with the metal silhouette design. It looked better with the venue."

"I can't wait to see the venue. I've only ever passed by that hotel, never been in it," I say, trying to keep this topic open. While I love my sister immensely, I don't actually care this much about the details of her wedding on Saturday. But it's keeping everyone occupied, at least.

I can't help but glance at Lexa again. She's staring at me with an amused look on her face. I shoot her a questioning glance.

"I just never knew you took such an interest in wedding planning," she says, somehow reading my mind.

"I have several interests in which you might not be aware," I reply, giving her my best smoky eye. She laughs, which wasn't my intention. She has the best laugh, though, and I always love to hear it, even at my own expense.

Having found a safe topic, we continue to talk about the plans for the wedding.

Thankfully, our food comes out in record time and we're

able to focus on that instead. I'm still not sure where all this weirdness is coming from—Lexa, Ansley and I have spent so much time together, and it has never been this awkward. Maybe it's Claire being here unexpectedly. Maybe Lexa somehow realized how I feel about her lately. Maybe I'm the only one that feels weird. Regardless, it's just another thing to talk to Ansley about when we're alone this afternoon.

The rest of the lunch passes easily, filled with idle chit chat and great food. I definitely needed this greasy goodness to get over the last hump of my hangover.

As we're paying our bills and sipping on the last of our drinks, I ask Ansley, "Do we have an appointment at this place or is this a walk-in situation?"

"We have an appointment at 2:15, and it's a five minute walk from here. So we still have a couple minutes before we have to head that way," Ansley answers, glancing at her watch. She then looks to Lexa and asks, "You still coming?"

So much for those burning questions.

Chapter 7

Lexa

Well yeah, at work last night when Ansley asked if I wanted to tag along for wedding errands, I thought it would be an easy afternoon. After that awkward lunch though, this might be more of a headache. Now that she's asking me in front of everyone, I can't turn her down now. *Oh well,* I reason, *at least she promised margaritas afterward.*

I look towards Drew again, worried for his reaction. He's been acting weird today, for sure. I'm almost positive there's something going on between him and Claire, I just can't tell if he knows what it is. Drew has never been the most observant when it comes to how others feel about him. Just look at our relationship. I've been crushing on this man for almost 10 years and I can guarantee he has no clue. Much to Ansley's chagrin, she has had to deal with her friends having a crush on her older brother since they were in elementary school. Which is another reason she has not been made aware of my feelings. I don't want our friendship to change over her brother.

Drew is staring down at his phone, unaware that I have been looking at him this entire time that I've been lost in thought. I smile to myself, shaking my head and turn to look at Ansley. Once again, she's giving me that quizzical look, but she swivels back to face Claire before I can figure out what that look is about. *Make that two Parkers acting strangely today,* I think.

We all get our cards back from the waiter and begin to stand, preparing to leave. It's only at this point I realize that we've made plans for after lunch that do not involve our extra lunch guest. *Well shit, this is awkward...again.*

As we're walking out of the restaurant it's painfully obvious–to me, anyway–that Claire is wanting to be invited on our next adventure this afternoon. Ansley, usually very in tune with her surroundings, seems just as unaware of Claire's intentions as Drew today. I just wave bye to Claire and tell her we'll be seeing each other again very soon as we part ways on the sidewalk.

✿

So much silk, I behold, as I run my fingers over yet another pastel tie. I'm so glad Ansley decided our dress colors for us, because there are frankly just too many options. She has honestly made this entire process so much easier for her bridal party. We all received a link to a site with the exact color we needed to purchase our dress in with a general description of what she would prefer–i.e., no low-plunging mini dresses. The guys were given a swatch of light gray suit material to take to their nearest tux rental shop and have matched and fitted. Ansley bought their ties for them so they wouldn't end up with different colors. The fact that Drew is the only groomsman that has yet to pick his suit up is not surprising in the least.

Drew likes to act like he's all grown up now that he's living in Dallas and works in marketing for one of the largest companies in Texas, but the man still has roommates. And plays video games. And obviously still procrastinates as much as he did in college. From what I remember, Drew was the kind of student who would stay up all night the last night before an assignment was due to start and finish it, rather than work on it all week. That's not to say that his grades reflected this *laissez-faire* attitude, he graduated cum laude and landed a great job immediately out of school. *Life really is unfair,* I remind myself.

My attention is suddenly captured by the image of Drew in an extremely well-fitted three-piece suit as he strides from the dressing room. My breath catches in my throat and dammit if I don't go red again. *This incessant blushing is ruining my life,* I brood.

Drew rotates towards me just in time to catch the blush spreading across my cheeks and probably down my neck, judging by the path his eyes are now traveling. His eyes make their way back up to mine and hold for just a fraction too long. I close my eyes to break the contact and when I open them, he's facing his reflection in the mirror.

The way Drew is studying himself in this suit is something utterly remarkable. I can't tell if he's purposely flexing his biceps and glutes as he turns this way and that, but I don't care. It's appealing either way. I can't tear my gaze from his body, as our eyes again meet in the mirror. *Shit,* I curse myself for staring.

A small smile forms on his lips as he holds my stare. *Is*

he flirting with me? No. No way. We're just friends and we will always be just friends. He's just being Drew and goofing around. *Right?*

Mercifully, Ansley chooses now to return to the room and immediately fixes her attention on Drew. She squeals with pleasure as he spins for her, showing off his suit and brand new dress shoes. *He probably forgot his dress shoes in Dallas,* I muse.

"Doesn't he look like the next James Bond?" Ansley bubbles.

"Maybe without that haircut," I retort. That earns me a scowl from both of them. They look so much alike when they're both glaring at me.

I want to say that he looks incredibly handsome, but I can't say that out loud obviously.

"He cleans up pretty nice," I settle on something kind but not too flattering. Apparently this comment is also taken too much to heart as I earn another half smile from Drew in the mirror. The way that he can so easily turn on his *sexy eyes* completely unnerves me.

Ansley rolls her eyes at me and begins talking to the tailor. Judging by the context of the conversation, it was her idea to have Drew fitted here in town, not his.

"Why here?" I ask, being nosy as always.

"This is where my dad bought his tux for our parents wedding," Drew answers unexpectedly. "We, well she, thought it would be nice to have that sentimental touch. Even if our family were the only ones that knew."

"Oh. Well that's incredibly sweet," I reply. "Did you just get fitted when you were here for Easter and then again now?"

"No, I got fitted at Christmas, again at Easter to be sure

and today just to show Ansley again," he responds.

That's more times than I've tried on the dress I'm wearing this weekend, I observe. Maybe Drew isn't as immature as he was in college after all.

☼

Now that we've picked up The Next Bond's suit, it's time for the much-anticipated margaritas. Our favorite Tex-Mex joint is a couple of blocks away. I loop my arm through Ansley's and begin to skip down the sidewalk like we used to in college. She obliges me and we are a block ahead of Drew before we realize he's not with us.

"Don't slow down on my account," Drew laughs. "I think I'm actually going to head home for the night, I was up a bit too late for my old age last night."

"Did you at least take a girl home?" Ansley teases, glancing my way.

It's Drew's turn to blush as he blurts, "Hell no, Ansley. What would even make you ask that?"

"Oh I don't know, the fact that you and Claire turned up together, looking well-acquainted and cozy," she snaps back.

"Ans, I was asleep on *your couch* when you got home this morning, remember?"

"Oh yeah, that's right. Weird then, that you and Claire just happened to get to the restaurant at the same time. Or that she even knew where to meet us."

"I told you, I ran into her leaving your building, she is staying near me and I walked her home. Then I went home and slept. *Alone.*" He asserts, before Ansley can respond. "And on that note, I'm definitely leaving. Have a great night you two." He spins on his heel and storms off down the sidewalk before either of us can say bye.

"Well that was weird," I say to Ansley, both of us watching Drew's fading form. "Why did you push him so hard about that stuff with Claire?"

Ansley slowly pivots towards me, then shakes her head and laughs. "I'm honestly not sure," she says, "He just seemed weird and uptight and I was trying to push his buttons enough to figure out why."

"Did you sniff out the answer, Scoob?" I ask, somewhat jokingly.

"No, actually. I'm still not sure what his problem was at lunch, or just now." She grins mischievously at me, "But I'll find out." And now I'm slightly scared for Drew.

Ansley's sleuthing skills are notorious in our friend group. Ansley is the friend you talk to when you think your partner is cheating on you and need evidence to corroborate. She once found the texts between our friend Weston's girlfriend and her *other* boyfriend, by reverse searching google from a screenshot of one message. It's FBI-level stuff, honestly. If anyone can get to the bottom of Drew's moods, it's Ansley.

As Ansley and I continue towards queso and margaritas, my mind can't get away from Drew. *Nothing a few margs can't fix,* I muse. I once again circle my arm around Ansley's and we skip off in search of happy hour.

Chapter 8

Drew

Tuesday

I'm glad I came straight home after the tux shop last night. I watched some TV, ate a light dinner and went to sleep pretty early. They aren't joking when they say hangovers get worse in your thirties. I feel great today, thank goodness. I might hit up the gym this morning and get a good sweat session in. Maybe the workout will help me work through some of what is going on in my head.

The way that Lexa looked at me when we sat down for lunch yesterday had me dreaming weird things last night. And now my brain is even more crammed with conflicting feelings than before. In my dream, Lexa was looking at me with those blown pupils and slightly parted lips that turn me on so damn easily. The same look on her face yesterday. Was she turned on by something? By me? I don't know what it means if the answer to that is yes. I have wanted this for too long to act rashly and screw it up before it can even begin.

This is why I need to keep myself busy this week. It's not going to do me any good to dwell on random looks Lexa gives me, trying to uncover their meanings. I still need to talk to Ansley about everything, but it can wait until her wedding is over. This week is about her, not some secret crush I've been harboring on her best friend for a decade.

Speaking of Ansley, I still have some wedding related errands to run. I did grab a new pair of shoes yesterday to go with the suit. Now I need some socks and I need to make sure my under shirt doesn't show through. I think I'm going to go get a coffee before I get started, caffeine being the essence of adult life apparently.

First though, shower and get dressed. I haul myself up out of the bed, planting my feet on the floor. I take a deep breath as I gaze out of my bedroom window. It overlooks the trees full of Spanish moss, which are swaying gently in the breeze. I'm suddenly back in high school, looking out my bedroom window at a different set of trees.

✿

The giant oaks in our backyard are so green this year. I can't believe I graduate in three weeks. I am stoked to be leaving this small town with these small people and be on my own. Ansley is right next door, as always, blaring her pop music. I love her more than life, but I can't wait for time away from her. God I'm so glad she wants to go to college up North. I can't even imagine if I had to share a campus with her, too. She is the most annoying little sister sometimes. I know they're programmed that way but she takes it to a whole other level on the regular. Without interference from our parents I might have drowned her in the pool. Speaking of, I think I'm going to go try to catch a tan. I need to be golden bronze for those college girls I'll be meeting soon enough.

✿

I snap back to the here and now, laughing at myself for my idiocy. I missed my home and my family, especially Ansley so much in the first month of my first semester that I drove 500 miles in the dead of night to come home. I acted like I was coming home to surprise my parents, but Ansley of course saw right through me. She made a pallet on my floor and slept in my room that night to keep me company. It did eventually get easier, especially once I met Landon and Jackson. Ansley came to visit me several weekends that first year and that probably staved off the homesickness just as much as going home.

These are the kind of thoughts that will have me moving back here, to be closer to my family again. Ansley and Landon are staying in Savannah after the wedding, not moving across the country like I did. I still don't think I'm ready to come back just yet. I feel like I have unfinished business left in Dallas somehow.

I stand, deciding to skip the shower and head to the gym first. I pull out my phone and get up to grab my ear pods. This means I'll be holding off on my caffeine run until later as well, but that's probably for the best. Getting a later start means I won't down 3 cups of coffee before noon. I snatch my ear pods from their charger in the kitchen and cue up my workout playlist on my phone. I let the music begin to pump me up as I pull on my shorts and shirt. I head towards the door to grab my gym shoes and pull my keys from the holder by the door. Locking the door behind me, I navigate the stairs at a jog, trying to get warmed up on the way. I like to jog to the gym so I can cut down on the time I actually spend there. I don't want to feel like I live there. The gym here is just a few blocks from the apartment I'm staying in and they let you get a membership by the week, which is convenient.

I jog past the road that Claire is staying on and reflect again on yesterday's lunch and Lexa's range of emotions. Was she angry at me for something I said? Or did? If I didn't know any better, I'd think she was jealous. Of Claire, though? She has to know that if I wanted to get with Claire, I could have a long time ago. She had a crush on me in college–Ansley told me.

I run faster, hoping to clear my head even quicker. I can't go the rest of this visit not knowing where I stand with Lexa. I'm going to have to talk to her since I can't talk to Ansley right now.

Gym first, then caffeine, then try to track down Lexa for a chat.

Chapter 9

Lexa

I wake up later than I planned to, which isn't shocking after how late we ended up staying at the Mexican restaurant last night. We went for happy hour, but closed the place down. I had a lot of feelings to drown and Ansley is always down for a cathartic marg. Unfortunately, there was a karaoke machine and I ended up on it, screeching out some horrid country song about falling for the girl you should be with. How ironic. I don't even want to call Ansley this morning like I promised I would. If she only suspected before, she definitely knows now. Something weird is going on between me and Drew and I need her help to figure it out. But she's the last person I want to talk to about this. I promised myself in college, I wouldn't be the girl that Ansley has to worry about with her brother like all of her high school friends. I'm Ansley's, not Drew's. *As much as I might like to be both,* my brain offers.

Ugh, I really need some coffee, I groan internally. Even when I'm not going to work, I still need a certain amount of daily caffeine intake to continue being human. Zombie-me is not very fun to be around. If I'm going to get my workout in, run my errands and make it to the airport in time to pick Jackson up this afternoon, I need to get started soon. I decide to get my workout in first, though. This way I can shower, grab coffee and get all my errands done after. I head to the closet to grab a pair of leggings and a sports bra. Today is core and I have all the equipment at home so I won't have to leave. I prefer to work out at home when I can. It unnerves me being around a lot of people at the gym and this time of morning, it'll be packed.

I turn on my favorite pop playlist and get started. 30 minutes and a lot of sweat later, I'm done and ready to shower. I strip off my leggings and slip my sports bra over my head, trying to avoid my hair if possible. Today is not a wash day so I don't want to soak it in sweat. I turn the knob to let the shower start warming up. I look at myself in the mirror, admiring the way the sweat defines my abs. I love to see my body post-workout, it makes me feel fit. I don't eat correctly to be able to keep my abs all day, so after a morning workout is the only time I see them. Over the past several years, it's taken a lot to get me to this place of acceptance–and sometimes love–of my body. I had a hard time in college, eating out with friends and drinking too much. I was under a lot of stress through nursing school and I would either eat too much or not enough. My weight fluctuated wildly and I couldn't keep my clothes fitting properly. I eventually resorted to the old standby of athletic shorts and a long t-shirt. It hid whatever damage I was doing to my body that month. Now that I'm out of college, I have the time and the motivation to train properly and I do–most days. There's still times when I come home from work and feel like a glass of wine and sleep will do me better than a workout, but those days are fewer than they used to be.

After checking that the water is warm enough to melt my skin off, I step in and let the shower do its magic. I immediately feel the tension leaving my shoulders and the grime leaving my skin. I luxuriate in the feeling for a few moments before turning to grab my body wash and loofah. As I scrub, my mind wanders. It quickly finds a place I have to pull back from sharply. My brain just supplied me with an image of sweaty Drew. An image I became familiar with in college, hanging out with the boys from the baseball team. But my devious brain took it a step further, giving me a 30 year old sweaty, half-naked Drew. I haven't seen Drew shirtless in person since my senior year of college when I accidentally ran into him getting out of the shower at his parents on Christmas Eve. *Is it sad that I remember the exact day,* I wonder. Seeing him so many times in just a few days is really messing with me. I switch off the water and step out of the shower, grabbing my towel. I dry off and tuck my towel around me so I can throw some dry shampoo in my hair. I spray my roots and stare at my flushed reflection in the mirror. I wish the blush rushing down my neck was solely from the heat of the water.

Trying once again to control the path my thoughts are taking, I move back into the bedroom to get dressed. I only have a couple of errands to run before driving to the airport, but I still want to be comfortable. I throw on my favorite sundress and sandals, throwing a thin sweater into my bag in case it's cold at any of my stops. Even in June in the South, I still get cold. I like to be prepared for the inevitable at all times. I run a brush through my tangled mess of hair, using a clip to pull the front away from my face and quickly roll on some lip gloss. I grab my sunglasses and keys and head out the door, already looking forward to my iced coffee.

I mentally scroll through my calendar for the day. I have a few hours to kill before needing to leave for the airport and the two errands I need to run are within a 10 minute walk of home. After some quick math, I get excited about the prospect of a little down time at the coffee shop. I'm so glad I keep a book in my bag. Like I said, I like to be prepared. As I step into the crisp air conditioning of the shop, I notice Mike is back behind the counter.

"Large cold brew, shot of espresso with a caramel drizzle?" Mike asks as I walk towards the counter.

"You got it," I reply. I smile, loving the fact that my barista knows my off day order as well as my work day order.

"It's wedding week, ain't it?" He asks while prepping my cup and waiting on the cold brew.

"It sure is. Everything is all lined up for a great party."

"I know Ansley is going to look gorgeous in her gown, but I can't wait to see y'all in your dresses, too."

"Aw, yeah I'm so glad she went with the blush color. It's going to look so good next to the guys in their suits."

He hands me my cup and motions to a table in the back that is being vacated. He follows me over to the small table and begins to wipe it down with a rag. I give him my most charming smile as he gestures towards the table, making a small bow and says, "Milady." I curtsy and giggle.

"I'll leave you to your book, my dear," Mike purrs, fixing me with another faux seductive smile.

I laugh and settle into the comfortable chair. I take out

my book and lay it on the table beside my coffee. I pull out my phone next, checking the screen for any missed texts or calls. I see a notification on my calendar app and open it up to see what's going on. And wow, it's a reminder sent to my calendar from Jackson to pick him up from the airport today. Lots of trust there, huh? I almost text Ansley about it, but stop myself. She doesn't need the stress of me whining about Jackson this week. I can do this one thing for her. Everything else I've done for the wedding, the shower, the bachelorette trip and everything in between, has been so easy because Ansley is so easy-going. She has no expectations and is so grateful, I've given it my all to make sure that she's gotten everything she deserves for this day. Picking up the best man from the airport is honestly the least that I could do.

Although if I would have known Drew would already be in town, I would have just made him do it. But with things already being weird between us, I don't feel like I can ask now.

I flip my book open and begin reading, becoming more and more immersed in the story. I'm fully into my adventure when I hear a faint ringing off to my right. I glance down at the table and I am immediately thankful that I set an alarm. I might have never made it out of the coffee shop. I reluctantly close my book and tuck it back into my bag. I grab my coffee and stand up, stretching. I sat in that one position for much longer than I probably needed to.

I take a sip of coffee and pull up my mental checklist of errands, already dreading having to leave my comfortable chair and book.

Chapter 10

Drew

With my workout done and my shower having rinsed off the rest of my stress, I get dressed—automatically putting on another pair of jeans and a t-shirt. I'm so much more comfortable in this than my regular work clothes and I would love to have a job that does not require a daily suit and tie.

I grab my phone off the bed, checking the battery after streaming music at the gym. It should last the rest of the day, so I head out the door. I lock the door behind me and make my way down the stairs to grab some coffee.

I need to text Lexa and see if she's available for a chat today. I remember she said she had plans this afternoon.

Today's Tuesday, so I'm pretty sure Jackson gets in tonight. I wonder if Landon is going to pick him up, I could ride with him and keep him company.

For now, though, I need caffeine. I'm so glad that a good coffee shop is right around the corner. I saw on their website that they have a new blueberry flavored frappe, which sounds so good for summertime.

I know I'm close to the cafe at this point, judging by the delicious aroma of roasting coffee beans. I tug open the door and look first towards the counter, assessing the line. There's only one person in line now, so I hop in, hoping to place my order and run to the restroom before it comes out. I scan the menu, including the new offerings to see if anything entices me more than the blueberry frappe. The woman before me finishes ordering and I step up to the counter. There's a different barista here today and I look down at his name tag as I start to say hello. "Hi Mike, how are you today?" I ask with a large smile on my face.

"I'm doing well," he replies. "What can I get started for you?"

"I saw on your social media page that you're offering a blueberry frappe this week? That sounds like heaven and I would love to try it."

"One blueberry frappe coming up, then. Can I get your name for the order?"

"It's Drew, thanks man."

I turn from the counter to head to the restroom. As I'm passing the back tables, I see a shock of red hair above a book and immediately know it's Lexa. I don't want to interrupt her just to tell her that I'm running to the bathroom. I know how she feels about getting pulled from her reading. I push open the bathroom door and catch a glimpse of my blushed cheeks in the mirror. *That has to be from the early morning heat of the city, not just from seeing Lexa,* I tell myself.

After finishing up at the urinal, I stare at my reflection as I wash my hands. I will my face to stop blushing and scrub some cold water on my cheeks. I need to head back out there and grab my coffee.

As I pass her table again, I notice Lexa is still absorbed in her book. I stand by the counter to wait for Mike to finish my drink and I am caught staring at Lexa's table.

"Yeah, she's always over there reading," Mike says when he catches me in the act.

"So she comes here pretty often?" I ask, already knowing the answer.

"Yeah man, almost every day."

I see him giving me the once over, meaning he probably thinks well of Lexa and is trying to determine if I'm the type of guy he should be giving information to. I guess he decides that I'm safe enough, because he says, "I never see her come in with anyone but her best friend. No one special from what I can tell. But you didn't hear that from me." At this, he turns and starts wiping down the counter.

Is it that obvious—even to complete strangers—that I'm interested in her? If so, how has she not noticed? Or worse, what if she has and is just choosing to ignore it? As I'm thinking over these burning questions, I see her check her phone and begin to pack up her things. I glance at Mike who is busy with the counter and then back to Lexa. I can see she's in her head, probably running down her "mental checklist" and she doesn't even glance my way. She walks right past me and I don't even say a word. *God I'm such a coward,* I berate myself.

I take a swig of my coffee and head to the table in the back that Lexa has just vacated. Mike looks up at me as I sit down and I only shrug. I pull my phone out to check my emails from work. As usual, I am carbon copied in several different email chains that don't even pertain to my department. I scan through the threads, just to be sure that I'm not missing anything. Luckily, I only have two emails that actually require a response. I type out my return emails and send them while continuing to sip my coffee. It's pretty good, though I'm not getting the caffeine kick from it that I was hoping. *Maybe I'll just keep drinking Lexa's cowboy coffee,* I consider.

While I have my phone out, I decide to shoot a quick text to Landon.

Are you picking up Jackson from the airport this afternoon? I type out.

He quickly responds with, *Nah dude, I think Lexa is actually grabbing him.*

Lexa? Why is Lexa picking up Jackson? Maybe they're closer now than I thought. My mind wanders to a deep, dark corner filled with images of Lexa and Jackson in college before conjuring up imagined pictures of now. I don't want to even acknowledge the vast well of jealousy already bubbling up to the surface.

I need to get a grip on myself and get these quick errands done. I might text Landon again later and see if he wants to hang out tonight, maybe hit up the batting cages. I guess my workout was not the full measure of stress relief that I needed.

Chapter 11

Lexa

I stare at the arrivals board, looking for the flight from Chicago that will be bringing Jackson. He texted me before he boarded saying it was on time. I scan the arrivals board one more time before I see it, the flight is still on time and should be landing in the next 30 minutes. *Perfect,* I think, *plenty of time to run to Starbucks.* I need another caffeine boost to get me through this reunion. I'm thankful the drive back is only about 20 minutes, with traffic. I grab another cold brew coffee and head to the gate to wait for him to walk off the plane. I pull my book out and set another timer on my phone so I'm not so engrossed in my book that I miss him. Not that he's very easy to miss. Jackson is 6'4", broad shouldered with caramel skin and eyes the color of honey. He definitely turns heads as he walks through a room. He caught my attention very quickly in college.

Ansley was dragging me along to yet another baseball game. She liked to have company and I liked hanging out. Also, who doesn't love a boy in baseball pants? She was crushing hard on one of her older brother's friends, Landon. So we went to pretty much every home game. About halfway through the season, Ansley and Landon began dating and of course that meant more games. We even started going to the close away games. With five games left in the season before playoffs, Ansley pulled me along to the dugout to see Landon and Drew after a game one night. It was a double header, so we were giving the boys some Gatorade and snacks. That's when the prettiest man I had ever seen leaned against the fence.

"Where's mine, gorgeous?" He asked.

I immediately blushed but I managed to get out, "Probably still in the fridge in that concession stand over there."

The tall, gorgeous man in tight pants laughed and then said, "I'm Jackson. You're Lexa, right? I met Ansley here a couple of weeks ago and she wouldn't shut up about you."

I gave Ansley a side-eye glare but smiled at Jackson. We ended up going on a date later that week and the rest is history.

We had a very easy relationship. But he wanted a lot of things that I didn't. It became more and more clear that we weren't on the same page. I wanted to stay in the South and have a career and a home. Jackson was very interested in his sports career and wanted me to move around with him in the MLB. As his graduation approached and he began talking with scouts from teams in New York, Chicago and California, I realized that I wasn't ready to change my whole life plan for him. We had already been drifting apart but that conversation ripped away the rest of our dangling threads. Within weeks, I was back out with Ansley, going to frat parties to try to decide what I really wanted from my college experience.

I'm still reminiscing when I realize that I never even opened my book and there's five minutes until Jackson's plane lands. I stuff my book back into my bag and head to the gate. I join the crowd at the gate–thinking that I should have made one of those corny arrival signs–when I see the top of Jackson's head coming our way.

He is still shockingly handsome. His eyes are as bright as ever, melted honey in its purest form. They meet mine and a large smile takes over his face. I feel my face stretch with a smile in return and I wave at him, even though he's already seen me. And I blush, again, of course.

He strides towards me, then sweeps me up into a huge hug. *This is weird,* I think, but I let him continue to hug me. I tap his arms, signaling that I want to be let go and he complies.

"Do we need to head to baggage claim?" I ask, eyeing his small carry-on.

"No need, got everything I need in here," Jackson states, patting said carry-on.

"Alrighty then, let's head to the car." I motion him along, walking back towards the parking garage and our ride home. "Where are you staying while you're here?"

"At Riverfront Village, you know it?"

"I've been past it but I've never stayed there."

"One of the guys from the team recommended it. It looked nice and it has enough room for me to spread out for a few days. My room is waterfront, which you know I love and there's a great restaurant downstairs."

The fact that he so casually mentions memories I *should* have of him tells more about how he remembers our relationship. I feel bad that I don't remember every small detail like that about him, but we were in school and there were always a million other things going on at all times. *I wonder if he still thinks about my small details,* I ponder as we make it to the car.

I pop my trunk and he throws his bag in. As we settle into our seats and I'm reaching for my seat belt, I can feel Jackson's eyes on my face. Seat belt still in hand, I turn towards him.

"What?" I demand, meeting his eyes.

"Nothing, you just look really good, Lexa," Jackson states, unflinchingly.

I blush, because that's what I do now apparently. "Thank you Jackson, you look good too," I reply, and mean it. He's definitely been keeping himself in shape since college baseball. His several year stint in the MLB probably didn't hurt either. He's working for the Cubs as a scout now, having injured his arm his fifth year in the big leagues.

He's still got nothing on Drew, my brain reminds me, ever helpful in these situations. This train of thought once again causes me to blush. I look away from Jackson before this conversation can continue.

"How is the scouting business?" I ask, attempting to ease some of the tension in the car.

"Oh you know, same ol', same ol'. I still love the job, don't get me wrong. I just don't know if I'm still in love with all of the travel. I remember when traveling the country by plane and bus was the only thing I wanted to do and now all I can think about is settling down somewhere."

"Well that's always an option. What would you do if you weren't traveling though?"

At this question, Jackson turns fully in his seat to look at me. "Find someone to love who loves me back and maybe even start a family. I would love nothing more in my life than a quiet small town to raise kids with my wife."

I can't even look at him, instead I keep my eyes on the road and reach over and switch the station to something that's screaming. I can't believe he just said that. His need for travel and reluctance to stay in one place longer than a week is most of the reason we drifted apart. I couldn't see myself flying all over the country following him or not seeing him for the entirety of baseball season. Is he serious? And why is he still staring at me like that?

Chapter 12

Lexa

Wednesday

I don't know that I even slept last night. The conversation with Jackson played over and over in my head. From his extremely intense looks to the way he was saying my name like a promise when he told me bye at his hotel. There's no way he is thinking of rekindling our relationship. I'm sure he has no trouble finding women on his adventures throughout the country. I used to see them hanging all over him on the covers of magazines when he was a star pitcher. And honestly, he looks even better in the suits he wears now than he did in the baseball pants.

I can't seem to shake the feeling that he's wanting me to tell him I still love him. I feel like he wants me to run up to his hotel first thing this morning and profess my undying love for him. *Well tough cookies mister, because that's not happening. That ship sailed long ago when you prioritized your career over us,* I silently steam.

Okay, so maybe I did have more feelings for him then than I've been telling myself. But they truly are gone. As great of a guy as he is, I'm no one's backup plan and I'm not going to go running back to him just because he's finally ready to be with me the way I need.

I decide to head to the bathroom, anticipating a nice long shower to ease some of the aches I put in my shoulders during my sleepless night. As I'm walking past my nightstand, I notice I have a text. *God don't let it be Jackson,* I plead. I unlock my phone and see that it's not a message from Jackson, but a text and a missed call from Drew.

I hope Ansley is okay, I think first, then *Why is he texting me so early in the morning if it's not about Ansley?*

I open up the message since he didn't leave a voicemail. *Hey, call me when you get a chance–not an emergency, D.* is all the text says. Great, real vague. I guess I have no choice but to call him before I shower.

I sit on the edge of my bed and tuck my feet up under me. I take a few breaths and hit dial. He answers on the third ring.

"Hello?" he answers like he doesn't have caller ID.

"Hey Drew, you wanted me to call?"

"Hey Lexa, yeah. Good morning! I was thinking of running to get coffee this morning and wanted to know if you wanted to join. There's that coffee place down the street from you where we ran into each other on Monday. I've heard since that it's the best in the city. My day is pretty open, I don't know about yours. What do you think?" he asks, seemingly breathless by the end of his spiel.

I think a minute on my plans for the day. I have dinner with Ansley and our nursing school friends tonight and then drinks with the girls from the bridal party after, but I'm pretty free until then. Maybe a coffee date with Drew is just what I need to get my mind off of Jackson. *Not a date*, I remind myself. Just two friends having coffee and catching up.

"Sure, coffee sounds great!" I reply, glancing at the clock. "I was just about to hop in the shower. Meet you there in 30?"

"Sounds great, I'll see you in 30 minutes!" Drew confirms.

I hang up, setting my phone back on the nightstand. I stare at the wall, contemplating my life choices for about a minute before forcing myself up and to the bathroom. As I turn on the shower, I'm again just blankly staring at the wall. I try to pinpoint the cause of my new anxiety and realize I'm nervous about this coffee with Drew. Something just feels different this week with us and I'm nervous that I'm somehow about to wreck our friendship. I can't continue living with this awkwardness that has settled between us.

I steel myself and hop into the shower while it's still a bit cool for me, too ready to make it to breakfast to wait on it to warm up further. I shiver slightly, letting the water rinse my hair. I can already feel it warming up so I stay under the stream until it's hot. I shampoo, rinse, repeat and condition, attempting to wash the nervousness away. So far, it's not working. I feel almost giddy with this energy. Maybe I don't need too much caffeine when I get to the coffee shop. A nice herbal tea perhaps. I know they have a great elderberry and lemon tea for stress. I don't know if it can manage this amount of stress, but it'll be nice to try.

With nothing left to scrub, I have to put my nervous energy elsewhere. I still have 20 minutes before I have to be at the coffee shop, so I hustle to my closet to begin trying to decide what to wear today. I throw on my favorite skirt that elongates my legs and search for a top. I try and discard four different shirts before I settle on a fitted crop that hits the waistline of the skirt perfectly, but allows a little midriff to show when I move my arms around. It's a cute off shoulder number, since I know Drew likes collarbones. *Why am I suddenly worried about giving Drew a view of my collarbones,* I question. And why do I remember that small detail about Drew but didn't remember that Jackson loves a water view in a hotel room?

I run some gel through my hair, scrunching the ends and decide to actually put forth effort and blow dry it today. Usually I just leave it alone to air dry since it always ends up in a messy bun anyway. But I have a skirt on, so I might as well complete the look.

By the time I'm finished with my hair routine, it's time to leave. I hunt down my keys and sunglasses and head for the door. I run back to my room when I realize I didn't put on any shoes. My nude flats are sitting at the edge of my closet, ready to be thrown on. I step into them, check that I have my phone in my bag and make my way back to the door. With my hand on the handle, I take a deep breath, telling myself that I need to calm down before I try to leave this apartment.

For Pete's sake Lexa, it's only coffee, I berate myself. More gently I add, *with the guy you've been in love with for almost 10 years.*

With that last thought in my mind, I walk out of my building and towards coffee with Drew.

Chapter 13

Drew

Bounce bounce bounce bounce bounce, my leg keeps a steady rhythm under the table. I got here 10 minutes early because once I got ready, I couldn't sit at home any longer. I put my hand on my thigh, trying to still the movement, but it resumes as soon as I pull my hand away.

Maybe caffeine was a bad idea this morning. I didn't realize how nervous I was going to be for this date. *Not a date dammit,* I remind myself once again. This is not a date because for Lexa this is just coffee to catch up with an old friend. Why do I have to keep telling myself that?

I can't stop thinking about Lexa picking Jackson up from the airport yesterday. Did she go to the hotel bar with him last night and catch up? Did they grab dinner? I'm sure they did. Last I heard, Jackson was single and there's no way he's over Lexa. She always says it was a mutual breakup, but I remember Jackson being crushed talking about it the next time I saw him.

✿

Jackson was pitching in a game against the Rangers one weekend about a year after we graduated. Landon flew into town and we got to watch Jackson play in the big leagues. We even bought jerseys with his name on them to wear to the game. They played Friday and Saturday but he had Sunday off so we got to take him out to lunch.

After we breezed through the "how the hell are you" and the "we're so proud of you" parts of the conversation, talk somehow abruptly turned to Lexa. Looking back, I think it was because Landon mentioned Ansley and Lexa starting nursing school.

"Oh the girls are starting nursing school, huh? So I guess they're really buckling down, probably studying a lot and not going out very much?" Jackson asked.

"I mean, they're still going out. You know Lexa loves a frat party," Landon replied.

"Do you know if she's–Lexa, I mean–like seeing anyone?" Jackson continued the interrogation.

"I mean, I don't think so, dude. She hasn't seemed serious about anyone since, you know, you"

I watched as Jackson absorbed this information, watched his face register something like happiness that Lexa wasn't with anyone else. By this point, I had seen every picture of every girl hanging on his arm and I was sure Lexa had too.

"Why, man? Just leave her alone," I said, a bit too harshly.

Jackson's face fell, "I didn't mean anything, I just miss her I guess and I wanted to hear how she was doing."

I felt bad for a second for snapping at my friend, but quickly realized that my reaction had a deeper meaning. I needed to tell Lexa about my feelings sooner rather than later.

✿

Shit, I think, *I should have said something to her so long ago.* All those Christmases spent at my family home, the summer days we spent in Texas when Ansley and Landon would come visit and she would tag along. We could have been together all along and I've just been wasting time.

I make a deal with myself at this coffee house table that I'm going to tell her how I feel. Even if she doesn't feel the same way, I have to tell her.

With perfect timing, Lexa glides through the door, looking like a summer goddess. Her curly hair is down and bouncing, she has on the sweetest skirt and top. And with her perfect shoulders and collarbones peeking over the top of the shirt, I can't help but stand up to greet her as she sashays towards the table and to me.

"Wow, Lex, you look amazing."

She blushes slightly, looking down. But then she looks back up, meeting my gaze with the full force of her beautiful jade green eyes. "Thanks Drew, you clean up pretty nice yourself." She sits and smooths out her skirt.

"What do you want to drink? Are you hungry? I was going to grab something light to eat," I ramble, trying and failing to calm down.

"Oh yeah, I am a bit hungry. I'll come up there with you."

She lays her light sweater on the back of the chair, saving our table and we make our way to the counter. I can't help but stare at the exposed curve of her shoulder blade as she pulls her bag around to the front to dig for her wallet.

"Don't worry Lex, I got it."

That amazing blush is spreading across her cheekbones again as she turns to me to say, "Drew that's not necessary."

"I know it's not, but I want to. Friends buy friends coffee

right?" Dammit why did I just overemphasize our friendship? I cringe inwardly, but smile at Lexa and motion her forward to order. As she steps up to speak to the barista, I notice for the first time that Mike is behind the counter again. We make eye contact as Lexa looks at the tea menu. Mike winks at me and I just shrug at him again. Apparently that has become my universal sign with this guy. He laughs and turns his attention back to Lexa, awaiting her decision. She must never order tea here for her to have to look at the menu for so long.

As I make up my mind to voice this observation, Lexa says, "It's so hard to decide which tea to order, I've never had any from here, but they all sound so good!"

Mike gives Lexa a once over and looks at the menu in her hands. "May I recommend the elderberry tea? It has wonderful stress relief properties and the lemon is great for immune support. Which you need to be doing anyway, all that hanging around in the ER with those sick folks," he adds.

This last comment pulls a smile from Lexa, and prompts her to reply, "Sounds wonderful Mike. One elderberry and lemon tea, please."

"Anything to munch on?" Mike asks, looking her over once again, probably trying to determine if she's been eating enough. He really seems to care for this girl, which makes me like him even more.

"Hmm, let me get a fruit parfait, Mike," Lexa says, pronouncing parfait in the most Southern accent I have ever heard.

I realize I'm smiling when Lexa turns to me with a quizzical expression on her face. "Are you planning to order or just stand there grinning like the joker?"

I bark out a very unflattering laugh and immediately feel a blush settling on my face.

"I'll have a tea as well Mike, and I'll take a breakfast panini."

"Sure thing, man," Mike says, putting our order into the computer and adding up our total.

We head to the pickup end of the counter to wait on our drinks while Mike gives our food orders to the kitchen. I turn to Lexa to try to start a conversation to dispel some of this nervous energy I feel hanging between us. When I meet her gaze again though, I'm speechless. Her pupils are blown in that oh-so-sexy way again and her lips are slightly parted. I try to understand her sudden change in mood, but she's just staring straight at me, specifically at the small section of skin showing above my waistband from my shirt riding up momentarily.

Unfortunately, the spell is broken when Mike yells out, "Lexa, Drew, drinks are ready!" Maybe I don't like the man as much as I thought.

Chapter 14

Lexa

Dammit. Why does this keep happening? Another wave of crimson is sweeping across my cheeks and I'm sure down my neck as well. Drew definitely just caught me staring at his abs that were peeking out under his shirt hem. I just happened to glance over while he was putting his wallet back into his pocket and saw the bottom of his shirt move and then I was staring at his toned and tanned stomach and then my mind immediately started going to deeper and much darker places. There is no way he didn't notice. *Shit, shit, shit,* I curse myself.

And another thing, with Mike reading my mind about the tea order, does that mean all of my thoughts are written on my face this week? I steal a glance at Drew and notice a distinct curve to the edge of his lips. So yes, every thought is being read like a page from a book.

Okay. Time to be a big girl. It's time to stop dancing around this issue and finally just say something to Drew about how I'm feeling. If not now, when? He's still in town for another week, that gives us plenty of time to talk things out.

We head back to the table with our drinks. Our food will be coming out shortly, but Mike will just bring it over. Knowing that we might soon have someone in close vicinity makes me nervous to begin this conversation, since I don't know how it's going to go.

As we settle into our seats, I place both hands around my tea cup, steadying myself and my breathing. I take one last deep breath and look up and into Drew's deep ocean blue eyes. I'm momentarily lost in the sea, but I recover quickly and say, "I think we need to talk."

"Whoa. That's never a good thing," Drew says, slightly taken aback.

"No, not like that. I just think…I just feel like…there's something different…awkward—ugh. This is not coming out right." One more deep breath and then, "I feel like there is a new and different energy between us and I want to talk about it because I think I know where it's coming from." There, that wasn't so hard. I continue to stare at Drew's face, searching for any sign that he's feeling anything similar. A small twitch of his right eye is the only indication that he's even heard me.

But then, "Lexa….I have something to tell you."

"Okay, now you sound like the one with bad news."

"No, it's not bad, not really. I don't know what exactly it is. I know that I'm having feelings that I think you need to know about."

Mike chooses this moment to show up with our breakfast. He lays our food down in front of us, smiling at each of us in turn like he can't feel the thick tension surrounding the table. Knowing Mike, he's been watching the whole thing and chose this moment to give us a breather before the rest of this weirdness continues.

"Thanks Mike, I think we're all set," I say, silently begging him to go back to the counter so I can hear what Drew is trying to tell me. Mike takes the hint and with a wink for me and a smile for Drew, he saunters back to the counter.

"You were saying?" I ask, not even looking at my food.

"Yes, okay. Lexa, you know I care about you. I always have. You have been a part of our family for so long. You are one of my closest friends. This is not something I want to say to make things weird between us but it's something I need to say. I have feelings for you. Like real feelings. I know this is probably not something you want to hear from me, your best friend's brother but—"

"Shut up, Drew. Stop talking. You are not saying this. Just hold on," I plead, trying to sort my thoughts. I thought this was a one-sided crush that I was harboring. I thought my feelings for him were turning our relationship into something awkward. And now he's telling me he feels the same way? Is this real life? Do I want this to be real life?

"I'm so sorry, Lex. I didn't mean to upset you. I know you—"

"No Drew, it's not that. I just—I feel the same way."

Complete and utter silence fills the space between us. We are intently staring into each other's eyes and I realize that we're both leaning halfway across the table, cutting down the distance between us. I inhale sharply and lean back in my seat. I exhale a small laugh and watch as the color rushes back into Drew's face. He begins to chuckle, too.

As the nervous laughter fades, I realize that this is an entirely different conversation than I thought I was going to be having today. I study Drew's face again, as if it's something I haven't already memorized in the last decade. I'm shocked to see he looks different now, with this new information. The gleam in his eyes and the slight smile on his lips is not because he cares for me like a little sister. It's because he has *feelings* for me. He's attracted to me. And I'm suddenly speechless again. How can this be happening? Drew—hot as hell Drew—is attracted to me. As in, wants to be with me. The look in his eyes right now is one of pure and unrestrained desire.

And then my phone starts ringing. Not just a text. A phone call. One I have to take. It's Ansley. *Great timing*, I think, silently promising to pay her back for this after the wedding.

"Hey bridezilla," I answer on the third ring, throwing a lopsided grin towards Drew and shrug apologetically.

"Lex, ohmygod I'msogladyouanswered," Ansley rushes out in a single breath. Uh oh, she sounds upset. This close to the wedding, my mind starts to spin through all the horrible possibilities–dress got destroyed, venue called to cancel, the ring bearer caught the flu–and I start working on solutions before I even know the problem.

"Breathe Ansley. Where are you? I'm near the park, I can be anywhere you need me to be in 5 minutes."

"I'm at home. Can you come over? I'm freaking out."

"Of course, I'll be right there." I don't even ask what she's freaking out about. I'll find out as soon as I get there. I hang up the phone and catch the stunned look on Drew's face.

"What's wrong with Ans?" he asks, concerned but obviously upset that I'm leaving now.

"I'm honestly not sure, she just sounded stressed and asked me to run over there. I'm so, so sorry that I'm having to leave.

Rain check on this very enlightening conversation? I have to go, it's T-minus-3 days to wedding and there's obviously something big happening." I push my chair back and stand, reaching for my bag and my sweater.

"Or something not so big, you know Ansley leans a bit dramatic at times."

I glare at him, hoping I didn't just hear him call his little sister dramatic because of a freak out the week of her wedding. He wilts under my gaze and says, "I'm sorry, but she is sometimes. I know this probably is a big deal though and you should go. We have plenty of time to catch up. Do you have plans tonight?"

I spread my hands on the back of the chair, clutching it for balance. "Actually yeah, dinner with the nursing school crew and then drinks with the bridal party. Speaking of, I thought the guys were going out tonight somewhere as well?"

"Oh shit, yeah we are. I completely forgot. I got a little too excited about possibly seeing you again tonight, I guess." Wow so we're already at the bald honesty stage. I blush on command and toss him a smirk.

"Well you'll see plenty of me soon enough I'm sure."

The wolfish grin that splits his face makes me aware of my phrasing, causing my blush to deepen and spread down my neck again.

I watch as Drew's eyes travel the path of the reddening skin down to my chest and across my collarbones. I could swear I see him lick his lips and I am almost undone in the middle of the coffee shop. Before I can further regret leaving, I flick my gaze back to his eyes and step towards him to say bye. Drew stands from his chair and pulls me into a crushing hug. I bury my face against his chest, breathing in his familiar scent.

The scent that has been haunting my dreams for almost 10 years. The scent that has been lingering in my mind for days since he arrived back in town. I squeeze him just a little tighter and then release him, afraid that if I don't let go now, I'll never leave and go to Ansley. I step out of his embrace and give him a small, secretive smile.

"See you soon." I turn on my heel and let my hips swish a bit as I stride towards the door. Always leave them wanting more, right?

Chapter 15

Lexa

By the time I walk into Ansley's apartment, she's pacing the floor in full-blown panic mode. I drop my bag and rush to her side, trying to stop her from wearing a hole in her new rug.

"What is going on?" I ask, concerned about how big of a mess I am going to have to possibly clean up.

"The caterer called. Lex, they ordered black cocktail napkins. I cannot have black cocktail napkins at my blush and champagne wedding. Can you even imagine the travesty? I don't know what I'm going to do."

I try to remember what color we were supposed to have and venture a guess to ask, "Rose gold?"

"Yes Lexa," Ansley all but wails, "rose gold is what we're supposed to have and we have black!"

Maybe Drew wasn't so far off about her tendency to slightly overreact about certain things, but that's what I'm here for. I level her out. I get to work immediately doing just that.

"Okay, sit. Let me grab you some water or–"

"A glass of wine would be better," Ansley counters, falling back onto the couch and letting her hand rest on her forehead in true Southern meltdown fashion.

I turn towards the kitchen, not letting her see my slight eye roll. I love this girl so much and I would do anything for her. But I got called away from a potentially very good breakfast over a napkin color. I sigh as I pad toward the kitchen, I grab her favorite wine glass ("You're like really, really pretty") and reach for the fridge door to grab whatever white she's got in there. My hand freezes on the handle as I stare at a picture of the man I just left at the cafe. It's the picture of me and Drew from college that I love so much. Our faces are smooshed up tight together and we look so happy. I remember being so excited for him that night and running out on the field to show him. I'm not sure why I ran to Drew first and not Jackson, who actually pitched a great one-hitter game. But the look on Drew's face when I threw myself into his arms is one that I will never forget.

I force my mind back to the here and now, grabbing the bottle of pinot grigio and pouring Ansley a half glass. She prefers white for day drinking, though she has a long day ahead of her so I won't be indulging her too much this morning.

As I head back to the living room, I glance one more time at the picture of me and Drew. I wonder for the first time why Ansley has it hung on her fridge and why it's the only picture on there. I'll have to ask at some point. For now though, we have very important matters to attend to.

"Alright so here's the plan," I begin, handing Ansley her glass, "call the caterer back, tell them obviously no black.

Ask what they have in stock as far as white, gold and rose gold. They should have plenty to make up the amount that we needed of just the one color. Whatever they don't have, I'll grab from the wedding shop down the street either this afternoon or tomorrow. They always have a lot on hand and I'll call them while you're on the phone with the caterer to let them know we might be coming by for a large pickup. Anything else you can think of that we need while I'm there?"

Ansley eyes me over the edge of her glass, mid-sip.

"What?"

"Nothing," she replies quickly, dropping her eyes back to her wine glass.

I laugh and ask her again what she was looking at.

"I just always forget how good you are in emergencies all the time, not just at work. I feel like I'm useless outside of work. Someone sick comes into the ER and I know exactly what to do, but as soon as something small–like a napkin mix up–happens outside of work, I crumble. It's so weird."

"Ansley girl, that is so not true and you know it. You handle everything well, that's why you're our charge nurse. And you are allowed to have freak outs this week. You are getting married in three days, it's normal."

She looks back up at me then and begins to giggle. "I am getting married in three days aren't I? And I bet I won't even care what the napkins look like."

"You definitely won't. As you always say, you're marrying your best friend, how will paper that everyone will toss anyway change that at all?"

With this, she's calmed down considerably. It is crazy how much this wedding has stressed her out. She's normally pretty level-headed and a quick decision maker. Every decision about these nuptials, however, has caused some sort of torment for her. It makes me not want to ever have a wedding. I honestly feel like I am much more of an elopement girl anyway. I laugh to myself a bit thinking, *most people find someone to marry before they start worrying about the wedding.*

With her sweet smile back in place, Ansley says, "Alright I'm calling the caterer. Wanna grab a glass and join me on the couch?"

I smile back and nod, heading back to the kitchen. I pull another glass from the cabinet ("Safety first, drink with a nurse") and pour a half glass of the same white. I take a minute to look at the Drew picture again, studying the smile on his face. I miss seeing that face as often as I got to in school. It's weird to think that now, after all this time, I might be getting to see more of it after all.

I'm blushing and smiling as I walk back into the living room. I fold my legs under me as I drop onto the couch beside my best friend.

"Okay great, thank you so much. We have a plan to get the rest of them, just email me with the final numbers of each color you have if you don't mind. And have a great rest of your day, see you in a few days!" She hangs up with the caterer and turns to me.

"They have almost everything we need there. I think we will only be about 50 short. They're going to send me the totals of each color so I can try to get them as even as possible."

"That's great news! I'll go ahead and call the store just to let them know the plan and that we'll be picking them up tomorrow."

I take my phone out to make the call and see that I have a

text message from Drew. I immediately blush again, before even reading it. I quickly swipe past the message, not wanting Ansley to see it. I find the number for the wedding shop in town and make the call. I tell them that we will be picking up 50 napkins the next day in an assortment of white, gold and rose gold and that I will call them later today with the exact totals of each color. They take my information down and I hang up.

I turn back towards Ansley, ready to ask what we're doing the rest of the day, but she's staring at her phone screen.

"What are you looking at so intently?" I ask, scared there's already another problem.

Ansley jerks her head up to look at me, startled out of whatever trance she was in. "Oh," she laughs, "I was just getting entranced by this video on how to make slime."

We burst into laughter and clink our glasses together. It's decided that we're going to spend a little time catching up on our favorite reality show this morning before I head back to my place to get ready for dinner and the after party.

I snuggle into my place on the couch and pull my phone back out to read the text from Drew.

It was great talking to you this morning, I can't wait until our next date.

Chapter 16

Drew

I ~~had a great time~~
~~When can I see you again~~
~~We should run away together~~
It was great talking to you this morning, I can't wait until our next date.

Wow. I don't think I've stressed over what to text a girl since I was in tenth grade. Lexa has me all screwed up right now. I can't believe she feels the same way. I sigh and drop my chin onto my palm, looking out the window of the coffee shop. I'm still sitting in the same seat, trying to remember all the details. This is a day I never want to forget. I'm still bummed she had to run off, but I know she had to. Ansley needed her and even if she wasn't the maid of honor, I'm sure she would still be hustling over there to help Ans with anything she needed. That's just how Lexa is. She's selfless and giving and way too good for me. That's something I've known for a long time though. Maybe she'll just never catch on to that.

I'll just have to spend the rest of my life making sure I'm trying my best to be good enough for her.

I sigh again, fully aware that I probably look and sound like an angsty teenager right now. But I don't mind, I have enough to think about other than what these coffee shop patrons are thinking of me. With that thought in mind, I decide it's probably time to head out and get on with the rest of my day. I have some things I need to do around town before I go out with the guys tonight. We're getting started relatively early and I don't want to be late.

As I'm leaving, I glance back towards our table, trying to memorize everything I can about this day.

✿

It's officially party time, according to Landon's last text to me anyway. I grab my keys from the ring by the door and lock up behind me. I know that tonight is going to be fun since all the guys are in for the wedding and it'll just be us, taking Landon out on the town and having a great time. However, a very selfish part of me wishes we were having a group night out. So I could see Lexa again.

I shake off the thought, aware that I will be seeing her all weekend, and there's no need to rush this. I need to get my mind straightened out before we get this guys' night started or Landon will definitely be asking me what's going on in my brain. He has the uncanny ability to sniff out my thoughts and worries, and he's been doing that successfully since college. I think he's the only one that knew how head over heels I was for Lexa while she was with Jackson. I could tell from the look of pity on his face when we were all together. It didn't help that I always ended up being the fifth wheel. While I dated plenty of young women in college, none of them lasted very long. They were all great in their own ways, but I could never quite get Lexa out of my head and it wasn't fair to them to have to compete against a ghost. At some point it just became easier to only hang out with Lexa in group settings and not even worry about bringing a date. If it was going to be the four of them, I started skipping out, which really only meant that I missed time with Lexa.

As I'm nearing the restaurant that will be our first stop of the night, I notice that only a few of the guys have made it on time. Landon is here, of course, with Jackson and Kurt. After that, we're waiting on Connor and Patrick with Weston joining us after his nursing reunion with our girls. *Our girls,* I think, *did I really just say that?* But I guess, she's always been my girl, even before I told her how I felt. I have got to get away from this line of thinking before Landon reads my mind.

Good thing tonight is all about getting drunk with my friends, I think, opening the door to said party.

"Look what the cat dragged in," Kurt says, by way of greeting. Him and Jackson stand up, ready to embrace me in a huge bear hug. I accept their show of affection willingly and return it with gusto. I guess I did miss these guys a bit. Kurt and Jackson were two of my best friends on the baseball team, along with Landon. The four of us made some pretty rowdy memories together.

Patrick is another friend from college, but he was brought into the fold after Landon met him in calculus during our sophomore year. Connor is a great guy that's new to us, he works with Landon but we've all met him and loved him immediately. We met Weston through the girls when they were all in their prerequisite classes for nursing school. He was the one who ended up hanging out with me the most when we both ended up as extras to the foursome of Landon, Ans, Lex and Jackson. All-in-all, a great group of guys to be around and a group that I'm very excited to have a reunion with tonight.

We all sit back down, following another bear hug from Landon, even though I just saw him a few days ago. He seems to squeeze extra tight tonight, and I'm not sure whether it's because he has a mostly empty glass in front of him already or if he's getting emotional about the upcoming wedding.

This guy is going to be my favorite brother for sure, well my only brother but that doesn't change the feeling one bit. He's felt like a part of the family for so long, this marriage just makes it legal.

"I'll have one of whatever that was," I say, laughing and pointing at his near-empty drink.

"Oh that? Yeah, it was pretty good. I may have drank it just a bit too quickly, but what the hell, it's my bachelor party, right?" Landon laughs and pretty soon, we're all served a glass of peach bourbon and coke. It is extremely tasty and I can immediately see why it went down so easily.

This is going to be a hell of a night and we're just getting started.

About half an hour later, Patrick and Connor come strutting in, looking like they just walked off of some business casual runway.

I mean, who has a right to look that good in a pair of jeans and a blazer? I'm also intensely jealous that they even get to wear jeans to work.

"Y'all late from getting so dressed up to meet us out?" I joke, knowing full well they both just came from work. I look down at my dark wash jeans and gray henley, knowing that I could have probably made more of an effort. But then I glance at Landon who is wearing jeans and a vintage Budweiser t-shirt and don't feel a bit out of place.

"You know we just like to make you commoners feel bad, hanging out with supermodels and all," Patrick retorts. It's only then that I remember he actually did some modeling in college. For like a catalog or something, but still. I laugh, openly enjoying this already. Apparently I didn't need more than a drink and some time with the boys to get my mind away from the all-consuming Lexa. Or at least stop thinking about her with every brain cell I still have.

I head up to the bar to order another round, and a round of water for those of us not just getting started. I need Landon to last the whole night, and at this rate he won't even make it to the third stop.

As I'm nearing our table, hands full of drinks, I overhear Landon asking Jackson about his ride home last night. I–somewhat ashamedly–eavesdrop, and don't love what I'm hearing.

"Yeah dude, I pretty much told her that I'm ready to settle down and I think she knows who I want to settle down with," I hear Jackson saying.

I almost drop the drinks in my left hand, focusing too intently on their conversation. I save them just in time to set them all down. I'm passing them around when I hear Landon's reply.

"Dude, you don't know that she's still into you. I mean did she say anything back, even?"

"Not really…but I could just see it in her eyes when she looked at me. I never forgot about her and I don't think she's written me off yet either," Jackson states, rather confidently.

I pass Landon's drink over to him, effectively ending their conversation as he looks up and meets my eyes. I can feel him trying to read me, so I smile and look at Jackson instead.

"How's Alisha or Megan or Kimmy? Are you still seeing all three of them?" I ask, in a not very kind tone. I chuckle to try to dispel some of the sudden anger and jealousy from my voice. I know that Lexa wants me, she just told me that. But what about her conversation with Jackson last night? Is she still interested in him?

"Dude, I ended things with them months ago. I was actually just telling Landon here how I'm thinking it's finally time to settle down, find someone to marry and have some kids," Jackson says, in a suddenly wistful tone.

I can't help the small derisive snort that comes out, nor can I seem to stop the next words that come out of my mouth, "Yeah you settling down? When hell freezes over, I'm sure." I immediately regret the tone and the hurtful words. I attempt to backtrack a bit, "Dude I'm sorry, that came out in such a shitty way. It just honestly surprises me. You've been living the bachelor life for so long and this is the life you've always dreamed of having. What changed so suddenly?"

Jackson, though a bit put off by my outburst, answers, "I don't really even know. A couple of months ago, I was at some random hotel in some random city, going to watch another high school baseball team when I just thought 'I don't want to do this forever' and that's when it started clicking into place that maybe I didn't even want to do the travel thing anymore at all. I started thinking about the last time I was happy being in one place and my mind took me back to the college years. Sure there was travel during the season, but we were home more often than not and I miss having some roots."

"I always knew you'd come around to our way of thinking, you're not really as much of a loner as you like to think. Have you thought of a place you'd like to settle?" Landon asks, throwing an arm around the back of Jackson's chair, always the big brother.

"No, but with my family spread all over the country, there's no one place that has ever felt like home. I did like it here in the South when we were in school, though. I wouldn't mind moving back here," Jackson answers, turning thoughtful.

"Well, another reason to celebrate then. We're taking two bachelors out of the game it seems!" I raise my glass to toast the group and receive a laugh from Jackson and a wink from Landon.

"May our lives be long and our drinks be strong!" Kurt yells, clinking glasses with me. Everyone dissolves into laughter at that and the rest of our night truly begins.

I'm afraid I won't be able to get Jackson's words out of my head the rest of the night, but around stop four, I don't have much of anything in my brain. My only thoughts include making sure Landon is having the time of his life, trying to get him to ride a mechanical bull and wondering how the girls are doing on their night out.

Chapter 17

Lexa

"What do you mean you're not with Brian anymore?" I practically yell at Grace.

"I mean that we broke up. It just wasn't working out anymore. He's all about getting married right this second, buying a big house and having kids. Like 4 of them. I'm just not there yet. I want him to be happy, and it just didn't seem like I was the person to do that for him anymore," Grace says, shrugging.

God, Grace and Brian had been together forever. I assumed I would be receiving a save the date in the mail anytime now. If people that seem perfect for each other can't make it work, how am I supposed to make a relationship last?

As this thought crosses my mind, I look at Ansley, glowing with her prenuptial excitement and realize that there are still plenty of examples of true love. Her relationship with Landon has renewed my faith throughout the years. The love and grace that they continually show each other makes me believe there really is someone out there for everyone.

This dinner has been so much fun and makes me even more excited for the next several days of getting to hang out with these lovely people. I missed all these sweet faces from our nursing school days. I'm sitting between Weston and Ansley and across from Claire. Grace is sitting across from Weston and he's the one she was originally talking to about Brian. Wes and Brian were friendly in college. I'm not sure they ever really talked afterwards and I didn't even ask before freaking out about the breakup.

"Was that news to you or were you still talking to Brian?" I ask Weston.

"I mean, it's been a few months. We were mainly only keeping up through random Snapchat stories," Wes replies.

Interesting, I think, *I guess he was already drifting off from everyone.* Wes is one of those guys that will maintain a friendship even if it's one-sided for him. He just believes in keeping up with people. So if he hadn't even heard about their breakup, I feel like that shows he was planning this for a while. I watch Grace again for any clues that she feels broken up about this, but she honestly seems fine. Another note for the mental sticky pad: *Check on Grace throughout the weekend.*

I turn my attention back to Ansley, looking to read her thoughts. I'm ready for this party to get started soon, but if she's wanting more of a chill dinner before getting a little wild tonight, I'll keep this tame. I see her foot tapping on the floor near mine and she's picking at her fingers while aiming a tight smile at me. *Party time,* I deduce.

I catch the waitress's eye and when she gets to our table with a huge smile in place, I say, "Five shots of Patron, please ma'am."

"Coming right up, my party people!" our sweet waitress

replies.

Claire catches my eye and we both begin giggling and I know our minds are in the same place. Our third semester of nursing school was filled with weekends off that we took advantage of by playing drinking games, usually with tequila shots. We would hang out Friday or Saturday and have a day or two to recover before class on Monday.

"Remember that weekend in the beginning of third semester, the three of us ended up having to pull an all-nighter that Sunday night to finish our clinical paperwork since we were too hungover to even look at it Sunday afternoon?" Claire asks, glancing between me and Ansley.

"If they don't, I wouldn't blame them. I remember having to do a Gatorade and french fry run for y'all that Sunday and the three of you looked half-dead," Weston says, laughing as he's slapping me on the shoulder.

"Oh God, that was such an awful day that we made even worse by staying up so late that night," I say, laughing again.

"Sometimes I think it's a wonder we even made it out of nursing school, much less are fully functioning adults," Ansley jokes.

"Hey, we did just fine!" I retort. "I mean, we all passed like way above the failing scores." We all laugh again, thinking about those days that already feel so far behind us. As I look around the table at all of these wonderful humans, I feel so lucky to have met each of them. It's probably true what they say about stress bonding—we have been through some stuff together and come through it with amazing friendships. I feel that way about Ansley especially. From nursing school to my dad's death to moving to a new city and working in the ER together, our relationship is stronger than any I've ever had.

I'm on the verge of tears, thinking about how much I love these people, when I see our waitress, Jen, heading back our way with some gorgeous gold liquid on her tray.

"Jen!" I shout, throwing my arms up in the air and effectively shoving these sappy thoughts away. Between that emotional breakfast with Drew and being around all of my best friends all in one day, I feel like there's a lot bubbling under the surface. While I'm known to be a bit of a crier when I start drinking wine, I don't want that to happen at the beginning of this shindig.

Jen begins passing around our shots, giving each of us a lime wedge and setting small cups of salt in the middle of the table. "Anything else I can grab for y'all?" she drawls.

"No, thank you! I think we're all set for now!" I say, giving her my best imitation of the Ansley megawatt smile.

Ansley laughs, knowing what I'm doing. She playfully slaps the back of my hand saying, "Stop that, you know I always feel like you're messing with me when you do that."

"Imitation is the best form of flattery, my dear," I reply, in a vaguely British accent (and by vaguely I mean just plain bad).

"Let's take these before they get warm!" Claire cheers.

We each take a lime slice, sprinkle salt on the backs of our hands and grab our shot glasses. We're all looking around at each other, trying to see who's going to toast first.

"To love, laughter and happily ever after," Grace says.

"To spending your days in happiness and surrounded by the ones you love," Claire says.

"To the same penis forever," Weston says, snorting. We all roll our eyes, then start laughing.

"To never having to go on another first date," I say, winking at Ansley.

"To having the best friends a girl could ever ask for," Ansley says, smiling at each of us in turn. We raise our glasses, lick the salt from our hands, clink the edges and give a hearty "Cheers!" before bringing the shots to our mouths and throwing back the throat-burning liquid. I immediately bring the lime to my mouth, sucking every bit of the sour taste into my mouth to not gag from the shot. I don't know why I always insist I love tequila shots, I almost always have to stifle the reflex.

But they're just so good at making you forget whatever shit you're holding onto.

Chapter 18

Drew

"Another!" I shout, in my best Thor imitation. I stop myself short of throwing the glass, setting it gently on the bar top.

"Do you really think we need another Irish Car Bomb?" Landon slurs, placing his hand on my shoulder to steady himself.

I give him a good once-over and reply, "Why the hell not? Are you suddenly no longer having a good time?" By the glazed look in his eyes and the huge grin plastered on his face, I can tell he's having a great time. I've been feeding him enough water between drinks to keep him on his feet. I've been drinking two waters for every drink myself, not wanting to lose him anywhere tonight.

"Man, I'm having the best time," Landon says, grabbing my other shoulder and forcing me to face him. "You're my best friend and I love you." His eyes start to well up, and I know this will not end well if he starts crying.

"I love you too, dude," I say, slapping him on the back. "If you really loved me that much though, I'd be standing beside you this weekend and not one person away." I laugh, knowing this will distract him.

"Ugh, I told you that it was due to the *aesthetics* and the *color palette.* Really, it's just whatever Ansley wanted because she's the one in control here. We all know it."

"I am just messing with you, my man. I don't give a shit. This way I didn't have to plan anything and there's way less pressure on me. Plus I know it's really just because you're self-conscious to be standing next to a beautiful man like me when you're supposed to be the center of attention." I wink at him and swat his hand away when he goes in for a soft hit.

"Okay then, another drink, maybe just a beer this time though."

"You got it." I sidle back up to the bar, catching the bartender's eye. I motion for two bottles and a water. I watch as he rings up the drinks on my tab and reaches into the cooler for the beers. As he pops the tops, he motions to Landon, "That's the lucky man, huh?"

"Yeah," I say, smiling, "That guy's marrying my little sister, so I'm not sure how lucky he is."

The bartender chuckles a bit as he's filling up my water glass. "Just 'cause she's annoying to you, doesn't mean she annoys him. I can guarantee that one."

I reach for the drinks, both of us laughing now. I turn towards Landon in time to see him hugging Jackson now. I laugh some more, realizing we're definitely in the portion of the night where he needs to make sure we all know how loved we are.

As I walk towards the group, I hear Landon telling Jackson just how much he cares about him and I watch as Jackson slaps him on the back while trying to unobtrusively slip out of the hug. Jackson has never been big on the touchy-feely stuff. Coming from a family of huggers, I'm just used to the full body bear hugs I get from Landon. He definitely fits right in with us.

Jackson sees me coming and gives me a look that I take to mean "please get me away from here" so I decide to be nice and save him. I bump shoulders with Landon, handing him the beer and raise mine to clink bottles. "To all that happily ever after bullshit," I say, grabbing him in a hug once I set my water on the table.

My eyes find Jackson's again and he's giving me a smile. *Why does Lexa want to be with someone who doesn't like touching,* I wonder. Maybe he's more touchy with her. Why am I even thinking about that right now? I realize I'm obsessing over their ride together last night again and what I heard him say to Landon tonight. I know how our conversation went this morning, but how about theirs last night?

I look Jackson over, trying to gauge his level of drunkenness and deciding if I really want to ask the question burning on the tip of my tongue.

"So I heard you hung with Lexa a bit last night…" I blurt, knowing that subtlety is not really my specialty. Jackson glances at Landon before meeting my eyes.

"Yeah, she picked me up from the airport. We talked a bit on the way home but she said she wasn't really up to hanging out at the hotel. Said she had a long day or something. It's fine though, I figure we have all weekend."

"That's true. The whole weekend's ahead of us."

"Do you still talk to her a lot? I mean I know she's your sister's best friend but are the two of you close?"

"I mean, I see her on holidays and stuff. She's still really close with my family. But it's not like we text a lot or anything." I'm not sure why I'm acting like me and Lex aren't close or like we didn't just have a life-altering conversation earlier today. Maybe I'm still trying to figure out where Jackson's head is. I know I'm probably coming on too strong to seem nonchalant, but that's what I'm going for. Just a mildly curious bystander to the entire situation. And maybe Jackson has enough alcohol in his system to buy it. I doubt it though, since I've only seen him drink three mixed drinks all night.

Not that I'm keeping tabs on him, I've just been trying to watch everyone, to make sure all the guys are having fun and not reaching their tipping point too soon. The night is still young.

Thank God I've been pounding water all night. We're in for a long one.

We still have to find that mechanical bull.

Chapter 19

Lexa

Thursday

*T*hank God I drank so much water last night, is my first thought upon waking with only a minimal headache. I'm still so glad we did the girls night out last night instead of waiting until tonight. I need to be on my A-game the rest of the weekend. The rehearsal dinner is tomorrow night with the wedding right on its heels on Saturday.

I turn over onto my left side and see that Ansley is still sound asleep. She's spending the night with me until after the wedding. Since her and Landon live together, they wanted to be somewhat traditional for this part. Landon still has to work today so she gave him the apartment for the rest of the weekend.

Ansley and I haven't had a sleepover in so long, so this is kind of exciting for us. Landon kept repeating how he felt like he was kicking Ansley out of their home. But I can tell she's relieved to not be living with a boy for at least a few days. While my apartment isn't spotless by any stretch of the imagination, at least I don't leave dishes piled in the sink or miss the laundry basket with my socks every day. My eyes travel from the chair in the corner of my room stacked with clean scrubs to the top of my dresser layered with books that I haven't shelved yet. I should probably get in a good day of deep cleaning while I have this time off work.

I twist around and grab my phone off of the nightstand, looking at the time as I unlock it. Wow, it's already 10 am. I haven't slept this late in forever. We did have a pretty late night though, so I'll give myself a break today.

I flip through some emails and then spend some time looking at my friends' posts online, catching up through social media. After a little while, I hear a growl and realize that I'm starving. I don't think we ate anything after our early dinner last night and now it's almost lunch time.

I gently untangle myself from the sheets, trying my best not to wake Ansley. The bride needs her beauty rest, after all. I tuck her back in, and tiptoe out of the room, heading towards the kitchen.

I'm relieved to see that I remembered all of our breakfast and lunch essentials for the next couple of days. I picked up cold brew coffee, instant cinnamon oatmeal with fresh blueberries, and avocado for toast. I also grabbed ramen and grilled some chicken that I picked up from the store. All of our struggle meals from college, but on a bigger budget.

I pour us each some cold brew, adding vanilla cream to Ansley's. Then, I pop some oatmeal into the microwave and begin slicing avocado for the toast. I grab the blueberries from the fridge and toss some bread into the toaster. The microwave beeps and I open the door, letting some of the heat out before taking out the oatmeal. I spoon it into two separate bowls and sprinkle the blueberries on top. The toaster pops so I snatch the toast and layer on the avocado. I dash the avocado with some everything bagel topping and grab a tray.

I gently place the breakfast items on the tray and carry them into the room. I set the tray down on the nightstand before crawling back under the covers. I look over to see that Ansley is still sound asleep.

I don't want to wake her too early, but she'll be grouchy if she doesn't eat soon.

I tap her arm a few times while saying her name. Nothing. I gently shake her, still nothing. I grab her arm and shake her a little harder while poking her face.

I hear a groan and then, "Why are you poking my face?"

"I wanted to wake you up and nothing else seemed to be working. I was this close to splashing water over you. That would have made more work for me, though, so I didn't get there."

"Thank God for your inherent laziness," Ansley mutters, still not opening her eyes.

"Hey, if I was lazy, would I have made you this?" I say, giving a full Vanna White to show off the breakfast spread.

She finally sits up, looking at the food.

"Okay, that looks and smells delicious. Gimme."

"Yes, ma'am madam bride."

"You're the worst," she says, laughing.

I lay the tray between us, watching her snatch up her coffee first. I laugh, seeing the look of true joy that crosses her face. She closes her eyes, smiling around the edges of the cup and takes a few more sips.

"Ah, coffee, my true love language," Ansley says, sighing.

"I've always known the way to your heart," I reply, giggling.

I reach for my toast and begin to nibble as she arranges her pillow behind her to more comfortably eat in bed.

"I love being an adult and getting to eat breakfast in bed."

"Me too. There's just something so peaceful about getting to munch on good food while in the comfort of your own sheets. But get your crumbs in my sheets and I will end you."

She snorts out a laugh and puts her coffee back on the tray, picking up her bowl of oatmeal. "You sound like my mother."

"I might take offense to that if I didn't love your mom so much. What do they have going on today?" I know tomorrow we'll all be wrapped up in wedding preparations with the rehearsal dinner.

"I think her and my dad are actually going on a little day date to Tybee to get away before our entire family descends on the city."

"God, your parents are sweet. It sickens me."

"I know, imagine growing up in the house with that." Ansley laughs before sighing wistfully and adds, "But it was a wonderful example of a loving marriage and I'm very thankful to have witnessed it as a kid."

"Yeah, of course I had a pretty different experience growing up. But you know my dad, he was wonderful. He definitely was the kind of dad that showed me how I'm supposed to be treated by someone who loves me. I'm thankful for him showing me how to know my worth in a relationship."

Ansley tears up a little and I realize that my eyes are welling up, too.

"Okay, enough of that. Eat your oatmeal and keep your crumbs on your side," I say, digging my finger into her ribs, making her laugh and almost drop her bowl.

"Okay, okay. What's on the agenda for today. I know we're stopping by the store for the napkins, anything else you need to get done today?" I ask Ansley, trying to run through my mental checklist to see what we're missing.

"I really think that's it. I might want to run to the shops just to do a little last minute shopping before we leave for Nantucket. I need all the preppy clothes I can get my hands on."

"Well I, for one, would love to accompany you in that endeavor." I love that Ansley and Landon are honeymooning in Nantucket. It'll be somewhere low-key where they can walk and bike and eat great food. She said she wasn't in the mood for a beach holiday since we live 30 minutes from a great beach. I love that they're staying state-side as well. It's just so different and I can't wait for pictures when they get back. I know I'm going to miss her greatly for the next week though.

"Well, we might as well get our day started. We'll head by the wedding shop first and grab the napkins. Then, we can spend the rest of our day perusing the racks. I might need to stop at the corner and grab another coffee though, I need a good caffeine kick to get this old body moving today."

"Sounds like a plan to me," Ansley says, grinning. "I'll go ahead and hop in the shower."

I take the tray back into the kitchen and I'm loading the dishes into the dishwasher when I hear my phone chirp.

What are you doing today? the text from Drew reads. And just like that, I'm blushing again. Why do I feel like a teenager?

Just clothes shopping with Ans, I reply.

Wanna grab food sometime today? Of course my sister is invited.

Sure! Let me ask her when she gets out of the shower. We could probably do a late lunch or an early dinner if that works for you?

Yeah, either sounds great. My day is pretty open, so just let me know. See you later, beautiful.

Heat rises to my cheeks and I know I'm blushing again. Yep, I'm definitely still a teenager at heart apparently.

I hear the shower shut off and put my phone down, determined to not let Ansley see the color staining my cheeks. She's too good of a sleuth to not figure out the truth if I don't work around this carefully. I'll have to think about how to casually suggest dinner with Drew without raising her suspicion.

Chapter 20

Drew

I roll over onto my left side and slit my eye open, peering at the alarm clock. I guess a late night makes for a late morning. It's already 10 am. I guess now is as good a time as any to get up and get going. I sit up, slowly so as to not disturb my head, just in case I didn't drink enough water last night. I stay there for a moment, feeling fine. So I stand, stretch, and head to the bathroom.

As I head into the kitchen, I see that Weston is still fast asleep on the couch. My place was a lot closer than his so he just crashed with me after the last bar. His leg is flung over the back of the couch and both of his arms are above his head. He's really just begging me to come slap his stomach. But, I'll refrain, seeing as we're not college dudes anymore and he probably needs the rest after the night we had.

I'm debating on whether or not to start a pot of coffee or run down the street to the cafe when I hear a loud snore rip free from Wes's mouth. *Cafe it is,* I think, not wanting to listen to that cacophony much longer. It's a wonder that sound didn't keep me up last night. But I guess I was pretty exhausted by the time we finally made it home.

I head back to my room and slip into the shower, trying to make as little noise as possible. Wouldn't want to wake sleeping beauty out there. I quickly dress and toss my hair around into some semblance of a style and grab my wallet from the dresser.

I sneak out the door, locking it almost soundlessly and head down the stairs.

I assume Wes will be sleeping for a little while longer, and if not, he knows to just make himself at home until he's ready to go.

Memories from last night are flooding back into my mind, from shots at the Irish pub to watching Landon hang onto a mechanical bull at two in the morning. We ended up finding the place when they were on their last leg of the night. They yelled last call maybe 30 minutes after we got Landon off of the floor by the bull, but we closed it down nicely. We all had a great time.

I still couldn't get Lexa off my mind though. All night, any time that I saw Jackson look at his phone, I was wondering if he was texting her. I need to talk to her again to see where she's at with all of this. We never got a chance to talk again after breakfast yesterday.

I'm nearing the coffee shop when I decide to throw caution to the wind and see if she wants to grab lunch or dinner today. I need to see her again and talk about all of this.

What are you doing today? I text her quickly, before I chicken out.

Just clothes shopping with Ans, she quickly replies. Shit, I forgot my sister was staying with her until the wedding.

Wanna grab food sometime today? Of course my sister is invited.

Sure! Let me ask her when she gets out of the shower. We could probably do a late lunch or an early dinner if that works for you?

Yeah, either sounds great. My day is pretty open, so just let me know. See you later, beautiful. Was that overkill? It probably was, but I'm glad I said it.

Now that that's settled, I open the door to the coffee shop and walk inside, inhaling all of the delicious aromas drifting towards me.

I see Mike is behind the counter again and I look around a bit as I walk up.

"I haven't seen her yet this morning," Mike says, giving me a devilish grin.

"Who?" I ask, trying and definitely failing to be nonchalant.

Mike just laughs, asking, "What'll it be today?"

"Um…what do you recommend? What's your favorite caffeine boost y'all got?"

"That would be the oat milk shaken espresso. Wanna try it?"

"Sure, sounds great. Medium, please."

"You got it," Mike smirks, looking towards the back table. I follow his gaze to see that the table Lexa and I shared yesterday is vacant. I decide it's fate and head that way.

Once I'm seated, I open my phone back up, navigating to social media. I don't think anyone would post too crazy of pictures from last night, but I want to make sure I'm not tagged in anything super embarrassing.

I see that Kurt posted one of just our glasses clinking, which all of our hands are tagged in. It's a pretty cool picture so I allow the tag. Connor posted a bathroom selfie of him and our handsome groom from the second bar we were at. Landon doesn't look too disheveled yet, but I laugh anyway, knowing where the night went from there.

I don't see any other posts from last night yet and assume that most people ended up sleeping in or had to drag themselves into work and weren't able to throw any pictures online yet. I took a few, but they're more suited to being made into memes to pass around our group chat rather than posted for mass consumption.

As I'm looking through the pictures on my phone from last night, I hear two very familiar voices walking into the cafe. Ansley and Lexa. Wow, they got ready for their day pretty quickly.

I get up from the table before they see me, putting my head down like I'm going to walk right past them. Before bumping into Ansley, I lift my head up to say, "Hey, watch where you're going. What do you think this is, your own personal runway?"

"Oh my gosh, I'm so sor–oh. It's you," she says, seeing me fully. "Asshole," she mumbles under her breath, but smiling at me all the same.

"Are you stalking me now?" Lexa says, pulling my full attention to her. She looks stunning today. Hair like fire pulled back into a high ponytail, a little black t-shirt dress and a pink bag across her chest, she looks like the dream girl next door.

She blushes as she realizes that I'm drinking her in. "No, you got here second, that means you'd be stalking me," I retort, in my best imitation of a fifth grader I'm sure.

"Good one, bro," Ansley says, huffing a laugh before turning to head to the counter.

"Great minds think alike?" I ask, turning back to Lexa, in time to see her smiling up at me.

"We needed a little caffeine after our night out. What about you?"

"Same, we were out pretty late. Weston is still passed out on my couch. I heard from Landon earlier, he barely made it onto his 9 am call, but he did. Luckily, that's all he had for the day and he's soundly back asleep now."

"That must be nice, being able to work from home when you can't go into the office. I wouldn't know. It's hard to do CPR through a video chat."

I laugh heartily, placing my hand on her forearm. "I can imagine that would be difficult. But, you wouldn't have it any other way and you know it."

"That's true," she says, "though it sure is nice to complain every once in a while."

"I know that feeling."

We're both quiet for a moment before Lexa looks down and realizes I already have my coffee.

"Oh, you already ordered? Were you on your way out?"

"Like I said earlier, pretty open day ahead of me. Are y'all posting up here for a bit?"

She looks towards the counter where Ansley is laughing with Mike. "I think we're just grabbing to go. But we're still meeting up to grab food later right?"

"Yeah, whenever y'all are free. I would love that." I smile down at her, catching a strand of hair that escaped her ponytail and tucking it behind her ear.

She blushes again, making the inside of my body heat in a very primal way. How can color going across her cheeks cause that strong of a reaction in me?

"We also need to talk some more, I think. But it can wait for a bit. I know y'all have a busy day," I say, quickly adding, "It's nothing to worry about, just want to talk some more about our little conversation yesterday." I quirk my mouth to the side in my most charming half-smile.

Lexa gently reaches out and places her hand on my stomach, just above my belt. "I would love to talk more about us," she breathes out, coming just a bit closer.

I want so badly to grab the back of her head and crush my lips into hers until we're both bruised, but now is not the time for a first kiss. We have so much time ahead of us and I don't really know how she feels about dramatic displays of affection. I stifle a shutter and she takes a small step back.

She smiles up at me with a devious gleam in her eye, knowing full-well the effect that little stunt just had on me. She steps back again in time for us to see that Ansley is about to be heading back in our direction.

That's one thing we need to talk about sooner rather than later, telling my sister.

"Here's a cowboy for you, my love," Ansley says, handing Lexa a cardboard to-go cup.

"Are you sure you need to be drinking that much caffeine on the regular?" I ask, knowing the kick that's in that cup.

"It's half decaf, half caffeinated with half the espresso shots that she normally gets. It's her off-duty cowboy as we call it," Ansley informs me. "Also, stop being so judgy."

Lexa just smiles at me again as they walk away.

"Hey let's do dinner tonight? I'll text you!" I say as they near the door. I get a thumbs up from Ansley and another sweet smile from Lex.

I take my phone out of my pocket, typing *Your butt looks*

really good in that dress before sending it off and putting my phone away. I laugh and turn to wave bye to Mike before also heading out the door.

I'll go wake up the sleeping prince and see if he wants to grab brunch before heading home. I'm suddenly ravenous.

Chapter 21

Lexa

Okay I officially love running into Drew at the coffee shop. Seeing him unexpectedly gives me all the butterflies. I'm so glad we're having dinner later. I'm even more glad that Ansley will be joining us. I feel like we might still need a buffer at this stage.

His "we need to talk" line really scared me and we're not even seeing each other.

And that hungry look in his eyes is really starting to wear me down. When he was giving me that sexy half smile of his and staring into my eyes with those burning blues, I thought I might jump him right there in the coffee shop.

I feel my phone buzz in my pocket. *Your butt looks really good in that dress.* Of course I can't keep the crimson from sweeping across my face. I feel guilty as I look up and see Ansley staring at me with a questioning look. I can't keep the fact that I'm in love with her brother a secret from her for much longer.

I know she knows something is up when she says, "Who

are you talking to, some secret lover?"

Luckily, I'm somehow able to stop from flushing this time and calmly answer, "No, just reading an email."

"Yeah work emails get me all hot and bothered, too," Ansley says, laughing.

Well, I think, *she's not wrong about my current predicament.*

I try to laugh it off, and attempt to change the subject.

"How far to Wedding Belles? It's only a five minute walk right?"

"Yes, Lex. Only five minutes. I really wish you would start running with me again. A five minute walk would seem like nothing."

"You know I only run for short sprints on the soccer field or if something is chasing me these days. And then only if there's even a chance of outrunning it."

"Lexa, my dear. How can you lift so much weight and do so many crunches but you won't go for a little run? Even with your best friend? It's such a good way to relax. It's just one foot in front of the other and you can clear your head."

"My head is clear," I say, knowing just how many thoughts are bouncing around my brain right now.

"Yeah, seems crystal clear. Especially since you just passed the turn to the shop."

Dammit. "I was just trying to get in some extra steps for the day. You know, build up that cardio so I can run as much as you one day."

"Yeah, yeah, yeah. Well let's take a left on this block instead of backtracking."

As we turn onto the main street, looking for the sign for Wedding Belles, I see a familiar figure walking towards us.

Having apparently spotted us first, Jackson is heading

directly towards us. I realize that I haven't talked to Ansley about what he said during our car ride the other night.

He's striding toward us, an easy grin on his face and gives us each a small wave.

"Hey, girls," he says, his velvet voice making those two small words carry more meaning. "What are you two doing out and about today? I assumed you might be sprawled in bed after your night out."

"We could ask the same of you," I retort. "I heard you had a pretty wild night yourself."

"You know I never get too crazy, Lex." He glances at Ansley and says, "Landon on the other hand…"

Ansley laughs, saying, "Yeah I saw some videos that Wes took. It looked like y'all had a great time. I can't believe you even got him up on a mechanical bull."

"Oh that was definitely a sight to see. I'm just glad I was there to witness it."

I think back to the video that I watched this morning on Ansley's phone of Landon on that mechanical bull. Ans and Jackson must have been thinking about it too, because we all burst into laughter at the same moment.

As we settle back down, I look up to see Jackson staring at me. I cock my head to the right and feel a small grin stretch across my lips. "What?" I ask, aware of Ansley's attention on me now as well.

"I was just wondering if you happened to be free tonight, or if the bride was keeping you all to herself."

"I am certainly no kidnapper, good sir. But we do actually have dinner plans with my brother," Ansley answers before I can respond. "But I'm sure he'd love for you to come, too!"

I shoot a death glare at Ansley, who is still smiling sweetly at Jackson, seemingly unaware of my unease.

Jackson at dinner with me and Drew? I can't even imagine how uncomfortable that would be. Especially with the things that Jackson said in the car Tuesday night. My mind flashes back to all the times Drew came out with me and Jackson and our friends and realize he was probably just as uncomfortable doing that. But he did it anyway, I'm thinking now though that it might have been just to be around me.

Before I can try to deter Jackson from this disastrous idea, he says brightly, "Oh cool, that would be great. Lexa, just text me where you're going and when and I'll meet up!" He flashes me a very disarming smile, gives Ansley a slightly more tame one and turns to head off to whatever his errands in town may be.

"What. The. Hell." I bite out, turning to Ansley.

"Whoa, what?" she stammers, genuinely confused.

I take a few deep breaths, reminding myself that Ansley is completely unaware of the weird love triangle that I have found myself in this week.

"Let's sit down over here real quick before we go into the store. I have a few stories from this week that I think you might be interested in."

Chapter 22

Drew

There's been a development, my phone pings with a message from Lexa.

Yo dude, it looks like I'm joining you for dinner tonight. Where are we going? says the message I get from Jackson at almost the same time.

I groan and drop my phone onto the table.

"Whoa, man. That was the most angsty groan I've heard since like high school. What's up?" Weston asks, eyeing me carefully like he's unsure whether I'm going to scream or never talk again.

"I really don't know how to even phrase this, but Lexa-"

"And you are finally hooking up?!" Weston half-yells in the crowded restaurant. I notice several heads turn our way and feel a blush creeping onto my face.

"I wouldn't say that exactly. But we did meet up for coffee and discuss the fact that we both have unresolved feelings for each other."

Weston cannot seem to contain his glee. "So what's the

problem exactly? I figured you would be freaking over the moon about this when it finally happened."

"Finally? What, like you just knew that this would come about somehow?"

Wes grins maniacally and says, "Uh, yeah dude. We all did. It was destined. Written in the stars, even."

"God, you're so sappy sometimes," I grumble, though I'm unable to contain my smile.

"Seriously though, you two have been in love with each other for so long and it's been torture for some of us just waiting for you to finally realize it."

I laugh, trying to wave him off. "Well I guess not everyone in the group was as observant as you. Those were texts letting me know that Jackson will be joining us for dinner. It was supposed to be just me, Lexa and Ansley."

"Well it's not like it was going to be a date with your sister there, anyway," Weston points out.

"True, but at least I would have been the only guy competing for Lexa's attention."

"I'm sure Jackson knows that you're into her. Unless he's blind of course."

"I think it's more just willful ignorance. He's still in love with her apparently, and he's intending to make sure she's aware of that fact."

"Oof. Well I love the guy, but he had his chance. This isn't about him. This is about how Lexa feels about you and you already know she's into you. So I really wouldn't worry about it too much."

"Yeah I guess," I say, looking down at my hands clasped together on the table. I realize that I've been picking at my fingers during this conversation, an old nervous habit of mine. I shake my hands out, attempting to break the tic.

I look back up and smile sheepishly at Weston, "This is the most nervous I've been about a girl in a long time."

"You sure have got it bad, man," he says, chuckling. "How about a drink to calm the nerves before dinner?"

"That sounds wonderful," I say, smiling for real this time and letting out a breath.

☼

I toss yet another shirt onto the bed. I have tried on and subsequently discarded five shirts at this point, trying to find something sexy but casual. *Has it always been this hard to get dressed?* I wonder, staring at my naked torso in the mirror. *Maybe I'll just go like this,* I think, laughing at myself. I mean, that would probably get Lexa's attention at least.

I shake my head, reminding myself that I already have her attention. I'm not competing against Jackson anymore. Lexa wants to be with me, or at least wants to feel it out. I am not screwing this opportunity up by acting like a jealous idiot tonight.

I look back over the pile of clothes on the bed, seeing a red t-shirt with a raw hem sticking out. I pull on the tee and reach into the closet to grab a gray and white flannel. I pull it on over the shirt and cuff the sleeves, exposing my decently muscular forearms. In this moment, I'm so glad I've been hitting the gym recently.

When I first started at my current job, I didn't realize how sedentary I was getting until one day I tried to play a game of ultimate frisbee with my roommates and was out of breath in the first 10 minutes. After that, I made it a point to get in some activity every day. Eventually, that led to a good routine of lifting at least three days a week and getting in cardio at least four days. It's done wonders for my endurance and gained me some pretty nice muscle tone along the way.

As I'm flexing and admiring my forearms like a high school junior, I hear my phone ping from the stand by the bed. I walk over and pick it up, reading a message from Lexa, *Hey it looks like we're going to be on time for once (yay!) so we'll grab a table for 4. Any seating preference?*

Anywhere near you, I type back, grinning like an idiot.

Idiot, she replies and then, *I'll save you a seat ;).*

This girl. I swear, she makes me feel like we're kids again. I can't wait to see her. I decide to send another quick message, before I finish getting ready and head to the restaurant. *I have a seat saved for you too, babe.* I snap a quick picture of my jeans and send it, before I put my phone back on the charger and walk to the bathroom. There is a flush warming my body that has nothing to do with the June heat.

Chapter 23

Lexa

The hostess leads me and Ansley to a back corner table, draped with a pretty pale pink table cloth and adorned with wildflowers. I can't help but look around at the other tables as we walk past, trying—and probably failing—to nonchalantly see what everyone's eating. As long as we've lived in Savannah, I've never been to this place. It seems like more of a date place, but being here in late afternoon gives it more of a laid back feel—the sun filtering in through the windows, highlighting the vases of flowers on the tables and giving the place a fairy cottage vibe.

Ansley and I are the first to arrive. We were actually both ready on time for once and we were both starving. With little to keep us home, we decided to head this way and go ahead and get a drink and an appetizer while we wait for the guys.

As we sit down, both picking up a drink menu, I hear a beleaguered sigh from across the table. I look up to find Ansley staring at me with an "I have something to say" expression on her face.

"Okay, what is it? Just spit it out so I can pick a cocktail please," I say, waving said menu around for added dramatic effect.

Ans huffs out another sigh before continuing the conversation we'd been having at the apartment. A conversation which I thought was over. "I just don't understand why you wouldn't tell me about Jackson. I mean I get why you weren't telling me about Drew, although, not completely—he is my brother after all."

"I told you that I was just waiting until after the wedding and honeymoon to talk to you about Drew. I mean dropping the bomb that I'm extremely smitten with your older brother two days before you get married seemed a tad selfish," I reply.

"It's not a bombshell if it's already public knowledge…" Ansley says, trailing off into a grimace at the end.

"I'm sorry, what was that?"

"Lex, come on. Everyone has known since college that you two are into each other. I see y'all together every holiday, you think I haven't noticed?"

"I didn't think it was that obvious, I guess," I say, shrinking behind the drink menu and attempting to hide the blush staining my cheeks.

"Oh girl, it is. Grace, Weston and I had a bet going of when you two would finally figure it out," Ansley pulls out her phone, checking the date, "and it looks like Wes was closest, dammit. You owe me $5."

"I am not giving you $5 to compensate for the fact that you lost a bet on your best friend and your older brother's love lives. That's just messed up," I say, laughing at the absurdity of this conversation.

This elicits yet another huff from Ansley. "So be it, I'll just have to use the fact that I was the first to know as a form of reparation."

"You are too much, bridezilla."

We both laugh, turning back to our drink menus.

Until Ansley obviously can't take the silence and says, "I just wish you would've clued me in to all of your relationship drama before I invited your ex to a dinner with the guy you're currently talking to. Your ex who happens to still be in love with you apparently."

"I would not say that he's still in love with me. He's just ready to settle down and thinks I'm an easy target for that since that's what I wanted in college," I reply, shrugging. "Can I look at the drink menu now before our waiter comes back?"

"Sure thing, toots," Ans says, "I'm looking at their signature drink, the Mockingbird. Sounds like something right up your alley."

It takes me a second to grasp her meaning, and I finally read through the menu. All of the drinks are literary themed. I flip to the front of the menu and read the name of the restaurant again, Pages. "Who picked this place again?" I ask.

"That would be Drew, and oh look there he is now!" Ansley squeaks out, waving Drew over from the door.

Drew picked out a book themed restaurant that I've never been to before? Maybe it's just a place he liked going to eat back when he lived at home.

I feel a strong hand graze my shoulder, dragging down to grip my arm. I look up into the most handsome face with startling blue eyes.

"Well if it's not the two most beautiful women in Savannah," Drew drawls, sending a shiver through my spine. From the way his hand tightens on my arm and the smoky look he gives me, he felt every bit of it.

I turn to respond when I see Jackson walking towards our table, an easy smile in place. Until he sees Drew's hand on me, at which point he ratchets the smile to its most dazzling level.

Once Jackson is at the table, he pulls Drew into a bro hug, effectively removing his hand from my arm. I look across at Ansley, who is smiling at me in a very strained and seemingly apologetic way. Jackson releases Drew who moves to sit beside me while Jackson pulls me up from my chair to give me a crushing hug, complete with a kiss to the cheek.

"You look even better than you did just a few hours ago, Lex," Jackson says, holding me at arm's length and repeatedly dragging his gaze up and down my body. I wish I could say this has no effect on me, but Jackson is still an extremely attractive man and I will always remember the way his body feels against mine. It's imprinted after years together, and of course, the feel of a first love isn't something you ever truly forget.

I feel myself blush again and look down, mumbling, "Hey Jackson, it's good to see you too."

I shuffle out of his grasp, dropping back into my chair as Jackson says hello to Ansley. I notice a distinct lack of prolonged contact and blush even harder.

I feel a hand on my bare thigh and glance down to see Drew's hand there, gently keeping me grounded. I'm almost too embarrassed by my obvious physical reaction to both of these beautiful men to look up, but when I do, Drew is staring at me with what I can only describe as a roguish look in his eye. I give him a small smile and place my hand on top of his. I squeeze once before letting go to pick up the menu again.

It feels like he can read my mind. Like he understands that this situation is just as uncomfortable for me and he wants to be here as someone I can lean on. He doesn't look jealous or upset like a lot of guys I know would. He's simply here to comfort me.

I guess he's also figured out that I told Ansley since they seem to be having a secret conversation through only sustained eye contact. Ansley's eyes flick down to where Drew's hand is resting on my leg and Drew's eyes flick over to Jackson before both siblings nod and look away. *I honestly don't even want to know*, I decide.

"So I guess you've been here before?" I ask, turning to Drew. "Ansley said you picked the place."

"Um, actually no I've never been here. I just read online that it was book themed so I thought you might enjoy it," Drew answers, turning a sheepish smile on me.

"Oh, well….oh. I mean yeah, it's really cool! I can't even decide what drink I want because three of my all-time favorite books are here."

"I figured you'd get the Mockingbird," Jackson states from across the table, reminding me that he knows all of my favorite things, too.

Without looking up from the menu, I can feel Ansley's eyes on me.

"Maybe you should try the Shire Fire, it sounds a little more impassioned," she says, drawing a glare from me.

I glance at Drew, watching a slow grin spread over his face. I know without looking at Jackson that he's either lost or not even paying attention. He was never great with the innuendos that me and Ansley speak in.

My eyes go back to skimming the appetizer menu, having finally settled on the Golden Gatsby champagne cocktail. It seems like an easy drink, with no ulterior motive for the order.

Once our waiter is back to check on us and take drink orders, normal conversation begins to flow again.

"Everything ready for Saturday?" Jackson asks, giving Ansley a big smile.

"Yeah, we're definitely ready. Anything that comes up now is just extra stuff anyway," Ansley replies. Looking at me with an innocent smile, she says, "As long as I get to marry my best friend at the end of the day, that's all that matters right?"

"If I had a nickel for every time I heard you say that phrase, I think I could quit my job," I say, laughing.

"At this point, I say it just for your benefit," Ansley says.

Drew squeezes my thigh as he laughs, sending shock waves to my core. *Has his touch always had this effect on me?* As I'm struggling to figure that one out, I notice that I must have missed a direct question. Ansley and Jackson are staring at me with an expectant look on their faces. I whip my head towards Drew who seems to be attempting to stifle a laugh. I cough and raise my head back to Ansley and ask with as much innocence as I can muster, "I'm sorry, what did you say?"

Ansley laughs but repeats herself in a very sweet tone, "I asked if you had any last minute items you needed to check off for tomorrow?"

"Oh, um, no I think I have everything and with us getting the napkin fiasco under control, I think it should all be settled," I say, giving her my professional best friend and maid of honor smile.

"Napkin fiasco?" both men ask.

"Yeah, we were delivered black napkins instead of rose gold ones," I reply.

"'Twas a grievous error, but one quickly remedied by my loving and ever-faithful handmaiden," Ansley intones.

"Handmaiden?" I demand.

We all fall into a fit of laughter at the drama we all know ensued.

"This wasn't by chance the emergency that pulled you from breakfast yesterday morning?" Drew asks.

I blush, remembering all too well the conversation I had to leave to be there for this catastrophic event. I nod and look at Ansley whose mouth has formed a tiny, perfect O.

"Wait. That's where you were when I called you? You left *that* breakfast to run to my apartment over napkins? Oh my God. I am a bridezilla." Ansley is looking back and forth between Drew and I, hand covering her mouth, on the edge of tears it seems.

"Girl stop. It's fine. Everything is fine. Your whole wedding aesthetic was in danger. We couldn't have that." This draws a laugh of relief from her.

I laugh and turn my head, catching Jackson's eye. Jackson is studying Drew with an intent gaze.

"You didn't mention you had all gone out to breakfast yesterday," Jackson says, first to Drew before turning a questioning glance to me.

"Oh it was just me and Lex," Drew replies, pulling his hand from its already obvious resting place on my leg to drop over my shoulders in a much more possessive gesture.

I can't help but be turned on by the outright claim Drew is making right now. He's saying *she's mine so back off* with one move.

I can see that the signal was not lost on Jackson. His entire countenance changes in a blink. His nice guy persona is quickly replaced by a predatory one. I can see from the new gleam in his eye and the hardened set of his jaw that if we were not in public, he might be swinging a fist towards Drew's pretty face.

And shit if that doesn't arouse me even more. *What the hell is wrong with me?* I don't want two men that I love fighting over me. I don't. I really–don't, right?

Two of the sexiest men I have ever seen, both wanting me at the same time? This is literally the stuff of those raunchy romance novels cluttering my night stand.

As Jackson's hungry gaze once again sweeps my body, I feel warmth start to pool in my core. His gaze lingers on my exposed neck and shoulders only a moment before Drew begins to knead his thumb over my collarbone. Jackson hisses out a small breath and drags his eyes to mine. The melted honey has changed to a molten gold and feels like fire, running down my skin to the roving hand still making my skin buzz. This is too much sensation at one time. I snap my eyes closed and take a steadying breath. I straighten my shoulders, stilling Drew's circling thumb and open my eyes to find a clear blue ocean looking back at me. Ansley is staring deep into my soul. Watching, waiting for her cue.

"Guys. Cut this shit out so we can eat in peace. Thanks," she snaps, looking at Drew and Jackson in turn.

Jackson has the decency to look slightly ashamed, while Drew just smirks at Ansley. They both mumble a halfhearted apology to me and Ansley. Drew pulls his arm from my shoulders. His fingers brush my left arm all the way down before settling back on his own leg. I immediately miss his touch but I also know that I need some time to reorient myself to my surroundings. I was so entranced that I didn't even notice the waiter bringing our drinks. I see Ansley's in front of her and realize we all have one.

Looking back to Ansley, I mouth a silent thank you. Aloud I say, "Yes, let's toast to the bride and have a drink for her happily ever after."

Ansley snorts out a laugh but raises her glass all the same. We clink our glasses and all sip in honor of our lovely sister and friend. I make the mistake of glancing at Drew first, who is eyeing me like he'd rather have me for supper than the dishes I see heading our way.

Dammit, I think, *why am I always blushing?*

Chapter 24

Drew

Well, that was intense. I don't really know what came over me.

Lexa is not a thing to be had or a possession to own. Why do I feel like I am trying to lay a claim? She already told me that she wants to be with me, right? Why am I suddenly feeling so territorial? *Maybe because this guy is the only ever person you've seen her be in love with,* I remind myself.

And suddenly I'm comparing the way she looks at me to how I used to see her look at Jackson. I want to believe that she's already in love with me but it's not like we've had much time to talk it through. Though, feeling the instant rush of electricity when I moved my hand to her shoulder, I have to think she's at least feeling part of what I'm feeling.

When I was using my thumb to stroke that baby soft skin over her delicate collarbone, I could swear I heard what sounded like a purr emanate from deep within Lexa's body.

But, being so caught up in the feel of her skin under my

hands that I forget we're at dinner with my sister and Lexa's ex–not good. I'm a grown ass adult man, not some teenager struggling to keep his hormones in check, for goodness sake.

I glance up, making eye contact with my sister. *Sorry Ans,* I mouth, meaning it.

She smiles, letting me off the hook but also reminding me that she's okay with this. I love my little sister more than almost anything in this world but having her blessing is something I didn't know I really craved until this moment.

I'm trying so hard not to look at Lexa again, but I can feel her body heat even from an arm's length away.

I risk a glance at her as she turns to look at me. Whatever she sees in my face causes a rush of heat to run down her body, showcased beautifully by the blush staining her cheeks and chest. I somehow resist the urge to reach out and feel the heat for myself. Maybe I'll see if she wants to come see where I'm staying after dinner.

Images run wild in my mind as she quickly rips her gaze away to turn to the waiter delivering our food. I somehow missed the drink drop but the smells rising from those platters almost rival the draw I'm feeling towards running my hands all over Lexa.

Food first, then play time–if I'm lucky.

I look up to see Jackson looking at me again. His eyes are narrowed, like he's taking the time to study the situation. His nostrils flare slightly, and an angry glint flashes through his gaze. It takes me a moment to gather the meaning in his look and when I do, my stomach drops.

He can't decide if this is new or a rekindling. He thinks we might have gotten together while they were dating. I open my mouth to refute the accusation but before I can, he stands and excuses himself, saying that he needs to run to the restroom to wash his hands.

I stand up to follow him, suddenly intent on making sure his mind isn't going where I think it is. But I feel a gentle hand on my wrist, stopping me before I can move away from the table.

"Another time," the words come from the most kissable mouth I've ever seen.

I give Lexa a gentle smile and sit back down, still facing her. "I think Jackson has the wrong idea about what's going on here. I'm afraid that he thinks we hooked up while you two were dating and I'm somehow rubbing that in his face. The look he gave me just before he went to the men's room was full of nothing but hatred. We were–are friends. I don't want him to hate me for something that didn't even happen. I was just going to talk to him and set it straight," I take a breath, realizing that I basically gave her a monologue. I smile, a bit self-conscious and shrug.

Lexa throws Ansley a sweet, apologetic smile and turns her body towards me. "Look Drew, do you really think you're the one he needs to hear that from?"

I think over her question and then shake my head, knowing and hating that she's right. She's going to have to be the one to talk with him. We haven't even gotten to eat yet and she's already having to clean up a mess that I made. I immediately feel guilty. I feel her pull away as she begins to stand. I raise my head to tell her that she shouldn't have to do this during dinner, but she is looking at me with every bit of patience and understanding in this world. I crack and let her walk away from me towards the hallway where the restrooms are located.

I swing my legs back under the table and look at my little sister. "I screwed up, didn't I?"

Ansley looks me over for a second before she replies, "No big brother, other's perceptions are not your responsibility. You know that."

I smile, still slightly ashamed of my behavior and ask, "So I guess she told you everything? And you're really okay with this, with us?"

Ansley laughs, taking a sip of her cocktail. "Of course. I'm more than okay with it. Lexa's always been like a sister to me, might as well make it official." She winks and laughs again. Ansley's laugh is so bubbly and contagious.

I let out a chuckle and say, "Whoa little sis, slow down a bit. Let's get through this wedding before we start trying to plan another."

Chapter 25

Lexa

I find Jackson with his back pressed up against the wall, eyes closed and looking like he's doing some kind of breathing exercise.

"Um, are you in line?" I ask, attempting to lighten the mood.

His eyes rip open and I'm suddenly not laughing anymore. He looks mad. In more ways than one. Angry, crazy and hurt.

"Please…just…" he starts.

"No, Jackson. Whatever is going through that beautiful brain of yours right now–it didn't happen. You can't possibly think that I would–"

His hand shoots out and grabs my wrist. He gently pulls me to him until we're sharing the same breath.

"Don't. I don't want to hear it. I know you didn't but hearing it said out loud feels like it would make the nightmare more real. It's not something I even imagined until today. Seeing the two of you together, it seemed so natural and effortless. My mind started giving me all these images of the two of you from college and how close of friends you were and I tried not to, but my brain connected the dots."

"There are no dots to connect, J. There was me and you and now there's me and him. Those two lines never intersect at any point. I promise you. I know I didn't always show it then, but I loved you. I loved you so much and I never thought that I would stop. I don't really think that I have. The love has changed over the years of course, but I will never not love you."

"You never stopped loving me?" Jackson's eyes shimmer light gold with the water rimming them.

I blink as my vision turns foggy with my own unshed tears.

"Of course not. You were my first love and that's not something you can get over easily. Especially with the way we left things."

"Do you think….do you think there's any way that I could earn a second chance to give you the happy ending you deserve?"

My breathing grows ragged and tears begin to spill down my cheeks. I should just say no. I want to be with Drew. But I also never even saw this ending as a possibility. I'm going to say no. *Then why am I hesitating?* "Jackson, I…."

"No, don't answer that right now. We have all weekend. And your best friend is out there waiting for you to have dinner with her. You have plenty of time to think about what I've said. I know I've been thinking about it for a while now." With that, he kisses my forehead lightly and pulls me in for a tight embrace.

✵

This is so not how I saw this dinner playing out. I imagined some good food, some laughing, some awkwardness. But not this. Not two men overtly trying to get me to commit to them over cocktails and seafood.

And as much as I thought Ansley would rescue me, she seems to be enjoying herself. *Asshole*, I think. What kind of friend wants to watch her bestie twist in the wind like this? Some kind of sadist, at least.

"Rehearsal starts at 5 tomorrow night, with dinner after?" Jackson asks, turning to face Ansley.

"Yep! Rehearsal really shouldn't take that long. But we have reservations at the hotel restaurant for dinner. So really as long as we're done with the rehearsal by 6, we're golden," she answers.

"I wouldn't think it would be too hard to figure out how to walk down an aisle," Drew says with a huffed laugh.

"Oh you'd be surprised," Ansley replies, "I was in a wedding that had the timing of each walkout couple synced to the words of the song. That one took forever to finish the rehearsals. I was on the brink of starvation by the time we finally made it to dinner."

I laugh, thinking about how hard that timing was to get through. The wedding she's talking about is one we were in last year. I remember afterward that Ansley went on and on about how she would not be that crazy when she finally got to plan her own wedding. And thank goodness she hasn't been. She's been a wonderful bride to be around and this weekend is going to be beautiful. That is, if I can get through it without having to declare my undying love to someone.

"You ready to walk in on my arm?" Jackson says with a smirk.

"I'm ready to walk down the aisle and be able to turn and

watch the most beautiful woman marry her best friend in the most gorgeous dress," I look to my best friend, "Ansley, I can't wait to see the full effect. You are going to be breathtaking. I'm afraid Landon might pass out."

Ansley laughs and says, "I don't know about all that. I am excited to see his face though. I've managed to keep the dress secret from him this whole time so it's going to be a huge surprise. I picked out the literal opposite dress of what I've always said I wanted. I put this dress on and immediately felt like a bride. I knew it was the one."

"Well sis, I absolutely cannot wait to see you in it. I know you're going to be beautiful because you always are," Drew says with a cute lopsided grin. I swear I see a tear sitting at the edge of his eye. But he blinks and it's gone. Maybe I imagined it.

Ansley beams, saying, "Oh Drew, you are so syrupy sweet. You gotta stop. I will not be ruining my makeup Saturday just because you decide to say nice things."

I notice the waiter looking over at our table. I look around and see that we've all finished our food and drinks. I turn back to signal him but I notice that he's already on his way over.

I glance over to see Drew making eye contact with the waiter. He drops his gaze to mine, and says softly, "It looked like you might be ready to go."

Giving him a soft smile, I nod. I close my eyes and turn back to the table. I wish tonight would have gone differently. After getting back from the hallway talk with Jackson, I think Drew could read my emotions on my face. He didn't put his hand back on my leg or over my shoulders. He barely so much as grazed my arm with his knuckles in passing. It felt like things were really building for us and now we've hit a roadblock. We really need to be able to talk about everything.

I turn to ask what he's doing after dinner when Ansley says to me, "Alright kitten, ready to get home? Big couple of days ahead of us."

Well I guess that settles that. Drew and Jackson both stand as we begin to get up. Ansley turns to say bye to Jackson and Drew scoops me into a crushing hug.

"Text me later, okay?" Drew whispers into my hair.

I just nod and hug him tighter.

Jackson comes around the table and holds out his arms, waiting for me to walk into them. I shuffle my feet a bit but I walk towards him, letting him enclose me in a hug.

"We'll talk later," Jackson states. Again, I just nod.

I didn't realize that emotional overload could make you mute.

Chapter 26

Drew

Friday

I'm awake before my alarm, which is unusual. I'm a decent sleeper on a normal day. But I had nightmares last night that kept me up and made it hard to fall back asleep. The nightmares centered mostly around Lexa deciding to get back with Jackson. I saw variations of her leaving me for him, some in a very harsh way and some in a very bizarre way. One time Jackson was the Cookie Monster and Lexa told me he gave her more cookies than I ever could.

I have never been this messed up over a woman before. And obviously I just want what's best for Lexa, even if that's not me.

I just plan on doing everything in my power to be the best for her that I can be.

I groan, reaching my hands up to scrub at my eyes. Even in the half-light of dawn, I can see that the sheets are all out of place, as if I was thrashing in my sleep. So much for being well-rested at the rehearsal tonight.

Maybe I just need a tough workout, a good breakfast and a cup of strong coffee.

With this plan in place, I throw my legs over the edge of the bed. I scrub my face with my hands again, hoping to rub away some of the fatigue. I groan again, aware that my effort was most likely in vain. I'm sure my eyes are packed for travel, designer bags and all. I almost don't even want to see my reflection before going to the gym. I also don't want to scare any young children I might pass on the way there.

I push open the bathroom door, willing myself to glance in the mirror. My hair is in complete disarray, I do indeed have dark circles under my eyes and my stubble looks more like a five day shadow.

I splash some water over my face and run my hands through my hair. I'll shave in the shower after the gym. I head back out and grab some shorts and a gym tank from my dresser. With my hair tamped down and some clean clothes on, I feel ready to at least face the beginning of my day. I stop by my fridge to fill up my water bottle, noticing the blank slate of the front. Maybe I'll hang up the wedding invite to give it some color. Maybe I'll see if I can go ahead and get a copy of that picture of me and Lexa. Then it can travel home with me too.

I realize that I've been staring at the front of the fridge, lost in thought, for several minutes now.

I really need to get out the door and to the gym. I need to burn some of this stress off. Maybe I'll even hit up the batting cages at lunch, focus on something else for a bit.

I think Landon is off after lunch today, I'll invite him for some good company.

As I'm walking into the gym, I glimpse a poster tacked onto the announcement wall that draws my attention. It's advertising a music festival in September that's being held in Atlanta. There's some pretty cool bands on that set list. That actually seems like something cool to check out. I grab my phone to leave myself a note so that I can remember to look it up again next week.

With that handled, I head over to the squat rack to get started on my leg workout for today. I'm loading my warm up weight onto the bar when I hear a familiar voice behind me. "You warm up with more than my body weight," Claire says, giggling.

I turn, feeling a small smile pull at my lips. "You're quite small, so that's not a high bar anyway," I reply.

"Oh okay, big man," she says, blushing and giggling again.

"You got a week's membership, too?" I ask.

"Yeah, I don't like going full weeks without hitting up a gym and the building I'm staying in doesn't have one. With this one within walking distance, I figured why not?"

"I feel that. You look great by the way, so your devotion is paying off."

Claire blushes heavily now, and bats her eyelashes as she looks down. "Well I'll let you get back to your workout and I'll see you tonight."

"Yeah, see you tonight!" I give her my half smile and turn back to my squat rack.

I catch her eyes in the mirror as I start my squats. Her eyes dip down to my ass, watching it through the movement before coming back up to my eyes. I wink, making her blush again.

"I just wanted to make sure you went deep enough," she

says, with a wink of her own. Claire giggles and gives a small wave before turning and heading to the cardio section.

I shake my head with a small smile on my lips. I'm used to being noticed by females, but having someone so blatantly check me out is pretty new for me. However, having Claire's eyes undress me only makes me want to see Lexa do it again.

Lexa was so responsive to my touch last night. Feeling her shiver just from touching her shoulder made my skin heat to almost uncomfortable levels. I need to explore that more and soon.

I wonder if there's a chance of getting her alone at some point tonight.

At least this has already gotten my mind off of Jackson and Lexa.

✧

Hey dude, batting cages after lunch? I type out and send to Landon.

I toss my phone onto the bed, heading to the bathroom to grab a shower. Even though I plan to get sweaty again after lunch, I want to be able to go to the coffee house and not run everyone off with my stench.

I peel off my sweat-drenched clothes and turn on the shower. As I let the water warm up, I spin and give my back and glutes a once-over in the mirror to check out my progress recently. I noticed my shirts are getting a bit tighter in the lat area and I can see some growth there now as I flex in the mirror like a 14 year old boy. I laugh at myself and check the water temperature. I'm thankful once again for great water pressure in this apartment building as I step under the stream. I feel like I'm actually getting clean rather than just rinsing off like I normally would at a hotel. I stand under the shower stream for a solid two minutes after rinsing the soap off, just letting the water sluice down my body.

I see Lexa's body tightening under my hands like last night, but Claire's wink and obvious flirting at the gym has her on my mind as well. I don't want to focus on anyone but Lexa this weekend, aside from Ansley and Landon of course.

I groan, putting my hands to the wall, letting the water run over my hair and onto my face. I feel like every dramatic scene in every romantic comedy I've ever been forced to watch. This makes me chuckle at least, and I reach down to shut the water off.

As soon as the noise from the shower is gone, I hear my phone ringing in the other room. I grab my towel from the rack, drying off as I walk through the room to my dresser where I dropped my cell.

Lexa's name is flashing across the screen. I smile and click answer.

"Well good morning sweetheart," I say.

"Good morning to you as well," she responds, and I can tell she's smiling. "Did you decide on any fun plans for your day?"

"I just got back from the gym and I was thinking of heading to the batting cages with Landon after lunch."

"Well that'll be tough, Landon and Ansley have decided to run away to the beach for a few hours before they have to be back to get ready for the rehearsal dinner."

"So I guess that means you're free, then?" I ask, letting hope enter my voice.

"Actually yes. That's why I'm calling. I didn't know if you wanted to hang out, maybe talk a bit."

I smile even wider and say, "I would love to hang out with

you Lex. Want to come here or me come there or go out somewhere?" I'm sounding a bit too eager at this point, but screw it. I'm not trying to play games. She already knows I'm crazy about her.

"Um…," she starts, hesitating, "what is it that you were saying about batting cages?"

I'm too stunned to speak momentarily, but I recover enough to say, "You want to go to the batting cages with me?"

I think she can hear the shock in my voice because she laughs. But then, "Yes Drew. I would love to go to the batting cages with you. Want to be here around 11 and we can grab lunch after the cages?"

"Sounds great to me!"

"Okay, see you soon cutie," she says and hangs up.

I can't stop smiling and I don't know what I'm going to do with myself for the next two hours before I leave to get her from her apartment. I pull my phone out to catch up on some emails for something to do.

24 unread emails from yesterday. I know none of these concern me, but I start reading through the threads anyway. The boredom this immediately causes almost kills my happiness, but luckily it doesn't succeed. All I have to do is think about Lexa's smiling face and the excitement is right back to its highest level.

Chapter 27

Lexa

I drop my phone onto my bed and squeal. I feel like I'm right back in school. I'm way too excited about the fact that I get to go on a date to the batting cages with Drew. That was a go to date night with the baseball boys but Jackson never wanted to take me. He always said that he would rather take me on a "real date." What he didn't understand was that I was happy to be anywhere with him and I didn't always want to go to movies and fancy dinners. I wanted to have fun, too.

I immediately rush to my closet to search for a perfect baseball date outfit. I find my pitching sleeve tee repping our college and grab my most comfortable jean shorts. I need to hop in the shower and shave my legs but before that, I definitely think I need some breakfast.

I head to the kitchen to check out a breakfast option. There's still enough bread and avocado for toast and I think I'll make some oatmeal as well. I brew some coffee and get to work on cutting the avocado. As I'm spreading the avocado, the coffee pot finishes its cycle. I grab my favorite mug and pour some up. I'm not feeling like black coffee this morning so I add a splash—or three—of salted caramel creamer and grab my bowl of oatmeal from the microwave.

I take my breakfast to the living room and set it on the table, reaching for the remote. I hear a small meow from under the coffee table and look to see Sneakers making his way out in a magnificent stretch.

"Well hey there sweet boy," I say, bending down to scratch my baby between his ears. Sneakers jumps up, finds his favorite spot next to the pillow and makes some biscuits. Once he feels like he's put in enough work, he circles three times and curls up with his head on the pillow. I smile at him and fall back into my spot on the couch.

I pull my knees up to cross my legs and tuck my feet underneath me. I balance my breakfast on my lap and flip through the channels, looking for something to help pass the time until Drew gets here.

I'm crunching on my toast when my phone starts buzzing against my thigh. I set my toast back on my plate and swipe my phone open to check the message.

Hey beautiful, didn't know if you might want to get together before the rehearsal tonight. Maybe practice how you're going to look on my arm? the text from Jackson reads.

Ugh, gross, I think. I'm not sure what part of me gives off the vibe that I want to be treated like arm candy but I don't even feel like that text deserves a response.

I turn my attention back to the home reno show that I love.

Buzz, buzz, buzz. And now Jackson's calling me. He gave me a two minute window to respond and he's already calling. I know that he's going to keep trying to reach me so I answer, although reluctantly.

"Hello?" I ask, trying to sound as annoyed as possible.

"Hey Lex, sorry about that text. It was a joke but I would love to hang out," Jackson says.

"Um…can't and don't really want to after that."

"Lex, come on, I was kidding. You know I don't see you as a trophy girl."

"Okay, whatever. But I still can't. I have plans. You know, maid of honor stuff."

"Oh okay, well are there any errands you want company for?"

I hesitate before responding, "You know, I think I'm alright. But I'll see you tonight! Okay bye!"

I hang up before he even says goodbye but I don't care. I feel irrationally mad over the fact that last night he was professing his undying love to me and today he's trying to act like a frat boy. I thought we were past this bullshit.

I roll my eyes, look at the time on my phone and toss it back onto the couch. I must groan without realizing it because Sneakers pops his head up to look at me.

"It's okay baby. Just men being stupid," I say to my favorite boy. "Unlike you of course, my super smart and sweet little lovebug." I reach over and give his ears a scratch and I'm rewarded with a long purr.

Assured that my sweet little man is happy, I turn back to my breakfast. I need to fuel up if I'm going to be keeping up with Drew. The home renovation show has done its job as well and I've zoned out enough to have just 30 minutes before Drew gets here. I stand up, intending to head to the kitchen when Sneakers pops his head up again, this time looking at the door.

Just then, a knock sounds. I look down and notice that I'm still in my pajama shorts and tank top with my hair up in a messy bun. I know that it's Drew at the door, it has to be. But why is he 30 minutes early? He has to know I wouldn't be anywhere near ready yet!

I set my plate on the table and pad towards the door. I take a quick steadying breath and open the door, hiding my unbound chest under my arm and coffee cup.

"Um, hi. You're early," I say.

I look up to see Drew's crystal blue eyes drinking me in. As I watch his gaze travel over my mostly naked body, I start to squirm. This seems to break the trance somewhat as his eyes snap back to mine.

"Oh, hi…yeah, sorry," he stammers. He even blushes, *oh God.*

Chapter 28

Drew

Mother of God and all that is Holy, I think. Lexa in the morning is delicious. From her tanned legs in those short shorts, to her peaked nipples that I can see through the thin fabric of her shirt, up to that mess of red hair on her head. It's an irresistible combination. I can barely think, let alone speak.

I manage a few more words, somehow, "Did I wake you?"

"No, I was up. I was just eating breakfast. Plus you weren't supposed to be here for another half hour…," she responds, trailing a bit at the end. She glances behind her and as she does, her coffee cup moves, exposing the outline of her breast against her tank. *Shit,* I think, *keep your eyes on her face dammit.*

I pull myself together enough to realize that the backwards glance might be because someone else is in her apartment. I instantly regret getting here early.

"Well I can run down to the coffee shop if you have someone–I mean something to take care of," I say, already taking a step back from her door. I don't want to leave but I also don't want to see who's in there.

Lexa narrows her eyes, cocking her head to the side before breaking into a huge grin. *What the hell?*

She's still smiling at me like a little devil when she says, "Oh come on Drew, stop being so jealous. Come say hey." She throws me a wink and turns before I can argue. I follow her into her apartment, still very unsure of what or who I'm going to find. It doesn't help that I can't take my eyes off of her ass as it bounces in her little pajama shorts. I think she's flouncing a bit on purpose but damn if I don't love it.

As we enter her living room, I look up and around, expecting to see Jackson. What I can mostly see are books and then a fluffy black cat staring at me.

I look at Lexa–the woman still giggling–who says, "Meet Sneakers, my main man."

I can't help but let out a chuckle as the fluff ball jumps down from the couch to come introduce himself. I stoop down, reaching my fingers out for him to sniff. As soon as we're acquainted, he drops his head to run it under my hand. I take that as my cue to begin showing him some love. As I'm running my hand down Sneakers's smooth back for the 20th time, I look up to see Lexa gazing at me with what can only be described as pure happiness. I give Sneakers a few more pats before standing back to my full height. I turn fully to Lexa and smirk. I'm rewarded with a purr and a rub on the leg from Sneakers as well as a deep blush from Lexa.

"What?" I ask, seeing Lexa shake her head a bit before smiling even brighter.

"Nothing…it's just that the only other man he's ever accepted that quickly was Landon. Normally he shuns any member of the male species," she replies, laughing again.

"Well maybe Sneakers is just a really good judge of character," I say, refraining from adding *and maybe you've been picking the wrong men.*

Lexa lets out a throaty chuckle and I'm sure she knows what I was trying not to say. I've told her for a long time that she needs to find nicer guys. I guess I was just hoping that she'd see that I was talking about me. At least I know Sneakers was holding it down while I couldn't.

"So you really just weren't ready yet? I'm so sorry. I know you don't get ready until the last minute and I should've waited. I was just getting a bit impatient and wanted to see you sooner rather than later," I explain, giving her a smile.

I'm treated to another beautiful blush as she says, "No it's okay, I'm glad you're here already. I was just about to throw my dishes in the dishwasher and get dressed. You mind hanging out here and keeping Sneaks company?"

"Of course not," I smile and turn my gaze to the couch. "You cool if I just settle in here?"

"Make yourself at home," she replies, giving me a sweet smile and an even sweeter view as she turns to walk to her room. She glances at me before going in, catching me in the act of once again ogling her. She tips her head back in a laugh, walks into her room and pulls the door behind her. However, it is left open a crack. I only have a second to wonder if this is an accident or not before I see her bare back through the door.

She's teasing me, mercilessly. I see the flash of a smile as she turns her face towards me and then she's gone out of view again. I realize I haven't even sat down yet. I move to the couch and notice that I still have a view through her cracked door. I hear the shower start up, and my brain supplies me with all kinds of unwholesome thoughts.

I shake my head, trying to clear them from my mind. I only succeed in zoning out for a minute, because suddenly she's back in sight, wiggling into a pair of jean shorts. I watch her shimmy the fabric over her toned thighs before noticing that she doesn't have a shirt on yet. Before I can see too much, she's turned her back again. She disappears for another second before returning to stretch a shirt over her shoulders and down to her slim waist.

I feel a weird sensation on my leg and it takes me too long to figure out that it's Sneakers purring against me. He's sitting right up against me, basically begging for attention. I look down to scratch his head some more when Lexa appears out of her room, dressed in the sexiest outfit that will ever grace a batting cage.

She's dressed down but it looks so good on her that I hope we're the only ones at the cages today. I won't be able to keep my hands off of her and I don't want anyone else's eyes on her.

I snap my eyes back up to her face to see her smirking at me. I don't even care that I've been caught staring, she's so damn cute.

"What?" She asks, still smiling.

"I was just thinking about how good you look in that baseball tee. You're a born cleat chaser," I say, grinning almost maniacally. I know she hates that term.

Lexa rolls her eyes, though she does chuckle. "Yeah okay, do you know the last time I dated anyone even remotely close to the game?"

I stop laughing almost instantly, "Is that what you want? To date me?" I'm looking down as I ask, acting like I'm staring at the cat when in fact I'm just being a coward and avoiding eye contact.

I look up to see Lexa giving me a soft smile, "I want to talk about all of that soon. Right now, I want to have fun and spend time with you. How do you feel about that?"

I search her face, hoping this isn't a way to dodge my question. But, all I can see is light and happiness. I realize then that I feel the same way. I want to spend all the time with her that I can. We have so much time to talk about all of the hard stuff later.

"I think that sounds great, Lex. Let's have some fun," I say. I love the way her green eyes light up when I say this. I would do anything to keep a smile on that gorgeous face. "Alright you ready to go knock some balls around?" I ask, giving my best wolfish grin.

"Oh my God, you're so cheesy," she replies, still laughing. "Let's go, you dork."

Lexa grabs her keys from the table by the door, and slides her phone into the back pocket of those cheek-hugging jean shorts. She turns in time to once again catch me staring at her ass. I just shrug and laugh. She shakes her head at me playfully as I reach past her to open the door. Our faces are inches apart and she takes a sharp inhale as her eyes dart down to my lips. I want so badly to kiss her but I don't want to push her too fast. I don't know if pulling her body to mine and crushing our lips together in a bruising kiss is what she considers *just having fun.*

I hesitate too long and the moment passes. I'm immediately kicking myself, knowing I should have just kissed her. But she's already turning away, ready to walk out the door. In that split second, I know I can't wait any longer for our first kiss.

I grab her forearm, spinning her back towards me before letting my hand drop to her lower back. I thread the fingers of my other hand into the hair at the nape of her neck, gently tugging her face up to reach mine.

Our lips meet in a crush of heat and fireworks explode behind my closed eyes. I can't even feel silly for thinking of it that way when all I can think of is the feel of her velvet soft lips on mine. I clench my fist in her hair, holding her to me. I inhale her spearmint breath as I push my tongue against her lips and she willingly opens for me. I slip my tongue past her lips, familiarizing myself with her mouth. I feel her body melt against mine and a low moan is pulled from my throat. Lexa fists her hands in the front of my shirt, pulling me even closer. Then, just as suddenly as it started, she releases me, pulling back and smiling.

Noah, I think, *that was one hell of a first kiss.* My second thought is, *why the hell is she pulling away?*

Lexa leans her head against my chest, wrapping her arms around my waist and hugging me to her. I rest my arms around her shoulders and try to catch my breath. After a few breaths, I place my hand under her chin, lifting her face so that I can see her eyes. Bright green, just like I was hoping.

"Hey pretty girl, you okay?" I ask.

"Yeah, better than okay. I was sorta afraid that if I didn't stop, we wouldn't make it to the batting cages. Or to lunch. And I really need lunch," she says, keeping eye contact and hugging me a little tighter on "need."

"We don't have to go to the batting cages and I can order you some pizza."

Lexa throws her head back laughing and says in that silly English accent she attempts from time to time, "Oh you naughty devil."

"That didn't sound like a no."

"It's a 'we should go to the batting cages as we planned,'" she retorts.

I heave out a sigh, squeezing her to me once more before saying, "Okay let's go hit some baseballs and not think about what could have been had we stayed here."

I motion for her to proceed through the still-open door and I follow her out. I swat her butt as she sidesteps me to lock the door. She snorts out a laugh and wiggles her cute little backside at me.

I shake my head at myself, once again wondering what I've gotten myself into.

Chapter 29

Lexa

I can feel Drew's eyes on my ass as we make our way down the stairs. That searing kiss that we shared in the foyer of my apartment left me near breathless. I knew that if we kept going I wouldn't want to leave.

As far as first kisses go, that one was spectacular. I don't know if it's the chemistry we already shared of the fact that I've been waiting to kiss those lips for almost 10 years, but something was definitely different. That saying about seeing sparks fly? Yeah, that's what happened the moment our lips touched.

I reach my hand up, running my fingertips over my bottom lip and barely containing a smile. I half turn back to Drew, to see if he's as lost in that moment as I still am. I catch his eye and the small half smile that he's giving me. I immediately blush and I can feel the heat running down my neck again. I can feel the warmth on my chest but also a warmth spreading through my chest. I don't remember a time recently that I've felt this...content. I turn again, giving Drew my best imitation of the megawatt smile. It makes him laugh, which warms me even further.

Once we reach the bottom of the stairs, I ask, "Which way?"

"Wait, you live here and you don't know where we're going?" Drew asks incredulously.

"Oh yeah, I mean I go hit some balls pretty regularly you know," I respond, letting my words drip with sarcasm.

Drew snorts in derision, "Right slugger, let's turn left and maybe you'll catch on soon enough."

We're a few steps into our adventure when I can't help but ask, "How long have you been thinking about how that kiss would be?"

"Only a decade, Lex," Drew answers immediately. He reaches toward me, threading his fingers through mine, "You?"

"Probably just as long," I answer honestly. "I thought that most of what I felt for you was just a deep friendship. And even though I do love being your friend, I love the rest of this even more. It's like I get to finally be my real and full self around you, not having to hold back that part of me that wants to run my hands down your abs when I catch you coming shirtless out of the bathroom on Christmas Eve morning." I blush, not realizing how specific that thought was going to be until it was out of my mouth.

Drew just laughs and says, "Yeah that morning was a lot for me too. I made a point to always put a shirt on before leaving a room when I knew you would be there. I didn't know it for sure at the time, but there was a lot of heat coming from your stare that morning and I'm not proud to say I had several dreams the next couple of nights we stayed there about what I wish I could have done in that moment. God I wanted to back you against the wall and–" He cuts off abruptly and I notice that he's turned a rather deep shade of red.

I pull up short, using our tethered hands to stop his forward progress. I swing him around a bit to face me before asking, "What Drew? Now you're shy?" I laugh, but realize that I'm also a little nervous that maybe I've pushed too far too fast.

Drew just shakes his head, laughing a little and says, "No, I just don't think I can finish that thought out loud without taking you back home now and showing you." As he finishes the sentence, his ocean blue eyes turn a shade darker and his lips part slightly, drawing me in. I'm close to pushing *him* up against a wall until I hear the honk of a car horn and the shout of a driver. The street noises pull me back to the here and now and it's my turn again to blush. We both know where those thoughts were taking us and how close we were to a very public make out session. We start to giggle like teenagers, caught in the act.

Drew tugs my hand saying, "Alright let's keep walking before someone's honking at us to get out of the road and stop staring at each other." He throws me a wink and his lip quirks up in that half smile that I love so much. I smile back and fall in step beside him, letting him lead me to our destination.

Minutes pass in a slightly awkward but not uncomfortable silence, punctuated only by Drew saying "turn here" or "take a right."

I'm still very unsure of why Drew thinks I have any idea where we're going. As I open my mouth to say as much, I notice a very familiar sign.

"Oh, the little league fields. Of course," I say with a laugh. I guess not growing up here, I forget about places like this."

"Yeah, I spent most of my weekends up here from ages 5 to 14, so this place ended up as a second home of sorts," Drew says, a touch of nostalgia entering his voice.

I glance up at him, trying to read his thoughts. Is this something that makes him miss home or just another memory that's filed away while he's back in Texas? He has such a sweet and dreamy, far off look in his eyes right now. I almost don't want to break the trance, I want him to be able to remember all of his years here in fondness without my interference. I feel like I'm intruding on something almost sacred to him.

I sweep my gaze over the clustered fields and try to see this place through a young Drew's eyes.

Chapter 30

Drew

The clicking and clacking of cleats as the other kids race across the pavement, their parents shouting at them to slow down before they bust their butts. The smell of freshly grilled burgers and hot dogs, hot popcorn and nachos. The taste of salt on your tongue as you shell another sunflower seed, spitting the hull in the grass like you saw your daddy do it. The whizzing of baseballs, the thud of the catchers mitt as another fastball is slung from the mound. The giggle of the little girls, come to watch their brothers play and flirt with the other boys on the team. That tangy taste of Gatorade mixed with your own sweat as you try to chug a gulp before grabbing your glove to head back out to the field. The crunch of the dirt beneath your feet as you hustle out to your position, ready to make that big play and win your team the game. The sound of metal striking the ball as what could have been your third strike soars over the fence, earning your team two more runs and cementing your home run record in the league this year.

✿

It feels like I could just step through the gates right back into my childhood.

I sigh, feeling like I'm letting loose a breath that I've been holding for far too long. It's been years since I've been back here. I can't believe I get to be here with Lexa, showing her something from my childhood. I feel a little…nervous I guess. Like maybe I'm showing her something personal that she could think is silly. But when I look at her face, I can see that she knows this is special.

"I've never brought anyone else here before. No other girl, I mean," I say, squeezing her hand. I want her to know how important she is to me.

I seem to have startled her from her thoughts, but she turns to me with the sweetest smile I have ever seen. "Oh Drew, I'm so thankful to be here with you now."

And I know. I know I love this girl. She knows parts of me that I barely even know myself. In this moment, I can feel her not just physically, but emotionally here with me.

I smile down at her, eyes roving over her face from lips to eyes and back again, as if trying to memorize it all. Like it's a face that I could even possibly forget. I have had this face in my dreams—day and night—for years now. But the absolute love and warmth that I can feel radiating from her now is almost overwhelming.

Before I do something stupid like blurt out the "L word" on our *first date,* I force myself back to Earth and give Lexa's hand another squeeze. I allow myself to plant a small kiss on her forehead before leaning back and turning back towards the fields.

"Alright slugger, you ready?" I ask, gesturing towards the batting cages tucked off to the side of the complex.

"As I'll ever be," Lexa says, sighing dramatically. Then, she giggles and tugs my hand before taking off towards the cages. I just stand there, watching her run for a second before I catch myself grinning like a maniac. I shake my head, let out a snorting laugh and take off after her. I know I'm faster than her, I mean her legs are so tiny. And while I'm usually the gentlemanly type, my competitive urge wins out and I'm racing her across the asphalt. We get to the cages, laughing and slightly out of breath. *Damn,* I think, *maybe I should be doing more cardio.*

I glance at Lexa to see her looking at the ground by our feet.

I smile and say, "Yeah, that's another reason I was so early. I came by here first to drop off the gear, that way I could hold your hand on the walk over rather than a bucket of balls."

The sheer astonishment on Lexa's face tells me that she's been dating some pretty indecent guys lately. This is such a small thing but the tear that I see welling in her eye makes it feel huge. Before I can even think of what to say next, she launches her small body towards me, arms outstretched and eyes closed. We meet in a tight embrace and I can feel how hard she's trying to hold onto me.

"Hey," I say, "do I get to breathe again soon or..."

"Ohmygosh," she rushes out, letting her grip slacken ever so slightly, "I guess I just wasn't expecting–"

"Me to be such a forward thinker?" I question, giving her a smirk.

"No silly. I wasn't expecting you to be this sweet I guess. It just caught me by surprise."

"Sweet as sugar, baby doll," I say, laughing. But the laughter dies down when I see the look she's giving me. Her pupils have dilated to almost drown out those gorgeous green irises. Her lips have parted ever so slightly and her hands are moving across my lower back, gradually easing my hips towards her.

I can't contain the amount of heat these signals send through my body and I shudder slightly before using one hand to tip her chin up and splay the other across her lower back to pull her to me. The feel of her entire body pressed up against mine is intoxicating, as is the feel of her breath tickling my lips.

I dip my head forward, needing to taste her again. When our lips meet, it's just as exciting as the first time. It feels like my body is being lit up by electricity while my lips try not to break the current. Lexa tilts her head to the side, slotting her mouth to allow me better access. As my tongue drags across hers, I feel like there's no way I'll ever be able to stop kissing this woman. I move my hand to stroke her cheek with my thumb, then ease it towards the back of her neck. I thread my fingers through the fine hair at the nape of her neck and she moans into my mouth. *Oh Holy God.* The growl that slips up my throat is nearly feral as I reach my other hand down to cup her ass and pull her into me as close as humanly possible.

I'm holding her halfway in the air by her butt when I hear the unmistakable sound of children laughing. I pull back sharply–still holding onto Lexa–to scan our surroundings. Luckily when we came over to the batting cages, we ended up behind some fencing and shrubs that mainly block the view of the parking lot. But I'm still able to see some cars pulling in from the road, meaning it's definitely not just us here anymore. I sigh, setting Lexa back on her feet. I smile as she reaches up to adjust her ponytail. I groan slightly when she pulls a thumb across her kiss-plumped lips and gives me a sultry look.

"Stop it," I say laughing, "We already almost put on a show for the pee wee teams and I can't help what happens if you keep looking at me like that."

"Fair enough," Lexa replies, flipping the end of her ponytail with a hand as she turns to walk towards the gear. I let my eyes drop down to the ass that was just solidly in my hands and silently curse the scheduling of little league baseball.

I huff out one last sigh before following her over to the ball bucket and bat bag.

I watch as Lexa opens the bat bag first, looking through the assortment of bats and gloves within.

"You still have this much stuff at home from high school just to be able to hit a few balls when you're home?" she asks, turning in her squatted stance to face me.

"I mean, yeah. It was actually all at Landon and Ansley's place. I grabbed it a few days ago, meaning to get out here. It's a solid collection of mine and Landon's high school and college gear."

She nods appreciatively as she continues to rifle through our stuff. She pulls out a smaller, battered glove and tries it on. I laugh as I realize that it's my glove from my last year of city league before I started high school ball. It fits her well though.

"Your hands are so small. I'm glad I still had my 6 year old glove in there."

Her face blanches as she looks from her hand to mine. I laugh heartily before saying, "Just kidding, that one is from middle school. But my point still stands."

Lexa gives me a rueful grin before saying, "Well at least I don't have big monster hands." She sticks her tongue out at me like she's actually managed to insult me somehow.

"Sweetheart, you know what they say about big hands…." When this statement causes the intended effect of making Lexa blush, I continue on with, "big mittens."

Lexa guffaws, losing her balance and toppling onto the bat bag.

"Noah there, Grace. Land on anything metal?"

She takes my outstretched hand, standing up and dusting herself off before answering, "No I don't think so. Luckily I had a lot of over-sized gloves to fall onto. What a cushion."

She turns back toward the bag with a smile on her face and I smack her butt cheek lightly. "Smartass." I bend down to start sorting out the things we'll need. I grab the dusty old mitt that fit her and my last college glove, along with three bats. I don't know what her swing is going to be like so I decided to grab a variety of weights.

I stand, ready to toss the bats into the cage and ready the balls to be put in the pitching machine when I glance at Lexa. She's looking very sheepish suddenly and a bit apprehensive.

"Oh no. Don't tell me you've never swung a bat before," I say, eyeing her suspiciously.

"Well," she starts, toeing the ground with her sneaker and looking all kinds of bashful. "I mean, I played tee ball when I was 4." She looks up at me then, obviously trying to gauge my reaction to this news.

"Tee ball? You mean where the ball sits in one spot on a stand and you get endless attempts to clumsily throw a bat in an arc in the ball's general direction? That's the tee ball you're talking about?"

"Yes, geez. I was more into soccer and volleyball, even basketball before everyone went and outgrew me. You don't have to act so high and mighty. Not everyone was a college sports star. And I'm reasonably athletic–"

"Yes, as your fall from a squatted position clearly showed," I remark.

Lexa's face goes red and I realize that she might actually be embarrassed by this.

"Oh baby, it's fine. I happen to know a damn fine coach," I say. I wink as I finish with, "And he happens to be a decent hitting instructor as well."

Lexa just rolls her eyes as she stalks towards me. "Okay coach, show me what ya got."

Chapter 31

Lexa

How did I know this coaching session was going to turn into a romcom montage? First there's the standing behind me, showing me where to place my hands on the bat. Of course, using every innuendo known to man while doing so. Next, there's the foot between my legs, moving them out and into their correct places to give me a perfect stance. Finally, there's the hands on the hips to show me how they should move as I complete the swing.

After all that, I think I'm ready to hit a ball from the machine. But no. First Drew wants to lob a few slow pitches my way from very close just to "check the swing." I groan but I let him do it, only because I'm actually still a little nervous about hitting off the machine. On my second attempt, I hit the ball solidly and Drew yelps in excitement. He eagerly tosses me several more, backing up each time until his back is close to the pitching machine.

"Okay, I'm going to throw some overhand for you to hit from the distance of the machine. It'll be a bit faster than the underhand tosses but just keep doing the same swing. You got this," Drew encourages.

"Okay, I got this. Just…not *too* fast okay?" I say meekly, giving him my sweetest smile.

"Okay not too fast," he laughs.

I look down at my feet, making sure they're in the correct position. I look at my hands on the bat to check the placement on the grip. I cock the bat back and look at Drew. "Ready," I say, feeling anything but.

Drew pulls back his arm and throws a ball *right at me.*

Okay maybe not right at me, but it felt close. I know it was right where the others had been, but seeing his arm coming over the top made it feel so much more intense.

I laugh, embarrassed by the yelp and scatter act that I just performed.

Drew smiles but drops his glove by the machine and walks to me.

He takes my face in his calloused hands and tilts my face up to look at him. "Hey, look at me. Do you want to just feed the machine and I'll hit? You've gotten really far today but I'm not trying to make you feel uncomfortable."

"No," I say, shaking my head, "I got this. I just got scared on that first one. I know you won't hit me and I know I can hit the ball. One more chance?"

"Of course," he says, placing a soft kiss on my lips before turning to walk back to his glove and the ball bucket.

I smile to myself before focusing once again on my feet, hands and finally, Drew.

He shows me the ball, cocks his arm back and throws. I put every bit of determination into my swing as the ball nears me. I let my hips lead and my hands follow, like Drew taught me.

The bat connects with the ball and sends it hurtling straight back at Drew.

I have a moment of sheer panic before Drew's glove comes up and easily fields the ball. He throws down his glove, ball still inside and races towards me, scooping me into his arms. He hugs me tightly before placing a much more fervent kiss on my lips. He pulls back, looking down at me with beaming pride and says, "My girl is gonna be hitting home runs before we know it."

I blush heavily, not just from the excitement of the hit, but also from what Drew just called me. *His girl.* I can't stop the huge smile that plasters itself across my face. I say, "Well I had an adequate teacher. Plus my natural athleticism–"

Drew shuts me up with another kiss. This one deeper than the last. I don't think I could ever get tired of kissing this man. Far too soon for my taste, he pulls back and says, "Ready for the machine?"

"Hell yeah, baby. Bring it on."

Drew chuckles and saunters back to the ball bucket.

"Alright this will be a bit different since you won't see the ball until it's leaving the machine okay? Why don't you step back and watch the first one go through so you can get your timing down?" he suggests.

I nod, suddenly more than ready to step back from the plate. I stand back, watching as he shows me the ball before it disappears momentarily. The ball reemerges just in time to be spit out by the wheel and thrown in my direction. I'm motionless as I watch the ball fly past me towards the back stop.

I don't realize that I'm still staring at the ball until I hear my name being called from the other direction.

"Lexa, hey Earth to Lexa, come back to me," Drew's saying.

I shake my head, trying to clear the daze and turn back to him.

"That was so fast," I say, in what sounds like a scared child's voice, even to my own ears.

"Okay, here's what we're going to do. I'm going to knock it down a few notches on the speed. You're going to continue standing where you are, but this time I want you to act like you're at the plate. Get set, get your feet placed and swing when the ball is at the point you want to hit it. That way you can feel the timing of the ball. I know it looks scary coming out of the machine but it's the most accurate way to do this. The ball won't hit you because it's going to travel the same path every time."

I look down for a moment before refocusing on Drew. "But…what if you just pitched to me?" I ask. Before he can mount a protest I say, "I watched you for years in college, and while I know you weren't a pitcher, I also never saw you throw an errant ball from center field. If you're that accurate from such a distance, I bet you can be accurate in this cage." He still looks a bit on the fence so I say, "Drew, I trust you."

Chapter 32

Drew

And that does it. Lexa placing her blind faith in me steels me to be able to do this. I don't know why I'm feeling so reluctant, anyway. Me and Landon pitch to each other all the time when we don't have a machine.

It's because you're afraid to hurt her dumbass, my mind snarks at me.

Okay, obviously. I guess I'm afraid that I'll hit her with a bad throw. Hitting Landon is one thing. Plus, I know he'll get out of the way. All I can really hope for now is accuracy on my part and quick feet on Lexa's.

"Alright, I'll pitch to you. But only because I'm never going to get to hit if we keep trying you out on the machine apparently." I laugh trying to ease some of the tension I'm feeling.

"Alright Babe Ruth, let's have it then," Lexa says, all grit and determination.

It's enough to make me lose my shit in a fit of laughter and spit out, "Babe was not a pitcher. Is that the only baseball player you know?"

Lexa turns red again, but I see her mouth draw into a firm line before she says, "Just throw like Jackson and we'll be fine." She uses one hand to tap the bat to the plate and the other to toss her ponytail back behind her shoulder. She slides her gaze back to me in a look of pure dare. *Oh it's on, baby.*

I move the pitching machine over so I have her square on before shucking my toe across the ground in a bad imitation of heating up the pitching rubber. I stare her down for a hard second as I place my foot on the rubber. I glance behind me, checking my runners and holding my glove close to my chest. I look back to Lexa, giving her my most evil grin before going into an MLB level windup. My arm arcs out and towards Lexa and I release at the sweet spot, knowing this one is heading right down the middle. In the split second it takes for me to celebrate my victory in this grudge match, I notice that Lexa isn't backing off. She's staring the ball down and her hips are already twisting, readying her body to punch the shit out of this one. If she connects, this is going to be a beast of a hit. Her eyes stay fixed on the ball as her hips start to pull her arms forward, bat level and held firm. The ball is a foot away as her stance tightens to punch the last bit of power from her arms before releasing all the power held in her hips. The bat makes it to the middle of the plate, connects with the ball on the front edge of the box and there's a loud *crack* as the ball's trajectory completely changes course. I can't even bother to look at the ball and I can only thank God it's not coming at me. I can't take my eyes off of Lexa. Her arms finish their arc, letting the bat take its natural follow through. *God why is that so hot* is the only thought crossing my mind.

I'm only half aware of the ball hitting the top back corner of the cage and then the ground because I've already dropped my glove and I'm walking towards Lexa.

She's wearing the biggest smile I've ever seen and only notices me when I'm a foot away. She gasps in surprise as I pick her up by her ass and rest her across the top of my hips. She's clinging to me tight as I push my lips against hers. Her lips part easily, granting me access. I stroke my tongue into her mouth, letting it glide along hers as I hoist her into sitting on one forearm. With my other hand free, I grab her ponytail and tug her head to the side. I use my tongue to explore the hollow formed by the dip of her collarbone, tracing upward and trailing kisses along her neck, ending in that tender spot under her ear. Lexa lets out another gut wrenching moan and I'm a goner. I continue to hold her and walk until we've hit the corner of the batting cage where the storage box sits. I place her onto it and put my mouth back on hers.

Lexa's hands are everywhere. My chest, my abs, my back and now my ass. I can tell she's trying really hard not to yank my shirt off. I spare her the decision by pulling up the hem of my shirt as her hand is gliding back up so she can touch without stripping me. Her hands are only inflaming my already scorching skin. I use my thighs to widen her hips so I can get even closer.

I'm thankful that none of the little league teams are taking batting practice over here because I can't seem to get a grip on myself. I'm rock hard against the fabric of my pants and the small amount of friction with Lexa's jean shorts is causing a large reaction in me. I can't seem to control the thrusting of my hips as I move between her legs. I deepen the kiss even further, using my hand on the back of Lexa's head to tilt her back slightly. If she would stop moaning I could maybe get an inch of self control. But as it stands, every time I try to pull away, she grabs another piece of me. This is the most intense takeout session I've had since I was in high school. But this is a million times better because we're not fumbling preteens.

And we fit together so damn well.

A rush of cool air suddenly hits my face as Lexa leans back and away from me.

"Noah whoa whoa. Not here," she says laughing. "Are you sure this isn't where you used to bring your high school conquests late at night?"

I shake my head, as much to clear it as to say no. I laugh and take a small step back, placing my hands on the outer parts of Lexa's thighs. I'm not quite ready to let go yet. "No but I thought it might be fun to have a different set of memories to add to this place." I shrug and give her a lopsided grin. "I honestly don't know what just came over me. Watching the sheer determination on your face and the rippling of your leg muscles as you swung that bat, it just hit a nerve. In the best way possible, of course. That was honestly one of the sexiest things I've ever seen. Maybe I should piss you off more often," I say with a wink.

"Yeah? Why don't you try that and see how it works out for you," she says, deadpan.

"I'm just kidding babe. But really, that was awesome. That ball would have been deep center if we would have been on a field. Maybe you really are just a natural athlete."

"Or maybe I just had a really good coach," she says, looking at me from under her lashes. Is this Lexa trying to flirt with me? Because damn if it ain't adorable. I love this woman.

Chapter 33

Lexa

After the Earth-shattering kiss that just happened, I expected Drew to want to leave and possibly continue the scene elsewhere. I was wrong.

Drew pats the outside of my thighs, squeezing once for good measure before pulling away from me to walk towards the area where he propped the other bats. He takes a second to pick his weapon before strolling back to the plate. He uses his foot to roll my bat away before looking up to smile at me with a look full of boyish charm.

"Okay sweet cheeks, my turn. You better roll that screen in front of you before you start putting balls through the machine," he says in a very serious tone, although his use of the silly nickname shows me he's still having fun.

"You're just wanting to impress me aren't you?" I ask, hopping down from my perch on the equipment trunk.

Drew chuckles before dropping his voice and calmly stating, "Baby I know I impress you."

I can't help the snort of laughter that comes out at that line.

"Geez, if I didn't know you any better I'd think you were a little cocky."

"More than a little," Drew says with a roguish wink. That one has my face going all shades of red. A nervous giggle escapes my lips.

I promptly turn to head to the pitching machine, not willing to give Drew the satisfaction of knowing that I'm thinking about how *not little* he is.

Once I get to the pitching area, I pull the machine back into position before rolling the screen over to protect me. I glance up at Drew once the screen is in place just in time to catch the self-satisfied grin stretching his cheeks.

"What? You think I'm just blindly obeying orders? I would have already thought of that. I'm not trying to have a black eye for this wedding tomorrow," I say, throwing my hip out and putting my hand on it to enforce the idea that I'm giving attitude.

Drew just continues smiling at me. Then, he ducks his head, shaking it slightly from side to side. He steps up to the plate before looking back up towards me. The mirth has left his gaze, leaving only pure determination on his face.

I love how competitive he is. I love the drive he shows, in every aspect of his life. There's something else behind his eyes, however—a different edge to him.

I step back out from behind the screen so there's no interference when I say, "Hey, where's your head right now?"

It seems to take a second for Drew to process that I've spoken to him. He shakes his head quickly, like he's coming out of a trance. "What?" he asks, still not fully in the conversation.

I take a step towards him, reaching out a hand. "Where's

your head at? What are you thinking about?"

Drew steps away from the plate and fully turns towards me. "Um, I'm not sure, really. I originally needed to come out here to burn off some steam because, well, work is kicking my ass. But then I kind of forgot about all of that…because you know…" he trails off but breaks into a small secretive smile.

I continue walking towards him, taking his hand once I reach him. "What's going on at work? Last I heard, you loved your job."

"Things have changed a lot recently. We have some newer managers that just got pulled up from the ranks that are running us ragged. It's like they don't remember being us just a year ago. The amount of emails that I get daily trying to micromanage every move I make, just makes me so irritated. I can't continue to be degraded through email and talked down to in meetings by people that are on a power trip with almost no real authority. And the part I loved about my job, the working with clients and realizing visions for marketing campaigns—isn't even what I get to do anymore. I got a 'promotion' which entails me overseeing other people's work and keeping tabs on their progress. I barely get to have client interaction and I haven't touched a new campaign in months. I want to be in the programs, working on the designs and the schematics, not reading someone else's work all day. And when I tried to talk to my new manager about it, she said that I should just be happy that I got a pay raise." Drew huffs out a sigh, squeezing my hand and pulling me to him.

I hug him tightly, trying to crush this sorrow out of him. I had no idea that he had been feeling this way. I wonder if he's even talked to Ansley about this. I honestly just hope that he's talking to someone. Knowing how Drew feels about sharing his feelings, I'm afraid that he's been keeping this in for a while without an outlet. I release him from my arms just slightly and lean back to look at his face. I see him staring past me towards the pitching machine. It dawns on me that he does have an outlet and I'm currently depriving him of it. I drag him back into a hug before fully letting go and turning to walk to the machine. I hear him shuffling around behind me as I walk and I let him have some space to himself instead of turning to look.

As I reach the machine, I inhale, letting my face fall into an easy smile before turning around. I take one look at Drew and I already know he's in a better head space. All I can see in his eyes is the calm determination. The errant waves of stress seem to have receded for now. I let a genuine smile fill my face before shouting, "Alright Babe Ruth, you ready?"

Chapter 34

Drew

I don't know if I've ever had that much fun in a batting cage, is my first thought as we're packing up to head home.

Lexa is amazing. It's like she took all that stress I was feeling about work from my body and released it into the atmosphere. Plus that takeout session was intense. It took everything I had not to just leave our gear behind and carry her straight back to the apartment.

She really does something to me. I don't think I've ever met anyone that can tangle me up and sort me out all at once. I'm excited just to get to spend more time with her tonight, around our friends and family. I also just can't wait to see what she wears. She sure knows how to pick an outfit that flatters her. Those cutoffs she's sporting today have my mind in so many places that do not warrant public access.

As if reading my mind, Lexa glances behind her to catch me once again obviously staring at her ass. She gives her butt a little wiggle and laughs, but turns so that I can gather her in my arms.

I pull her to me, letting my hands fall to their preferred position near the back pockets of her shorts. Lexa places her tiny hands on my chest, and I feel her butt flex as she stretches up to her tiptoes to kiss me. I love how small she is. It ignites every protective instinct in the caveman part of my brain.

I dip my head to deliver a long, sweet kiss. I pull back, just long enough to say, "Thank you so much for today. You don't know how much this meant to me."

"Anytime, babe. I loved it too. It was just what I needed," Lexa replies, smiling sweetly up at me before stretching up for another kiss.

I cup the bottom of her cheeks, squeezing once before gently releasing. As much as I don't want this moment to end, I know we need to get back and start getting ready for the rehearsal.

I let Lexa go, keeping hold of her hand—still not ready to fully release her. Lexa in one hand and my baseball bag in the other, I feel a huge grin stretching my face. I inhale deeply, letting the smell of the freshly cut grass and tilled dirt wash over me and fill me. Today has been a great day.

✿

After dropping Lexa off at her apartment with another wonderful kiss, I came back to mine to start getting ready for tonight. It's hard to even shower without thinking of Lexa. Now that I've felt how her body fits against mine, I can't think of anything else. I want to take my time with her, we have no reason to rush things. At the same time, I feel like I can't wait another minute to really be with her. Maybe we've waited long enough.

I try to shake off these thoughts so that I can use my mind

for other things. Like what I'm going to say in my toast tonight. Since I'm the brother of the bride and a groomsman, I'm giving a toast tonight at the rehearsal. Exciting, right?

I honestly tried before today to get this figured out. I tried to work on it at home the week before I left, on the plane on the way here and every spare moment I've had since I've been here. And while I don't want to use Lexa as an excuse, I know that I've been a bit distracted since I've been in town.

But once I get out of the shower, I have two hours to get this toast outlined, get ready and get to the rehearsal venue that's only 15 minutes away. That's plenty of time. Especially since all I have to do is say some sweet things about two of the people I love most in this world.

After an inordinate amount of time, I finish my shower and head to the kitchen to grab a water before I get started writing. With my towel still wrapped around my waist, I fall back onto the couch, water in one hand and phone in the other. I just want to outline this toast in a note on my phone so all I have to do is glance at it before I head to the mic. One upside of my current job is that I've gotten pretty good at presentations. Before I was moved to more of a supervisory position, I was the man they asked to throw together a last minute slideshow and bring around a tough client. Because of that, I know I can quickly throw some notes down and have my whole toast prepared in minutes.

I take a sip of water, pulling up my notes app. I see a note at the top, *ask Ans about pic,* and chuckle. That's a picture I definitely want in my possession now.

I once again tell myself to focus on the task at hand. Toast time.

I type out a few quick notes, *joke about Landon, joke about*

Ans as the annoying little sister, sweet something about knowing they were soulmates at the beginning, what true happiness looks like, what I aspire to, love wishes and cheers!

That oughta do it really. I don't want to overdo the outline. I know the best parts will come to me in the moment. I should probably check in on Lex tonight, make sure she's getting along okay on her toast. I know she suffers from a bit of stage fright and I'm sure she's getting a bit nervous about this.

Now that my major responsibility of the night is handled, I think I'll watch some TV until I have to get dressed. I wonder what Lexa's doing right now.

Chapter 35

Lexa

Oh I don't know why I thought that two hours would be enough time. Today is wash day for my hair so I have to wash, put in the product and diffuse to get my curls going strong. I also need to finally decide what I'm wearing tonight. I need to eat a small snack so I'm not starving when I get there and I still need to work on my toast for tomorrow night. I haven't had to speak on command in front of this many people since my sophomore speech class in college. I hate public speaking. But I'll also do anything for Ansley.

At least I have another day. Drew has to talk tonight. I doubt he's that nervous though. Judging by what I've heard from Ansley, Drew was a born orator. *Lucky ass,* I silently seethe. Maybe I can siphon off some of his confidence tonight–I doubt he'd miss any. With a chuckle at that thought, I decide it's time to at least start trying to get this shit show going.

First up, shower. As much as I would love to take a long

and luxurious shower, reminiscing on the feel of Drew's hands running over my body, I would never get ready in time. So instead, I rush through the shampoo, conditioner and washing to just get it done. I have to get my curl routine done today so that I can style the curls in a half up, half down look for the wedding tomorrow.

I rush to my closet while I wait for my hair to dry just a bit. I have three different dress options for tonight. Normally I would just call Ansley and get her opinion but obviously that's not in the cards. She reiterated the dress code for the rehearsal to me several times, but I still don't know how dressy or casual I need to be. I throw all three options onto my bed, and pair shoes with them in the hopes that seeing a complete outfit will help me finalize the decision. I'm getting frustrated with myself for not being able to choose a dress when I realize it's time to start on my hair. Okay, dressing myself will be saved for later.

I don't want to rush my hair routine since I need these curls to last and look good for several days. I take my time with the products and the drying process, making sure every curl is defined and ready. I breathe a sigh of relief once that's done. My hair on wash day always takes the longest to get ready. I check the clock and I still have 45 minutes before I need to leave. With a clearer head, I walk back to the bedroom to pick a dress. It can't be that hard right?

As I'm walking into the room, a slant of sunlight streams through the window, falling on a dress. It's my emerald green cocktail dress that I wore to Jackson's senior baseball banquet. I do love the way that dress looks with my hair. The sun picking a dress seems like reason enough for me to wear it.

With my outfit finally picked out, I head back to the bathroom to throw on just a little makeup–eye shadow, lipstick, the basics and nothing too crazy. I know I'll have a lot of makeup on tomorrow so I don't want to bury my skin two days in a row. With 15 minutes left, I pull my dress on and slip into my black heels.

I glance at the clock before strolling over to my full-length mirror to look at the final result. I still have a couple of minutes so I give myself a full spin, trying to catch all my angles and make sure nothing is out of place. My reflection does make me smile. I clean up pretty nicely, if I say so myself. Not that tonight is about me in any way, but I definitely don't want to be the reason that Ansley's pictures from the event look bad.

I chuckle, thinking about the prom pictures she showed me where her big hair was permed and pulled up into a horrendous up-do. She said her mom even did her makeup in an 80s style, regardless of the fact that this was in 2012. I burst out into full laughter thinking about my poor girl in that poofy dress with big hair and blue eye shadow looking miserable in that picture with all those well-coiffed people she went to high school with. Knowing her mom like I do, I'm not surprised that she wanted to dress Ansley like it was still the 1980s. Mrs. Parker has been stuck in that time period since I met her. She still wears the stirrup leggings and scrunchies. Luckily for her, these things are coming back around.

I hear my doorbell ring, accompanied by a knock. The sounds immediately startle me from my thoughts. Who would be knocking right now? I swear, if it's Mr. Schwartz from downstairs telling me that my heels are too loud on the floor again…

I open the door to see Jackson, all polished and pretty with a panty-dropping grin on his face. *Shit,* I think, *this man sure knows how to work his charm.*

"What are you doing here?" I ask, shock written all over my face.

With his grin still in place, Jackson says, "Well I figured you wouldn't want to walk or drive in your heels and since I rented a car, I thought I'd come pick you up."

"How did you know I'd still be here and wouldn't have left already?"

"Because I didn't have to be there early either. And I know you like to be just right on time for everything so you wouldn't have left already." He flashes me a shit-eating grin, seeing my look of surprise.

"Yes Lex, I still remember things about you," Jackson says, laughing. "Well, do you want a ride since I'm already here?"

"Um, yeah sure," I say, still struggling to get my act together. Why do I feel so affected by this act of chivalry? Maybe it's just the sheer surprise of it.

I step back so that Jackson can come into the apartment. As he steps in, he looks around and I realize that he's never been here before. I'm immediately self-conscious of my place in a way that I was not when Drew was here. I feel like he's probably judging my crammed bookshelves and the coffee cup I've left by the sink so I can use it again in the morning. I'm afraid he's looking at my small, cozy home with disdain and that makes me uncomfortable. I love my place and my life and everything about it here. I feel immediately on the defensive just watching his eyes roam through my apartment.

The fact that he seems rooted to his spot by the door

instead of looking around makes it worse. It's like he doesn't want to get too close to my mess.

This is the moment that Sneakers decides to announce his presence with a loud purr and stretch right beside Jackson's foot.

"Oh God, what's that?" Jackson half-shouts as he pulls his foot away from Sneakers.

"That would be a cat, Jackson. A very cute, cuddly and sweet one, in fact," I reply. Letting the ice take over my tone. I scoop up my sweet fur baby and snuggle him into me, letting him glare over my arm at Jackson. "I'll be right back, let me just grab my purse," I say, not turning to look at him.

Ugh, the nerve, I think as I walk into my bedroom. I gently set Sneakers on my bed, giving him a few more pets and turn to my dresser to grab my purse. Pulling my black clutch from its spot, I stuff my phone in and try to take a deep breath before going back out to face Jackson.

Once I feel that I've calmed enough, I trudge back out to the living room to see Jackson scrutinizing my coffee table. He's not touching anything. He has his hands clasped behind his back, leaning over and peering at what I have set on the table top.

I glance at the coffee table, making a quick assessment of the book, Starbucks cup, two remotes and collection of cat toys sitting there. *God he is such a cleanliness snob,* my brain reminds me in quite a derisive tone.

I'm now remembering every trait of his that I just couldn't stand. I like to look back on our relationship with a different view sometimes, thinking it was just the distance and the difference in our wants for the immediate future that caused our downfall. But oh my, it was so much more than that.

Jackson's head whips towards mine as he realizes that I'm watching him critique my space. His face reddens momentarily before he collects himself and can plaster a smile back on.

"Hey there, beautiful. You ready to head out?" Jackson asks, trying to seem as casually charming as possible. It feels cheap though, and fake.

I smile back, weakly, and nod. "Yep, ready when you are," I finally say. It feels like getting my heart broken all over again, remembering that a lot of Jackson's personality these days is fake. Being splashed across TV and the magazines made him different, even though he'd never admit that. Jackson was the "Hottest Rookie of the Year" in more ways than one. It was something that the owners were able to cash in on for years.

With another smile that I'm afraid isn't quite reaching my eyes, I stretch out my hand towards Jackson. With a grin that seems more real than anything else I've seen tonight, Jackson takes my proffered hand and we walk together towards the door. As much as I don't want to lead him on, I don't want to crush his hopes tonight, just before watching his best friend get married. Plus, who knows, maybe some time around real people will bring his genuine side back to us.

We head out the door, down the stairs and out to his waiting car. I guess it will be nice getting driven to the dinner, anyway.

Chapter 36

Drew

The first thing I notice is how amazing Lexa looks in that dress. The second thing I notice is that she walked in with Jackson. Did they ride together? She didn't mention that she'd be riding with him the whole time we were hanging out today. What does that mean?

But God does she look great in that green dress. It looks familiar and it takes a moment to place it. She wore it to our senior year baseball banquet. And she was on Jackson's arm then too.

Oh shake it off Andrew, I chastise myself. She's not here *with* Jackson. She just showed up with him. I'm sure he's still trying his hardest to win her back, even if that means picking her up tonight.

In an attempt to appear unaffected, I turn back to the table I'm sitting at and try to catch the thread of the conversation. Unfortunately, everyone seemed to have noticed the same thing I did. I hear Claire say "No way, they are not back together" and I hear Amanda say "Oh *that's* Jackson? Well

191

they do look good together." I feel Wes's eyes on me but I don't want to see what he's thinking. I turn to Connor, seeing that he seems lost with this conversation topic, thank goodness.

"So, how's work been man? We didn't get to talk a whole lot the other night," I ask, trying to distract myself.

Connor sets down his beer before huffing out a breath. "It's been alright. I'm not really loving it right now. Me and Patrick have been throwing around the idea of starting something of our own. We'd need a few more people obviously. But the idea of working for ourselves has become more and more appealing recently. How about you? Still loving working and living in Texas?"

With what I hope is a subtle glance at Lexa talking to Ansley, I say, "Not as much as I used to." I shake my head, clearing my throat a bit before continuing, "If y'all need someone in marketing, I'd be willing to throw my name in the ring. I could work remotely until I know if or when I'm moving back this way."

I realize this is the first time I've started making any plans to move back to Georgia. I don't know if it's something that I've actually been thinking about or if it's Lexa that's spurring this decision. Either way, it doesn't hurt to keep my options open, especially for my career.

"Really? That would be amazing! We'd love to have you on the team. When I get back to reality on Monday, I'll shoot you over an email of what we have worked up so far. If you're looking to get in on the ground floor, that would be great."

"Cool man," I say with a chuckle. There's a bubble of excitement forming in my chest that I haven't felt in a long time when thinking about work.

With my mind elsewhere and a small smile on my face, I look up to see Lexa. She's standing 10 feet away, red wine glass in hand, head cocked slightly to the side and staring at me with a sexy pull to her lips. The look in her eyes is full of questions but I'm more entranced by the halo of light around her soft curls and the way her emerald green dress is hugging her frame. It looks even better on her now than it did 5 years ago.

I stand from the table, excusing myself without breaking eye contact with Lexa.

"Hey gorgeous," I say, using Lexa's free hand to pull her towards me. I release her to place my hand on her lower back. Her palm lands on my chest and she lets out a soft exhale. When she looks up into my eyes, it's all I can do not to dip my face to hers and kiss her in the middle of this room. While Ansley knows about us, I don't think our parents do and almost none of our friends are aware. I don't want to announce our budding relationship at my sister's rehearsal dinner. I use the leverage of my hand to pull her towards me for a quick hug before releasing her and taking a half step back.

"Well hey stranger. Long time, no see," Lexa says, somewhat breathless. Her cheeks are stained crimson and I know immediately that her thoughts are back on our time in the cages today. She laughs once, before saying, "So what is the protocol here? I know we're not trying to be too public tonight, but I still get to hang out with you right?"

"Of course! You think I don't want you right beside me? I was sitting over here with some of the bridal party and there's still a few seats left at the table. Wanna join?"

"Lead the way," she says, dipping her head in deference.

We weave back through the throngs of party guests, arriving at the table to see two seats left. Sandwiched between Jackson and Claire. I look to Lexa to let her choose her seat and I see that Jackson is already motioning her towards his side. Knowing Lexa like I do, I know that she won't want to be rude. I take the seat between Lexa and Claire. I'm immediately tapped on the shoulder and I hear a shrill "Hey!" from right next to my ear.

"Hey Claire, how are you? You look great tonight," I say, turning towards her. I sweep a cursory glance over her dress, so it looks like I'm not giving a fake compliment. She does look great though, she always does. And until I knew I had a shot with Lexa, I probably could have seen myself with someone like Claire. She's a lovely person and all, just not my type–my type being fiery redheads, apparently.

"I'm doing great, I've loved being in Savannah. There's so much to do and see here. I'm still looking forward to our coffee date next week," she says, blushing.

"Oh right, yeah you'll have to let me know when you're free," I reply, immediately regretting that invitation from last week.

"You're taking Claire out for coffee next week?" I hear the smooth voice ask from my other side. I turn to see Jackson leaning slightly across Lexa, a burning look in his eye.

I clear my throat before saying, "Claire and I are going to get coffee next week and catch up before we both have to fly home."

"Oh, I wasn't aware you two were close. I never really saw you hang out much together," Jackson says with a dismissing wave of his hand.

I open my mouth to reply, but decide now is the time to

be the bigger man. So I turn to Lexa and say, "If you're free, we'd love to have you join us. Plus I know you can't really turn down midday caffeine."

Lexa lets out a chuckle, replying, "Of course, that sounds great."

I turn in time to catch Claire's face fall just a bit before she plasters a smile back on. She leans across me and says to Jackson, "How long are you in town for?"

I am not prepared to be in the middle of Claire trying to flirt with Jackson, so I gently push my chair back. I look at Lexa as I stand, "Need anything from the bar?"

Lexa's eyes fill with gratitude and she takes my offered hand. "We'll be right back, anyone need anything?" she asks before we step away. No one responds so we make our way across the room to the bar.

"We better get the actual rehearsal started soon or there's going to be some very intoxicated people trying to remember where to stand," Lexa says, laughing.

I motion to the bartender for two drinks and look back to Lexa. "Well at least all you have to remember is to walk out before the bride and stand by her."

"So true. To be honest, though, I am a little nervous about tomorrow," she says, anxiety clouding her features.

"Why? Afraid you might be prettier than the bride?" I ask, trying to make her laugh. It works, but earns me a slap to the bicep.

"No, oh my gosh, why would you even say that?" she says, still laughing.

"Just to hear that laugh I like so much come from those lips I'm dying to kiss," I say, my voice dropping a few octaves.

Predictably, a blush colors her cheeks and it takes every

bit of willpower I possess not to brush my thumb across her cheek and kiss her now. My hand is halfway to her face when I hear the music stop and the MC starts making an announcement. I can't even comprehend what he's saying because Lexa's breath has hitched and she's staring into my eyes with unrestrained want.

"Come on, you two. Rehearsal time," Ansley says, breaking the intensity of the moment. Lexa's breath huffs out all at once and my hand drops back to my side.

"Oh look, the twerp found us," I say, pulling Ansley to me for the hundredth huge bear hug of the weekend. I still just can't believe my baby sister is getting married.

"You're going to mess up my hair," she says, laughing against my chest before shoving me away. "Now come on, we're rehearsing so we can eat and keep drinking. If we wait any longer, no one will be sober enough to remember their cues."

We all laugh, knowing how true this is, especially with our group of friends.

Lexa loops her arm through Ansley's and I follow right behind. Lexa says, "You know, I think that's why most people wait until rehearsal is over to start serving alcohol."

Ansley laughs, saying, "Yeah, but where's the fun in that?" She winks at Lexa and they both dissolve into giggles.

I can't help the stupid grin stretching my face right now. Two of the women I love most in this world laughing and bonding even more right in front of me. Both so happy and carefree in this moment. It's truly beautiful to be able to have these types of experiences in life.

Chapter 37

Lexa

Okay, at this point I'm almost convinced that Jackson keeps messing up his cue so that we have to remain beside each other, arms linked and separated from everyone else.

No, that's crazy, I remind myself. He wouldn't do that. Especially when it's so clear that everyone else is ready to get to dinner.

"Hey, what about I just signal you when to meet me here and then we'll be good to go. It looks like everyone else is ready to eat," I say, flinching from some of the stares aimed at Jackson.

"Just watch you until I get to walk to you, I think that's something I can handle," Jackson says with a smirk.

I look to Ansley and say, "Okay I have a plan. Once more and then we're done."

We all line up on our sides, ready to meet in the middle and walk each other down the aisle in front of the beaming bride. I signal Jackson when it's his turn to walk and he meets me in the middle with impeccable timing. We finish our walk and make it to our spots. I glance behind Jackson to see Drew rolling his eyes. I let out a silent giggle and focus on the back doors as Ansley makes her entrance. It's not even the real wedding yet and I'm already getting teary-eyed. I'm going to be a mess tomorrow. I look over at Landon who is smiling so big, I'm afraid his face might get stuck that way. I love these two. They are so perfect for each other and I am so happy they found each other.

Once the fake vows and rings are exchanged, we all let out a big cheer. We make our way back up the aisle to more upbeat music. We walk as a group back across the street to the restaurant where we're having the rehearsal dinner and find our tables again.

I reclaim my seat between Jackson and Drew, hoping the latter will get here soon. I saw him stop to talk with his mom after the rehearsal.

"You look so good on my arm, Lex," Jackson purrs against my ear, reaching his hand out to rest on my forearm.

I chuckle, because I'm so caught off guard by this sudden change in demeanor. When I look over, I notice that Jackson's eyes have gone a bit glassy. When did he get so drunk?

I'm contemplating my next words when I feel a strong hand on my shoulder. I look up to see Drew smiling at me, "Wanna dance while we wait for our food?"

I lean my head to peek past him and notice that there are several people already on the dance floor. I perk up, saying, "Sure, lead the way!"

I let Drew pull me from Jackson's grip. I don't even turn to look at him as we leave. I'm not sure what's happening with him, but I know I want to be with Drew and I don't want him messing that up.

I let my gaze fall to Drew's outfit, taking in the nice fit of his dress pants and the broad shoulders under his shirt. This man sure knows how to wear some pants.

I giggle, thinking of his butt in all of the pants I've seen it in. Baseball pants, dress pants, sweatpants…but my favorite has to be his worn-in jeans. My mind wanders to the way his jeans are worn just enough around the back pockets to accentuate his tempting ass.

I'm pulled back to the now by a tight squeeze on my hand, dragging me onto the dance floor. I feel my face stretch into a smile as my eyes meet Drew's baby blues. His attention is solely on me and I feel the blush stain my face. I look down, feeling embarrassed. A finger touches the underside of my chin, gently pulling my face back up. I let Drew pull me back to him, as he says, "Hey, let me see those beautiful eyes."

I blush again, putting my free hand onto Drew's shoulder. When we're standing this close, he feels impossibly tall. His thoughts seem to be running in the same direction because he laughs, saying, "You feel so tiny when you're up against me like this."

"Tiny? Really?" I demand, faking an affront.

"Tiny and cute?" Drew asks, letting his free hand fall to my waist. He uses that leverage to pull me even closer. The upbeat pop song we came out to dance to inevitably changes to something slow and Drew smiles wide. He drops his mouth down to my ear and whispers, "Tiny and incredibly beautiful…and a little scary."

I can't help but laugh at this description, knowing he's only half joking. I like it when he calls me beautiful though, and

I'll gladly listen to that all night. I also don't mind him calling me tiny, I like being tiny compared to Drew. It makes me feel safe to be enveloped by him.

In the comfortable silence that follows, I close my eyes and try to just savor this experience. Dancing with Drew is nice, really nice. He holds me to him, but not too tightly. His arms feel warm and secure. I let the music fill my head, finally hearing the lyrics.

My eyes fly open, immediately searching out and finding Ansley. She's looking directly at me with a sweet and loving expression on her face. This song was one that me and my dad used to dance to when I was young. I can't believe she remembered and played it for me tonight. I start to tear up, remembering when I learned to dance while standing on my Daddy's feet. I close my eyes, letting the tears fall down my cheeks and a smile form on my lips. I feel a gentle pressure on the back of my head, easing my cheek against a warm, solid chest. I blink through the tears and tilt my head to see Drew smiling down at me with ocean blue eyes. I rest my head back down on his chest and I feel him gently set his lips against my hair. The rightness of this moment hits me and even more tears begin to escape.

As the song ends, I squeeze Drew to me tightly, silently thanking him for the dance and the safe space to think about my dad. For some reason, tonight is the first time I've really registered the fact that I won't get a first dance with my dad at my own wedding. That's why Ansley wanted me out here to dance tonight, to remind me that she'll always be here for me.

Realization dawns as I look up at Drew again and ask, "Is this what you were just talking with your mom about?"

Drew's eyes are focused only on mine when he says, "We were making sure the timing was working out for me to pull you out here for this song. You know my family is your family and we just wanted to do this for you. The anniversary is so close so we wanted to honor him in some way. It was okay, right?" Drew suddenly looks nervous, thinking maybe I'm upset for the wrong reasons.

"No, no it was perfect," I say, sniffing again and smiling. The Parkers have got to be the sweetest and most thoughtful family on Earth. I glance around and catch Mr. and Mrs. Parker's eyes, fixed on me and Drew. I feel my grin falter for a second with a new wave of tears before it stretches to fill my face again. Mr. Parker pulls his wife closer to his side as they smile at me with so much pride on their faces.

I feel a tug on my arm as I hear one of my favorite voices say, "Okay big bro, she's mine now." I flip around and land in Ansley's outstretched arms, hugging her with as much love as I can put into the gesture.

"Okay, let's do this Bridezilla!" I say, pulling away and spinning Ansley to pat her butt in an attempt to get her moving to her table. I sit in the open chair beside her, waiting for whatever she's wanting to talk to me about. We don't have anything planned for tonight that she'd need my help with. Now that the actual rehearsing is over, we're eating, drinking and hanging out.

"So," Ansley starts, "I have a big favor to ask." She looks at me with such hopeful nervousness that it scares me a bit.

"Anything Ans. You know that," I say, meaning it.

"Well…so…you know how we're having y'all announced as you walk into the reception while with your pair? Well we were hoping to do this cute idea that we saw in a movie earlier this week," Ansley says, still a bit hesitant.

"Yeah? What is it?"

"Well so once you walk in together, you all do a few dance moves to a slow song that will be on. So you know, a little side stepping and a twirl or dip or something. But I know how that might be uncomfortable for you with Jackson." Ansley gives me a small, sweet smile at this.

"Ansley, doll, it's your wedding day. I would walk over hot coals in my bare feet for you on a normal day. Of course I'll pull a few dance moves with Jackson." Ansley's face splits into a grin with this.

As she squeezes my hands in hers, I can't help but go over the last few hours in my mind. Have I been that obvious in my discomfort around Jackson tonight? I don't even feel that out of sorts around him, just annoyed with his attitude tonight. I make a mental note to do better the rest of the night so Ansley has one less thing to worry about tomorrow.

I give Ans my rendition of the megawatt smile and pull her into a crushing hug. I love this girl. "I love you so much and I can't wait for tomorrow. It's going to be amazing."

With a parting hug and smile, Ansley releases me with a flick of her glance over to my table for the night. I follow her gaze to where Jackson and Drew are steadily ignoring each other while sitting one foot apart. I head back towards my spot and silently praise the fact that it's finally time for food.

Once I reach my chair, I watch as two beautiful pairs of eyes turn in unison to where I'm standing. I try to smile, but my face feels just as frozen. Drew breaks the silence and eases the tension by standing to pull out my chair. My eyes pull to his handsome face, watching the corner of his mouth quirk up into a lopsided smile. Seeing it instantly warms my heart and melts the ice I felt building in my veins. I keep my eyes on Drew as I drop into my seat, grateful to be off my feet for a little while and eat.

Working the night shift, I end up not eating on a normal schedule, but I am starving. The almost overpowering aroma of braised beef and brown gravy swims around my head as the servers lay plates in front of us. The fluffiness of the mashed potatoes and vibrant green of the grilled asparagus is causing me to salivate. I absolutely adore the catering company Ansley is using. They cater a lot of the work events that we attend and they have the best down-home Southern dishes, but elevated with gourmet spices and cooking methods.

I dive in as soon as my plate is set in front of me, feeling like I'm not even pausing for air as I inhale my food. I didn't realize how hungry I was, I guess. I'm halfway through my meal before I even glance up, catching the eye of Amanda from across the table. She's laughing and giving me the "slow it down" motion. I start laughing as she starts telling a story about me choking on my food at work because I eat too fast sometimes.

"Side effect of the ER," I say with a shrug, as Amanda falls into easy conversation with my seatmates regarding life at the hospital.

Chapter 38

Drew

As we're finishing up eating, I notice that Jackson seems to be sobering up a bit. *Thank God,* I think. I really didn't want to deal with a drunk Jackson the rest of the night. Since no one has to be here to start getting ready until the girls get here at 10 a.m., we're all going for a night cap. If he wasn't the best man, I wouldn't even think he'd make it out with us tonight. Of course I'm looking forward to spending more time with Lex, but I need to save some focus for Ansley and Landon as well.

My thoughts are pulled back to the present when I hear the MC call my name. *Oh shit, it's toast time.*

I get up from my seat, throwing a nervous smile and Lexa. She just holds my eyes and gives me a sweet grin before mouthing, "Good luck."

I amble towards the front of the room, stopping to drop a kiss on the top of Ansley's head and give Landon's shoulder a squeeze. I take the mic from the MC and inhale a deep, steadying breath, closing my eyes. When I open them, I start talking.

All I can think of afterwards is I hope that I said something good, because I don't remember a word of it.

When I finally recover my senses and walk back to the couple's table, I see tears in Ansley and Landon's eyes and know I must have at least said something sweet. Ansley squeezes my hands and drops her face against my side. "That was so beautiful, I can't believe that came from you," Ansley says with a watery laugh.

Damn, I'm going to have to request the tape from this part of the night. The only thing I remember is saying how much I loved these two, surely that wasn't what caused the waterworks.

I turn to Landon who stands and wraps me in a fierce bear hug, slapping me on the back a few times for good measure. "I love you so much bro," Landon whispers against my shoulder. Shit, they're gonna make me cry.

I make it back to my seat, not really wanting to meet anyone's eyes for fear they'll see the tears in mine. But I feel a warm hand slip into mine and look up to see Lexa gazing at me with the warmth of the sun in her eyes.

"That was wonderful, Drew. I don't know how I'm even going to follow that tomorrow night," she says, giving my hand a squeeze.

"Wanna know a secret?" I ask, leaning in closer so that my breath is tickling her ear. I hear her intake a sharp breath, which instantly makes me smile.

"Of course," she says, still a bit breathy.

"I have no idea what I said. I blacked out once I started talking. I can only hope I followed my outline." Lexa guffaws at this, laughter shaking her body as she throws her head back.

"Are you serious? That was one of the most eloquent speeches I've ever heard and you're not even sure what you said? I can't believe it. All that does is make me more nervous!"

I can't help but laugh with her as all the anxiety releases from my body. Lexa is so great at making me feel relaxed, she's like a drug that I don't want to quit. Hopefully I won't have to go through that withdrawal.

The rehearsal dinner winds down and people begin to clear out after the speeches from some of the other family members. It's time to blow this joint and head out for some time out on the town in our formal wear.

✿

I'm sitting with Landon, talking about anything and everything sports related when I hear a sweet voice yell from across the bar, "Hey, if you can't take the heat, stay out of the kitchen!"

I turn to find Lexa pointing the end of her cue stick at Wes, who undoubtedly just accused her of cheating her way to a win. From what I saw during the game, I can't necessarily say he's wrong. Lexa has a very particular way of playing games that always edges on rule-breaking. Wes should remember that from college. I look back to Wes to see him backing away, hands up, but with a smile on his face. At least he's not taking it too seriously.

I laugh, turning back to Landon to see him doing the same.

"Maybe you should rescue our man," Landon says, slapping me on the back and winking at me.

"Yeah cause we all know Lexa is not the damsel in this situation," I reply, standing to make my way to the pool table.

I'm cut off by Jackson who doesn't even seem to see me, his gaze locked on Lexa. I stand back, knowing what's on his mind and wanting to see where this goes.

Jackson and Lexa used to always slink away to the pool table when we were in college, playing each other in a decently competitive game before inviting people to play against them. It was some of the only times I saw Jackson display any outward signs of affection towards Lexa. They were never very big on the PDA, but when they played pool there was always a lot of touching. The light touches to the waist as he would "position her for a shot" or a hand ran up an arm as he "showed her how much pressure to apply." It seemed like she enjoyed it, she would shiver and smile. But it always drove me crazy, watching him touch her and knowing this was all she would get from him. Not that I really think I could have watched them kiss and cuddle constantly like some couples do.

I know that's exactly what's going through his mind right now. He's seeing Lexa as she bends over the table, imagining standing behind her and leading her through the motions again. I'm not mad, he told me his plan for this weekend. I'm just curious to see Lexa's reaction after feeling how she came alive under my touch today.

He's circling her like a shark while she's lining up a shot. He looks up long enough to meet my eye, give me a wink and a smile with a hint of challenge.

I sit down by Wes, who pushes a full beer towards me.

"She cheated again, huh?" I ask, tapping his beer bottle with mine.

"Hell yeah, you know she always does. It's so hard to argue with her though. I just need to get better and then I can beat her without a problem," Weston says, laughing.

My eyes wander back to the pool table and I feel Wes go still beside me. Jackson is leaned against the pool table, hands braced and butt on the edge. He's bent down to where Lexa is chalking her cue and basically whispering in her ear. She shakes her head, but smiles up at him. Lexa bends over to line up another shot and Jackson moves easily to brace one arm on the table and rest the other on her lower back. I glance at Lexa's face just in time to see her eyes close. *Is she enjoying this?* I wonder. I don't have very much time to think about it before I see her gently push back from the table and whip around towards Jackson. I can't hear what she's saying, but I can tell from the set of her jaw that she's talking through her teeth. She looks pissed.

Jackson's hand flies off of her like he's been burned. He forces a smile onto his face and says something that I assume was supposed to be funny because he's laughing, but Lexa isn't. I move to the edge of my chair, preparing to get up when I feel a hand on my shoulder. I look back at Wes and Landon with what I'm sure is anger in my eyes. Wes handles it well though and just says, "Dude, just wait."

I look back to Lexa and see she has Jackson backed up against the wall with his hands up between them. I can tell she's giving him a piece of her mind now about what he's trying to do. I watch as she rips a cue stick from the holder, thrusting it into Jackson's hands. I can only assume she said something along the lines of, "Play or leave."

I watch as Lexa continues playing her game, only pausing once to look up at me and smile. I smile back, lifting my drink up to give her a "cheers."

Chapter 39

It's about two minutes before I feel Jackson move behind me to start playing. I feel slightly bad about the interaction we just had. But, he needs to understand. He can't treat me like I'm still his girlfriend. If he's really trying to have a chance with me again, he has to actually try. He can't just walk back into the spot he vacated that easily.

I see him move around the table and bend down to grab the rack so we can get a new game started. I look around to make sure that no one is waiting on the table and notice that Drew is still watching us out of the corner of his eye. I see him smirk when he realizes I'm staring at him. I laugh and shake my head, turning my attention back to the table.

I lock eyes with Jackson. He's staring at me with an odd expression in his eyes. Like a mixture between determination and resignation. I'm having a hard time figuring out his game plan here. He's been all over the place.

Before I can think any more about Jackson's behavior, he's drawing me back to the present by gesturing to the waiting game. "Ladies first, Lex," he says with a dramatic sweep of his hand over the table.

"Ever the gentleman," I reply, sashaying over to the table to line up for the break.

"I'm just giving you the go-ahead so you can get at least one shot in before I run this table," Jackson replies, calling up trash talk from years ago.

"You would think you had gotten better banter material playing a professional sport," I snark.

"Just go ahead and lose and it won't matter what I have to say." Jackson has a shit-eating grin spread across his face when I look up at him.

I lean back down, readjusting my grip once more before striking the cue ball. I'm rewarded with a stripe careening into the corner pocket. I stand up, brushing my hand across my opposite shoulder. "Glad I could at least take one off the table for you."

I bend back down, lining up my next shot. Over the next couple of minutes, I sink three more balls, all stripes. Leaving Jackson with all seven of his solids. Luckily, I didn't set him up for anything easy with my last shot.

Jackson easily knocks in four solids before missing again, leaving me with an easy shot for my next strike. Two more stripes in. Just one more to go before I can take aim at the 8 ball.

As I'm lining up my shot for the 11 ball, I feel heat enclosing my space again. I turn my head to the side to see Jackson staring at the end of my stick. "Something wrong Sharky?" I ask, not yet turning my head back to the game. Jackson's jaw is so close to my mouth. He's leaning fully over me without touching a single part of me. His body heat is radiating off of him in waves, coating me in warmth.

"Hmm? No, just watching," Jackson replies, his eyes roaming my face before landing on my lips.

I intake a sharp breath before shaking my head. I turn my attention back to my shot, taking a deep breath to center my focus. I want to beat Jackson even more now that he's intentionally distracting me like this.

I pull my arm back and thrust the stick forward through my outstretched fingers, making solid contact with the cue ball. I watch as the cue ball connects with the 11, spinning it onto the perfect path towards the side pocket. As the ball sinks into the pocket, I pull back from the table to celebrate. I'm immediately stopped by the feel of a very hard body against my back.

"Good girl. Now make that 8 ball and put me out of my misery," Jackson purrs under his breath. I shiver as tingles run up my spine.

I decide to try to diffuse this ticking time bomb and spin out of Jackson's arms. "Oh so it's miserable to have to hang out with me now?" I question, throwing every bit of brattiness I can into my voice.

Jackson just smirks as he lets me walk away from him and towards the other side of the table. I hold his eyes as I lean over the table to line up my final shot. I watch as his gaze dips down to my open neckline, climbs back up to my lips and settles back on my eyes.

"Well," Jackson says with a hand gesturing to the table, "call your pocket babygirl."

I smile sweetly, using my cue stick to point to the pocket near where Jackson's other hand is resting on the table.

I drop my smile, checking and rechecking my angle. I

aim, shoot, and watch in nervous anticipation as the 8 ball approaches the called pocket. It stops on the edge for just a moment before finally sinking out of view.

"Oh hell yeah!" I shout, throwing my fist in the air in victory.

In the next moment, I'm swept up into strong arms and being pulled off the ground. I open my eyes to see Jackson's face lit up with joy, huge smile stretching his face. There's a beautiful light in his eyes and when he notices that I've opened mine, he says, "I love when you beat me. You always get so excited and God, do I love that smile." With the last word, he drops his gaze to my mouth again. I feel the smile melting from my face, replaced with an open-mouthed anticipation. *Is he going to try to kiss me in front of everyone?*

I'm saved from that knowledge by a shrill voice yelling, "Are you going to hog the table all night?" I turn in Jackson's arms to see Ansley shooting a look filled with surprise and warning.

I tap Jackson's shoulder, signaling him to put me down. I turn fully to my best friend with palpable relief.

"As far as I understand the rules of the game, winner keeps the table."

Ansley takes my hand, dragging me away from Jackson and back to the rack. "Alright then winner, it's my turn to take you on."

"Yes ma'am, Bridezilla," I say with a laugh. I'm absorbed by the game and by Ansley in no time, almost–but not quite–forgetting about what just happened.

Chapter 40

Drew

Saturday

I'm so thankful to be a guy this morning. I don't have to be at the venue until noon. We're eating lunch and then getting ready. We have to be ready for pictures by 3, which means the girls all had to be there at 10 a.m. I'll never understand why it takes women five hours to get ready for wedding pictures, but I'm probably better off not knowing.

Without realizing it, I've grabbed my phone to text Lexa. *When did I become an every morning texter?* I wonder, still holding my phone. I decide to go ahead and text her, against my male instinct to not show vulnerability by being too available. *At least I'm self-aware.*

Good morning, beautiful. I can't wait to see you in another pretty dress today. And take pictures with you ;), I fire off, knowing that she's awake but probably way too busy to text back.

I stand and stretch, knowing I stayed out too late last night.

Once Lexa left, I noticed most of the other girls had already gone as well. As I looked around, I saw that aside from me and Wes there were a few other guys from the wedding still here. We all seemed to sense it and pulled our chairs closer together. A round of toasts to the wedding that brought us all together began, ending several drinks later. A couple of hours more had us stumbling our way out of the bar, laughing at nonsense and thankful we were already walking home.

It hits me as I'm walking into the bathroom that I never saw Jackson leave. I remember Lexa coming to tell me she was leaving and getting a hug from her and from Ansley. Landon wasn't long for the bar after that. But I don't remember if I saw Jackson leave before Lexa or after. *Did he go home with her?*

With that disturbing thought in mind, I jump into the shower. Watching Jackson with Lexa last night was a little rough, seeing how much he obviously still likes her. But she's changed since college and I really don't think she's all that into him anymore. I also know that shared history sometimes makes it hard to live in the present.

I decide the best course of action is to try to forget about this less than desirable thought train as I start getting ready for Ansley and Landon's big day.

✿

We're gathered in the groom's room, a bunch of guys half dressed in their formal wear and drinking beer. Hair of the dog and all that. I look around, watching as the faces of my best friends crinkle with laughter. I watch the light in Landon's eyes as he sees his friends all here for him on the best day of his life. I wouldn't want to be anywhere else right now.

I raise my beer and say, "Well since I've already completed my real toast, this one will be for free." I wink at Landon who laughs and then I continue on, spilling my guts to my friends. "As I look around at you guys, I realize that there is no greater love than that you have for your bros." I can't contain my laughter at that, giggling with the group for a minute. "But seriously, Landon, I can't wait to watch you marry the love of your life today. Y'all truly are an inspiration and I'm so glad she tied you to our family forever. I can't survive those Christmas family dinners without you anymore."

As I finish, I see a tear glistening on the edge of Landon's eye. I hadn't meant to turn mushy but weddings bring up all those crazy feelings.

I step over to Landon, pulling him into a tight hug.

"Love you, dude," Landon says, squeezing even tighter. Before he can make me cry, I pat him on the back and release him. Everyone raises their beers and takes a deep slug.

I walk back to where Weston is sitting, laughing as he uses the back of his hand to wipe the beer foam from his face.

"Sup?" he asks, patting the edge of the seat by him.

I reach my bottle out to clink with his as I sit. "Oh not much, just trying not to turn into a blubbering mess before the wedding even starts. You?"

"Dude same, so many feelings in this room. I love it though. I love you guys," Wes says, clinking bottles with me again.

I look up to see Jackson laughing and talking to Kent. I realize I haven't forgotten the thoughts surrounding him and Lexa from last night. I turn back to Wes with my mouth open to ask a question. I notice he's already staring at me with a very odd look on his face. "What?" I ask.

"Well I just saw the look on your face when you saw Jackson

over there, I was wondering if something happened."

"No, nothing happened. Not that I know of at least," I say with some question in my voice.

"What is that supposed to mean?"

"Well, I remember telling Lexa and Ansley bye and then Landon shortly after that. But I can't remember when Jackson left and for some reason it's throwing me off pretty badly today."

"Because you think he left with Lexa but can't remember?" Weston asks with a knowing look on his face.

I drop my head into my hands before saying, "Dude I'm such a mess."

I feel a hand land on my shoulder and squeeze once before Wes says, "Just to put you out of your misery, I saw Jackson leave and it was way before Lexa. He didn't look happy."

I feel slightly bad for the momentary happiness that flits through me at that. "Okay thanks. I guess I should have just asked her about it." If she was texting me back. I glance up at the exact moment that I see Jackson send a text and then look up at me and smile.

God I need to get that guy out of my head. It's time for us to finally finish getting ready and head toward the front of the space where pictures will start.

I shake my head, trying to get in the head space I need to be in and getting excited to see Lexa again.

Chapter 41

Lexa

"Yeah he said he'd save a dance for me," Claire continues on her soliloquy about Drew. Apparently they hung out a bit at the bar last night after Ans and I left and now she's pretty sure they'll be dating by next week. I guess she doesn't read signals very well. But then again, maybe I'm the one misreading. I got a text from Drew this morning after we got to the venue to start getting ready. I texted him back but never heard anything else. I'm sure he's busy over there with the guys. It's about time for pictures.

This morning has flown by in a blur of makeup brushes, hairspray and mimosas. We already had our sweet getting ready pictures in our matching pj sets with our over-the-top smiles in place. I always love the "look at the bride and laugh" command from a photographer. It starts out so fake but ends with real laughter and joy that the photographer is able to capture.

Amanda wanders over and breaks me from my thoughts. "Hey you know that music festival you were talking about?

The one in September? I checked into it and I am so down," she says, excitement breaking out on her face.

"Yes!" I exclaim, pumping my fist in my Tiger Woods celebration pose. "We're gonna have such a great time. We'll talk hotels and tickets and everything later this week at work."

"Sounds perfect. I just wanted to mention it before I forgot. I'm honestly not even sure what brought it to mind," Amanda says with a laugh.

"Maybe all the chaos of the morning?" I respond with my own laugh.

We're pulled back to the present by Susan, the fearless wedding coordinator. She has made wrangling this group look like a cake walk so far. "Okay my beauties, time for the first look with the groom. It'll be right outside that window if anyone is interested in watching," she adds with a wry smile, knowing we're all about to rush over there and paste our faces to the window. "But first, here's your bride," Susan continues, sweeping an arm towards the small area partitioned off from the rest of the room.

Ansley walks from behind the screen to a series of awed gasps and some stifled tears.

"Oh my God, you're gorgeous."

"Oh Ansley…"

"You are by far the most beautiful bride I have ever seen," I say, emotion choking my words. I then add, "That Landon is one lucky guy."

The girls around me all giggle, some still obviously trying not to openly cry at the sight of our breathtaking friend.

"Ready to go see your groom?" Susan asks her.

Ansley nods emphatically, looking around at us with tears

welling up in her eyes as well.

"Hey none of that yet," I say, handing Susan a handkerchief to help Ansley catch the tear before it falls. "We have so much more to go before we let that amazing makeup get ruined."

"You're right," Ansley says with a breathy chuckle. With a sniff, a smile and a nod, she turns back to Susan, "Lead the way."

As Ansley leaves the room with Susan, us bridesmaids rush to the window to watch the first look. These things always bring me to tears and I know Landon is going to cry. He's such a huge softie.

We watch as Ansley gets closer to Landon's back and I can see that Landon is already tearing up. *Uh oh,* I think, *here come my waterworks.*

Once the first look is over with Landon, the groomsmen come out to get pictures with him and Ansley is coming back inside to have a first look with her dad. While they're having their private moment, it's time for us to get zipped into our dresses and strap on our shoes.

With our hair sprayed to near hardness and our waterproof makeup in place, we begin the downstairs trek to the meeting spot for our group pictures. First up is the bridal party and the bride, then us with the groom. Then the groomsmen with all of us and a picture with the boys and the bride. Then we're excused long enough for the family pictures.

I catch a glimpse of Drew smiling, looking at Ansley with so much love and affection. There's no place he'd rather be right now and that is the sweetest thing I can imagine. As I'm watching my favorite set of siblings laugh and talk, I hear, "Watcha looking at with that cute smile on your face?"

I turn to see Jackson watching me, eyes scanning my face.

I feel myself blush, caught in the act of staring. My eyes track up his fit body, wrapped in a well-tailored suit.

"Oh nothing," I reply, "just watching my beautiful best friend."

Jackson hits me with a quick, too-sweet smile, dipping his head in an awkward pause before saying, "Um, sorry about last night. I wasn't really in the right frame of mind for a party I guess."

"What does that even mean? You've been here all week, you know what this week is about." I pause, gathering my thoughts and trying to breathe before I say something stupid. "It's okay. I know things get overwhelming with this many people involved. Though you think you'd be used to that kind of pressure from the league."

"Well yeah, I guess you're right. What I'm really trying to say I guess is that I wasn't in my best form last night and I'm sorry about that," Jackson says, regret shadowing his face.

Lifting my eyes from my feet, I connect with his torn gaze. I smile tentatively before reaching over to bump his arm with my elbow. "I've been a bit scattered this week, so I understand."

"Scattered or spread thin…?" Jackson says, suddenly unable to keep eye contact.

"Excuse me?" I demand, taken aback.

"Is there a problem? What's wrong Lexa?" I hear from behind me as a hand lands on my shoulder, gently pulling me back a step into a hard chest.

Chapter 42

Drew

I pull Lexa one step further back and place my other hand on her hip. I walked up to say hey to Lexa and Jackson and caught the tail end of the conversation. I didn't hear what Jackson said, I only heard the indignation in Lexa's voice and the sudden change in her posture that I've noticed means trouble.

Lexa turns her vivid green stare to my face, scanning from my eyes to my mouth and back again. I lean my head down towards her ear and softly ask, "You okay, baby?"

I feel her shiver in my grip and I watch with fascination as her cheeks flush. She seems to struggle internally for a second before shaking her head and saying, "Yeah, no everything's fine. We were just…talking."

I peel my gaze away from Lexa long enough to look at Jackson. He's staring at us like he's seen a ghost. Eyes wide and fixed, he takes a small step back before shaking his thoughts loose. He finally makes eye contact with me and I can tell he's not okay. He's…angry? Jealous? It's hard to tell with his face so closed off. He eventually opens his mouth to add, "Just having a conversation about the past." Lexa shoots a near-lethal glare in his direction before swiveling back to me. God I love that face. She's so angry but it's so damn cute. I know I should feel angry for whatever she's mad about, but it's honestly hard to concentrate with her intense green eyes penetrating my mind like they are.

"What, you freak?" Lexa chirps, fully turning toward me, my hands falling from her.

I realize then that I have a half smile pulling up the edges of my lips. I quickly release the grin, reaching out to touch her again. I don't want to lose contact right now. As I grasp her toned forearm in my hand, I say, "You look gorgeous."

That beautiful crimson stains her cheeks again and she tries to look down. I can't take that so I place my fingers under her chin, gently tipping her face back to meet mine.

"Thanks," she says, before adding, "You look rather handsome yourself."

She steps back from me then, much to my chagrin, and turns to include Jackson back in the conversation. I'm still not sure what he said to piss her off so quickly but I know she can handle herself.

"You both look very handsome," Lexa says, with a little less warmth in her voice than two seconds before. Jackson smiles at her and I force a fake grin.

I bend at the waist in a mock bow, saying, "Milady, we humbly offer our gratitude for such high praise." Thankfully this earns a small laugh from her as well as a smile. I turn to Jackson to see the blankness has returned as he stares through me. I shoot him a quizzical glance before I hear our names all being called for the group pictures. I offer a smile and my arm to Lexa before sending another glance over my shoulder towards Jackson. All I see in that short look is pure anger. And it rattles me.

✿

With group pictures done, Lexa is excused while we take the family shots. I shoot her a little smile and wink as she waves at me before walking away with Amanda and Claire. I see Weston scooping Jackson up and taking him back towards the groom's room. The fact that Jackson won't be able to corner Lexa again for the moment does little to ease my worry about the situation that I walked into earlier. There was so much heat coming off of that conversation and I haven't had time to even attempt to decipher the meaning of it. There's so much history between those two, I can't get a good read on her current feelings towards him.

"Andrew Parker," a voice cuts into my thoughts and I snap my head towards Susan. She is on top of things today. I have never been more scared of someone dressed in a sweet summer dress with bouncing blonde curls. But man, she's intimidating.

"Yes ma'am…?" I say, hoping she hadn't just asked a question.

"Are you planning on joining us on this plane of existence or living in your head for the rest of the day? I just need to know whether I need to get you cropped out of these later." Scary, like I said.

"I'm here. I'm focused. Smile? Okay, let's do this," I say, laughing and turning to Ansley. She's staring at me with the oddest expression on her face. I used to be able to read her like a book, but I guess the recent time apart has changed that. And there's another tally to add to the self-loathing column.

I focus on my baby sister, bringing my hand to rest on her upper arm. "I'm here. I'm focused. Smile." Ansley laughs at that before spinning back to Susan and our wonderfully patient photographer. I beam at Ansley and then for the camera. All other thoughts but love for my little sister and my best friend wiped from my mind.

Chapter 43

I t's finally time. We're all lined up outside the doors, ready to walk down the aisle. I turn to Amanda standing beside me with a smile and say, "You think the boys will remember their cues?"

"Oh they better. We practiced it enough thanks to Jackson," she replies, laughing.

My laugh gets caught in my throat, thinking about how our conversation ended earlier. I know what he was implying with the "spread thin" comment, I just don't understand why he even felt the need to say it. Does he honestly think that he stands that much of a chance at getting back with me? I don't even know what I've done to give him that impression.

I hear the music change, signaling the doors to open on each side of the aisle. I look around the line of women in front of me to see the guys standing there, some of them looking a tad bit nervous. I smile, thinking how cute they are for it. The cues for the first couple come, and they walk out to meet each other. Thankfully both of them remember to smile. I whisper to the girls in front of me as they file out, "Smile girls, smile big." As the line before me shortens, I see Jackson talking to Drew. They both look over at me and smile. I grin, waving before looking back to Claire. She's the last bridesmaid before me. I see her walk out to meet Drew, who is still looking at me. At the last second he drops his gaze down to Claire, smiling at her as he reaches out his arm.

My eyes track back to Jackson, standing alone. He's no longer smiling, instead he seems to be contemplating something as he stares at me. I nod, trying to signal him to walk to me. I start to step over the threshold before I notice that he hasn't moved. I stop, widening my eyes and nod again to get him moving. This time it works because he's in motion. We meet in the middle of the aisle, a small smile tacked onto his lips that doesn't seem to reach his eyes. He lifts his arm for me to take. I smile up at him, eyes still widened and place my hand into the crook of his elbow. As we turn to walk down the aisle, a more normal smile stretching my lips, Jackson places his other hand over mine. I'm stunned momentarily at the proprietary feel of that hand. I keep walking, smile straining as I glance towards the altar. Drew's eyes are fixed on Jackson's hand covering mine and he does not look happy. His eyes track over to me and immediately find my gaze. I hold his stare as I continue down the aisle toward him.

Once we reach the end, Jackson squeezes my fingers and releases me to go to our places. I look at Landon, standing there waiting for his future, and I smile widely at him. I see Drew glance at the back of Jackson's head and then turn to look back out at the crowd. I realize he's looking at his mom, who I notice is watching this scene unfold with a slightly amused expression on her face. I only have a moment to wonder what's on her mind before the music changes and we all turn to look at the main doors, waiting for our bride to enter.

The bridal march swells and the doors open, revealing a vision in white. I watch as gasps spread through the gathered crowd. Hands fly to mouths and handkerchiefs wipe away tears as Ansley and her father make their way down the aisle to us. I look away for only a minute to see Landon's face. His eyes are glistening with tears as he tries to hold it together. My head swings back to watch Ansley finish her walk. Mr. Parker has tears in his eyes as he looks down at Ans, getting ready to give her away.

The ceremony is just as beautiful as the couple we're here to celebrate. They wrote their own vows and hearing them exchange such heartfelt promises has everyone here sobbing. These two are truly such an amazing couple.

After we witness the first kiss for the married couple, one in which Landon dipped Ansley deep to roaring applause and several loud whoops, I hand the bridal bouquet to the newly minted Mrs. Blake. The beautiful couple walk back down the aisle, raising their joined hands in victory for having the hard part of the night over. It's all partying from here.

The bridal party makes our way to the cocktail hour while Ansley and Landon head outside to take some pictures.

I trek to the bar, needing some social lubricant for whatever awkwardness I'm sure will ensue with Jackson and Drew tonight. There's a sweet older couple in front of me, ordering some wine and talking about how wonderful the ceremony had been. I smile to myself, listening to them chatter. They walk away and I step up to the bar. I feel a hand on my lower back and a deep voice behind me says, "We'll have two of the bride's drinks, please."

I turn to find Drew smiling down at me. "What if I wanted something else?" I tease.

"You didn't. I know the spritzers are yours and Ansley's favorite drink," Drew says with a laugh. I can't argue because it's true. I shrug, accepting the glass from the bartender.

I swing back to Drew, "Did you just come talk to me so that you could skip the line?" I wink and laugh, watching his face split with a smile.

"You caught me, I had no other motivation to come up here. Definitely not for an excuse to see you and touch you." He pauses for a beat before saying, "It feels like it's been too long even though it was just yesterday that we were together."

"I know what you mean. I missed you a little, too." I look down, not willing to meet his eyes with that admission. I feel the crimson blush staining my cheeks as warm fingertips brush the already heated area.

"Have I ever told you how much I love when you blush like this? It makes you look even more beautiful than you already are," Drew says, tipping my face up so that our gazes are once again aligned. I want to look away again but the absolute sincerity radiating from his stare has me transfixed.

"Flattery will get you everywhere, my dear," I say, putting as much smoke into my voice as possible. I let my lips turn up into a half-smile that I'm hoping looks more seductive than deranged. It must, because Drew's breath hitches on a sharp inhale.

"Okay, so let's talk about tonight. We already know we have to do the first dance with other people but I expect you to be in my arms the rest of the time," he says, holding my chin between his fingers. I melt, loving this slight possessiveness coming from him.

"Yes, sir," I say with a wink.

Drew releases my chin, only to place his hand on the back of my neck. With a gentle pressure, he pulls me to him, bending to whisper in my ear, "Don't play the good girl, we all know you're a little brat."

I laugh, shoving him in the chest. He threads his fingers into the back of my hair, tugging once before releasing me.

"You better be glad the pictures are over, considering you released approximately eight bobby pins with that gesture."

Drew shrugs, "Worth it."

Chapter 44

Drew

I need to get a grip. Cocktail hour is almost over, meaning we're about to have the call outs and the first dances. I look over to where Claire is sitting, almost wishing it was anyone else that I would be dancing with. It's not that I don't like her or think she's cool, Claire's great. But she's not Lexa and I definitely felt some animosity between them at lunch the other day. I never noticed it before so I'm assuming it's new. And there's a chance it has to do with me. I know that we made the right choice by not announcing our relationship before the wedding, but seeing Jackson still adamantly pursuing Lexa is killing me.

As this thought crosses my mind, the devil himself appears at Lexa's shoulder. I glance his way, causing Lexa to turn. She doesn't completely turn her back to me, thankfully. I'm still near enough to hear the conversation.

"Ready for our dance, Lex?" Jackson asks.

"Yeah, sure. It's nothing complicated, just a little twirling and whatnot," Lexa replies, turning to smile up at me.

"We could always make it a little more interesting," Jackson says, winking at her. I shudder, but Lexa just smiles and says, "Sure, Jackson. We'll see."

He reaches down to place his hand on her lower back and leans into her ear, whispering, but maintaining eye contact with me. Whatever he says makes her gasp and blush. My eyes narrow into slits with a challenge. Once Jackson can see that he's riled me sufficiently, he smiles and straightens back up.

"I'll see you out there soon, babygirl," he says and throws his most dazzling smile at her.

"Babygirl?" I ask, pulling Lexa's attention back to me.

Her face is still slightly flushed as she turns fully back to me. "Yeah, an old nickname."

"Interesting, not something I usually call my friends," I say with a small smile.

Lexa huffs out a laugh, "Yeah you know Jackson definitely thinks of me as a friend."

"That's what you are though, right?" I question, hating that I'm letting some jealousy slip through.

"Yes, Drew. As far I'm concerned, me and Jackson are just friends. He's been trying his hardest this week to show me 'what I'm missing', but I don't think he understands I have everything I've been missing out on already."

I smile for real then, reaching my hand out to squeeze hers gently. She squeezes back before saying, "Well I think it's time for us to head to the staging area for call outs."

I don't want to let go of her hand but it would be harder for her to move through the crowd holding her dress and her drink in one hand. I give a final squeeze before dropping her hand for us to move to the back of the reception area.

After making our way through the crowd, we step through the doors and see the newlyweds with the widest smiles I think I have ever seen on their faces. It's hard not to believe in true love and ultimate happiness when looking at those two. Since the day they met, Ansley and Landon have seemed damn near inseparable.

"God, I'm so damn happy for you two," I say, embracing them both in my arms. I look down at my baby sister who has tears welling in her eyes. "Hey none of that, can't ruin your makeup before the first dance."

"Well stop being so sweet and I'll stop crying," Ansley replies, choking up just a bit with her laugh. I release her into Lexa's arms and throw both of mine around Landon.

"Congrats bro and welcome to the family–finally," I say as I feel tears pricking the back of my eyelids.

Landon hugs me back, hard. "Thanks dude," he replies.

I step back, patting Landon on the back and smiling over at Lexa and Ansley. Their hands are clasped and heads bowed together whispering. They look like teenagers again in this moment and I love that about their friendship.

I glance at the doors as the rest of the bridal party starts trickling in. Once everyone is accounted for, we see Susan's blonde bobbed head pop around the door. "Alright guys and gals, line back up in your pairs, same order as the wedding. You'll hear the DJ make the announcement for call outs, then he'll call your names. Walk through, wave and smile. Stand near the head table but don't sit. Cheer for the beautiful couple as they are announced and then watch the first dance. The DJ will call y'all again when it's time to join in the first dance. And once again, smile," she emphasizes the last word and I wonder how many times she's had people walking around weddings looking like *Walking Dead* extras.

I line back up with Claire, right in front of Jackson and Lexa. I feel a hand on my arm and look down, seeing Claire's fingers splayed on my bicep. I look back up, meeting her gaze. "You ready to be presented, cutie?" she says, with a wink.

I laugh and reply, "I was born for the spotlight."

I glance back at Lexa, who is talking with Jackson, Landon and Ansley. Claire draws my attention back to her by placing her other hand on my forearm. With my arm locked in a death grip, I'm basically only able to look at her. She smiles up at me with perfectly white teeth, saying, "I'm really ready for our dance. Hopefully it won't be just one."

"Sure, we'll see. If you can pull me away from the mashed potato bar, that is," I say, chuckling.

"Oh I'm up to the challenge."

I hear the DJ start calling names, beginning with Kurt and Amanda. Soon enough, it's my turn to lead Claire through those doors. This feels way more nerve-wracking than the ceremony since people are actually paying attention to us this time.

"Next up, we have Claire Anderson, escorted by the brother of the bride, Andrew Parker." With the announcement, we make our way through the double doors, smiling big and waving at those that we know. Claire's grip on my arm has only lessened slightly, and I feel like she's trying to hold me in place next to her. We arrive at the head table and Claire still has not taken her hand off of my arm. I'm not rude enough to jerk it away and it's not bothering me enough to really mention it. I turn back to the doors as I hear the DJ say, "Concluding the bridal party are the maid of honor Lexa

Chase and the best man Jackson Roberts."

Lexa sweeps out from the doors, all smiles and radiance. I can't take my eyes off of her as she waves at her friends in the crowd. Looking between her and Jackson, I have to admit that they are a pretty couple. Their differences seem to complement each other. I look around the room and notice people whispering after they have passed by. I can only speculate that their thoughts are in the same vein as mine.

The doors open one more time as the DJ announces, "And now, it's my pleasure to present, for the first time, Mr. and Mrs. Landon Blake!" Applause and whoops spring from the gathered crowd as the glorious couple makes their way to the dance floor for the first dance. Their faces are lit with dazzling smiles and their love for each other shines so brightly.

"Ugh, they're so beautiful it almost hurts to look at," Claire whispers, laughing.

"Yeah, they really are," I respond, barely looking away from them.

All too soon, their first dance ends and it's time for us to join them.

Chapter 45

Drew

I watch in fascination as Jackson swings Lexa around the dance floor. Claire and I have mastered the sweeping sidestep but we are not in the same ballpark as them. I'm transfixed by the fluid movement of their bodies in time with one another, their grace and their presence. I know I'm not the only one here staring at them. As Jackson leads Lexa into yet another graceful turn, I notice that Lexa hasn't looked away from his face once. I know it might just be that she's trying to keep up, but it doesn't seem like it's that hard for her.

They just flow so well together. Each movement looks natural, not choreographed. I am torn in half by the languid smile gracing Lexa's face. She's enjoying herself and I'm glad for that, but dancing is something she obviously loves. And I can't dance like that.

The song is beginning to wind down, and I finally look back down to Claire. Her hands were a constantly moving presence on my arm and back during our dance. Claire is smiling up at me, all melty charm and gorgeous eyes. I decide in that moment that maybe I should let Lexa have some room to work through everything from this week. And I don't want her to not dance just because she'd have to be swaying with me.

I glance back to Lexa once more, just in time to see Jackson dip her low and swing her back up, placing his forehead against hers. There's lots of clapping, but I know it's all for them.

I turn to Claire, "Care for a drink?"

"Absolutely! Lead the way!" she says, grabbing my hand to let me pull her through the throng.

Now that cocktail hour is over, it's time for our buffet style dinner. People are milling about near their tables, no one rushing to eat. I, however, am starving. I make a beeline for the buffet, grabbing some meat and mashed potatoes. Leave it to Ansley to serve comfort food instead of a gorgeous sit down meal.

I find Claire back by the bar and tell her that I'm going to sit down and eat real quick. She smiles and waves me away sweetly.

Once back at our table, I glance around to see who will be sitting around me. Of course Claire, but Wes and Kurt will also be here which makes me happy.

I dig into my plate, noticing that others have now made their way to get food. I smile at some of our distant relatives that pass by, only clapping me on the shoulder, obviously trying to leave me to my food. But then I see someone sitting down next to me, a flash of red hair against a bare shoulder and I'm staring into Lexa's jade green eyes.

"Are you avoiding me?" she asks, tilting her head to the

side like she's studying me.

"No, why would I be doing that?" I ask. I give her a small smile, but don't reach for her like I have been this weekend.

Her head tilts the other way and her mouth forms a thin line. "I'm not sure, you just seem suddenly distant."

"If anything, I just figured you might want a break from me. I've been monopolizing your time. And I know there's other people here that want some of it, too."

At this, Lexa rolls her eyes, but doesn't say anything else for a moment. I tentatively go back to eating, glancing at her in between bites. I can't read her well enough to know what she's thinking right now, but I'm hoping it's not anger that I'm seeing flit across her features.

Chapter 46

Lexa

Ugh, guys can be so infuriating sometimes. How is Drew going to act like he can't get enough of me one moment and then push me away the next? Did he get scared? Is it the wedding, making him feel like there's pressure on us when there's not? I don't want to have this conversation right now at my best friend's wedding and in front of their entire family. We can talk about it tomorrow, I guess.

All I can do right now is watch him while he eats, trying to read his face in those small glances he's giving me.

I sigh, knowing I can't just sit here and stare at him all night.

"Are you wanting to dance again? I need a break after that first dance, but I bet Jackson would take you out there," Drew says, a tight smile on his lips.

"What? What happened to the whole 'you're mine all night' thing from earlier? Are you already tired of me?" I ask, indignation and embarrassment at my own whining voice coming through.

"No, of course not. I just know that you really like to dance and it seemed like Jackson did, too. Might as well have two happy people here tonight," he answers.

Having no idea where his head is right now, I realize it is not the time for this conversation. I move to get up from the table. I feel Drew's hand circle my wrist for just a second, but by the time I look down, he's already dropped it back into his lap.

I cast one last glance over my shoulder, hoping to see something on Drew's face that tells me what is going on. All I see is the top of a head with light brown hair, ruffled like hands have been run through it. *His hands,* I wonder, *or someone else's?*

I shake that thought from my head at the same moment that I feel a warm hand glide down my spine before settling on my low back. The tingling sensation raises goosebumps on my arms and brings forth an involuntary shiver. The shiver intensifies as a hot breath whispers against my ear, "Are you all alone out here? That's a shame with how gorgeous you look in this dress." With the last word, Jackson uses the tips of his fingers to brush at the exposed skin of my lower back from the cut outs of the gown I'm wearing.

"Well, I guess I'm date-less, if that's what you're asking," I reply, turning to meet his golden-eyed gaze.

A smile curls his lips as he says, "Well then, follow me."

Without another look towards my seat, I do just that.

After several songs of twirling around the dance floor on Jackson's arm, I look up to see Drew staring at me. It doesn't feel warm and sweet like it did at the bar last night. He looks angry, but I can see it's not with me. His eyes burn as he stares above my head at Jackson. I turn to look up at Jackson's face, hoping I won't see him smirking like an asshole. When I see the slight pull to the left side of his lips and the glare in his eyes, I know he's antagonizing Drew. I whip my head back towards Drew, but by the time my eyes make it to our table, he's up and moving towards Claire.

I had noticed at cocktail hour that Claire seemed to be at the bar more often than not and she seems to now have a new drink in her hand every 15 minutes. I know she's an adult and can hold her own, but I also don't want her to get sick like she used to in college. Hangovers at our age are so much worse.

Claire is swaying on her feet, but straightens up immediately when Drew approaches her. I see her eyes light up as he bends down to speak with her. She's laughing in a beautiful and carefree way that I'm not sure I've ever mastered.

I look down at my shoes, not wanting to see the way he looks at her, in case it's with the warmth that I'm missing. I feel Jackson's arm circle my waist to turn me back to him. Using his finger and thumb, he gently guides my face up, searching out my eyes. I give them to him, letting him see the hurt I'm feeling. I see his eyes flick over my head once to where I know Drew and Claire are, but I don't follow his lead this time. Instead, I lay my head on his chest and sigh.

"What's wrong, babygirl?" he asks, placing one hand against the side of my head, stroking my cheek with his thumb.

I'm quiet for a moment, contemplating what led me here, to Jackson's arms instead of being with Drew. I close my eyes, letting my mind wander back over the last several days.

"We don't have to talk. Just having you in my arms again

is enough," Jackson says, continuing to run his thumb over my cheek, using his fingers to dig into my hair lightly. I'm glad that he's basically hiding the side of my face that isn't against his chest as I feel burning against my eyelids and wet warmth tracking down my cheeks. I'm not even sure why I'm crying. I can't sort out my varied emotions enough to determine if it's sadness, anger, or possibly embarrassment.

Could I have made what I felt between me and Drew a much bigger deal than it was, or was it one-sided and I just deluded myself into thinking he felt the same way?

Regardless, I leave my head against Jackson's chest for several more songs, letting my tears dry. I eventually raise my head, giving him a smile when I met his eyes.

"Sorry about that, I didn't mean to get the front of your shirt wet," I say, glancing down at the small spot on his dress shirt.

"Babygirl, you know I don't care. I'm sorry you are feeling this way. I wish I could help, but I'm starting to think that maybe letting you go is the only way that I can," he replies, emotion coating every word. I'm going to start crying all over again.

"Jackson, you know I love you and I always will," I say, gripping his hand just a little tighter, "but…"

"No buts, I understand. I will always love you Lexa. I see that you've chosen someone else and I think I'm now just standing in the way." Jackson gives me such a sad smile, I'm afraid he's going to start tearing up.

Thankfully he doesn't, because I don't think my heart could take it right now. I nod, knowing this is what needs to happen, but still being sad for another end.

"Well, I guess I should let you go hunt him down. God, I

hate losing and I hate losing you even more. But Drew is such a good guy and he deserves the happiness that I know that you'll give him."

With one final spin and a tight hug, Jackson releases me to go find Drew. I turn back once to smile at Jackson before heading for my table.

I pick up my drink from the table, noticing that it's warm in my hand. I was dancing for longer than I thought. I look around the table, seeing purses and jackets on the backs of chairs but no party-goers. I take a sip of my warm spritzer and cast my gaze around the dance floor, thinking maybe I missed him while I was coming off. I see Ansley and Landon, smiling at each other with so much love in their eyes. I glance at my phone to see that the last dance of the evening is coming up soon with the sparkler send-off only 20 minutes away.

I spur myself into action, looking for Drew so that I can have the last dance with him tonight. I check the bar, the groomsmen room, even call into the bathroom for him. I text him and try to call him but his phone goes straight to voicemail. I head outside to check the parking lot in case he stepped out for air, still not finding him.

I step back inside, finding Weston coming out of the restroom.

"Hey, have you seen Drew?" I ask, catching his forearm mid shirt tuck.

"Uh, not for a bit. Last I saw, he was heading outside with Claire. She was pretty wasted," Wes answers.

"Oh, okay thanks." I release his arm and wander back inside. I see Amanda sitting at the table she was sharing with Claire.

"Hey girl, have you seen Drew lately?" I ask, trying to sound nonchalant.

I must look on the verge of tears again because Amanda gives me a small smile of condolence when she says, "Yeah he left with Claire probably 10 minutes ago. She wasn't feeling well and she was ready to go."

I feel my face drain, knowing that a drunk Claire is a handsy Claire. Did she ask him to go home with her and he was so angry with me that he did? What does this mean?

Chapter 47

Drew

Claire stumbles for the hundredth time since we left the reception, or at least that's what it feels like. I have caught her from busting her ass so many times, I might as well just cradle carry her at this point. I'm trying to maintain my air of gentleman's kindness that led me to offer to take her home, but this is getting ridiculous. How do you get this drunk at a friend's wedding?

"Ddd-dd–oo knnooow hh-how cuuuute yar?" Claire slurs at me. Again. Along with the tripping and the stumbling, this seems to be the only thought on her mind.

"Yeah, thanks Claire. How about you watch where your feet are going instead of looking at me?" I ask, still holding her under her arm to try to steady her.

"'Cuzzzz I canstop lookin' atcha," she replies, blinking one eye repeatedly, I'm assuming in an attempt to wink.

"Alrighty well I'm going to continue just holding your arm here until we can get you into your place."

"Ar-areyou comin' up?" she asks, turning her fully dilated

and very glassy eyes on me yet again.

I catch her from tripping over a crack in the sidewalk and say, "Only long enough to get you on the couch and put a trash can near you. I'm pretty sure you're going to get sick."

"Buuut youcouldstay," she rushes out, trying not to trip over another crack.

"No ma'am, I can't. I'm still trying to get back in time for the send-off. I only offered to bring you home because I didn't think you could handle another second in there. And honestly, I thought the fresh air might help a bit."

We are finally at her building and I release my grip on her arm long enough for her to dig out her keys. She drops them on the ground and I reach down to pick them up. As I raise back up, she grabs a fistful of my shirt, bringing me towards her.

"I've alllssss luhhvv yew," she slurs into my face. I try to gently push her away but I'm too afraid she'll fall to actually put any force behind it. That was a mistake on my part because as I try to tear her grip from my shirt, she plants a wet kiss against my mouth.

I grip her shoulders, pushing her away from me, a little more firm this time. "Claire, stop. You're drunk and I'm not doing this," I say.

Claire nods, then ducks her head.

"Ready to try the stairs?" I question gently, trying to bend down enough to see her face.

Claire lifts her face enough for me to see her wobbling lip and reddened eyes. *Oh no,* I think, *here come the tears.*

"Oh no no no don't cry," I say, attempting a smile.

"Buh-buh-buh-but you haaaaaate meeee," Claire begins wailing. Oh shit, what am I supposed to do now?

I pull her to me, tucking her face against my chest and rubbing her upper back, trying to console her. "Shh, it's okay. It's okay," I mumble into her hair. I let her cry into my shirt for several minutes before I start trying to put her key into the front door lock. I'm able to get the door unlocked, maneuver her up the stairs and into her own apartment before she stops for a real breath.

"Are you just going to leave me here?" Claire asks, still crying.

"I have to get back to my sister's wedding. There's only 20 minutes until the send-off and it's a 10 minute walk back," I say, as gently as I can while trying to untangle myself from her.

I lead her over to the couch, take off her shoes and put a blanket over her. I go into the room I'm assuming is her bathroom and hunt through the medicine cabinet before I remember that she's only here for a week so all of her stuff is probably still in a bag.

I head back out to the living room, carrying a small trash can that I found by the toilet to place by the couch. "Do you have any Advil in your purse or bag?" I ask the prone form.

"Bag by bed," comes the muffled response.

I find the small bag on the nightstand and dig out the Advil bottle. I grab a water glass from the kitchen and place it along with the bottle on the table for when she's sober enough to reach for it. I stand there for a moment, trying to decide if I really should stay when I hear soft snoring from under the blanket. She's already asleep. I make the decision to come over and check on her first thing in the morning.

Just in case, I leave her phone by the water and I write her a sticky note saying to call me as soon as she's awake.

I lock the door knob behind me and pull the door closed. Walking down the stairs, I'm full of worry for what could happen while Claire is home alone in this state, but I know that my sister would kill me for missing the send-off. Plus, Claire has made it through plenty of nights in this condition I've heard.

The 10 minute walk back to the venue feels shorter than it should. My mind is jumping all over the place, from what happened tonight with Claire to my worries about how Lexa is feeling about me. I don't know what came over me, but just watching her dance with Jackson, I realized that maybe she should be with him instead. They have so much history together.

Maybe I was just making a bigger deal out of our little takeout session than she was or maybe all of these feelings were just in my head. Either way, I know I just need to get back to that venue for the sparklers.

Chapter 48

Lexa

Knowing that Drew left with Claire and that he hasn't come back yet has drained me emotionally. I know that all I should be feeling right now is elation for my best friend but it's buried under my own selfish bullshit.

Jackson has been giving me some space since I found out about Drew and Claire but I can tell that he's worried.

Luckily, it's time for the sparklers and getting our girl in the car on her way to the honeymoon suite. I put on my biggest, brightest smile and head out the door. Grabbing a sparkler from the bucket, I make my way to a spot beside Amanda. She's smiling and laughing with Weston. I see Jackson approaching my side so I turn to smile at him. He lights my sparkler with his own.

"Want a ride home?" he asks, sensing that I probably don't want to walk home alone right now.

"Yeah, that would be great. Thank you," I say, offering a genuine smile this time.

I feel a nudge from Amanda and hear her say, "Here come

the newlyweds!" I turn with my real smile still on my face to see my beautiful best friend and her wonderful new husband coming through the door, hands held high and smiles lighting up their faces.

We cheer as they walk through the arch formed by the light from our sparklers. Ansley and Landon stop halfway down the aisle for a kiss. Landon dips her low, kissing her deeply. The cheers from the crowd grow even louder. When they come up for air, they're both laughing. I can't stop the smile straining my cheeks. This is what love looks like.

I watch the happy couple walk the rest of the way down the sidewalk, Ansley turning once to wave back at me and at her mom standing opposite me. We both wave back and blow kisses. I turn back to Jackson, seeing if he's ready to leave. That's when I notice Drew is back. He's between Kurt and Patrick and looking directly at me. I shiver involuntarily from the look in his eyes. He looks vacant and emotionless. When he sees me looking at him, he offers me a weak smile. He raises his hand in a small wave but doesn't attempt to walk over.

What the hell changed so much in the last 24 hours? It's like as hot for each other as we were yesterday, we're now frozen. Neither one of us seems willing to make the move to break the ice.

I lift my hand in a wave back, then turn to Jackson. "I'm ready to go when you are. Let me just pop back in and grab my stuff," I say.

"Do you want me to go with you?" Jackson asks. "I threw all my stuff in the car right before the ceremony."

Hmm, thinking ahead, that's new, I ponder. But I shake my head in answer, "No, thanks though."

Amanda taps me on the shoulder. "I need to go grab my stuff, yours is still in there right?"

"Yep, that's where I was heading," I answer. She threads her arm through mine and we weave through the crowd toward the back door of the venue.

It only takes a few minutes to gather our things, luckily we had all packed up before we left for pictures.

"So, I know it's really none of my business, but I kinda thought you and Drew were together but tonight it seemed totally different," Amanda says as we're looking around, making sure we aren't leaving anything behind.

"Oh. Yeah I actually thought we were, too. I'm not sure what happened. Maybe all the emotions of his little sister's wedding day got to him or something," I say, shrugging.

"You don't have to act like you don't care about what's going on with you just because it's Ansley's wedding day," she says, rubbing her hand on my upper back. "Your emotions are important too."

"I know, I just honestly am ready for life to go back to how it was last week when we were cleaning butts in the ER. So much less emotional involvement."

Amanda laughs before saying, "Don't wish too much for that, you know we're right back there later this week."

I laugh too, before reaching out to hug Amanda to me. "Love you, girl," I say, and mean it.

"I love you, too. Now let go of me with your butt-cleaning hands!" We both dissolve into giggles and make our way back out into the warm June night.

I immediately spot Jackson standing by his car, waiting for me and smiling. I turn back to Amanda, "Need a ride?"

"No thanks, my ride is already here," she says. I watch her

walk off towards the road where a ride-share is waiting. She waves back at me before climbing in. As I'm watching her car drive off, I see Drew approaching me with a wary look on his face.

"Do you need me to walk you home?" he asks, sounding uncertain.

"Not if you have somewhere else to be. I have a ride anyway," I say, hooking a thumb over my shoulder towards Jackson.

"You're going home with him?" Drew asks, slightly indignant.

"If you choose to see it that way, then sure. But he's just giving me a ride to my place. My feet are hurting too badly from these heels to walk."

"Oh. Okay, then. Well I'll see you tomorrow morning? Breakfast is still on, right?" Drew glances down at his shoes, unable to hold eye contact.

For whatever reason this only serves to anger me, making me feel like he's hiding something.

"Yes, breakfast is still happening. Claire knows where it is, so you can ask her." And with that, I swiftly turn on my heel and walk towards Jackson's car.

What the hell changed?

Chapter 49

Drew

What the hell? Is she angry with me? What was that last comment about?

Wait, does she think I hooked up with Claire? *Well shit,* I curse myself for not catching that fast enough to correct that assumption. I still don't think I understand what even happened tonight. How did we go from making out in a batting cage yesterday to being less than friends tonight?

Maybe our relationship wasn't meant to even make it this far. Maybe we'd always been doomed from the start.

I watch as Lexa walks away from me. I'm not sure why but this feels like goodbye.

The walk back to my apartment is quiet and lonely. I can't help thinking about what may or may not be happening a few blocks away. It's taking every bit of my willpower not to walk those few extra blocks and knock on Lexa's door. She doesn't need that from me though. If she chose Jackson, then she deserves a chance at happiness with him. She doesn't deserve some guy banging on her door in the middle of the night trying to explain something that he can't even put into words.

My first thought upon entering my bedroom is that I wish I would have drank more. I don't think I'm going to fall asleep anytime soon.

I slowly unbutton my dress shirt, leaving it hanging open with the vest still on top of it. I want to get undressed but I'm suddenly lacking the motivation. I sit down on the edge of the bed, staring at the doorway for who knows how long. At some point, I fall back onto the mattress, legs still over the side, and spread my arms out from my body. I lay there staring at the ceiling, thoughts running rampant. I must have fallen asleep because when I come back to consciousness, there's sunlight pouring in through the window. I pull my arm up to glance at the time on my watch. It's 8 a.m. Breakfast starts at 8:30. *Shit.*

I grab for my phone, trying to remember the name of the restaurant that Ansley picked. I go to my messages, thinking to text Lexa and see that I typed out a message to her yesterday morning that I never hit send on. *Double shit.* I guess that's why she never texted me back. I wonder if that's what began some of the tension between us yesterday.

I don't have as much time to think about that as I would like since I still don't know where we're eating. I want to just text Lexa but things ended so off between us last night. I'd rather just talk to her in person this morning.

As I'm staring at my phone, trying in vain to remember the name of the breakfast place, I see an incoming call. I groan inwardly, but sigh, knowing I need to take this call.

"Hey Claire, how are you feeling?" I ask.

"Not too great," she says weakly, letting out a small laugh.

"Yeah I bet. I'm glad you're up though," I say honestly.

"I think the water and Advil you left beside me saved my life. I downed the glass sometime in the early morning and woke up with only a slight headache. I could really go for some food though, I think," she sighs.

"How fast can you get ready? I just woke up myself and we're invited to the bridal party breakfast."

"Pretty quickly if I don't have to get too ready. I can just touch up my makeup and throw on a sundress. Do you know where we're going?" she asks.

"Um, actually no. I was hoping you might," I say, chuckling awkwardly.

"Hold on, I have it in a note on my phone. Looks like… Crack Some Eggs? Does that sound right?"

"Oh yeah, that's the one. It's pretty new. I knew it had something to do with eggs," I say, laughing. I hear Claire laugh too and then there's a short moment of silence. I clear my throat and then ask, "Do you want me to swing by in about 10 minutes and we can walk together?"

"That sounds wonderful," she replies, suddenly sounding more energetic than before.

I rush into the bathroom, quickly pulling off my suit from last night. I know we have to return them soon but that's not happening this morning. I shuck off my vest and shirt, drag my pants and underwear down in one swoop and then pull off my socks, leaving it all heaped in the floor. I turn on the shower and then face the mirror to see how my face looks after not getting great sleep last night. It's a little puffy, but I'm sure I won't be alone in that.

Once the shower is warm enough, I step in and run my hands through my hair to wet it. I quickly shampoo and condition, not spending the amount of time on either that my greasy hair probably needs. I wash my body and decide to skip shaving my face.

Stepping out, I dry off, tousle my hair with the towel and toss it over the shower rail. Back into the room to grab a pair of jeans and a light shirt. I'm sure the June sun is baking the concrete already.

I brush my teeth as fast as possible, noticing the stubble I should have shaved and the too-tousled hair that I don't have time to worry about.

Then it's shoes on, out the door and I'm walking to Claire's, realizing way too late that I forgot my phone on the bathroom counter.

Chapter 50

Lexa

Sunday

It took me way too long to fall asleep last night. As evidenced by the bags under my eyes and the amount of effort I did not put into getting ready this morning. I'm glad I at least scrubbed off my makeup last night, even if my hair is in loose messy curls from the up-do.

I wish I was tired for better reasons. I wish I was tired from being kept up by Drew's hands and mouth, not the thought of them on someone else. I couldn't shake the image of him and Claire going home together last night. I know he took her home and came back but the place she's staying was between the venue and his place. It'd be easy enough to just stop back by and stay there.

I still can't decipher the signals he was sending last night. He went from possessive and hot for me to cold and pushing me off on Jackson. Maybe he just felt more for Claire after they danced together. Or maybe I really was reading more into what was happening between us. Either way, I am not ready to see him again this soon.

Regardless, I was slightly disappointed not receiving a text from him this morning. Not a good morning, not even a hey what's the name of the restaurant. But what did I expect? I did tell him not to bother me. I hate these games. We're adults and I'm sitting around waiting for him to want to text me instead of just texting him.

I look up at the sound of door chimes, seeing who just came into the restaurant. I jump to my feet to run to Ansley who is positively radiant this morning.

"Hey married woman!" I shout, throwing my arms around her neck. She giggles into my hair and squeezes me back.

I hear someone clear their throat to my left and I peel myself off of Ans long enough to see that Landon is standing there, looking expectant. I huff out a laugh and sling my hand out to grab him and drag him into the hug. "And married man!" I say, laughing.

"Thanks, Lex. And thanks for getting here so early to secure our table," Landon says, gesturing at the packed restaurant.

"Oh, we had reservations. I just…was up earlier than I planned on," I reply, starting to regret the half of a mimosa I had before they even got here.

I lead them back to the table, sitting them across from each other in the middle so we can surround them. We go ahead and order mimosa pitchers and greet the others as they begin to arrive. I'm laughing with my head thrown back by the time her parents arrive and grab me up into a bear hug after Ansley.

"Good morning, darling," Mrs. Parker says, hugging me

tightly. "You look so beautiful. I wish I could take my hair down from a bun and have those gorgeous curls framing my face. Alas, I was cursed with straight hair," she says, flipping her elegantly styled long bob.

"Thank you, but I feel like a bridge troll this morning. I didn't get a lot of sleep last night," I say, unable to filter my thoughts through my exhaustion.

Mrs. Parker just smiles a knowing smile and releases my shoulders to grab my hand. "Oh that's okay, dear. As long as you had fun," she says, throwing me a wink. I stand there for a minute, too stunned to speak. What is that supposed to mean?

"Where is Drew, anyway?" she says, cluing me into her thoughts.

"Oh, I'm not sure. Probably still at home, showering," I answer, laughing nervously. "You know his love of nice long showers."

"Oh yes, we're aware," Mr. Parker says, laughing heartily.

"I saved y'all some seats right by us," I say, giving them my best smile.

I turn back to the door as the Parkers take their seats, anxious for the last two people to arrive.

Claire texted me this morning to say she was alive and going to be here. I'm so glad she's okay after last night. I was afraid for her possible hangover. She must have drank less than I thought.

Drew still hasn't texted me, so I'm not even sure if he's awake or why I care so much.

"You know you can come sit down right? Whoever is still coming can probably track us down," I hear Ansley say from behind me. I want to turn and walk towards her. I want to sit down and smile at her and cheers her and the wonderful new groom. I want to laugh with her parents and our friends and not care about anything else. But all of that is made impossible when I see who walks through the door next.

I see Claire's beaming face first, followed by a well muscled arm resting on her lower back and guiding her in. My eyes track up the arm to a scruffy, chiseled face with the most gorgeous tousled hair above it. Deep blue eyes swallow mine as Drew locks onto my gaze, stopping in the doorway. All the energy I just stored by being rooted to my spot comes out in a burst as I smile and then turn on my heel and hustle to the restroom. I'll later be told by Ansley that I looked like a ghost running to haunt the stalls.

As I stare at my reflection in the mirror, willing my cheeks to return to their normal color instead of the death-like flesh they are currently covered in, I take slow and controlled breaths.

I am not entirely sure why I am so shocked. I knew he took her home, I assumed he went back there, why would they not show up together? Him freshly showered and glowing like a god and her in the same hair and makeup as last night but with a fresh-faced dewy happiness making her look brand-new? It's so obvious they hooked up last night and I am unable to fully comprehend this entire situation. Why would he feel the need to rub this in my face? Is he blind? Did I not make it obvious enough that I was into him? Maybe he thought he wanted me and then once he had me, he realized that I'm not who he thought I was.

Maybe I'm just not enough. I'm not in any way conceited about my looks or what I bring to the table but I thought I was at least what Drew wanted. But I guess not. He wants something else. Not a red-headed, freckle-faced nerd with swamp water green eyes.

I'm resigning myself to these thoughts, still staring at my reflection. I decide that while Drew is everything I know I want, maybe I'm not it for him.

I splash some water on my face, thankful once again that I took off my makeup from last night and try to regain some of the composure that I felt before *they* walked in together. One more deep breath and I push away from the sink. I square my shoulders and practice my best fake smile in the mirror. "You got this," I say aloud to myself. I laugh at the absurdity of this moment. I have to stop giving myself bathroom pep talks.

I put my hand on the doorknob, taking one last breath. I walk out into the hallway, immediately running into Jackson.

"Hey Lex, are you okay? You look shaken." And with that, I crumble. Tears start coming and I can't seem to stem them.

"Oh shit, okay. Hold on," Jackson says, sneaking a quick glance behind him. He discreetly pushes me back into the bathroom, checking for any other life before locking the main door behind him. "Noah, whoa, shh, shh, shh," he croons into my ear and I realize he's holding me. Not just hugging me, but has pulled my feet off of the ground like I am a child.

"Hey stop it, I'm here. Do you need me to go get Ansley or Mrs. Parker or someone?" he asks, swinging my dangling feet a bit.

I laugh despite myself and shake my head. I sniffle a bit, feeling slightly self-conscious for the blubbering that just occurred. "No it's okay. Apparently I just needed to release some of the pressure behind the floodgates."

"Well, I'll always be available as a snot rag if nothing else," he says, laughing and looking down at the tears wetting his shirt.

"Oh my gosh, I am so sorry!" I say, aghast. But I giggle anyway, relieved that I'm out of the woods a bit on the whole crying-in-front-of-people thing.

"Can I say something without you getting mad at me?" Jackson says, ducking his head to meet my eyes.

"Um…no promises in my current emotional state, but go on," I reply.

Jackson takes a small breath before continuing. "I think you really like him and you should pursue that rather than letting whatever happened last night cause this to end. I've never seen you this emotional–happy or sad–about anything and I've known you pretty intimately for years."

I drop my head, my mirth quickly subsiding. "Yeah, I do, but I don't think he feels the same way. And I'm too happy with myself to try to make me into someone he wants," I say.

"And what makes you think that you're *not* what he wants?" he asks.

I just shake my head and shrug. I can't go into this with Jackson. I don't even want to think about this myself. "Hey, when did you become so in touch with emotions?" I ask, trying to lighten the mood.

"When the girl of my dreams moved on before I realized that I missed the most important opportunity of my life," Jackson says, hugging me one last time before releasing me and turning to unlock the door. "I'm going to head back to the table and order you something a little stronger than a mimosa. Stay here, wipe your face off and come out when you're ready."

With that, Jackson exits and I start to realize that even though we will never be together romantically *ever* again, I want him around as a friend. He's genuinely a good guy and I do miss him.

Chapter 51

Lexa

By the time I make it out of the bathroom, breakfast is in full swing. Mimosas are flowing and there are fancy egg dishes covering the table. I'm glad I was able to order before my breakdown, because stuffing my face is preferable to answering questions at this moment.

I slide back into my chair, noticing the Bloody Maria sitting in front of me. Tequila on a Sunday morning? Ehh, can't be that bad. I shoot Jackson a quick nod of thanks and take a sip. I dig into my plate, letting the conversation flow around me while I try to find my equilibrium.

Halfway through my drink, I finally take my eyes off of my plate. I look up to see Ansley and Mrs. Parker staring at me from across the table. Both have troubled expressions on their faces.

"What?" I ask, pulling my mouth from the straw.

"Nothing, you just look…haunted," Ansley answers. Mrs. P slaps her arm before offering, "Sweetie you just look like you're bothered by something, is all."

"Oh, no I'm good guys. Really," I reply, knowing that I don't sound convincing to anyone. Least of all my best friend and surrogate mother.

They let me off the hook though, thankfully. "Well, at least you don't have to work for a few days, you can get some rest," Ansley says.

"Yep, for sure," I reply. Knowing full well that I will be trying to pick up extra shifts this week while Ansley is gone. I can't be by myself right now.

"What time do your flights leave this afternoon?" Mr. Parker asks, saving me from having to talk for now.

"Not until 5 p.m.," Landon says, smiling at Ansley. "We're going to head to the apartment and grab a nap and then head to the airport early. Grab a drink at the bar or something to begin the celebrations."

"Any specific plans for tonight in Nantucket?" Amanda asks, coming into the conversation.

"Just some lobster bisque, that's all I want," Ansley says with a full laugh. "Our place is on the water, string lights and a hot tub on the beach. I imagine it won't be too hard to find some time to relax."

"That sounds heavenly," Grace groans. Everyone around the table laughs and conversation veers off into everyone's dream vacation spots.

"Where do you want to go?" Ansley asks me.

"Somewhere tropical. Blue waters and drinks in coconuts," I say wistfully.

"Now *that* sounds heavenly," Weston says, causing laughter to ripple along the table.

✿

The rest of breakfast passes without incident. Lighthearted

conversation flows while I become increasingly more aware that I will be without my best friend for the next week.

Once it's time for everyone to be going their separate ways, I hang back as Ansley hugs all of our wonderful friends.

"You know we'll be back on Saturday? It's not even a week," Landon says, pulling me into a tight side hug.

I laugh but my face won't pull into a smile. "I know, but that's the most distance we'll have had between us since we met. I'm just trying to adjust," I answer. I look up at Landon who is smiling down at me, but with a distinct sadness in his eyes.

"If you need us this week, call us. Call her. You're family. I know you need her just as much as she needs you," he says quietly.

"I am not going to bother y'all on your honeymoon. Not happening," I say, throwing my hands up.

"Hell, I'd ask you to just come with us if I thought that you would. So calling us is not any kind of bother in the least."

I laugh, knowing that they would ask me along on their honeymoon with no reservations. That's just how they are.

"Well after this last week of fanfare, I'm actually looking forward to some downtime with Sneakers and a good book," I reply.

"You think it'll only be Sneakers beside you on the couch?" Landon asks with a pointed look towards the direction that both Drew and Jackson are standing.

I shove him gently before saying, "Yes I'm sure. Sneakers is the only man I need in my life." I cross my arms and turn my chin up in my best show of indignation that I can muster.

Landon ruffles my hair like a big brother would and hugs me again. "Go tell your sister bye so we can go home and take a nap."

Chapter 52

Drew

I think those may have been the most meaningless conversations I've ever had in my life. Trying to talk to Claire, Elsie and Connor, two of whom I barely know and still look for a way to speak with Lexa turned out to be an excruciating exercise in futility.

Once she came back to the table, Lexa barely turned her head. She didn't just not look our way, she didn't glance at the other side of the table where Jackson was either. If she raised her head enough to engage in conversation, she was looking straight at Ansley or my parents.

It only took me a half of a second to realize the mistake that I had made by walking here with Claire. To me, it had seemed simply a nice thing to do since I was walking past her building to come here anyway. But seeing the smile turn into a grimace and the color drain from Lexa's face when she saw us walking in together, I knew she assumed the worst. Knowing what didn't happen last night, I was unconcerned how our arrival would look to everyone. I just didn't count on Lexa already having that thought in her head.

I will be honest though, seeing Jackson chase after her when she ran to the bathroom didn't help either. I don't understand how she can judge me for something that didn't even happen when I saw her and Jackson together and he's literally always with her. *Whatever.*

We're adults. If she wants to talk to me, she will. I'm in town for several days and Ansley told me that Lexa doesn't have to work for another couple of days. She's off Saturday to pick Ans and Landon up from the airport so I guess she works Wednesday night through Friday night? That gives me a few days to talk to her.

As everyone is preparing to leave, hugging the newlyweds and wishing them a great time on their honeymoon, I can't take my eyes off of Lexa. She's keeping herself in the background and not talking to her friends like I know she normally would be.

I watch as Landon walks over and has what appears to be a pretty deep conversation with her. I watch as she laughs and smiles. It warms my heart even though it isn't in any way directed towards me.

I walk towards them but I'm intercepted by my parents. "Maybe I'm having a stroke but I'm very confused why you showed up with Claire instead of Lexa this morning," my mother states.

"Mom, don't even joke about that," I say, trying to look offended, but it's probably coming off more guilty. "And what are you even talking about?"

"Oh you know," she says cryptically, narrowing her eyes at me. I skirt her long enough to reach my baby sister. She's locked in a fierce embrace with Lexa and I stand there, unsure what to do with myself.

I clear my throat, like an asshole, and wait for Ansley to turn towards me.

"Yes?" she says, obviously irritated.

"I just wanted to tell you guys bye," I say, not making eye contact.

"Mkay, well bye," Ans says, giving me a squeeze before turning back to Lexa.

"Bye, bro," Landon says, pulling me into a bear hug. "Don't worry about her. She's just worried about Lexa. By the way, is there something that I should be worried about as well?"

"No no, everything is fine. I'm just exhausted. Probably need a nap myself," I reply, shrugging.

I turn back towards my parents, my mother with her all-knowing and judging eyes and my dad who just looks like he's happy to have us all in one place. "What are your plans for the rest of your stay here son?" my dad asks.

"Nothing too concrete. I was thinking of hitting the golf course tomorrow. Interested?"

"Always," he replies, clapping me on the shoulder. I pull him into a hug and then pull my mom into my chest. "Love you both, I gotta head home and get some sleep. Long night last night."

As I'm walking out the door, I miss the pointed glance my mom throws at my dad.

✿

I don't wake from my nap until it's already dark outside. I guess I really did miss out on some sleep last night.

I roll onto my side, checking the time on my phone and notice there's 4 missed texts. There's one from Landon and one from Ansley, both telling the group we're in that they made it to the airport and they got their celebratory drink alone. I have one from my dad confirming a tee time for the morning. And I have one text from Lexa. All it says is *hey*.

It's from 3 hours ago. I open it first and quickly type back, *hey, what's up?*

And like a fool, I sit there and wait like she's going to immediately text me back. Part of me wants to call her. The other part wants to act like this isn't a big deal. I decide to take the middle road and head into the kitchen to start fixing dinner instead of staring at my phone.

I want so badly to be able to talk to her again in person before I leave this week. But I'm also not about to push her past a breaking point. Maybe by Tuesday, we'll both be in the head space to make that happen.

Chapter 53

Lexa

September

Thursday

"I'm sorry, what do you mean you can't come tomorrow?" I demand, making Amanda cower into the corner of the break room.

"I just can't go. Something came up and I'm so sorry. I paid for my ticket and my half of the room so you're not out any money."

"That's so not the issue," I whine. "You know I can't go to this thing by myself."

Amanda scoffs, "If anyone here can go to a concert by themselves, it's you."

I roll my eyes and cross my arms, "But I don't *want to.*" I laugh, knowing this is a silly argument. I'm just blindsided by the fact that I'm going to the music festival by myself this weekend. It's not that I won't still go, I just want someone to enjoy it with.

"I know, and I don't want you to. If it was within my power, I would be going with you. You know I love these bands too," she says.

"Ugh, fine. I get it. But you owe me a fun experience," I say, pulling her in for a hug.

"Anytime, girl. Anytime," Amanda says, squeezing me hard.

"I love you so much but I want to strangle you a little right now," I say, laughing.

"I totally understand," Amanda responds, pulling away from me. "Good thing we have a whole shift ahead of us for you to forgive me."

"Well the rest of this one at least," I reply. "And then I'll sleep all day today before waking up to drive *by myself* to Atlanta tonight to get to the hotel for the shows starting in the morning."

"Maybe our super sweet charge will let you go home early if you ask nicely."

"Highly unlikely with the influx we had in the last hour. But I already know how you're going to make this up to me. I need a coffee from the machine on the third floor. The good coffee."

"The forbidden roaster?" Amanda gasps.

"The forbidden roaster," I say with a mischievous grin on my face.

✿

Once Amanda is off the floor on her nearly impossible task of obtaining me the good espresso from the third floor machine, I walk over to Ansley's desk.

"Ugh, I just got bailed on for this weekend. I wish you weren't working," I complain.

"As much as I hate that for you, I'm glad I am. Two days of bands I don't enjoy sounds like torture. I grew up listening to that music from next door and it would only give me flashbacks to nougies and smelly teenage boy rooms," she says.

As much as I've tried to stop it from happening, my thoughts tend to lead back to Drew throughout the day and having a full explanation of his teenage habits doesn't help. I flinch internally but smile at my best friend before saying, "Drew listened to this kind of music, too?"

"I'm pretty sure it's still the only music he listens to. That pop-punk, metal-core, screamy stuff."

"Okay that's so not what's going on this weekend. It's just like punk rock. That's it," I say laughing. "I won't be dressed all in black and banging my head so hard that I break my neck."

Ansley laughs and says, "Now I can't get that out of my head. You dying the ends of your hair black, smearing all that dark makeup on your eyes and just head banging for 48 hours straight. Now I kind of want to go just to see you."

"Ohmygosh. I just told you that's not the vibe! I'll be in shorts and converse and a band tee. Nothing crazy. I'm not 20 anymore."

Ansley laughs again before saying, "You know, I bet Drew would die to go to these shows with you this weekend. I know for a fact that he's off tomorrow."

I shiver and say, "No thanks, I don't need a pity date. You know me, I'll find friends there. And I'm staying at the hotel right by the park. Not much chance for me to get lost."

"That's not what I'm saying and you know it. I just know you two used to be close. And in June it looked like you were getting even closer. Are you ever going to talk to me about what happened that week?"

"While you were living your best life in Nantucket with your brand new husband? Unlikely. Mainly because nothing happened. And that's the truth. Nothing."

"Mkay, whatever," Ansley says, finally willing to change the subject. "Did Dr. McKay tell you that she was ready to sedate 18 for the procedure?"

"No and thanks for just now telling me," I say, rolling my eyes in mock annoyance. I playfully punch Ansley on the arm as I walk past her to head to the room. I stop into the doctor's area to let Dr. McKay know I'm heading into room 18.

"Great, Lexa. I'll be right in there!" she says, smiling brightly. *The coworkers really make the job*, I think as I walk into the patient's room.

"Hey there Mr. Sutton, you ready to get that hip popped back into place?" I ask, checking the IV, setting the vital sign machine to give me a blood pressure every 5 minutes and logging into the computer.

"Been ready, honey," he says, grimacing as he tries to chuckle.

"We'll get you fixed up, good as new," I say with a big smile. I'm not sure why, but my Southern accent is always put on so thickly when I talk to patients. It seems to calm them a bit though, so I don't try to check myself anymore.

As we go through the checklist required before we can get started, all thoughts of the weekend leave my mind. My only focus for the next half hour is getting Mr. Sutton out of pain and on the mend.

After the satisfying pop of his hip going back in, Dr. McKay orders a little more pain medicine, just to help him get some rest. I leave the room to grab the medication and see Ansley on the phone in the break room. I never see her on her phone at work, I hope the family is okay. I don't have too much time to focus on these thoughts as I rush back into the room to administer the medication.

"I know y'all keep telling me you did, but there's no way you already put me under and popped that pesky hip back in. I would remember," Mr. Sutton is saying to Dr. McKay as I walk back into the room.

Dr. McKay laughs and says, "That's the beauty of the medication my dear. You don't remember and we get to do our jobs quickly and quietly."

We all chuckle and I give Mr. Sutton a dose of the pain medicine the doctor ordered. "Okay sweetie, you get some rest and I'll be back in here in a bit to check on you," I say, patting my sweet patient on the forearm.

After finishing up with the sedation charting at bedside, I head back to the desk in search of my water bottle and my best friend. I see Ansley in a room across from the nurses station helping another nurse start an IV. I smile, grab my water bottle and walk into the nourishment room to refill with some ice cold water.

"Here, fill mine up while you're at it," I hear from the doorway. I swivel to see our new hire, Josh, smiling at me.

"Hmm, considering the seniority I have over you here, I think you should be filling mine up."

I see heat flash through Josh's eyes and a sexy smirk quirk on his lips.

I flush, realizing how that just sounded. I throw my hands up in front of me and say, "Wow I did not mean that to come out like that. I would never…I'm not…"

"Noah slow down," Josh says laughing, "I didn't take it that way and if I did, it's not like it would be an unwelcome advance." He winks at me, leaving me speechless. I feel my cheeks burn even hotter before I duck my head and hightail it out of there.

I mean it's not that I don't think that Josh is attractive, because who wouldn't? It's just that I'm not a huge believer in office place romances. I already felt weird even thinking about being with a coworker's brother, I couldn't date someone that I actually see at work.

Who am I kidding anyway? I haven't had a successful date since that day in the batting cages with Drew. Every guy I've had coffee or lunch or dinner with since then has failed to elicit any of the bodily or emotional reactions that Drew did that week. I don't know if I just need more time or if I need to lower my standards, but for now I'm definitely on a hiatus from the world of dating.

Back at my desk, I spend several minutes catching up on charting and checking on orders for my other patients. I got all of the initial things squared away before going into the sedation, so I'm really just waiting on test results for everyone.

I see pink scrub-clad hips slide onto the desk beside my keyboard before I hear Ansley say, "Hey boo, if you can get your people out of here before 0300, I'd like to let you leave a little early. That way you can catch a nap before you have to drive later. The lobby has been clear for a while and everyone's sections are emptying."

I look up into my best friend's eyes and smile. "You know, you're a real sweetheart, no matter what they say about you."

We both laugh, knowing that's all anyone ever says about her. And they're right. Ansley is one of the most unselfish and sweetest people I know. I don't know how she does it.

"Well don't thank me just yet, I may have gone against your wishes and kind of told Drew about this weekend…." Ansley says, mumbling a bit like I won't be able to hear her this close.

"I'm sorry. I must have misheard…you what?!"

"He texted me about coming in this weekend to hang out and I called him to tell him that I'd be at work and then I accidentally said something about the concert and you going alone now and…sorry. But don't worry! He said he's just going to wait until next month to come visit anyway, when I'm off work. So he's not even going to be in state!"

I glower at her all the same, really letting her feel the full weight of my irritation at this news. "Why were you talking to your brother about me anyway?"

"Well, he asks about you. How you're doing, how you seem and if you're seeing anyone….those kind of things," she answers.

"If he really cares, he could ask me himself," I say, icily.

Chapter 54

Drew

Is there any way we could talk? has been sitting in my drafts folder since June. I have wanted to check on Lexa so many times since that week that everything fell apart. But every time I try to send that text, all I can think about is how she looked at me during that breakfast, thinking I'd already betrayed her. I need to figure myself out and what my feelings for her mean before I try to talk to her about it.

That's where my thoughts are when I get a call from Ansley at 1 a.m. I'm sitting on my bed, still awake. I haven't slept well for a few months now. Ans never calls me this late. *I hope everything is okay,* I think, picking up my phone.

"Hey Ans, what's up? You okay?" I ask, concern flooding my voice.

"Hey bro, yeah everything's fine. I was just wondering if you were still thinking about coming to town this weekend? I won't be able to hang since I have to work but Landon is free," she says, trailing off a bit.

"Um I don't think I'm coming in this weekend, especially

if you're at work. Why are you calling me about this right now? Aren't you at work?"

"Yes I'm at work, or you know I wouldn't be awake. I just…was thinking. So Lexa was supposed to be going to that concert thing in Atlanta this weekend with Amanda but Amanda can't go anymore and Lexa is having to go by herself. I was just going to say if you were going to be in Georgia anyway…but you're not, so never mind!" Ansley finishes somewhat breathlessly.

"Oh," I say, unable to think of another response.

"But like I said, no biggie since you won't be in town anyway. It's that festival with all those bands you used to blast through my walls in high school," she says, laughing.

"Yeah…hate I'm missing that really," I say. Why is she calling me about this in the middle of the night? Did she really think I was coming home this weekend or is she just trying to give me some insider information? "Anything else you're wanting to talk about? I was heading to bed soon…"

"Oh no, that was it! Sleep tight big brother. Love you."

"I love you, too. Goodnight," I say, hanging up but not putting the phone down immediately.

Before I realize what I'm doing, the web page for the concert festival this weekend is pulled up. I do like these bands, love them actually. It was something I had thought about going to when I saw that poster this summer. But I'm not flying to Atlanta for two nights to see some bands. Not that that's why I'd be doing it. It *would be* a chance to see Lexa again. A chance I'd very much like to take.

I lay back on the pillow, letting my mind wander down paths I've been trying to avoid these last few months. With the musical roster still illuminating my screen, I fall asleep with thoughts of Lexa running through my head.

Those thoughts led to dreams of her. Dreams or memories, I'm not sure. I see the replay of our date in the batting cages that Friday afternoon. I feel the touch of her lips on mine and the feel of her hand in mine as we danced together. I smell her wonderful lemony scent that always reminds me of a warm summer's day.

I wake later in the morning than I intend. I must have not wanted to wake myself from such pleasant dreams.

I feel my phone still resting in my hand and pull it towards my face to check the time. 9 a.m. Thursday morning.

Attempting to shake the fog of sleep, I open my phone to scroll through social media. However, when my phone unlocks, the website for the music festival in Atlanta is still pulled up. With the dreams of Lexa still fresh in my mind, I give into the impulse and purchase the two day pass. Next, I hop on another site and search for cheap last minute flights into Hartsfield Jackson Airport and another site to book a hotel room with a good cancellation policy in case I change my mind.

With a flight that leaves in four hours, I wrestle free from my sleep-tangled sheets to get a start on getting showered and packed. Suddenly, I'm filled with an energy I haven't had in months.

Chapter 55

Lexa

My fairy godmother of a best friend sent me home a few hours early so I could get some sleep before making the drive to Atlanta. I was exhausted by the time I got back to my apartment and I ended up only getting a quick shower before collapsing on my bed. I'm almost afraid to even see what my hair looks like right now, knowing I fell asleep with it so wet.

With a groan, I force myself to roll out of the bed. I trudge into the kitchen, staring at the fridge door for a good two minutes before remembering what I came in here for. Caffeine, of course. I open the refrigerator, grabbing the cold brew mix and the creamer, hoping to put a little pep in my step. Honestly, I just want to get to Atlanta, get checked into the hotel and pass out on that bed. Without Amanda being with me, I have no need to go out tonight. I can save all of my extroverted energy for the actual music festival. The farthest I plan to get from my room tonight is the hotel bar for a beer and some grub.

With my first sip of coffee hitting my tongue, my brain wakes back up. My mental checklist begins flashing before my eyes, making sure that I'm not forgetting anything crucial.

I go over the schedule of the festival in my mind, seeing the outfits I have planned and packed. Making a mental note to pack two extra pairs of socks in case it rains or my feet just get too hot. Luckily the bands I'm most excited for are either in the morning or late afternoon and night. The bands performing midday aren't on my list and that will give me time to head back to the hotel, eat, rest and re-hydrate. I learned that lesson the hard way in my early twenties, hitting up a festival at the last minute with some friends. We thought we would be fine staying out all day in the heat and not drinking enough water to even live. Since then, I have invested in a water cooler backpack and enough cooling towels to keep some companies in business. With God as my witness, I will never get that hot and thirsty again.

Now that my melodramatic Scarlett moment is over, I can move on to remembering my phone charger. I'd hate to lose my phone battery and not be able to act like I'm taking a call to get out of an uncomfortable situation this weekend. The go-to move of any twenty-something alone in public.

As I walk back and forth through my room, scanning my belongings, I receive an alert on my phone. I drop onto my bed for a minute to rest, reasoning that I still don't have to leave for another hour. The notification pops up as a reminder from the festival. *Don't forget to pack sunscreen and water party people!* I laugh, thinking about all those newbies that will be rocking a burn by the middle of the first day. September in Georgia can get hot.

I'm still sitting on my bed, scrolling through social media

at this point when I suddenly remember that I need to pack a swimsuit. There's a pool and hot tub at the hotel and I plan to take advantage of the amenities. I hop up off the bed and walk into the closet, towards my rack of swimmies. Living next to a beach, you tend to accumulate several sets over the years. I would say I have somewhere in the range of 15-20 different suits, including one pieces. I grab out my three favorite sets, the ones that are comfortable but flattering, and tuck them into my suitcase. I let my hands rest on top, pondering any other needs. I tend to stick with my father's advice—"you can probably just buy it there"—in situations such as these. Anything I forget, I'm able to purchase at any local store. I'm not too high maintenance in that department. With a sigh and a shrug, I zip up my bag and grab my pillow from the bed. Another memory of my dad flashes into my mind, making fun of me on every trip for bringing my own pillow. "You know the hotel actually has those for guests, it's pretty cool," he would say, laughing like it was the funniest thing he'd ever come up with. I, of course, would just roll my eyes and say, "Right but none of those are *my* pillow." I would love to have my dad make fun of me for taking my own pillow to a hotel right about now. I'd just love to have my dad. Even though it's been years at this point, I don't think that pain will ever fully ease.

✿

After getting my bag unpacked and having a glass of water, I decide it's definitely time for a nap. It's mid-afternoon so I have plenty of time for sleep and fun whenever I wake up. I reach over to the nightstand and grab my phone. I set an alarm for 6 p.m. just in case I haven't woken up by then.

I assume that since I'm exhausted, I'll fall asleep quickly.

But my brain has other plans. With my head on my pillow and the plush hotel sheets pulled up around me, my thoughts spin back to the summer. Scenes of dancing and batting cages and stormy ocean blue eyes flash across the back of my eyelids. I groan and open my eyes.

I pull my phone off the nightstand again, finding a calming and hopefully mind-numbing sound to play from the white noise radio app. With sounds of crashing waves and falling rain, I feel myself start to drift off into oblivion.

✿

What is that sound? Where am I?

I'm instantly awake and sitting up in an unfamiliar bed. I look around at the hotel room and reality begins to flood back in. Wow, I sure was sleeping hard before my alarm went off. I probably needed it. But now my heart is pounding from the scare I had upon waking.

I feel remnants of my dream trying to leak into my conscious mind. Once again, I see those blue eyes, haunting me.

I wish more than anything that I could get over Drew, get past him and move on. I have noticed that every guy I try to date, I compare them to Drew and how he makes me feel. It's unfair to them but also to me. I don't want to settle for something that makes me feel less, but I don't want to be alone for the rest of my life either.

Maybe I'll meet someone this weekend. Now that I'm here alone, I'll have to make friends. Where better to meet someone than at a concert for bands that you both love? Instant connection, right?

Chapter 56

Lexa

I use my hands to rub the sleep from my eyes, regretting not getting up immediately to just wash my face. After my alarm went off, I stayed in bed for another 30 minutes, scrolling on my phone.

Ugh, I think, *time to get up and be a human being.*

I roll out from under the plush white comforter and shuffle to the bathroom, needing to take care of a few human needs first. I flush the toilet and turn to the sink. I make eye contact with myself in the mirror, seeing red where white should be and a new puffiness underneath. I sigh, realizing that I need some water, some more sleep and probably an eye mask tonight before I can even think about having fun tomorrow.

I run a comb through my hair, resigned to pulling it into a messy bun tonight since I let it dry while sleeping on it. My curls are everywhere, making me look like a bad imitation of Ms. Frizzle. I throw a little mascara on my lashes and smack on some lip gloss. *Good enough,* I reason. Next to the dresser to grab a pair of leggings and my favorite cropped sweater. It's by no means cold outside but I know it will be downstairs. I slide into my brown booties to add a touch of style to the outfit and check my reflection in the full length mirror on the closet door. *Definitely good enough,* I laugh. I am just going downstairs to get a drink and something quick to eat. I don't plan on meeting the future Mr. Lexa Chase down there or anything.

I'm close to walking out of the room when I realize I don't have my room key. I shove my hand back against the door at the last second and accidentally throw it all the way open, banging it against the doorstop, and causing myself to jump. *Whoops.* I slip back in, locating my key card on the nightstand where I left it this afternoon. I slip it into my wallet, looking around one last time to make sure I don't have to come back for anything else tonight. With a final glance towards the bed I'm already longing to crawl back into, I make my way out the door.

I love hotel carpet and the way it sways a bit under your feet as you walk on it. It's so different from home carpet–another thing I said to my father that earned a chuckle from him in the past. I punch the button and wait for the elevator to retrieve me from the 6th floor. My legs are too tired from the hustle at work last night to want to walk these stairs right now. I watch the LED display change from 3 to 4 to 5 and then finally 6 and I sigh as the doors slowly open onto an empty elevator.

Empty elevators are a catch-22 for me. I love not having to share it with anyone, but sometimes they creep me out due to the insane amount of elevator scenes in scary movies. Such as *The Eye.* I can't not assume there's a ghost floating behind me because of it. I laugh at myself, shaking off the irrational fear and press the lobby button.

When the doors slide open on the bottom floor, I breathe in the scent of freshly brewed coffee mingling with the smell of seared salmon and roasting potatoes. My mouth immediately starts watering and I am so glad I came downstairs for dinner instead of ordering pizza like I had thought about doing.

I make my way over to the little restaurant and to the hostess stand. There's a gorgeous blonde behind the counter and she's smiling at me for a minute before I realize she's asked me how many will be in my party.

"Oh, uh, just me," I say, smiling brightly back at her. "I can just sit at the bar if that's okay."

"Absolutely ma'am!" the blonde says, immediately making me feel old. I laugh at myself for caring and then follow her outstretched hand towards the bar area.

I turn back and offer another grin, "Thanks, have a good evening."

"You too!" she replies, still smiling.

I turn back to the bar, scanning for seats. I see an opening of about 5 chairs on one side and make my way over. I leave one seat between me and a couple and 3 seats on my other side in case more people show up. I reach to the back edge of the bar and grab the menu sitting there. I'm still trying to decide which specialty cocktail I want when a low voice asks, "What will it be tonight, beautiful?"

I look up into smoky gray eyes and I can feel the blush spreading across my cheeks. "Um," I say, eloquently. "I was trying to decide between the cucumber margarita and the strawberry mojito. I'm looking for something refreshing."

"If you're looking for something more on the minty side, I

would definitely recommend the mojito. The margarita is slightly sour," the extremely attractive bartender replies.

"Mojito it is, then…?" I say, hoping he'll tell me his name.

He doesn't disappoint. "Zane." He winks at me before throwing his bar towel over his shoulder and moving to make my drink. He is every cliche romcom character in one, but I'm here for it. He can tell I'm checking him out, but he seems to enjoy it. He continually makes eye contact with me while he muddles mint leaves and uses the cocktail stirrer to mix in the strawberry. I watch in fascination as he spins the rum bottle through his very dexterous fingers.

I feel slightly ashamed at my gawking, until he throws me another wink and bites his lower lip to hide a smile. His muscular forearms flex as he rattles the cocktail shaker. I may or may not lick my lips, inviting further staring from Zane whose gaze is now laser focused on my mouth.

Maybe I should have at least worn lipstick, I think, regretting my choice for no makeup at this moment. It doesn't seem to deter Zane, however, so I quickly let it go.

When he sets my drink down, I reach to grab it but Zane doesn't move his hand away. Our fingers brush and I look up to see him beaming at me. I want to say that I felt a spark, but it would be a lie. I decide in this moment to stop caring whether there's fireworks and instead focus on the solid warmth. I smile back and he releases my drink to me. I take a small sip and let the flavors fill my palette.

Letting my eyes fall closed, I sigh. It's definitely refreshing, and probably dangerous. It's very smooth.

"And?" Zane asks, wiping his hands on the bar towel. As he does, I notice the tattoos peeking out from under his rolled up dress shirt. I also notice a small vine creeping up his shoulder behind left ear. I have the sudden urge to uncover him and see what else lies beneath.

I shake myself back into the present and smile, saying, "It's really good. Thank you, Zane."

"You never told me your name," he says, arching a thick black brow.

"It's Lexa," I reply, blushing again.

"Well Lexa," he starts, leaning his forearms onto the bar, "I'm off in an hour if you're sticking around for a bit."

My face flushes crimson and I watch as his eyes devour the trail of red down my neck. "Um, yeah. Actually I was planning to eat down here, too. So I'll be around for a while." I turn my eyes towards my lap for a minute, feeling shy suddenly. I see the menu cut into my field of vision and I look back up to see Zane smiling at me again.

"Well what are you thinking? Or would you like my recommendation on that as well?"

"I smelled the salmon and potatoes as I was walking in. Is it any good?"

"I hope so, it's our best seller," he says, running a hand back through his roughly tousled black hair.

I laugh, "Well I'll take that then."

"Any other sides? Apps?"

"No thank you, I'll just sit here and sip on this delicious drink for now." I smile and Zane winks again before walking across the bar to put my order into the computer.

This is the first real connection I've felt with a new guy in forever. I run through a quick pro/con list in my head of hanging out after his shift is over. He didn't invite me anywhere or himself up to my room. We could stay here at the bar if he's okay with that. That's not too fast. But it still leaves the opportunity open.

Why the hell not? What do I have to lose? I raise my eyes to see Zane glancing back over at me and this time it's my turn to bite my lip, hiding my smile. I put my mouth back to work sipping on this amazing cocktail.

Chapter 57

Drew

With the short flight and the change in time zones, I land in Atlanta in the early afternoon. But with no real plans from here other than making it to the shows tomorrow, I decide to head to the hotel I have booked for the weekend. It's right next to the park, I'm surprised they still had rooms left but maybe Lady Luck is with me. I don't know how to hunt down Lexa without outright telling her or Ansley I'm here. I don't feel like talking to Ansley about my rash decision making right now, even if she's the reason I knew Lex would be here alone.

All there is to do is occupy myself until I can find Lexa at the shows. I pull up my phone, trying to see what is going on tonight that will distract me. The first thing that catches my attention is that they're having a horror film festival at the old theater in midtown. That's definitely something I'd love to see. It looks like they're having a Stephen King theme tonight, *The Shining, Misery and Salem's Lot* are all playing.

I check show times and see that it starts in a couple of

hours. I smile, thinking that it sounds like a great way to spend the night. I love old horror movies, especially King's.

My stomach begins to growl as I'm planning my night, making sure that I remember to feed it. Since I already have my phone out, I pull up restaurants in the area, hoping to have a good meal before I chow down on popcorn and candy for the rest of the night. There's several on the street that I'm staying on that just so happen to be on the way to the theater. I'll just drop my bag in my room, make sure I don't look too travel worn and then head to grab an early dinner.

I make it through check-in without issue and up to my room with no major disturbances. Not that I thought there would be too many, I just tend to plan for the worst.

I make it through my door then head straight for the bed to drop my bag. Then to the bathroom to freshen up just a bit. I notice that my t-shirt is a bit rumpled from travel, so I grab a fresh one from the top of my bag. I change out of my tennis shoes and into my casual boots and grab the flannel from my backpack in case it's cold in the theater.

I perform my pocket pat-down, phone and wallet accounted for. I check my wallet for the room key, see that it's also there and shove the wallet into my back pocket. Flannel in hand, I head to the door.

Once I make it back to the lobby, I glance to the desk and see the cute brunette that helped me earlier smiling at me. I grin back and wave, continuing towards the door. I feel her eyes follow my progress, but I don't turn back around. I'm in the mood for distraction, not disaster. And that's all it would feel like with my mind so hyper focused on Lexa like it is.

I take up a leisurely pace as I stride down the road, looking at the various places to eat. It doesn't take long before a delicious scent assaults my senses. I follow my nose to a little hole in the wall American type eatery. As soon as I open the door, the smells engulf me and I feel immediately at home. There's a small bar along one wall, but with so many craft beers on tap I can't even count them all. I wait to be seated, as per the directions from the sign, and I'm led to a cozy booth in the back. As I thank my host, he hands me a menu and asks, "Would you like a beer menu as well, sir?"

"Oh, absolutely. Thank you," I say, accepting the smaller menu. I skim the selection, noting there's several local breweries on the list. When I see a brewery with the location listed as Savannah, I do a double take. *That must be a new one, I think, it's not one I've ever heard of or been to.* "PaCo Brewery" is the name and I pull out my phone to do some research.

"Are we boring you already?" a smooth voice asks. When I look up, I see a stunning smile under an equally gorgeous pair of eyes. The mouth moves again, but I'm not sure what it says this time. I shake my head to clear it before asking, "I'm sorry, what?"

"You just got here and you're already pulling your phone out. I was wondering if we were that boring of a place. Maybe we need adult coloring books on the tables or something," the beautiful eyes crinkle at the edges with the smile that follows the joke.

"Oh, um, no I was actually about to look up this brewery in Savannah that I've never heard of."

The too-attractive waitress bends over slightly to see which place I'm referring to. "PaCo? Oh yeah it's super new. I don't even think they've fully opened. One of their owners is friends with ours so we're putting some of their stuff out for people to try. It's a pilsner if you're into that kind of thing," she replies and I get the distinct feeling she is *not* into pilsners.

I chuckle and reply, "Yeah, I am. I'll take the Savvy Pils from PaCo."

"Coming right up. Any appetizers catch your eye or did you only make it through the beer menu?" *Oh she's sassy, huh?*

"I'll have the mushroom caps, please," I say, arching an eyebrow in return.

She just winks and sashays away. Wow, I can't decide if I was being flirted with or castrated there.

With the disappearance of that strange creature, I refocus on the food menu. My mind whirls with the possibilities presented. This place is obviously one of those fancy takes on comfort food types and I am here for it. I locate a chicken sandwich that has my mouth watering. Grilled chicken topped with provolone cheese and sauteed mushrooms on a brioche bun. *Yes, please!*

I notice a screen behind the bar, playing funny videos of animals. I apparently fixate for a while because the next thing I know, the bewildering beauty is back with my beer and my stuffed mushroom caps.

"Ah, thanks. That was quick!" I say, accepting the beer and appetizer.

"Yeah, I mean, I didn't make either, I just brought them out here. But you're so welcome. Any chance you're ready to order your food or were the tiny kittens too distracting?" she asks, reaching for her notepad.

"For your information, I looked at the menu before I started watching the adorable fluff balls, thank you. So yes, I'm ready to order." I expect a retort from her but when all I get is a slightly amused but mostly blank stare, I clear my throat and say, "I'll take the smothered chicken sandwich with grilled asparagus."

"Sounds great, I'll get that right out. Enjoy the entertainment in the meantime."

I look back to the screen and notice that the videos have switched to people doing dumb things and getting hurt. My favorite. It's hard not to laugh aloud at some of the stupidity.

With a good meal and an even better beer in my stomach, I look around for the smart-mouthed waitress, hoping to go ahead and get my check. I spot her across the restaurant, seemingly totaling out the bill. I watch as she prints it, slips it into the check cover and then interestingly enough, takes off her apron and sets it on the counter. It looks like she has applied a small amount of lipstick since the last time I saw her and done something to her hair to make it bigger. I assume she's getting off work and is wanting to leave as soon as she can get me out of here. I have a smartass remark to make concerning not asking me if I wanted dessert when she slides into the booth opposite me.

"Um, hi?" I say, lifting my left brow to indicate my confusion.

"Hey, so I'm getting off work. What are you doing tonight?" she asks, as straightforward as I've come to expect.

I'm momentarily taken aback at her approach but I feel like I'm into it as well.

I clear my throat and then thrust my hand across the table. "Hi, I'm Drew. And you are?"

"Yeah okay. I guess we should know each other's names or whatever. I'm Ari. Nice to officially meet you, Drew," she says, ever the sass-hole apparently.

I stare at her for a minute, still unsure what this is. She interrupts my train of thought with, "So what are you doing when you leave here? Going back to the hotel to prepare for some boring business meeting?"

"No," I respond, rolling my eyes. "I was actually heading to that horror movie marathon at the theater down the street."

"Oh cool, I was wanting to go to that anyway. You ready now?" Ari asks, starting to get up from the table.

"Well I need to settle my tab, but then yeah I guess. You're going to the movies with me?"

"What a sweet way to ask me on a date, Drew. I'm blushing, really. Yes I'm going. I have nothing else to do tonight and you're hot. And you seem mildly interesting. A movie date means we don't even have to talk if we decide we hate each other."

I'm once again stunned to silence. I glance down and see she's still holding the check folder. I reach my hand to my back pocket, intending to grab my debit card and pay.

"Oh, it's on the house. The owner liked that you ordered the new beer so he comped your meal when I told him you were taking me out tonight," Ari says with a shit-eating grin on her face.

"A bit presumptuous, aren't you? How did you know that I would even agree?" I ask, slipping my wallet back into my pocket and moving to stand up from the booth.

"Um…look at me," Ari replies, waving a hand to present herself to me, as if I hadn't already noticed how gorgeous she is.

"Right," I say, not willing to give her the satisfaction. "Well let's go then."

Chapter 58

Lexa

*N*ote to self, screen the potential date options before *blindly saying yes.* If I would have done so, I may not be sitting in a musty old theater watching the creepy twins in that gross carpeted hallway scene that's so famous. I might not have told Zane that I'd love to hang out with him if I knew it meant reheated popcorn, expired candy and *The Shining* playing on a screen that should have been retired by now.

I sigh, slightly exasperated with myself. But then I look over to Zane to grab a handful of popcorn and see the huge smile on his face, directed at me. I smile back and laugh, saying, "So this is your move?"

"Not usually," he admits, before adding, "but you seemed like you needed to get out of your head for a little bit and this is the best place to do that."

I let a real smile stretch my lips and see Zane's eyes dart to my mouth before returning to my stare. I quirk an eyebrow in question. He simply shrugs before turning the popcorn bucket towards me for easier access.

I glance around the darkened theater noting that there are actually quite a few people here and honestly I've spent worse nights with much worse company. And Zane did buy me my favorite candy. Speaking of which, I elbow him in the ribs and turn my palm face up in the international sign of "gimme."

Once the cookie dough bites are secure in my grasp, I quickly tear into the package. With a laugh and a side-eye glance, Zane quietly "tsks" me. Apparently I'm making too much noise in this not-very-quiet theater.

"Sorry mister," I say, earning another chuckle. Zane is easy to be around. And funny. And very good at his job that he seems to love. So why do I feel so ready to shut this down? As I mull over this question, I realize that the half of the soda I drank has already run through me. Or it could be the couple drinks I had with dinner. Either way, I need to find the restroom soon.

I quietly make my case to Zane, giving him my sweetest smile in apology. He halfheartedly rolls his eyes but he's grinning back as he moves his legs for me to slide by.

I duck and weave to avoid the other movie-goers, eventually making my way out of the theater and into the slightly less dark hallway leading to the bathrooms. I absentmindedly pull my phone from my back pocket to check the time and make sure I haven't missed any important messages (I haven't). I'm scrolling through old notifications when I run straight into a hard chest.

"Oh my God, I'm so sor–," I start, pulling up short when I see the face connected to the aforementioned muscular chest. "What the hell, Drew?" I demand, causing the man to stumble back.

"Hey Lex," is all he says. Drowning me in his baby blues and turning my insides liquid with that sexy half-smile.

And suddenly, I understand why I can't fully connect with Zane. It's because of this asshole.

☼

We must have been outside the theater for longer than I realized because next thing I know, Zane is walking out, looking around like he's searching for me. He catches my eye and walks over, looking somewhat uncertain about Drew and says, "Hey Lexa, I was kind of worried you got lost trying to find the bathroom." He looks between me and Drew again, I think somehow sensing the tension.

"No, um actually," I start, and then clear my throat, "this is my friend Drew. I didn't know he was going to be in town this weekend and we just ran into each other."

"Literally," supplies Drew, unhelpful as ever.

If looks could kill, I think he'd be smoldering in a pile of ash right about now. I turn my gaze back to Zane saying, "Sorry you had to come looking for me. I didn't realize I'd been gone very long."

As my eyes swing back to Drew, they're pulled to an absolutely stunning blonde walking out of the theater and seemingly towards us. My mouth opens in preparation to ask Drew why he's here when she makes her way fully towards us. My mouth stays open, apparently unable to close on its own until I look at Drew who is looking at our new arrival like they know each other.

I immediately snap my mouth closed and turn my eyes down. I'm suddenly jealous—and quickly embarrassed of said jealousy. *What,* I ask myself, *was he supposed to wait*

299

forever for me to decide to come back? This really just goes to show that it wouldn't have worked out. We run into each other in a random city and we're both with other people. This is fine, really.

As I'm trying to decide what to say–to Zane or to Drew, I'm not entirely sure–the woman that's just joined us says, "Is this her?"

My head snaps up so fast I'm afraid I have whiplash. I turn rounded eyes on Drew, who for once looks very bashful. "Yeah, it's her. This is Lexa." I can't remember what happens next, which makes sense considering I pass out from holding my breath.

Chapter 59

Drew

"I bet you have girls fainting over you all the time, don'tcha?" Ari asks rather sardonically.

"Um no, but this isn't the first time Lexa has passed out from situational tension," I reply, still holding Lexa with her back against my chest and seated on one of the benches lining the hallway. Brushing her hair back from her face, I notice that she has bangs now. Her hair doesn't usually fall into her eyes like this. It makes me wonder what else I've missed over the past couple of months.

As I'm searching her features, wondering what shade of green her eyes have been recently, I see them begin to open.

"Hey sleepyhead,'" I say, easing her away from me so she doesn't feel uncomfortable. "I know you like to nap but it's not necessarily cool to do it on a theater floor." This gets a chuckle from our audience. I had almost forgotten about Ari and the guy with Lexa. My attention is drawn to said guy momentarily, looking over his muscled and tattooed physique. My gaze meets his gray one, noting that there's no animosity towards me, only curiosity. *Maybe they just met then,* I think.

My eyes track back down, immediately locking onto Lexa's, which are thankfully wide open now. Even though I attempted to move her from my chest, she's leaned back into the position she had been resting in. She's basically looking at me upside down, jade green eyes alert and searching.

It makes me instantly happy to see her eyes so light. But in the next second, everything shifts. Lexa sits up so sharply, I'm afraid she's going to fall again and swivels back to me with a glare.

"So what are you doing here again?" she asks me, glance sweeping toward where Ari is standing. I look to Ari who just stares impassively at me, *okay thanks for the help there Ari.*

I turn back to Lexa, take a deep breath and say, "I came to find you."

"You brought a date for that?" Lexa asks, gesturing towards Ari.

"I didn't bring a date, I was eating dinner and she was the waitress and—actually can we not have this out right here? Plus it kinda looks like you brought someone as well," I say, waving a hand towards her dark and broody friend.

"Well, why shouldn't I? Am I in a relationship that I was unaware of?" Lexa spits at me.

At this, I notice her date noticeably fidgeting. I look at him and Ari, seeing them exchange very meaningful glances.

"Hey Ari, I'm so sorry. I didn't–," I start, but I'm cut off.

"Dude, it's fine. I knew we were just hanging out, watching movies." Ari turns to face Lexa head-on. "By the way, you're all he's been talking about tonight. Don't give him too hard of a time, okay? He seems like a decent guy."

With that, she nods at me, then Lex and Lex's date and then just turns and leaves. Shaking my head to clear it, I face Lexa. But she's looking at her date with pleading eyes. "Can we have a minute?" she asks. It takes me a second before I realize she's talking to me. With a grunt, I get up and walk towards the bathroom, just trying to give them some privacy. What is she telling him—"Sorry my best friend's older brother is here and we had this weird fling over the summer and I feel like I need to talk to him but I'd rather be with you"? It's taking everything in me not to turn around and try to read her lips. I'll just have to be patient. Not one of my strong suits, if I'm being honest with myself.

"Drew?" I hear a soft voice just behind my right shoulder. I slowly turn, afraid of what she might say next. Reluctantly, I let my eyes travel to where her date was standing, immediately noting that he's not there any longer. My eyes flash back to Lexa's face. Her skin is flushed, but I can't decipher the meaning behind the crimson staining. Her light jade eyes are staring up into mine, open and ready.

It takes me a moment longer to collect my thoughts and stop staring at her so blatantly. But damn, she is breathtaking. I gently reach out a hand towards her, letting it fall before touching her arm. I just feel so unsure right now. I know that I came here to see her. I know that I want her. But I don't know how she feels about me.

"So um, would you want to maybe go somewhere and talk?" I ask, feeling the edges of my lips curl up at my accidental cliche.

Lexa laughs, filling my chest with warmth, and replies, "Sure Drew. Let's just head back to my room. I'm tired and it's just down the street."

"I'm just down the street, too," I say, realizing that she's still not aware that I booked a room and bought festival tickets just for a chance to see her. I duck my head, trying to hide my thoughts. We can go through all of that as soon as we're sitting down and talking face to face.

Lex hooks a thumb over her shoulder, indicating the way to her hotel, or really just the way out of the front door at this point.

"Lead the way, captain," I say, smiling and signaling her to go ahead.

Chapter 60

Lexa

I keep my head down as we exit the theater, watching my feet on the uneven sidewalk and trying to decide what to say next. There are so many thoughts screaming through my head right now. Ranging from *how are you* to *why the hell would you pick up a girl if you were here to see me.* But we'll get to the hard stuff before long, I'm sure. So I decide on an easy question for the walk back.

"How are you?" I ask, turning to catch Drew in my peripheral vision. I see his eyes searching my profile, studying me.

"I've been okay. How about you? Aside from the occasional update from Ansley, I don't really know anything going on with you lately," he responds.

For whatever reason, I feel immediately defensive. "Yeah she told me she's been filling you in on my life. If you were so curious, you could have texted me. You've been pretty silent yourself."

"Yeah? Well it kinda seemed like you wanted nothing to

do with me the last time we saw each other."

I scoff, *seriously?* "Okay so we're doing this now? In the street? Fine. At least I didn't hook up with someone else the night of the wedding after leading someone else on all week and acting like you cared about me–them," I finish, stumbling over the end.

Drew stops dead in the street. I stop and turn to face him, hands finding a resting place on my hips. He opens his mouth, then closes it. I wait a beat before popping an eyebrow and flipping my wrist into a, "What Drew? Just say whatever you were going to say. I'm tired of acting like I don't need to talk about this."

"I just can't believe I'm being accused of hooking up with Claire when you were all over Jackson on that dance floor," he says, blue eyes flashing dark with the storm brewing in them.

I flinch slightly, but recover enough to throw back, "Are we still talking about Jackson? I thought we were past that. God Drew, I wish you could focus on yourself instead of other people. Do you even know what you want? It's high time you figure that out." I'm fuming but hold my ground, not ready to give up yet. Until Drew says something that breaks my heart.

"At least I moved away and found my own life. I didn't just follow the only friend I've ever made back home like a sad puppy."

My mouth falls open and I take a step back. I feel like I just got punched in the gut and I can't breathe. *Is that really what their family thinks of me? Is this how Ansley feels?*

I snap my mouth closed, placing my hand over my lips like I'm on the verge of hurling my dinner. Which honestly, I could right now. I feel physically sick. I meet Drew's eyes, but I can't really see him through my tears. I shake my head and start to back away. Drew reaches a hand out like he'll try to stop me but I sidestep him and turn. I run back to my hotel, not stopping to see if he's trying to follow. I hope he's not.

I somehow make it back to my room. I stumble to the bed, not even turning on a light. I collapse onto the comforter and proceed to dissolve into a puddle of tears. I can't stop thinking about all the things he said, but especially that last part. I know Ansley loves me but my anxiety has forced its way into our relationship in the past and now it is taking complete control of my mind. I relive every conversation I've had and every secret I've shared with my best friend. Was she just humoring me this entire time? Were her parents just letting me come around for holidays because they pitied the little orphan girl?

The Parker family is too nice and loving for any of that. Well everyone except one member, obviously.

I cry until I feel like there are no more tears left in my body. I cry until it is physically impossible to continue. I cry until I have felt every hurt and every fear all over again. And then I make a promise to myself. Never again. No more chances. I'm done.

Chapter 61

Drew

S*hit.*

What did I just do? I am never going to be able to take back what I just said. I don't even know why I said it. I was just getting so angry and then she told me I needed to figure out my own life. For whatever reason, that was my breaking point.

I can't even follow after her because there's nothing I can do to fix this. I am so far past fixing this now.

I stand in the middle of the sidewalk, staring after her for so long my legs go numb from not moving. Did I just screw up my entire life in two seconds? Because that's how this feels.

Shit.

Chapter 62

Lexa

April

S even months of radio silence. Seven months of absolutely no word from Drew. At first, I was glad because it makes it easier to ignore him if he's not actually contacting me. But now I'm mad. Mad at the way it ended, mad about what he said to me and mad at myself for not being able to let any of it go. Seven months ago I swore to myself that I was done with him. But obviously I'm not. I had to work Christmas Eve and Christmas Day so I didn't go see the Parkers until the weekend after and he had already returned home. He didn't come home for Easter.

I still haven't told Ansley what he said. She seems to know at least some of what happened because she refrains from mentioning him unless necessary. I feel bad that she's having to monitor her words around me. It was rough when I first got back home, she came over and we talked, cried and laughed. I told her how the rest of the festival I spent screaming my heart out to my favorite songs and actually making some new friends. Since then, we've been as solid as ever, even having movie nights and sleepovers again like in college.

I would say we're back to normal following me almost dating her brother, but she's been acting weird this week and it's making me nervous.

Speak of the devil and she shall appear. Ansley's long strides bring her around the corner as I'm leaving work this morning. I receive a bright smile, and a quick wave before she's caught up to me.

"Hey girly pop," she says, slinging an arm over my shoulders, "got a minute to talk?"

"I have every minute to talk to you," I say, returning her smile. She releases me as we walk through the lobby doors and out into the spring sunshine.

"So, we're coming up on our anniversary in a couple of months," she begins.

"The anniversary of the time we tried to chug two liter cokes and burped so loud our neighbors thought someone was dying?" I ask sarcastically.

"No you weirdo. Mine and my husband's wedding anniversary? You remember? Same time period as that wonderful party you helped me plan last year?"

"Oh right! I remember. You made me wear a dress and do my hair and makeup and all that stuff. How could I forget?" I say, laughing.

"Well anyways," she says, rolling her eyes with a laugh, "we have something we're trying to plan and I want you to be there."

"Okay, you know I'd love to already. What is it?" I turn to

fully face her as we stop by my car.

"So you know we have plans to go to St. Croix? Well, we just heard from our travel agent that the waterfront villas around us that had been booked by a big party have recently come available. And since it's so close to time, they're wanting to get them rented out—at a discounted price. There's five available in our pod, all sharing a common walkway and fire pit and stuff. We want to get the bridal party–those that can make it–and take y'all with us. What do you think?"

It takes me all of two seconds to process St. Croix with my best friend. "Um yes, obviously. How do I get booked?"

Ansley laughs brightly before grabbing me into a huge hug. "I'll let our travel agent know and she'll send you an invoice. I'm glad we haven't scheduled for June yet so you don't even have to rearrange your work schedule!"

I hug her back tightly before releasing to look at her face when I ask, "What was Drew's answer?"

Her face falls slightly before resuming a somewhat strained smile. "He's going to be there, too."

"Is that why you've been acting weird this week?" I interrogate.

"Yes, I should have known that you would notice. I was just nervous to ask you and have you not come because he'd be there. I don't know all the details, but I know that y'all haven't spoken since September."

I shrug, saying, "If he wants to talk, he knows how to reach me. But I would never miss out on an opportunity to travel with you because of a guy. You know that."

"I know, girl. I know. I love you," she says, another real smile taking over her beautiful face.

"I know. I love you, too. Go home and get some sleep and we can gush over this trip tonight. You know I need all the details."

Chapter 63

Lexa

June

Tuesday

With a final mad dash around my room, making sure I didn't leave my favorite bikini and making sure I packed my razor, I think I'm finally ready to head to the airport. With not a minute to spare, either. Ansley and Landon are picking me up in five minutes. I scoop Sneakers up, hugging him and reminding him to be good for Mrs. Reynolds. She's coming to pick him up later this morning to take care of him while I'm gone this week. I won't be getting him back until Monday morning so I give him an extra three kisses on his furry little head.

My phone beeps on my bed, I pick it up to see a text from Ans. *We're here. You better be ready.*

I'm coming miss ma'am. Hold your horses. I shoot back. I grab my bag and my backpack full of all my plane activities and make my way to the door. I check the thermostat and recheck my bag for my ID and my phone. Both there.

"Bye Sneaks! I'll see you on Monday. Don't miss me too much!" I say over my shoulder, blowing one last air kiss his way. With that, I'm out the door and down the stairs.

As I'm nearing the car, it takes me a second to realize there's a third person in the vehicle. Ansley is in the back seat. Sitting in the passenger seat, head resting in his hand and eyes facing resolutely forward, is Drew.

I stop in my tracks, my eyes widening. Movement in my peripheral vision causes me to turn my head, catching Ansley's gaze burning into mine. She somehow got out of the car and over to me silently.

"Need help getting your bag in the trunk?" she asks, already moving to take the handle from me.

I shake my head to clear it, "No, I got it. Thanks though."

She follows me to the trunk and watches as I stow my suitcase alongside hers. There's just enough room for me to throw my backpack in as well. Empty-handed, I turn back to Ansley, not yet closing the trunk lid.

"I didn't know he was riding with us until this morning when we picked him up. Landon swears up and down that he told me last week that Drew was flying in the night before and riding to the airport with us, but I have no recollection of this alleged conversation," Ansley says, resting her hand on my forearm.

"It's okay Ans. He's your brother. And it's not like it's a surprise that we're going to be seeing each other on this trip," I reply, turning my hand over to grab hers. With a quick squeeze, I release her hand and then close the trunk. "Let's get going. Don't want to be late for our trip to paradise!"

✿

"What the hell are you reading?" I hear from over my shoulder. I turn to see Drew's deep blue eyes looking at my book. I didn't even notice him standing there.

"Um, the Wraith Chronicles. Why?" I reply, bringing my gaze back to the page.

"The one with, like, the vampire queens and the talking spiders?"

"One talking spider. And he used to be a human," I respond, a little too snappy even to my ears. I soften my tone a bit and add, "It's fun to read fantasy because it's an escape from real life."

Drew doesn't say anything, but he squeezes my shoulder as he passes my seat. I don't look up, too scared to meet his eyes. I'm afraid he might see how much that small touch just affected me. *Shit,* I think, *it's going to be a long week.*

I must fall asleep at some point over the water, because the next thing I know, our pilot is on the intercom, telling us to buckle our seat belts for the descent.

I shift around in my seat, noticing that Amanda slept through the announcement. I gently shake her awake and relay the message. Once buckled in, we both become giddy with excitement.

"I've never been outside the southeast. I am so excited I feel like I might throw up," Amanda says, practically bouncing in her seat.

"I know, this is going to be such a great time and we have such a fun group! I'm so glad you could make it," I say, reaching over to squeeze her hand.

Our hands remain locked as we touch down in St. Croix.

✿

Because of the layover we had in Atlanta, we made it here mid-afternoon. Plenty of time to go get checked in, settled in and ready for dinner. Maybe even time for a quick trip to stick my toes in the water. Moving to Savannah has turned me into such a beach bum but this is on a whole other level. As our taxi makes its way to the resort, all I can see is blue ocean stretching to the horizon. I roll my window down, breathing in the salty sea air and feeling the sun and wind on my face.

Chapter 64

Drew

It's so hard to keep my eyes off of her as the wind flows through her red hair and the sun shines on her beautiful face. She's angelic and I don't want to stop looking at her. But if I'm going to succeed in my mission this week, creeping her the hell out is not the best way to get started.

I rip my gaze away from freckled cheeks and cherry red lips to concentrate on the plan. Mission L.O.M.L. starts now and I need to be focused.

As we pull up to the gates of the resort, I hear Ansley and Landon discussing the rooming assignments. Knowing that Jackson and Claire are together and actually *seeing* them together are two different things. Ansley filled me in on that topic a few months ago. She said Lexa seemed genuinely happy that they found each other. I was happy for other reasons. Jackson and Claire sharing a room made it easier for Lexa and I to have rooms to ourselves instead of sharing with someone. That simplifies things, mission-wise.

I guess I have Ansley to thank for her help thus far.

Especially since this trip is supposed to be about them. But my little sister is the most unselfish person I've ever met, not that this is news to me. She knows how much I want this to work out and she's been so supportive. She loves Lexa just as much as she loves me and Ansley is truly convinced we can make each other happy if we can just get out of our own way.

Lexa's last words to me haunted me for months before I finally let them sink in. I really took a look at my life and re-examined my priorities. I made some changes that have improved my quality of life but I was still missing the most important piece. But this week, I win her back for good.

I steal one last look of Lexa, face turned to the sun, radiating the beauty of the world. I sigh, hoping that's a sight that I'll get to see for the rest of my life.

Chapter 65

Lexa

This resort is one of the most beautiful sights I've ever seen. The main building is all glass and open air. There are beautiful flowers, trees and birds surrounding the area. Our villas are located right on the edge of the sparkling and amazingly clear water, connected to a common area by little boardwalks. The whole place is just the epitome of tropical wonder. I feel like my mouth hasn't stopped gaping open since we walked onto the sprawling grounds of the retreat.

I finally force my mouth closed, only to have it drop open again when we make it to the villas. Each place is slightly different in style, but all cohesive. The first villa is for the Blakes. Next is Amanda and Grace. After that it's me, then Weston and Patrick, then Drew and then rounding out the semi-circle are Jackson and Claire.

Claire and Jackson will be the next arrivals with Grace, Patrick and Weston getting in just before dinner. Coming from so many different time zones, it's amazing that we were able to get flights landing so close together.

I haven't seen Claire and Jackson since the wedding, but apparently they started talking last July, just messaging back and forth about some shared interests and then were able to make the move to be together. I've talked to Claire several times in the last few months and they're living in Chicago—Jackson is stationary now and she's loving it there. I'm so happy they found each other and I can't wait to see them in person. Patrick apparently went in on some big business venture with Connor and that's going really well. Weston and Grace have been taking road trips and travel nursing contracts around the country together, they swear they're not seeing each other but I'll be the judge of that once I see them.

Ansley told me Drew has made some kind of big change, too. I'm mulling over all the major life events that have happened for everyone else over the past year and wonder if I should be trying harder to make a difference in mine. I feel somewhat stagnant, but also so content in some aspects that I'm not willing to rock the boat just yet. But that's not saying that I wouldn't uproot if I found someone that I wanted to do that for.

I make my way to my bed in my villa, suddenly not in the party mood. I'm going to have to change that before dinner, but for now, I can just change into a bathing suit and head to the water. Salt water fixes everything.

✿

Clad in my favorite green bikini, I lay sprawled on the sand, soaking in some sun rays through my 50 SPF sunscreen. Being of the fair skin population, I will have to be vigilant this trip if I don't want to end up with major burns. One more minute and it's time to get it in the water and then under an umbrella. I feel the warmth of the sun heating my skin and melting my worries. With a deep sigh, I heave myself into a sitting position and look out at the water. There aren't as many people out here as I thought there would be. I just assumed the beach would be packed. I see a couple swimming about 20 feet offshore and another sitting on their towels and reading. After another minute of people-watching, I climb to my feet, dusting the sand from the sides of my arms and make my way to the water.

The cool water momentarily takes my breath away, but as I wade further, I let my stress drift out on the current. I sink into the water and then turn on my back to float. I let the gentle waves lull me into a quiet retrospective. My mind wanders through the past, drifting as aimlessly as I am through the sea. Images of my mom's sweet, smiling face and the sound of my dad's boisterous laugh fill my head. Even though I miss them more than life itself, I have so many good memories. I try to stay thankful for that.

As I'm letting my memories flood through me, I feel a disturbance in the water near my legs. My immediate irrational thought is that there's a 16-foot Great White Shark sniffing my feet. My eyes fly open to see a brunette head looming over me. I scramble to my feet, inhaling a little bit of salt water in the process.

"You good?" Ansley says, laughing and trying to help me stand up and slapping my back as I cough.

"Uh yeah. I'm fine. I just thought you were…not you," I splutter, coughing once more. I think that's it but I definitely need some water to soothe the burning in my throat.

"You thought I was Jaws huh?" she says, still laughing.

"Maybe. But I mean, who wouldn't? You can't sneak up on people like that!" I exclaim.

"I don't know if *sneaking* is the correct term. I walked towards you in broad daylight in the open water. It's not my fault you were so lost in your head you didn't hear me calling your name or slapping the water before I got close. I had to resort to the foot tickle."

I huff out a sigh, wanting to argue. But she's right.

"What were you thinking about so hard anyway? The water was boiling around you with the effort," she says, earning an eye roll from me.

"Just the past. My parents and stuff," I say, not wanting to really get into all of it right now. It's hard sometimes to explain to someone that has both of their parents how much you miss yours but that it's not always sad thoughts keeping you in your head.

Trying to shake my mood, I grab Ansley's hand and start running deeper into the water. "Race you to the shark nest!" I scream, letting go of her hand and diving into the water, heading for the buoy in the distance.

Chapter 66

Drew

Why am I so nervous? I feel like I'm about to swim with sharks, instead of going to a dinner with friends…and the love of my life. What if it's too late? What if I fucked this up beyond repair already?

I stare at my reflection, hands resting on the counter. Time for a pep talk.

"You are worthy. You are kind. You know who you are and what you want," I say to myself, never breaking eye contact with my double. Along with making the big life changes over the past several months, I've started trying to do this whole positive self-talk thing. Getting to really know myself has been hard but worthwhile. I realized that I was running from my past, not embracing my present or planning for my future. But all that has changed. And I couldn't be happier. Well I could be, but I guess that depends on how this week goes.

I straighten up, adjust my cuffed sleeves and fix myself with a meaningful stare. With a final deep breath to settle me, I turn to slip on my loafers and grab my phone. Not that I really need it, everyone that I would be talking to is here tonight. I guess it's still better to carry it, just in case of emergency. It's not that big of an island, but technically you can get lost anywhere, right?

I make my way down the walkway connecting my bungalow to the common area. I notice that they've already come to light our fire pit, as they said they would every night there's no rain. Tonight is going to be beautiful if the clear sky over the sparkling water is any indication. The radar showed no rain in the forecast until an early morning shower. Thank goodness, it's been an unusually wet summer in Georgia so far. Add to that the fact that I haven't had a chance to even get out much with my new job. Head of Marketing is a much more demanding position, but I'm loving it so far.

I haven't told Lexa that I moved back to Georgia yet. Not that we've talked recently anyway. But I wanted to wait until it felt like the right time. I've been back for a couple of months now, living in an apartment just outside of Savannah. Something that I'm very surprised Ansley hasn't told her best friend. Maybe she's actually respecting my wishes. Or she just thinks I'm stupid and doesn't want to tell me. Either way, Lexa doesn't know yet and that's the more important piece.

I'm almost to the restaurant when I see Claire and Jackson strolling down the beach towards the place. To my surprise, I'm genuinely happy to see both of them. I let a smile overtake my face and jog to meet them.

"Hey y'all! I am so glad you're here!" I say, enveloping them both in a hug.

"Yeah man, we're happy to be here," Jackson says, wrapping his arm around me to embrace me more fully.

I let go of Jackson, grabbing Claire by the shoulders to look her over. "A lot has changed since last year, huh?" I say, pulling her into another hug.

"It has, and I'm so happy to see you! Without you, me and Jackson would have never connected. I am still so glad that you even thought to hook us up. I don't think I realized how much we have in common," she says, staring lovingly up at Jackson. Who, in turn, is looking at her like a lovesick puppy. I am so glad I gave her his number that week when we met up for coffee. They look so happy together.

"Shall we?" Jackson says, gesturing ahead towards the restaurant.

"Yes, wouldn't want to keep anyone waiting," Claire responds with a wink towards me. I guess she remembers that in addition to supplying her with Jackson's number that day, I also spilled my guts about my feelings for Lexa. I just roll my eyes and wave her off.

As we walk into the beach side eatery, complete with linen tablecloths and fishing decor, my eyes immediately fly to the red-headed beauty in the blue dress. She looks like she may have gotten some sun today, her freckles across her cheeks and shoulders are more pronounced. *Dammit*, I think, *I knew I should have gone down to the water this afternoon.* I was just too nervous about how this week would play out. I spent more time picking out my outfits for this trip than I think I have ever spent on any work project in my life. But we're here now and I have to relax and try to play this cool.

That thought flies out the window as bright jade green eyes meet mine and the sweetest smile lifts the most perfect mouth I have ever kissed. It seems like I may have stopped breathing for a minute because my next thought is my brain screaming at me for oxygen. So much for playing it cool.

Chapter 67

Lexa

I feel him enter the room before I see him. I feel that familiar shiver run up my spine to the back of my neck. Feel his phantom touch on my skin. It takes everything in me not to just whip around in my seat and search him out. Instead, I take a sip of my drink and slowly turn towards the entryway.

My eyes find his immediately and the hungry look in them has a quick blush running over my cheeks. I duck my head down, suddenly shy.

I look back up and Drew is still staring at me. But the look in his eyes is different now. The hunger and desire are still there, but burning underneath is something I'm not familiar with. He seems…sure of himself. Like he finally made up his mind.

My thoughts flash back to the conversation I had with Ansley in the water today. She said Drew had changed since last summer. She mentioned he had made some "big moves" and whether she meant metaphorically or physically, I never got to ask. I guess I'll have to find out from the man himself. He seems determined to rekindle a relationship with me. I haven't deciphered if that's friendship or something more. But for now, we'll just have to take it one day at a time. With this in mind, I wave at him and motion for the open seat next to me.

As he makes his way to the chair, eyes never leaving mine, I finally notice the movements of the people behind him. Claire and Jackson are waving at everyone, huge smiles plastered to their faces and hands clasped together. I can't help the large grin stretching across my lips or the excitement that causes me to jump from my seat. I hear Drew chuckle beside me as he brushes his body past mine, igniting all kinds of heat inside me. Ignoring my baser instincts, I rush to Claire and wrap her in a big hug.

"Hey girl!" I say, pulling her even closer before whispering, "You look good, and so, so happy. You're glowing."

"Thanks, Lex. I've missed you so much," she says, crushing me to her.

"That makes two of us," I hear a deep voice say, just seconds before I'm lifted off of the ground into a pair of stronger and much taller arms.

"Hey, Jackson," I say, giggling as the air is pushed from my lungs at the force of his affection. "It's good to see you. But I won't be seeing you much longer if you continue to deprive me of oxygen."

"Oh, sorry," the big brute says, setting me down gently.

I smooth out my dress, a little self-conscious now that I'm on the ground and facing the both of them. The stilted way everything ended last year fills me, before I realize that we're all different people now. And they have obviously moved on from it, so I will too. I straighten up and smile again before saying, "Well, have a seat so we can get this party started. I'm ready for a drink."

"Amen, sister," Ansley says from behind me, raising her water glass in a salute.

As I sit back down, I feel Drew's arm come to rest on my chair, just so slightly grazing the bare skin of my shoulder blades. I shiver slightly, feeling crimson flare across the exposed skin. That much heat should not be radiating between barely touching skin. I sneak a glance towards Drew, trying to see if he can read my face, but he's laughing at something Landon said. *Dammit.* I need to pay attention. I can't fall straight back into the trance that I was in last summer. I shake my head to clear it, take a deep breath and turn to Ansley. Who is, of course, staring straight at me. I blush, knowing she's noting my reactions to her brother and fix her with a stare of my own. I feel her thoughts in my head and I know she catches my drift from my narrowed eyes. *Don't say anything,* I think at her. She just smirks and says, "Hey Drew!" I snap my head around in time to see Drew's eyes leave the back of my head and flash up to his little sister. "Hey Ans, you look radiant tonight, as usual," Drew says, letting his hand lightly brush over my exposed shoulder as he says it. I shiver again, but I'm given full body chills when he leans down, whispering into my ear, "And you look gorgeous. I love this dress, is it new?" His hand gently eases from my shoulder to my back, leaving a trail of goosebumps.

"It is," I reply. I know he likes green on me, but I went for blue this time.

Somehow reading my thoughts, Drew says, "You know, I

think blue might be my new favorite color."

I can't help but turn my head, facing him. He doesn't move an inch and suddenly our mouths are so close we're breathing the same air. Or, we would be if I could breathe.

His fingers continue their gentle path along my shoulders and back, "Relax, Lex. Breathe."

So I do. I let out a breath and a little chuckle. *Shit, what is he doing to me?*

"What do you want?" he says, raising his eyebrows, face still way too close.

"Um, you want to talk about that now?" I say, incredulous that he's ready to talk right here, right now.

Drew lets out a small laugh, pulling away from me a little before motioning to the waitress who is patiently waiting for my drink order. I flush from head to toe and jerk back from Drew, much to the amusement of our friends. *Ohmygosh.* Everyone at the table just witnessed that scene. I stutter about trying to find the drink menu, before I hear Drew say, "She'll have a glass of champagne."

I finally make eye contact with the waitress, who is now raising an eyebrow at me, asking me if that's correct. "Yes ma'am," I say, suddenly Southern, "a glass of bubbly, thanks."

I lean back in my chair and huff. This is so not how I saw tonight going. What happened to my cool, calm, and collected attitude I was trying to put forth? It's shot to hell now. Oh well, I might as well have fun.

Chapter 68

Lexa

I haven't laughed this much in a long time. Being back with our friends has put me in such a great mood. And everyone seems so happy. There's no random arguments, there's no tension and there are so many big, genuine smiles. Ansley has such a great group of friends and I am so proud to be a part of it.

Looking around the table, I notice that there's more flirting than I expected, too. Grace and Amanda are giving both Patrick and Weston some looks. I'm not sure if it's the impressive amount of alcohol we have consumed tonight or the overall romantic feel of this island, but there may be more couples leaving than when we arrived.

Speaking of, I don't know that Drew's hand has left my vicinity tonight. Even when we were both eating, he kept one hand either on my chair or resting on the table beside my arm so that every time I moved, we would touch. Not saying that I mind it, but there are some serious things we need to discuss before I melt back into his arms. Which is why I started drinking water an hour ago. I need to be as clear-headed as possible tonight. I'm not drunkenly doing anything that I'll regret.

With that thought in mind, I hang around a little longer than necessary when we decide it's time to leave. I want to have Ansley near me for moral support. She notices my lingering and comes to my side.

"What's up buttercup?" she asks, looping her arm through mine. The island life is already treating her so well. She is glowing and even more gorgeous, somehow.

I smile before replying, "Oh nothing, just trying to stay in a crowd. Buddy system and all."

"Trying not to get snatched?" she asks, pointedly glancing towards Drew.

I feel my face heat with a blush. "Something like that," I say, not lifting my eyes to meet hers.

"Well you know I'm always here for whatever you need, love." She plants a kiss on my cheek, making me giggle.

As we make our way out of the restaurant, arms still linked, Landon sidles over to us. "Interested in a night stroll by the water?" he asks Ansley. Ansley quickly glances towards me, but this is her anniversary trip. There's no way she's sacrificing even more for me than she already has.

I lift her hand and unwind our arms, giving her to Landon. "Y'all get out there and do some really romantic shit. I can't wait to hear all about it in the morning." I wink at Ansley who throws her megawatt smile my way.

As soon as they're gone, I release a sigh. Alone again. *Well not totally alone*, I remind myself. When I look back to the path in front of me, there's Drew. Thumbs hooked in his back pockets, broad chest on display under his not-fully-buttoned shirt, hair tousled by the wind and grinning in that devilishly handsome way of his.

"Hey," he says, taking a step toward me.

"Hey yourself," I reply, closing the distance with another step.

"Want an escort home? I'd hate to think of you all alone out here, just waiting for some handsome guy to come take you back in for a drink." With this, he raises his hand and brushes a stray piece of my hair from my face. He lingers as he tucks the strand behind my ear.

A sharp inhale leaves me, but I don't make any other move. "Sure, wouldn't want some hot guy to walk up and sweep me off my feet." Still barely breathing, I reach my hand up to touch the back of Drew's. "Especially not a guy that can shake me with a single small touch."

This time it's Drew who seems unable to control his breathing. "Right, wouldn't want to feel an instant connection with someone and have to wait a decade to even make a move. That would be frustrating." His crooked smile pops onto his lips, drawing my attention from his eyes.

Those lips are trouble. From the words they speak to the way they move against mine. "Wouldn't want to fall for the guy and then have them up and leave again, either. Even more frustrating." That gets him. He snaps his hand down and tilts his head to the side.

"That's not fair, Lex," Drew says softly. "That was a year ago and things are different now."

"Okay, so tell me. Are you still in marketing? You hate that job."

"I don't hate marketing, it's my passion," he says, somehow answering the question without really answering me.

I purse my lips, ready to argue that point when Drew says, "Trust me, things have changed. I've changed. I've figured out who I am and what I want. Just like you suggested I do back in Atlanta."

"Yeah that's what Ansley said," I say, unwilling to look back up and make eye contact.

"Oh so you and my sister have been talking about me, then?" he asks.

I raise my head, catching the joking smile on his face. "Obviously. But I've made some changes, too. I've applied to a few travel nurse job postings across the country. I need to see more places and meet new people. Can't rely on my best friend to supply my entertainment forever, right?" I didn't mean to add that last part, but what he said in Atlanta still gets to me sometimes.

Drew's hand reaches out, grabbing my fingers. His other hand leaves my cheek to rest under my chin, gently tipping it back. "Hey, I need you to forget I ever said that. I know you probably can't forgive the action, but forget the words. I was wrong and it was mean to say. I can't imagine what Ansley would do without you."

I nod my head, tears starting to form along my lash line.

"Well," I say, "ready to head back to the rooms? We have a pretty early start tomorrow."

"Sure," Drew says, stepping beside me without releasing my hand. "I'm pretty sure we're neighbors anyway."

We walk in silence for a while, both staring out at the moonlit water. The way the light ripples across the dark waves has always mesmerized me. But the quiet serenity of this place adds beauty that I could never have imagined.

Chapter 69

Drew

The moonlight shining on Lexa's face is a breathtaking sight. I want to see the light change on her face every night, every morning and every moment of every day. I still haven't let go of her hand since we left the restaurant, and she hasn't made a move to take it back. I wish I could read her thoughts as we stroll along the walk back to the bungalows. She looks so serene and just absolutely beautiful.

"Gorgeous, isn't it?" she asks, eyes never leaving the water.

"Stunning," I reply, eyes never leaving her.

We make it to the fork in the road between our separate rooms much too quickly. I still can't think of what I need to say in this moment.

But it seems that I may be saved the trouble of having to formulate any kind of sentence when Lexa turns to me, jade green eyes full of fire. She's either about to kill me or kiss me, and it could honestly go either way. As soon as this thought flits through my mind, she leans toward me, rising onto her toes the slightest bit. She turns her face up to mine and her eyes begin to close, ever so slowly. *Oh thank God,* I think. I move to sweep her into my arms and kiss her when I hear a loud scream and a splash. I'm jolted enough that I draw my face away from Lexa, but reach my arm out for her in protection.

"What the hell was that?" she says, looking around wildly. Just then, we hear Weston's voice float to us from their villa. "I thought you said you couldn't swim! I had to make sure we wouldn't have to be saving your ass all day tomorrow."

I hear another splash and what sounds like someone scrambling onto the dock, then Patrick saying, "You are the worst. I said I couldn't swim in the open ocean, not that I couldn't swim at all. You heard me."

Weston laughs loudly before replying, "Yeah, maybe I did. I just thought you needed practice anyway." I hear both men laugh, way too loudly.

"I guess they're having a good night," Lexa says, already two steps away from me.

"Yeah, it sounds like it," I say, wanting so badly to close that distance.

"Well I'm exhausted from the trip and we both need some sleep. Big day tomorrow. See you bright and early for the boat trip!" she says brightly. She's backing away from me, but I refuse to let her lose eye contact. I may have lost the opportunity for a goodnight kiss, but I know I'll still be dreaming of her.

Chapter 70

Lexa

Wednesday

Just as my dreams were, my first thoughts of the morning are haunted by the look on Drew's face as I walked away last night. The almost-kiss interrupted by Weston and Patrick is right there with it. I can still see the absolute relief on his face as I leaned towards him. The intensity of it scared me a little. I think that's why I ran as soon as the distraction ripped me back into reality. I thought I was ready for this, but I'm scared it could all just end the same way as last summer. Granted, Drew seems a lot different, a lot more sure this time. But I had thought he was sure about us last time, too. Maybe with less distractions, we'll finally have the opportunity to feel this out. I'll just have to have patience and a little bit of trust I guess.

Lost in my thoughts, I almost forget why my alarm woke me up so early. And why I'm in an unfamiliar room. The realization jolts me from bed. Boat excursion from the island, that's right. I laugh at myself a bit and blame the jet lag after working all weekend. Maybe I'm getting too old to be working the night shift, or maybe I shouldn't expect to have a normal life outside of it anymore. Either way, I'm finally up and out of bed, roaming around the edge of the room until I find the light switch. The room is immediately bathed in a warm light. *Even their lights are cozy here,* I think. My thoughts wander to where I can find these light bulbs at home as I get ready to start the day.

I hop in the shower to quickly wash and shave my legs again. The fact that hair can grow so fast really frustrates me sometimes. Since we're going to be out in the water all day, I'll be waiting to wash my hair until tonight. I step out of the shower and into my brown bikini that I plan to wear for the day. I braid my hair into two plaits, letting them fall down my back. I find my trusty cream cover-up and my brown baseball hat. I slip my tan sandals on and go to town with the sunscreen. SPF 1000 would suit me better, but I'll have to stick with 50. I slather it on, making sure I pack the tube in the small bag that I'll be carrying on the boat. I grab a towel from the room, stowing it beside the sunscreen. I find my water bottle, fill it up and shove it in the bag. I pull on my cover-up, hat and backpack and look around the room for my sunglasses. It takes me a second to find them. They somehow fell to the bottom of my suitcase when I got back from the beach yesterday.

I glance in the mirror, turning to admire the scooped out back of the cover-up and all it does to highlight the *assets* that I work so hard for. I chuckle and then my thoughts immediately go to Drew. *I hope he likes this suit,* I think. Then shaking my head, I tell myself that I like this swimsuit and that's what matters anyway. I give myself a big smile in the mirror and with that, I'm ready to meet up with everyone.

I close my door behind me, making sure the automatic lock is engaged. I'm so glad they have the keypad entry here, I hate carrying around a key. It's still a little dark outside as I make my way to the middle of our circle.

Ansley and Landon are already there, and I can tell my best friend is equal parts excited and exhausted.

"Just how late did you two stay out last night?" I say, laughing.

"Honestly, not that long," Ansley says, "We just didn't go straight to sleep when we did get back." She throws me a wink as Landon says, "Babe!" We're both laughing now, a little too loud for this early in the morning.

"What's so funny?" Amanda asks as she walks up to our little group.

"Oh nothing. Just Ans spilling the beans about Landon keeping her up all night," I say.

Landon rolls his eyes and tries to ignore us. It's hard though, especially once Grace asks, "God you two are still in the honeymoon phase aren't you?" She pulls a disgusted face but then starts laughing and says, "We already know you're perfect. We came on this trip expecting to watch you two swoon all over each other. As gross as it is, it's also incredibly cute and inspiring."

"Aw Grace, you're so sweet," Ans says, moving to wrap our friend in a hug.

Patrick and Weston arrive just as I see Drew making his way down the boardwalk towards us.

"Well good morning," Drew says as he reaches me. It's not lost on me that his eyes never left me as he was walking to the group and he addressed me first. I redden slightly, before replying, "Good morning Drew, sleep well?"

"You were in every one of my dreams, so you tell me," he answers in a hushed tone, reaching his hand out to trail down my upper arm. My blush deepens and I shiver at the touch.

"Well that makes two of us," I say, smiling up at him and letting it really reach my eyes.

From behind me I hear, "Just join us when you can!" I whip around to see Jackson and Claire, blush spreading across the latter's face as they make their way from their room.

"We had a late night," Jackson says, looking down at Claire with a smile dripping in seduction. I can see it working on her as her blush deepens to a dark crimson. I laugh, and go to Claire.

"Get away from my friend, she needs some rest," I say, jokingly pulling her away from Jackson.

"Hey she knows what she signed up for, don't you, baby?" he asks, winking at Claire. We all burst out laughing and turn towards Ansley and Landon.

"Well then, now that we're all accounted for, ready to head out on a boat and maybe catch a sunrise?" Ansley asks, taking charge.

"Ready!" we all answer in unison, like some kind of field trip group. With that, she turns on her heel and we all walk toward the dock near the resort.

Chapter 71

Drew

I'm once again transfixed by the light glowing on Lexa's face. I'm so glad we made it out on the water before the sun rose. The gorgeous early morning rays are dancing across the water and reflecting onto Lexa. It looks like she's some mystical sun goddess, being lit from within. As that thought crosses my mind, the goddess herself turns her attention on me. Her smile is somehow brighter and more magnificent than this sunrise. I don't take my eyes off of her as I take the few steps to close the distance between us.

"You look like a sun goddess," I say, reaching out to touch her. As my hand reaches her arm, she shivers but her smile grows impossibly brighter.

"I don't think a sun goddess would require so much protection from its rays," she says with a laugh. She steps away from me only momentarily to bend and reach into her bag. As soon as she stands, she takes the step back to me. I see she has a bottle of sunscreen in her hands. "Think you could get the top of my back?" she says, brushing her beautiful auburn hair over her shoulder and exposing her delicate shoulder blades.

"Of course, I'd be honored," I respond, taking the bottle from her hand to squirt a dollop into mine. I warm it with my hands for a second before placing my palms over her bare skin and feeling the deceptive amount of muscle underneath the surface. I spend longer than I have to rubbing the lotion onto her, but she seems to be enjoying the pressure I'm applying. She's so tight in her shoulders and if I can give her a moment of relief, then I'd do this all day.

"Ugh, this feels so good. I've always held so much tension in my shoulders. But don't let those hands get too worn out, this is going to be an all day process," she says, turning to me to ask for the lotion bottle back.

Leaning down so that I'm close to her ear, I whisper, "Oh I could go all day, don't you worry." I pull back in enough time to watch that delicious blush steal over her cheeks.

She won't meet my eyes as she says, "Well thanks. I'll come find you when I need more sun protection." She smiles up at me and finally meets my eyes. Hers are such a fiery and bright shade of green right now, it steals my breath away.

We stand there leaning against the balcony and alternatively staring at each other and at the ocean view as we cruise out to the area we'll be diving at today.

Our peace is interrupted by the loudest gag I've ever heard. I turn to see Amanda holding her hand to her mouth, face green and puffy. *Oh no, she's going to barf.* Amanda rushes over to the other side of the boat and promptly empties her stomach into the surf. I look to Lexa before realizing she's probably too used to this kind of thing to feel squeamish about it. Lexa is looking at Ansley and they're having some sort of silent eye conversation before both click into action. Lexa goes to Amanda and Ansley goes to the cooler to grab her a water. They settle her onto the cushion directly in front of the captain's area, looking straight out over the water and where the rocking doesn't feel so bad.

I glance around at the rest of our group, not knowing who might have a weak stomach or if someone is a sympathetic vomiter. Just then, I see Patrick and Weston running to the rail, too. I make my way to the cooler to grab some water and check on them.

"I didn't know y'all got seasick," I say, handing Patrick a water bottle as Weston continues to hang over the edge of the boat.

Patrick gulps the water a few times before saying, "I don't usually. My stomach was feeling kinda iffy this morning. Maybe the drinks were a little stronger last night than I thought. Thanks for this," he says, holding up his half empty bottle.

I nod and turn back to the rest of the boat. Lexa is watching me like a hawk, probably wondering if I'm next. I smile at her and just shake my head. Well that's almost half the group down. I'm sure they'll feel better once we get in the water.

The three vomiteers were rallied with the water it seems. I watch as Amanda and Grace join Patrick and Weston to put on their gear for snorkeling. Jackson and Claire are talking on the bench at the front of the boat and Lexa is standing by Ansley and Landon. I walk over to that group so I can put on my fins and mask. "It's pretty ironic that there were three people that get seasick who decided to join us on a boat this morning, huh?" I ask as Ansley hands me my mask.

"I don't know, I've been on a boat smaller than this with Amanda and Wes before and they were fine," she says, handing Landon a pair of fins.

"Well I heard Pat say he wasn't feeling too hot before getting on the boat. Maybe he ate something weird at the airport yesterday," Lexa says, shrugging.

"Yeah, maybe. Didn't y'all say there was a stomach flu going around the hospital last week?" Landon asks the girls.

"Oh yeah, there were several people who had to call out last week. But we'll be fine. Immunity of the gods, right Ans?" Lexa asks, grinning and laughing.

"Right, Lex. I honestly don't remember the last time I caught something from work."

"Well…babe the last time you got sick, you actually caught it from me while you were off. So I guess let's just hope I don't get it," Landon says, reaching to pull Ansley into a hug.

With that, we waddle our way to the back of the boat to get into the water. Our captain is staying with the ship, but they have an instructor that will be showing us around. As I try my best to pay attention to the safety demonstration, I keep catching movement from the corner of my eye. Lexa can't stay still. She looks like a kid of Christmas, hopping from fin to fin.

I lean over towards her and whisper, "Hey calm down, your movement is going to attract the sharks."

She slaps my arm but leans into me, "Shut up, I'm just excited to snorkel for the first time and this honestly seems like the perfect place for a first time."

I look back out of the crystal clear water and take in the beauty of the reefs just under the surface. There's millions of fish and other marine life just going about their days. It's captivating from the boat, so I can't even imagine how amazing it will be in the water. I turn back to Lexa and offer a sweet smile and I'm graced with one in return.

"Okay guys, remember to stay with the group! Keep a member of your party within sight at all times. We don't want anyone swimming off," our instructor is saying when I finally tune back in. "And what's the most important rule?" he asks, looking around the group.

"Don't touch the coral!" several people shout in unison. *Oh good,* I think, *I actually already knew that rule.*

We're led off the edge and into the water. I see Ansley and Landon splashing in first, followed by Jackson and Claire. The rest of us file behind and hop in. The water feels amazing and I'm tempted to just float on my back for a second, soaking in the sun when I remember how fantastic the view below is. I fit my snorkel into place and flip over, immediately greeted by a world beyond imagination. I've snorkeled before, but never in a place like this. The water is so clear you can see the ocean floor and every bit of life thriving in their element. As I paddle around lazily, trying to keep a member of our party in sight, I see colors I've never seen before. The fish are even brighter than they are in the aquariums and the coral is home to so many different species.

I spend close to an hour in wondrous awe of the teeming life under the sea before I even try to make my way back to the group. When I surface, I notice they're all crowded in one area. I swim that way and see everyone's heads in the water, staring straight down. I refit my snorkel into my mouth and have a look. Below our group is a huge turtle. Bigger than me and swimming along like it hasn't a care in the world. I look to my left underwater and see Lexa and Ansley holding hands and pointing. I am so glad they're getting to have these kinds of experiences together. This is honestly magical.

Eventually, our new turtle friend tires of being a spectacle and swims away and we all surface in a pod.

"Oh my God. This is just amazing," Ansley says, face lit up with wonder.

"It really is. I'm so happy to be here with all of you and doing something so great," Weston says.

"What a sap," Patrick says with a laugh, before continuing on to say, "but I second that."

"Aw, how sweet of you," Claire says, splashing Patrick gently in the face.

"Well it looks like the rest of the tour is heading back to the boat. I believe that means it's time for drinks and lunch, correct? And preferably in that order," Jackson says.

The boat has a bar onboard but they don't serve anything until you have the excursion. I would assume it has something to do with people not getting so drunk they can't snorkel.

"Oof, I think I may have had a bit much last night. My stomach is starting to feel a little uneasy, too," Grace says.

"Hair of the dog and all that, right?" Jackson says.

"Is having a drink called a Painkiller really the best option at 10 a.m.?" Claire asks.

"We won't know until we try," Lexa replies. Everyone laughs a bit as we clamber back on board, fins in hand.

We're all one painkiller in by the time the boat docks for lunch. And one is probably enough. That is the strongest drink I have ever tasted in my life. The rum they make on this island is not for the faint of heart.

We all feel a bit tipsy as we climb over the boat railing and onto the dock. We're at a really cool lunch spot that's almost on its own island. You can get here from one road as long as it's not raining, but otherwise it's boat traffic only. Once our party has fully disembarked, we head to the restaurant. There's plenty of shade to sit in while eating and I'm starving. After placing our orders, we amble over towards a large table set underneath a sprawling mangrove.

We each have a beer and a water, for hydration of course. I raise mine to the group and say, "To the couple that brought us all together and the friendships that have brought us here." Everyone clinks their glasses together and I see smiles all around. These are some of the best friends I've ever had, that's for sure. And my sweet sister is the catalyst that brought us all together.

Chapter 72

Lexa

While we're eating, I've noticed that a few people aren't really touching their food. Wes and Pat are eating, which is good. But Amanda and Grace are barely nibbling. I look around again and notice that Jackson has a certain green sheen to his face that wasn't there before. I glance at Claire, but she's already turned to him to ask what's wrong.

"Are you feeling bad?" I ask quietly, not wanting to draw too much attention. Before he can answer me though, Jackson has pushed away from the table and ran to the far edge of the tree where the roots are in the water. Whatever he just ate is no longer in his stomach. With that, I turn to see Amanda and Grace getting that look on their face. And Weston and Patrick have suddenly put down their fish tacos and pushed away from the table as well.

"Oh no," I start, turning to Ansley. But she's staring at Landon, whose face is lit with a green glow, sweat pouring from his forehead. *Oh no, not Landon.*

Before I can even think of how to stop this, they are all at the water's edge with Jackson. I slump in my seat, trying to sort out my own body, determining if I feel sick. I would think it was something we had last night but we ate family style and all shared food. It has to be that stomach bug.

I lift my head, catching Drew's eye. He looks cool, calm and collected. A normal color and not sweating profusely. All good signs. I turn toward Claire, she looks fine, other than her worry for Jackson. And then Ansley. Not sickly but horrified.

"Hey, Ans. It's gonna be okay. I'm sure everyone will feel better tomorrow. We already did all the fun stuff we had planned today anyway," I say, scooting down the bench to comfort my friend.

"Of course, yeah. I just feel…responsible somehow," she says quietly, so that only I can hear.

"Ansley, look at me," I say and wait for her to lift her head. Once she does, I continue, "This is in no way your fault. You didn't cause this and you couldn't have prevented it. These things happen."

"You're right, I know. I know," she blows out a breath and looks toward Landon, who is now sitting on the ground by the shore. The whole group of them just look drained all of a sudden. "Let's get everyone back on the boat and the sooner we can get them to their rooms, the sooner they can start recuperating."

"That's the spirit," I say. I can't help but think of my coworkers that called in sick with this same virus last week. They said it lasted for several days.

Chapter 73

Lexa

Once we have everyone back on dry land, Ansley and I help get water, washcloths and buckets for the infirm. We make sure that Claire doesn't need any help with Jackson and then we get Grace and Amanda settled in.

"You go ahead and get back to Landon. I'll go check on Wes and Patrick," I say, pulling my friend into a tight embrace. "Watch yourself and wash your hands. I don't need you getting sick, too."

"Yes ma'am," Ansley replies, hugging me back fiercely. "Same to you."

We part at the fork between their bungalows and I walk down the boardwalk to Patrick and Weston's place. As I'm raising my hand to knock and make sure they're decent, the door swings open. Drew is standing in the doorway but he's facing into the room.

"Guys, I'm serious. If y'all need literally anything, just call me. Or text me. But I'll be here. I feel fine and I'm not about to not take care of you," he says with a stern tone. He looks pretty good giving orders, I'll have to give him that. I don't tear my gaze away from his face quick enough before he turns to leave and almost runs me over. He stops dead in the doorway and stares at me for a full minute before saying quietly, "What are you doing here?"

Matching his volume, I whisper, "Checking on my friends, is that not allowed?"

He just shakes his head and smiles at me before throwing over his shoulder, "And Lex is here to check on y'all but I'm not letting her in since you're naked. But she says she loves you both."

I smile and just stare up at him. "Are you going to move so I can close the door?" he asks.

Shit. I'm such an idiot. I stumble backwards too quickly and trip over the step. I feel my feet leave the ground one second, and the next I'm pressed against a hard chest and wrapped in warm muscular arms.

"Are you trying to hurt yourself so that I have to take care of you, too?" Drew asks, much closer to my face this time.

I'm breathless, whether from the near fall or his sudden proximity, I can't tell. I huff out a laugh and say, "I just can't help falling for you." I give my best doe eyes and bat my eyelashes several times before Drew finally–regretfully–returns me to my standing position and releases me. We walk back towards our rooms in comfortable silence until we get to our intersection.

"Well," I say, looking him fully in the eyes, "I guess we might not have very many dinner companions tonight."

He laughs before replying, "You're probably right, but that shouldn't stop us from eating."

"Very true. But not before a nap. That sun drained me today."

"Same. Okay so naps, then dinner? Sounds like a perfect plan to me. I'll meet you here around 6?" he asks.

"Sounds great," I say, giving him my megawatt smile before turning to head to my villa. I don't hear his footsteps and when I turn around, he's still standing in the same spot, just smiling at me. I feel the heat rise on my cheeks but I keep walking, telling myself I need a shower and a nap before any other decisions can be made today.

Chapter 74

Lexa

I wake to the sound of Juice Newton singing "Angel of the Morning" to the room. I stare at the ceiling for a moment, getting my bearings. It always takes me a second to fully come out of a midday nap. Rolling onto my side, I reach for my phone to silence the alarm. Once the music is no longer playing, I can hear the sound of the waves lapping against the shore by my room. It's incredibly relaxing and it takes a herculean effort to not fall back asleep. Instead, I toggle to my messages, seeing that I have one from Ansley and one from Claire in our group chat for the trip.

Ansley wrote, *Hey guys, y'all are gonna have to do dinner without us. Landon is still bad and I'm starting to feel a little symptomatic as well.*

Yeah, Jackson is just now starting to fall asleep so I'm going to stay here with him, Claire said.

I type back to them both, *Oh no guys! I'm so sorry to hear that. Let me know if y'all need anything. Claire, do you want me to bring you some food?*

I decide I might as well get up and start getting ready since I'm meeting Drew in 30 minutes. I check my phone just to make sure Claire hasn't already texted me back. I turn my ringer on in case any of them try to call me while I'm getting dressed and trying to decide what to do with my hair. It didn't really dry all the way since I fell asleep with it wet and it looks like a rat's nest.

I stare at my reflection in the mirror, noting the new freckles that have sprung up since we've been here. Just a little time in the sun brings them out. Curses of being a redhead, I guess. But the slight amount of sun has also soaked into my skin a bit, giving me a healthy glow. I smile at myself, and enjoy the way my eyes crinkle at the corners with a real smile. I don't mind the crows feet I'm already collecting if it's from smiling too often. It's a good problem to have. "You are beautiful and worthy," I say out loud to myself. Positive self-talk is so important for good mental health. With that in mind, I reach to the side of the sink and pull my cleanser out of my toiletries bag. I like to compliment myself while cleaning my face of any amount of makeup I'm wearing. It really has helped me to not feel like I have to cover my imperfections.

I clean my face, scrubbing in the cleanser and repeat my mantra a few times. "You are worthy, you are kind and you are smart. You are beautiful, you are a good friend and you are clever. You are worthy," I say to myself as I scrub. Washing off the bubbles, I smile at my reflection again.

My eyes drift to my hair, causing me to laugh. It's worse than I thought. I grab my comb and start working out the tangles. My curls are out in full force with this humidity and the salt water that it's been soaking in. I use the comb to pull the front of my hair away from my face and grab a small claw clip to hold it back. I'll leave it the rest of the way down for now. I pop a ponytail holder onto my wrist, just in case.

Now, onto the outfit. It's just an informal dinner with Drew, so it's not like I have to get too dressed up. I still reach for a dress in the closet, a casual dress. I hold the cream-colored shift against myself, testing the look. It looks nice with my new tan, so I slip it off the hanger and over my head. I glance at my phone, no new messages. And I have 5 minutes until I need to meet up with Drew. I head back to the bathroom and search through my cosmetic bag until I find the peach lip gloss I was searching for. I apply it with a flourish and smack my lips together a few times to make sure there's proper coverage. I give myself another smile in the mirror.

A knock at the door startles me from my thoughts. I look at the time, I still have 2 minutes, I guess Drew just got impatient. I chuckle as I walk to the door. Sure enough, I can make out Drew's outline in the tempered glass of the window.

I open the door with a smile on my face. I try to say hello, but I'm instantly breathless from the sight of him. He's wearing blue shorts with a white button up, sleeves rolled to his elbows showing off beautifully tanned and toned forearms. His shirt is unbuttoned enough to see his chiseled chest and I can't stop my eyes from tracking down his body to see what else is exposed. His shorts are short enough for me to get a glimpse of his very muscular thighs and I'm on the verge of salivating.

"Hey beautiful," Drew says, leaning down to catch my eyes.

I rip them away from checking him out with a blush

coloring my cheeks. As I do, I'm distracted again by the gorgeous smile stretching his very kissable lips. This man is undoing me without even trying. I don't think it's fair to the human race for him to be this good-looking. When I'm finally able to look him in the eyes, I see the smile reflected in the depths of his ocean blues.

"Well hi," I say, still somewhat breathless. "I thought we were meeting in a few minutes."

"To be honest, I was tired of waiting. I was ready to see you again," he says, his smile morphing into a seductive smirk.

"Oh yeah? Well here I am. Are you ready for dinner?" I ask, trying to decide what to do with my hands. I settle on dropping them in front of me and grabbing my wrist with the other hand. This effectively binds me from reaching out to run my hands over the magnificent man standing in front of me.

Drew's tongue darts out to wet his lips and my eyes track the movement. He laughs before replying, "Well I actually already went and picked up food for us. I thought we might have a picnic on the beach?"

My eyes fly back up to his, searching. There's so much heat behind his gaze, it's melting me.

"Yes," is all I can get out in response.

Drew reaches out his hand, grabbing mine and taking it away from its secure position on my wrist. He smiles down at me again before pulling me to him and folding me into a hug. He releases me way too soon, but keeps hold of my hand.

"Off we go then," Drew says, pulling me along like a lovesick puppy.

Chapter 75

Drew

We walk along the boardwalk in silence, but I can feel the nervous energy pouring off of her. I know I'm not helping, I can't seem to keep it together around her this week. All of my plans to play it cool and try to be her friend first again have blown up in my face. She's incredible and now that I know how she feels pressed against me, I can't keep my mind off of her when I'm not with her.

As we reach the sand, I step to the side and grab the basket of food I had stashed on the steps. Just as I'm about to lead her out onto the sand, she suddenly stops, pulling me back by the hand.

"Oh, I left my phone in the room and I was waiting for Claire to text me back about bringing her food!" she says, obviously feeling guilty that she forgot.

"I already dropped food off for her. Jackson was asleep but he looked pretty sick still," I reply, not letting go of her hand. I don't want to lose any of the proximity I've been given now.

"Oh. That's so…so sweet Drew. And thoughtful."

"You sound shocked," I say with a chuckle, but I'm a little surprised by that reaction. Does she not think of me as a thoughtful person?

"No, I just forget how great you are sometimes. I get too used to other guys and how they act when you're not around to remind me there are good men in this world," she says, meeting my eyes and squeezing my hand.

Oh. "Well maybe I could be around more often…to remind you."

"I'd like that," she smiles so brightly I'm blinded for a moment. I shake my head, trying to remember what we were doing. Oh right, food, eating, catching a sunset.

I use her hand to pull her to me again, this time wrapping my arms around her lower back and pressing a kiss to the top of her head. She giggles and snuggles into my embrace a bit before pulling back to look into my eyes. Her eyes stay on mine for a while until she's distracted by something behind my head.

"Oh! The sun is going to set soon! It's going to be wonderful to watch it out here!" she says, almost bouncing with excitement.

"That was the plan," I say, smiling and leading her to a blanket I had placed out here before coming to get her. I motion for her to sit and I watch in fascination as she dusts off both feet before gracefully sinking down onto one side of the blanket, smoothing her dress out under her.

I set the basket down and kneel on the blanket. I pull out two glasses and a bottle of wine. I pour hers and hand it over, giving her a wink as I meet her eyes. After filling my glass and setting it to the side, I begin to unload the food. From the restaurant down the way, I got some cheddar biscuits, grilled salmon and asparagus. I stopped by the small store on the resort property to gather some grapes and strawberries. I leave the fruit in the basket for now, that will be our dessert.

As I lay out the fish and sides from the restaurant, Lexa groans. A noise that sends signals straight to my groin. I sit still for a moment, soaking in that unexpected reaction. I blink a few times and take a deep breath. When I look up and into Lexa's eyes, I can see heat there that wasn't there before. What does that mean? Can she read what she's doing to me and my body?

"Drew," she starts, staring straight into my soul, "I need to tell you…"

"Shh, let's eat first and then we have all night to talk, yeah?" I say, not ready for this moment to end and I'm too scared that's where Lexa's thoughts are heading.

Lexa smiles at me a bit sheepishly, but nods. "Okay, sure. Let's eat and enjoy the sunset then."

I smile back, trying my best for one of reassurance. It's kinda sad, how I'm trying to prolong a picnic just to keep Lexa with me for as long as possible. I'm scared that once we are actually sitting down to talk, she's going to be telling me all of the reasons this won't work out. I'm not going to force her into a relationship she's not ready to try. But God, if she is willing, I will not quit until I make her mine.

Chapter 76

Lexa

I'm not sure why Drew stopped me from speaking earlier, but now I'm glad he did. I would have probably embarrassed myself by professing my undying love for him when he's just here for dinner. I still don't know if I'm reading the signals correctly, and I'm so scared to possibly find out that he's not ready to really give us a try. Long distance sucks but we can make it work. As many reasons as there are to not try, I have about a million reasons that we have to.

I don't know that I can continue to just live my life without the warmth, energy and love that Drew brings to the world. I don't want to.

My thoughts have started running away from me, but I'm jerked back to the now by a large and warm hand settling on my thigh.

"Hey there astronaut, want to join us back on Earth?" Drew asks, one hand on my leg and the other bracketing my hip closest to him. This position effectively has him hovering just in front of my face. I can't help the impulsive move that I make next. I lean forward and let my lips touch his. Not so much of a kiss as just a brush of our mouths, but for one sweet moment, I'm blazing with an internal fire. I pull back almost instantaneously, just to meet Drew's blown pupil stare. His quick puffs of breath make me realize I'm near-panting just from that small amount of contact. My skin feels overheated and my brain feels fuzzy, but I can't seem to back away from Drew and put any of the needed space between us.

I open my mouth to apologize when his hand leaves my thigh and thrusts into the bottom of my hair, gripping and pulling my face back to him. I close my eyes, unable to believe the scene unfolding in front of me. I feel the velvet soft touch of his lips on mine before I feel him shift his weight from his arm, bringing his body closer to mine. His free hand finds my cheek and he softly caresses me as his lips continue to explore mine. I can't help the small whimper that escapes my throat but it seems to do something to Drew. Suddenly, the soft touches are gone, replaced by hungry pulls of lips, with his teeth sinking into my bottom one. His hands are moving down my back, drawing me even closer as he carries on with the assault to my mouth. His tongue is now running along the seam of my lips, seeking entrance which I immediately grant. As his tongue drags across mine, he gently lowers me fully onto the blanket.

I'm gasping as he pulls away from me to look at me. There's a look of uncertainty on his face as he tries to read my thoughts. Whatever he sees on my face, he must take as approval. Within seconds, he's laid himself out over me, holding most of his weight on his forearms. His mouth is blessedly back on mine while my hands roam his broad back and shoulders before finally sinking into his soft hair. His mouth starts to move away from mine, to my jaw and then to my neck. He's licking and sucking gently and kissing me in that spot that drives me absolutely crazy. Before I know it, I have handfuls of his hair, dragging him inexorably closer still. I moan, causing a reciprocal reaction from Drew. The delicious sound that comes from him ignites a sudden unquenchable fire in my lower belly.

I release his hair to move my hands to the buttons of his shirt. I need it off now. I need his skin on mine, not all these clothes.

"Lexa," he groans, releasing my neck and moving to my exposed collarbones.

And then the sky opens up. I hear a loud crack of thunder and we're suddenly being drenched in a warm tropical rain.

I squeal and squirm as Drew hops up and starts to grab our food. I grab the wine bottle and the glasses that are both thankfully empty and once the food is up, I scoop up the blanket. We take off running towards the villas, both laughing like maniacs and not even able to cover ourselves. Not that it would matter, it's really coming down now. Drew rushes into his bungalow, holding the door open for me to run through. Once I'm under cover, I shake off some of the water and set my items down on the nearest surface.

The laughter on my lips dies as I turn and see Drew, shirt open and soaking wet. It's plastered to his body like a second skin. There are raindrops racing down his abs, towards his shorts that I am more than ready to rip off his body. The heat in the room is nearly suffocating as my gaze tracks over his sculpted chest to meet his eyes. His ocean blue eyes that are melting the clothes right off of my body. I barely have time to take a breath before his hands are on me, fast-paced but gentle movements slipping my wet dress from my body. As the fabric slides over the swells of my breasts, I hear Drew gasp when he realizes I'm not wearing a bra. He falls to his knees, attempting to free my hips from the clinging material. He works the linen over my thighs and down to puddle at my feet. He doesn't rise from his knees, but offers me a hand to help me step out of the dress on the floor. His eyes are on mine, searing into my gaze, warming me despite the chill racing across my bare skin.

Drew presses soft kisses to the inside of my thighs, trailing them up and over my right hip as his hand grips my ass hard on that side. His other hand slides to my hip as he nips my skin with his teeth, pulling a startled whimper from me.

Drew starts to stand, placing kisses across my abdomen, hands never leaving my hips. The feel of his lips on my skin is like heaven. His barely-there stubble scratching in perfect contrast to the softness of his lips. Losing myself in the sensation, I'm shocked when his lips leave my skin. My eyes fly open, searching for where his amazing mouth went. Drew is smiling at me broadly as he rises to his full height, taking me into the air with him. I squeal as I'm lifted into his arms as if I'm feather-light. I smile back, meeting his lust-glazed gaze.

"I want this off," I say, pushing his shirt over his shoulders and letting it hang on his arms. I drop my mouth to his bare shoulders, worshiping his skin like it's the only sustenance I'll ever need. I lick the rain from his chest, pulling another fierce groan from him.

"All in good time, baby. We'll never make it to a soft surface with your mouth on me like that," Drew husks out.

"Soft surface?" I ask, pulling my mouth away from nibbling at his neck.

"Honey, I'm not taking you for the first time on the floor. I've been dreaming about this day since the moment you walked into my dorm room. This is going to be a marathon, not a sprint so we might as well be comfortable."

Good God, this man is about to wreck me and he's barely touched me.

Chapter 77

Lexa

Comfortable is not the first thought running through my head as I'm lightly dropped onto Drew's bed. More like *hell yes* or *why is he still clothed?* He begins to take care of the second thought by pulling off his skin tight shirt, first down one arm and then the other. A torturous grin stretching his lips. Oh he's going to play it that way, huh?

I take control from him by sitting up and tucking my feet under my ass, getting myself onto my knees. I let him settle his eyes on my exposed chest before I drop onto my hands and begin to crawl the length of the bed towards him. He's breathing hard, fingers still gripping his discarded shirt. As I reach the end of the bed, I thrust my hands out, looping my fingers into his waistband. I tug him towards me and let his off-balance stance help me pull him onto the bed beside me. I rip the shirt from his hands and straddle his hips. With no hesitation, I lean down and press our chests together, crashing my mouth onto his. I steal his breath for the next several moments, enjoying the feel of his heartbeat thrashing against his chest. He's definitely just as affected by this as I am.

I pull back and watch in fascination as his head falls back against the comforter, his breathing ragged. His hooded eyes watch me as I edge backwards slightly, hands on his shorts. I need these wet things off. Then we'll at least be on more equal footing, both just in our underwear.

"Off now," I demand, pulling the wet material over his muscular thighs.

"Yes ma'am," Drew says, scooting up the bed to help the shorts come off.

Once he's only in his *very* form fitting briefs, I sit back on my heels and admire the most beautiful man I have ever seen.

"What are you looking at?" he asks, his lip quirking up in embarrassment.

"Oh, just the man of my dreams," I say, not letting the words settle before my mouth is back to exploring his body. My lips run over his muscled abdomen and I nibble slightly at the waistband of his briefs before I'm being hauled up his body by my waist.

"Oh no, me first. I insist," Drew says, tossing me onto my back. I don't even argue as he trails hot kisses from my mouth, to my throat to my chest. He cups my right breast in his hand, thumb toying with the nipple as he takes my left in his mouth. He sucks and swirls as all thought leaves my brain. I have only one focus in life now and it is the inexplicable pleasure Drew is wringing from me.

His hand leaves my breast and flattens across my stomach for a moment as he switches his mouth to my right. His hand then continues its exploration down my body, lightly tugging my lace underwear down. His silent urging has me lifting my hips, letting him strip me bare. He tosses my panties aside and brings his hand back to its original destination. He fills and stretches me, using his thumb to circle that tight bundle of nerves before releasing my nipple with an audible pop of his lips. Then his mouth is on me again, this time licking and laving in time with his fingers. I'm pulled to the edge and then shoved over with one more touch of his thumb. I shout his name and tremble around him. I can feel him smiling against me before he licks one more time.

"I like hearing my name fall off of your lips like that. Full of satisfaction," Drew says, leaning down to put us face to face. I struggle momentarily to get his briefs off of his hips, but he leans back to take care of the rest. I can still hear the rain drumming against the roof and the windows. But all at once, every sense beyond what I can feel is blacked out as Drew enters me for the first time. *Absolute bliss.*

Chapter 78

Drew

Thursday

I'm so thankful we still had that food from the picnic. After round 3 we were both ravenously hungry and could no longer ignore the other needs of our body. We poured some more wine and grabbed some water bottles to take back to bed with us. We had a naked picnic on the comforter–now one of my most favorite memories. We fell back into bed, exhausted but quite sated.

I drag my eyes open, finally ready to face the day, hoping it wasn't all a dream. The first thing I see is a spread of auburn hair over the pillow next to me. My gaze drops to the soft skin of Lexa's shoulder and finally down the curve of her tightly muscled back. I can't help but watch the gentle rise and fall of her breaths, but I can't control the movement of my hands either. She's so at peace, and I hate to wake her, but I need to touch her.

I let my hand rest on her back, trying to let her get the

sleep I know she needs. But as soon as she feels my touch, she wakes and turns toward me with a sleepy smile on her face.

My God, she's gorgeous.

"Sorry baby, I didn't mean to wake you," I whisper, brushing her hair back and tucking it behind her ear.

She smiles but I can see a hint of embarrassment in it when she says, "You should be. I was having this great dream."

"Oh? What was your dream about?" I ask, unable to control the smile taking over my face.

"Well you were there and I was there and we were…actually you know what? I think it might have actually happened." She laughs at her own joke, causing me to laugh right along with her.

"Do you need some assistance remembering whether it was real life or not? I don't mind helping with that," I say, winking wolfishly.

Her face heats with a beautiful blush as she bites into her kiss swollen bottom lip.

"Maybe after some breakfast. I'm absolutely starving," she says, letting her full smile free.

"We did burn some calories last night, that's for sure. Let's see what's stocked in the kitchen," I say, patting her butt for good measure as I move to get up.

I turn back to look at her a moment and see her gaze on my naked body. "After some food," I promise, with another wink.

Crimson spreads from her cheeks to her neck when she realizes I caught her devouring me with her eyes. She tracks her gaze back up my body, lingering on my chest before finally finding my eyes. Her jade green eyes are heated to an inferno and her pupils are blown so wide they have almost taken over her irises. "Don't look at me like that or we're never eating again. Food that is," I say, earning a dark chuckle from her. This woman will be my undoing, I swear.

I finally make it to the kitchenette and pull open the fridge to see what the resort stocked us with. "Eggs? Bacon? What are you feeling?" I ask in the direction of the bedroom.

"Whatever's quickest," I hear from just behind my shoulder before I feel a pair of warm hands wrap around my torso. I turn and see Lexa there, in my t-shirt with her just-had-sex-hair flowing down over her shoulders.

"Cereal it is," I laugh, gathering her into my arms and planting a kiss on the top of her head. I spin her until her back is against the counter, then pluck her up off the floor and place her ass firmly on the granite.

I use my position between her legs to reach for the bowls above her, the cereal box behind her and finally stretch over to the fridge for the almond milk, making my already awake crotch come into contact with her heated core. I groan, sending a shiver down Lexa's body before I back up just an inch to give us room to breathe. I was serious about us eating before we engaged in more fun activities. We will be drained at this rate.

Lexa chuckles, but lets me back away, reaching over to grab her bowl and dump in the cereal. As she adds her milk, I spread her legs further apart. I reach in between her thighs and her breath hitches, but comes out in a laugh as she realizes I'm just opening the silverware drawer under her.

"A little tightly wound this morning, dear?" I ask, letting my hands skim back up her thighs and nestling myself back in her embrace. "Need to find some release?"

"Oh no you don't. You said food first," she says, taking a big bite of cereal.

"Right, and you're eating," I reply, letting my gaze fall to the apex of her thighs. My hands follow my eyes, spreading her legs back out to allow access. "Now I'll have my breakfast, too."

"Oh my God. You did not just say that," Lexa says, on a breathless whisper.

Chapter 79

Lexa

I throw my head back with no thought of the cabinets behind me as Drew's mouth closes over me. His tongue is driving me wild as his hands knead deeper into my thighs, baring me to him.

I'm moaning and grabbing his hair in my hands. All thoughts of breakfast cast aside. He pushes me to the edge so fast, almost painfully fast. I'm panting, closer and closer to the precipice when a loud knock on the door shakes the villa.

"Oh shit," Drew and I whisper in unison, staring wildly into each other's eyes.

"Were you expecting someone this morning?" I ask, hands on Drew's shoulders as he quickly scoops me off the counter and sets me onto my feet.

"No, shit. I bet it's Ansley. Checking on me since everyone else is sick. Shit, shit shit," Drew curses under his breath as he hustles around trying to find a pair of pants. I would laugh if I wasn't terrified.

I cannot let Ansley see me standing here in Drew's room, in just his t-shirt, hair messed up with flushed skin. I scamper towards his bed, which is thankfully blocked from the front door. But if she walks anywhere into the villa, she will see me. Or my clothes scattered around, *shit.* I pick up what I can as I run towards the corner of the bedroom that is hidden. I pass the bathroom and decide that's an even better option. With one last look at Drew, I wave and disappear into the bathroom and close and lock the door. I put my ear up to the thin door, hoping I'll still be able to hear through it. If I can slow my heart rate enough that it's not beating through my chest, that is.

"Good morning, big bro. Just came by to check and see how you're feeling this morning," Ansley says, a smile evident in her voice.

"Oh thanks, yeah I'm great. How are you feeling? Get any sleep last night?" Drew asks and I can hear the stress in his tone. I hope Ansley can't.

"You look a little flushed. I hope you're not popping a fever. You don't feel nauseous or anything? Have you eaten breakfast yet?"

I hear the stutter and the choked laughter from Drew before he finally replies, "Just a light one, but yes I feel fine. I just got a little overheated in my sleep last night I think. I forgot to turn the air conditioner on when I got in."

I'm shaking with barely contained laughter, Drew is killing me slowly. Thankfully, I'm able to keep silent.

"Alright," Ansley hesitantly begins, "well if you do start feeling cruddy, let me know."

"You'll be the first person I call," Drew promises. "You take it easy today and tell Landon I hope he starts feeling better soon."

"Will do. Oh, by the way, have you talked to Lexa this morning? I tried calling her but her phone is going straight to voicemail and she didn't answer her door."

"Oh. No. I haven't. I haven't seen her since yesterday. Um, did you try the beach? Maybe she went to catch a sunrise?" Drew lies, but not very convincingly.

Ansley must buy it though because I hear her mutter something about checking there next and then she's saying goodbye. I hear the door shut and the lock turn a second before there's a soft knock at the bathroom door.

"What's the password?" I whisper, giggling.

"Cereal?" Drew guesses.

I open the door a crack, just enough to see his ocean blue eyes and his brilliant smile. "Wrong, but I can't stay in here any longer."

Drew gently pushes the door open and I step back with a smile on my face. "Well that was weird," I say.

"Extremely," Drew replies. "I felt like a teenager being caught by my mom." He laughs nervously, but reaches for me. I step into his arms and let myself relish the heat from his bare chest.

I hug Drew to me, squeezing one last time before pulling back to look at his face. He looks contemplative and still a bit on edge. "You okay?" I ask, "Regretting last night already?"

"Hell no," he growls out, crushing me back to him. "You never have to ask me that. I loved every minute of it."

I smile, appreciating his quick response. "Me too, baby," I reply. "But I do think I should head back to my place, get ready for the day. At least shower." I shrug at the last part, pulling a laugh from Drew.

"I can clean you up real good," he says, running his tongue over his lips.

"And with that, I am officially out of here." I pull away and try to run from Drew, but he catches me from behind, hands wrapping around my stomach. He presses a kiss to my neck, making me groan.

"We probably do need to get ready for whatever today's activities are. Do you remember what we're supposed to do today?" Drew asks, still hugging me to his front.

"No and I don't have my phone to check, either. I need to go home," I say. Though, there's not enough heat behind my words to convince even myself.

"Well my phone is right there. I'm going to release you, you better not run again," Drew says, pinning me with a hard stare.

"Yes sir," I simper.

"God bless, woman. You will be the death of me," he groans as he releases me and stalks toward the night stand where his phone is charging.

Drew pulls up the itinerary, scrolls a bit and then starts laughing.

"What?" I ask, walking to him and trying to catch a glance of the screen.

"Jet skis. I doubt any of the infirm will be out there, it could be just us. Let me text Ansley real quick," he says, still smiling.

"I'm gonna head back and get ready then. Text me when you find out where we're meeting!" I say, picking up my clothes from the floor and trying to hunt down my shoes.

"Will do!" Drew says, looking up from his text thread to shoot me a dazzling smile. I blush automatically and then roll my eyes at myself. Will that ever stop?

I finally locate my shoes, right beside the door. Exactly where Ansley was standing when she was talking to Drew. There's no way she didn't notice my sandals sitting there. Would she recognize them? *Oh Lord.*

Chapter 80

Lexa

I take my time getting ready for our day on the jet skis. According to the text I got from Drew, we don't have to meet up until 9:45. I need some time to decompress from last night's events.

When I got back to my room, I had 10 texts and 3 missed calls from Ansley before my phone died. I texted her back and apologized, claiming I forgot to throw it on the charger before I crashed last night. She let me off the hook, as I knew she would. I hate lying to her, but for right now it's the best option. Drew and I haven't even talked about what this means.

We went from hanging out with the intention of reacquainting ourselves with each other to learning every part of the other's anatomy. Not that I regret last night in the slightest. I just need some clarification on what this signifies. Obviously some major change in our relationship, but what kind of change? Are we friends with benefits? Just a fling for the trip? Something more? God, I'm hoping for something more. As much as I haven't wanted to admit it, I am craving something so much more with Drew. I want more than just his body. I want his mind, heart and soul. I want everything with Drew.

Hence, the long ass shower I am currently taking. I need to collect my thoughts before I spill something that big into a normal conversation with him. There's a decent chance of that happening today. The adventure for this morning will just be the two of us. The sickies are on the mend but they still aren't up to jumping waves and going fast. Which I know will be mine and Drew's main objectives. We have an hour of playing on the jet skis and I can't wait. I know we're going to have fun, we always have fun together.

Having fun together now includes sex, I remind myself. Of course, this makes me blush, again. Just thinking about the last 12 hours gets me hot, leading me to turn the shower water cold. Once I'm properly chastened and shivering, I shut the shower spray off and step out to towel dry.

I catch sight of myself in the mirror and grin at the obvious glow I'm radiating. If Ansley sees me today, she is going to know immediately. If she doesn't already…I know she had to have seen my shoes by the door. I keep waiting for the texts from her to roll in, all the jokes and the memes. Hell, I'm even expecting a song or two. But so far, radio silence on that front. I'm not sure whether to be pleased or scared.

Either way, I still get to spend the whole day with Drew. We have the hour on the water then we'll be hitting the beach until it's time to come back up and get ready for dinner. We have reservations tonight, not that I think the rest of our party will even be able to join, but there's always a chance.

✿

"This life vest doesn't really match my swimsuit," Drew says with a cute little hand flair to signal the offending article of clothing.

"Well Drew," I say, laughing as was his intended purpose, "you shouldn't have worn ceil blue bottoms, they don't go with anything."

"I can always just take them off," he replies, switching gears.

I blush, more from memories of him stripping last night than the suggestion of seeing him sans swimsuit right now.

"Sir we have a strict policy against nudity at this resort," the attendant says, unsmiling.

"He was just joking, trying to get me to blush and as you can see, it worked," I say, gesturing to my face which is still beet red I'm sure.

Once we're strapped into our vests and informed of every safety protocol from emergency shut off to how to flip a jet ski back upright, we're ready to begin. The sullen attendant waves us away with a "Please don't do anything stupid," and then we're off.

The feel of the ocean water spraying my face combined with the heat of the sun is an instant cure-all for any woe. I'm ready to get out of my head and have some fun.

I look over at Drew, a huge smile on his face and years strip away. I feel like we're kids again. The wind is rushing through his chestnut brown hair and he is glowing. The sun is shining out of him rather than on him. It's a sight to see.

He turns and catches me smiling at him and his answering grin is brighter than the light on the sea. He looks so at home here.

"How have you stayed landlocked for so long?" I ask, pulling up to idle beside him.

"Hmm? Oh Dallas? I mean, it's not *that far* from the beach. A quick little weekend trip. But honestly, I don't know. I do love the water. Growing up in Savannah and being able to run over to Tybee anytime the mood struck…" I study Drew as he seemingly gets lost in thought. He shakes his head and then turns back to smile at me again. "Either way, we're here now. And I'm about to dust you in a race, so let's go!"

I squeal as he revs the engine and turns, splashing water up onto me. He speeds off, laughing maniacally as I try to catch up. Oh it's so on.

Chapter 81

Drew

The hour flies by, full of laughter, insults and me beating Lexa in every race. The resort has little tracks set up with buoys for those of us that possess a competitive nature. We tried all of them and Lexa lost each time. That didn't stop her from trash talking with the best of them, though.

We're still laughing as we return the jet skis to the dock and hand our life jackets over to the surly dude running the thing.

"Have fun?" he asks, sounding like Eeyore.

"Um yeah, it was great. Y'all have a great setup here!" Lexa answers, much more enthusiastic than our host.

"Great," Eeyore answers.

"Alrighty then…well we'll be going now," I say, putting my hand on the small of Lexa's back, trying to lead her away from this increasingly awkward conversation.

"Bye! Thanks again!" she says, waving at the attendant, who not surprisingly, does not respond.

"You are too much," I say once we're out of earshot.

"What do you mean?" Lexa asks, whipping around to see the smile on my face.

"Just so sweet and happy, even if you aren't getting the same energy back."

"There's no reason for others' negativity to affect my outlook on life. And who knows, maybe my sunshine will brighten his day," she replies with a shrug of her slender shoulders.

"Well it's brightened mine considerably," I say, pulling her to me for a hug and a quick kiss. "What do you say we settle under an umbrella with some fruity drinks?"

"That sounds perfect," she replies, stretching up to steal another kiss.

✿

"Do you think you could apply some to my back? It's kinda hard to reach," Lexa asks, holding out the sunscreen bottle. I hate to admit that it takes me a second to process her request. As soon as she unzipped her long-sleeved rash guard and I saw the tiny baby blue bikini top that was underneath, I couldn't really focus on anything else.

I shake my head, probably looking like a damn teenager seeing boobs for the first time. If we were in a cartoon, my eyes would be stretching out of my head and I would be wolf-howling. But luckily, this is real life and I have some control over my reactions. Instead, I calmly say, "Of course, you can go ahead and lay out if you want."

"Thanks, Drew," she says with a very knowing smile plastered on her gorgeous face. Dammit, she knows I'm ogling her. But it's not like I'll ever get tired of seeing her either. Fully clothed or not. She truly is sunshine incarnate.

I watch as she gently lays out on the chair, arranging the towel and her arms under her chin so she can stare at the ocean.

I take the tube of sunscreen, squirting some into my palm. Then with the grace of a prepubescent acne-ridden teenager, I begin to rub the lotion on her back. She shudders under my touch, squealing a bit at the cold temperature of the sunscreen. But once it begins to warm, she relaxes and lets my hands glide over her body. I move her bikini string and make sure to get the lotion underneath. I wouldn't want her burning anywhere. Then I work the sunscreen down to her bottoms, letting my finger run just under the waistband. She shivers again, but for entirely different reasons this time.

"Did you get your arms and shoulders already?" I ask, my voice a little too husky.

"Oh um, probably not well enough. If you don't mind going back over it?" Lexa says, but when she looks at me, there's a deep fire in her eyes.

It's all I can do not to grab her and run back to one of our rooms. But somehow, I manage. "Of course, love. You lay that pretty little head down and just let me take care of you," I say with a wink. That line draws an adorably frustrated sigh from her which only serves to make me laugh.

"You know there's no way we'll be able to get through dinner with Ansley without her catching onto us, right?" Lexa says.

"Yeah, but so what if she does? Maybe she doesn't need to know all the details but it's not like she doesn't know we're hot for each other."

"I guess you're right, I just don't want her to feel weird. Though, that ship has probably already sailed," she says, muffling her voice as she presses her face a little further into the towel.

I sigh, my hands pausing on her back but not moving away from her. "You probably don't want to hear this but she's not going to feel weird or awkward or anything because she's fully aware that this is my plan and I have her full support."

Lexa turns slowly, my hands staying on her, not ready to let go. Once she's on her side and staring into my eyes, she says, "Your…plan?"

Chapter 82

Lexa

Wait, *what?* "What is your 'plan' exactly?" I say, somewhat belligerently.

There's absolutely no reason for me to be reacting like this, but also *what?!*

"Um," he begins sheepishly, "well, I thought that this trip would be a good opportunity for us to hang out again and without other distractions and things. I don't have like a crazy diabolical master plan to make you fall in love with me if that's what you're freaking out about." He huffs like he's exasperated.

I swing my legs around to sit up, effectively removing his hands from me. I immediately miss the warmth, but I need a clear mind for this conversation and that is one thing I cannot have with his hands touching me.

I see the hurt flash in his eyes at my sudden movement, but I need to see his face while we talk. I reach my hand out to him, trying to communicate that I'm still here and I just want to talk.

He gingerly reaches back for me, sinking his hand into mine. I squeeze it for good measure before saying, "Drew, what of this has been planned and what has been spontaneous? What about last night?"

Fear flashes across his face, suddenly realizing why I'm so on edge. Did I fall into a trap? "No, no baby. The only part that was 'planned' was having our villas beside each other. I wanted us to have to see each other on the way to and from places. I thought running into me more often would encourage more conversation. But never in my wildest dreams did I imagine what would occur yesterday and last night. I am just as off balance as you are right now. Scouts honor," he finishes, holding up the 3-finger salute and letting a small smile shine through.

I laugh, a bit hesitant, but say, "You weren't even a boy scout!"

We both laugh and he squeezes my hand to make me look at him. I raise my head, meeting his eyes and holding them. I'm immediately lost in the ocean blue of them. The storm of emotions rolling through them moves me. I have my arms around his neck before I even have a second to think. His lips are crashing into mine, his arms pulling me closer and his hands sinking into my hair.

"Get a room!" someone jokes from behind us, but it's enough to break the spell. I huff out a laugh as we pull away from each other.

"Maybe we should still be careful out here, since we haven't told any of our friends yet," I say, keeping his hands in mine.

"You're right, of course. But that's just making me want to go back to the villa," he replies, winking.

"All in good time," I flash him a grin and resettle onto my

chair. "Now get back to protecting my ghost skin."

"I think you mean this gorgeous porcelain skin, right?" Drew asks, slathering some extra sunscreen onto my shoulders.

I laugh and swat playfully at his hands as I turn to look at his face. I want to call bullshit but the way his eyes are devouring me right now, maybe he's serious. I nestle back down into my chair. Making sure to keep my face shaded with the towel and then I promptly fall asleep.

☼

I'm awoken by a gentle hand on my back, and a decadently rough voice saying, "Lexa baby, you might want to get out of the sun for a bit." I sit up, turning to Drew and thanking him with a smile. I would have probably laid out here all day if he wasn't watching out for me.

I sink down into the low chair set under the umbrella and accept the cold rum drink that Drew obviously just ordered before waking me. I can't help the huge smile taking over my face as I think about just how sweet this man is. And how thoughtful. I've never met anyone else like him.

I'm pulled out of my trance by the sight of Drew standing and stretching. His muscles tightening and releasing in the most delicious sequence. I think I'm drooling. I quickly snap my open mouth closed, not wanting to be caught salivating over him.

"I'm gonna cool off in the water real quick. You need some more sunscreen before going back out there, though. Want me to get you covered and then you can join me when you're ready?" he asks, hooded eyes tracking my movements.

"That sounds marvelous," I reply, reaching into the bag for the sunscreen.

Once I'm lathered up and letting it soak into my skin, I get to enjoy the view. Watching Drew pick his way over the sand and wade out into the water is like something out of a movie. He could've starred in *Baywatch* with that body.

I flick my gaze to the side to see other women eyeing him as well. And it doesn't make me as jealous as that would with other guys. Because as soon as I look back to him, Drew is smiling at me, making it obvious that I'm the only person here that he's looking at.

Chapter 83

Lexa

"I wonder if anyone will be able to join us tonight. I'm really hoping they're starting to recover," Drew says, grabbing my hand as we walk towards the villas.

"Maybe we'll at least pull Ansley and Claire out tonight so they can have a good meal," I shrug.

Once we're back to my door, I punch in my code and turn the knob. I'm immediately greeted by the sound of my phone ringing and it's Ansley's ringtone. I rush in, not wanting to miss her call. I answer breathlessly, turning back to look at Drew. "Hey girl, what's up?" I ask, holding the phone away from my mouth as I breathe a little too loudly.

"Hey! I was just calling to check in and see how the jet skis were. And I was going to see what your dinner plans were," she says.

"We were just talking about that!" I say, before realizing that I'm telling her me and Drew are still together. "Me and Drew had talked about that when we were getting off the jet skis," I try to amend. "Any chance you're feeling up to going out with us? There's apparently a little place on the water closer to where we were racing. It looked quaint and smelled yummy!"

"That sounds great! I think Claire should be able to join as well! Landon is definitely feeling better, but not really enough for island food just yet," she explains.

"We can bring him back some grilled chicken or something."

"I like that idea. Wanna meet in the middle around 6 and we can all walk over there?"

"Perfect! You want to text Claire and I'll let Drew know?" I ask, feigning nonchalance.

"Sure thing, just let him know he'll be the only guy there. Can you ask if he minds stopping by and checking in on Weston and Patrick?"

"Of course, and I'll go check on Amanda and Grace in a little while, make sure they're still alive," I reply. "See you at 6!"

She says bye and hangs up. "Looks like we'll be having some dinner companions after all!" I say to Drew.

He smiles, slipping his arms around my waist and pulling me to him. "Yeah I kinda gleaned that from your side of the conversation," he says, laughing. I huff out a laugh and snuggle closer into his arms. I soak up this wonderful feeling of just being held for a moment before I can't ignore the heat between us any longer. I reach up and gently cup his scruffy cheek with my hand. It trembles a bit as I take in the intensity in his eyes.

Suddenly his mouth is on mine, tongue sliding against my lips, asking for entrance. I grant it and quickly get swept up in the feeling of him in me and all over me. His hands are roaming like they can't decide where to settle. He decides on leaning down and gripping my ass, lifting me up into the air and pressing me back against the wall. I can feel all of him against all of me in this position and it causes a moan to escape from my throat. He swallows it with his kiss and pushes into me even more.

I have my hands fisted in his shirt, trying to pull him into my skin. I'm breathless as he pulls back and looks into my eyes. His pupils are so blown, I can barely make out an edge of darkened blue around them.

"I think we have time for some fun before we have to go check on the sicklings, right?" he asks, peppering kisses down my jawline and nipping at the sensitive spot where my shoulder meets my throat.

"Yes, please yes," I whimper, pulling a groan from him.

"I can't make it to the bedroom this time," he says darkly before he's pulling his trunks down and my bikini bottoms to the side.

"Oh shit," I nearly scream as he slams into me, pushing every thought besides him out of my head.

✧

"Did you two have a good day?" Ansley asks as we're walking towards the restaurant.

I feel a blush making its way across my face as I answer, "Yeah we had a lot of fun on the jet ski courses."

"You look like you got some good sun today, too," Claire says to me, running her hand lightly over my exposed shoulder.

"We laid out for a bit on the beach after we got done riding," I respond with a smile towards her.

I hear a muffled chuckle behind me, causing another blush

to steal over my skin. Of course, Drew is going to take any chance to point out an innuendo. And it's only taking me back to the afternoon we spent together before rushing out to check on our friends. We barely had time to shower and make it here from our respective villas so they wouldn't see us coming from the same one.

I'm ready to talk to Ansley about this and hopefully sooner rather than later. I am not built for secret-keeping. But I also don't want to tell her until I'm sure it's real this time. She had to deal with a lot of my bullshit over the last year while I was hung up on her brother. It's not fair to her to drag her back in until we're sure.

I drop back from walking with Ansley and Claire, lowering my voice to talk to Drew. "We need to talk to her, but I want us to have that full conversation first. I know we talked some today, but there's still more to iron out," I say.

"I would love to talk," he replies, "And whatever else may come to your mind."

I laugh loudly, causing the girls to spin around, looking at me quizzically. "Oh!" I fumble, "Drew was just complaining about how many times I beat him on the courses today!" I elbow Drew in the ribs, pulling a curse and a dark chuckle from him. *Shit*, that sends shivers down my spine. Sensing my reaction to him, Drew leans down as the girls turn back around and growls in my ear. My whole body trembles and it's a miracle that I don't jump him on the spot. *We're like hormonal teenagers,* I think to myself as I try to steer my thoughts toward safer ground. Maybe a dinner of spicy island food and a stiff drink will clear my head enough to talk to my best friend about my budding romance with her older brother.

Chapter 84

Drew

Watching Lexa talk to Ansley and Claire is all the entertainment I need for a night out. The three of them fall into easy conversation, talking about everything from work to men to the shoes they're wearing to a wedding next month. It's amazing the amount of topics women can cover in one meal. I'm not sure that I get a word in for most of dinner, but that's okay with me. I'm very content to just watch. Especially if I'm getting to watch Lexa as she laughs so hard she cries or when her smile lights up her entire face or when she's trying to be serious but can't and her laugh cracks through. She is so stunningly gorgeous, but especially when she's happy. Her light jade eyes track back to me more than I think she realizes, but every time I see them I smile. I hope I'm at least some of the reason she's happy. Because she makes me ecstatic.

As dinner winds down, Claire and Ansley both order some food for the guys. When we checked on everyone else before dinner, they had all ordered in. We couldn't find Grace and

Amanda at first, but they were hanging out with Weston and Patrick. So everyone is on the mend, it seems. I'm glad. That means everyone will be along for the hike tomorrow. We stop outside at the intersection to all of our rooms. The sound of ocean waves crashing on shore is so soothing, I could be lulled to sleep just standing here. And with the stars and moon reflecting off the water, this place looks like something out of a painting.

"This was so nice,"Claire says, hugging me as Ansley talks with Lexa.

"It was great, I'm so glad you and Ans didn't get sick. And I'm even happier that all of my friends are getting healthy again," I reply, hugging her back and dropping a kiss to the top of her head.

Then she's over to Lexa. I look up to see that Ansley is staring deep into my soul. "Yes?" I ask, trying to break the hold she has on me right now.

"You look different today," she says, eyes narrowed in suspicion. "And so does Lexa."

"Yeah? Well we did get some sun today?" I suggest as a possibility.

"Hmm, yeah no. I think it has more to do with the goofy ass smiles you both have plastered over your faces. Does this mean what I think it means?" she questions, inching closer and dropping her voice so she won't be overheard.

I glance toward Lexa, making sure she's not listening to us and respond, "Maybe but she wants to be the one to talk to you. So don't breathe a damn word about it until she does."

"Oh my God," she whispers. "OhmyGod. Ohhhh my Godddddd." She's hyperventilating a bit and I'm nervous that Lexa is going to look over at any second so I wrap her into a tight hug and spin her so Lex can't see her face.

"Shh. Shut up. She's going to hear you. It's not officially official yet. But we're working on it, okay?"

"Shit. What's to work out? You live in Savannah now and–"

"And she doesn't know that yet. I don't want to tell her until she decides how she feels about me. I don't want her to feel like she has to choose me now that we'll be in the same city."

"Drew. Seriously? That's the stupidest shit I've ever heard. It would probably make her decision that much easier."

"Just…let me do this, okay?" I plead.

My little sister steps away from me, looking up into my face. Her eyes roam across my features, taking in any information she can find. "Okay," she says, "do whatever you think is best. I'll support you regardless, you know that."

"I know that. Just like you know how much I love you, right?" I squeeze her hard, trying to make her feel just how much she means to me.

"I know bro, but you're currently crushing the life out of me," she says, obviously having a hard time breathing.

I release her and we both laugh as she lightly punches my shoulder. "Okay well I'm gonna get this food to Landon. Y'all gonna behave without further supervision?" she asks, eyebrow quirked.

"As much as we've already been behaving," I reply with a roguish wink.

She fakes a gag and then laughs before turning to face Lexa and Claire again. "Okay girly, you ready to head back to our guys?" she asks Claire.

Claire smiles, hugging Lexa again before skipping forward to link arms with Ans. "We're off to heal the wizards," she giggles and winks at us.

"Um ew," Lexa says, but laughs. "Y'all get some rest! I expect to see everyone bright and early for our island hike!"

"Yes ma'am!" the girls call over their shoulders as they head back to their villas.

Once they're out of earshot, I lean down and place my lips near Lexa's ear, whispering, "My place or yours?" I watch in delight as a shiver runs through her body and she leans back into my chest slightly, watching her friends amble toward their respective rooms.

"Mine, but I wish they would walk faster," she says, sighing.

I bend down and scoop her up into my arms. She lets out a cry and whips her head towards me and then back towards the dwindling shadows of Ansley and Claire. Neither turned and she visibly relaxes, sinking down into my hold. She turns her face back up to mine, running her hand along my jaw and into my hair. "Need anything from your place first? Pajamas?" she asks.

"For the sleep I don't plan on getting?" I say, dropping my mouth onto hers and devouring it in a way that shows her my intentions for tonight.

"Well when you put it that way," she laughs, "what are we still doing out here?"

I growl into her ear and take off towards her bungalow. I set her down just long enough for her to type in her door code and then she's back up in my arms. As soon as we're inside, I drop her onto her bed and begin divesting her of these pesky clothes.

"We're going to be around the whole group again tomorrow, so we're going to have to behave," I say, pulling her up to rip her dress off.

"So your plan is to what? Try to satiate ourselves tonight so we don't look like horny teens groping all over each other?"

I pause and look down at her, savoring every inch of exposed skin. "Oh I'll never be done with you, I'm just hoping I can make it through the hike without pulling you into a cave like a barbarian."

She giggles at that and reaches up to help me with my shirt. I grab the hem and tug it off over my head and quickly step back to do the same with my shorts and briefs.

"I'm glad you didn't stop to get pajamas," she says, heat taking over her eyes and her hands reaching to pull me closer.

Chapter 85

Lexa

Friday

My alarm blares through the darkened room, making me groan. I roll over to turn it off, but I'm stopped by the weight covering my back. Drew has an arm and a leg thrown over me in a delicious display of muscle. I groan again, for entirely different reasons this time. I'm able to scoot over enough to hit the button on my phone, silencing the music. I turn back to Drew and see that he's awake. His eyes are still closed but his lips are tipped up in a dreamy smile. *I could get used to this.*

We didn't talk much last night, but we did actually get some sleep, despite his threats. I laugh to myself and reach out to run my fingers through his disheveled hair. "Hey sleeping beauty, fancy a shower before we grab something to eat? We have a little bit before we have to meet up with the group," I say, twisting some of the longer strands of his hair around my finger.

He pops one eye open, lets the smile take over his face and says, "How long is a little bit?"

"Not nearly enough time for activities that don't include showering, dressing or eating," I say, fixing him with a look that I hope is at least a little authoritative.

He groans, the sound going straight to that pit in my belly. *Ugh, what is wrong with me?*

"What if we use some shower time for other activities? I can be quick," he suggests.

"We have to make it out of bed before we can even discuss this and so far, you haven't moved a muscle."

He stretches, his briefs not doing much to hide what he's pressing against me. "I could definitely use some muscle movement, you?"

I slap his arm but can't help the laugh that spills out. "You are the worst, get your heavy leg off of me so I can shower!" I'm still laughing as he lets me squirm out from under him.

I turn back to the bed, to ask if he's going to join me, but I lose my train of thought as I note the hunger in his eyes. He's raking his gaze across my body like he's trying to memorize every freckle. I feel my face heat under the attention, drawing his stare up to my cheeks and then my eyes. He must see something in my expression, because he grins and in a sudden movement has pounced from the bed, sweeping me up into the air and taking me into the attached bath.

He gets the water warm enough and reaches down to strip me from my underwear. He leads me under the stream and leans down to kiss me, just as the water hits my back. I groan, loving the feel of the water and of him.

I feel him reach around me, and I hear a cap pop open. A

moment later, he's lathering soap onto my body. My hair is up in a bun and allowing him full access to my neck and shoulders.

"This is all I could imagine doing when I was putting sunscreen on you yesterday," he says, continuing to wash me. His hands slip from my shoulders, lowering to my breasts where he runs his thumbs over my already hardened nipples. One hand slides to my lower back as the other skims over my belly. In the next moment, both hands are kneading my ass, massaging and pulling another groan from me. "Just making sure your muscles are all warmed up for the hike today," he husks into my ear.

"Uh huh," I mumble, relishing in the feel of his hands on my body. He bends onto a knee, making sure to wash every inch of my legs. As his hands slip closer to the apex of my thighs, I feel my hands moving without my consent. By the time his lips are meeting with my tender skin, my hands are gripping his hair. He gently pushes my back up against the wall. The sudden chill of the stone provides a stark and welcome contrast to the heat blazing through my body. Drew works his fingers and tongue in a motion that has me crying for relief within minutes. In a swift movement, he's up, one thigh gripped in his big hand. He pushes into me fast and hard. It only takes a few minutes before we're both panting and swearing. I'm riding the edge hard, craving the friction he's providing with every thrust. He changes the angle slightly and we're both shattering. Hearing my name pour out of his mouth would be enough to undo me without even a touch.

"Told you I could be quick," he says, still breathless as he holds me up against the wall.

"Yep, still plenty of time to get you showered off, too," I say as he releases my thigh and steps back an inch or two.

"No way. If we're going to make it out of this shower, much less this room, you're not touching me anymore," he says, picking up the soap bottle and cleansing himself. *At least I get to watch,* I muse.

☼

We shockingly make it to the meeting spot on time. We had to run by his room after I got ready so he could change clothes. He's wearing something akin to what I would imagine you'd wear on a safari. All neutral colors and rugged clothing, finished off with a bucket hat. I laughed my ass off when he came out of the bathroom, but he only smiled and said he'd be getting the last laugh when everyone else was uncomfortable.

I'm wearing one of my more athletic swimsuits with a gauzy button down top and some loose khaki shorts. I have my thick-soled sandals that I love to hike in and I feel ready to go. I even remembered a water bottle.

"Thanks for letting me borrow a hat," I say to Drew as we're approaching the group. I can't believe I forgot one, but I'm thankful that he brought some extras.

"It looks better on you, anyway," he replies, reaching up to tip the brim back, eyes roaming my face. "You did put sunscreen on your face, right?"

"Yes, dear. I always wear sunscreen on my face," I say, rolling my eyes.

He flicks the brim of my hat down, causing it to fall nearly into my eyes. "Brat," he mutters.

I laugh and fix my hat, turning to face our friends. I see them all staring at us, eyes flicking between me and Drew.

Great, I think, *way to not rouse any suspicion.*

To draw attention from us, I run up to Amanda and Grace, throwing my arms around them. "It's so nice to see you two back in the land of the living!"

They laugh and hug me back, both thanking me for checking on them and bringing them supplies while they were holed up.

"No problem, my loves," I say and swivel to see everyone else. I smile big and say, "I'm so glad all of you are feeling better. I can't wait to see this gorgeous island with y'all!"

With that, Ansley claps her hands together and gets the group's attention focused on her. "Okay gang, we'll be hiking some well laid out trails today. We have maps, so we shouldn't be getting lost. I expect us all to stay together. Speak up if you need a break. A lot of you just had your first full meal last night. We will not leave anyone behind and we will not be sneaking off anywhere." She fixes Drew with a stare as she says the last part, making me wonder why she thinks he'd be the one to stray from the group. If anyone gets lost, I'd be betting on Weston. We lost him a lot in college. He's a wanderer.

Ansley hands us all a map, under the assumption that someone will indeed wander off from the group. I laugh, but take my map, knowing I'd rather have it just in case.

"Any last questions, thoughts, concerns?" Ansley asks, making eye contact with each of us briefly.

"No sir, commander. Let's roll out," Patrick barks in his best commando impression.

Ansley rolls her eyes and laughs. "Okay well let's get going then. We'll be out here for several hours, so ration your water and snacks appropriately, please."

Chapter 86

Drew

I'm doing my level best to keep my hands off of Lexa, but for as athletic as she is, she's very clumsy when she hikes. I'm not sure if it's those sandals she's wearing or if she just doesn't watch where she's stepping, but she's tripped on almost every possible obstacle.

Every time she trips, my hand flies out to stop her from falling. Most of the time, it's not needed. But I have saved her from actually face-planting twice so far. I would be annoyed if it was anyone else, but she's just so damn adorable in her clumsiness that I can't stop laughing. I joked that I could just carry her if that would make it easier. All I got in return was the cutest angry face I've ever seen.

The hike has been relatively serene otherwise. There have been several areas where I could hear running water, but couldn't see any of the waterfalls they are supposed to have here. The cool air in the shade of the trees is a balm for the oppressive heat in the sun. Wearing a long sleeved shirt was definitely the move today. I've been trying to discreetly keep a watch on Lexa, making sure she's not burning. I know she's a big girl and can take care of herself, but getting burnt will make her miserable and I don't want her to have to deal with that. Plus, on the more selfish side of things, she probably wouldn't want me to touch her if she was too burnt.

I hear a yelp and immediately whip my head up, fearing that Lexa will be skidding along the ground at any minute.

"Oh shit man!" I hear Patrick yell. I look around at the group, trying to see who or what they're looking at. I finally see Lexa at the edge of the group, almost on Landon's back. I follow her eyes to the ground, towards the large iguana scurrying across the path.

"I didn't know you were that scared of lizards," I hear Weston chuckle from beside Lexa. She's still ghostly pale and trying her best to scramble up Landon's back and away from the ground. The iguana has now stopped on the path and is—I swear—staring straight at Lexa.

With a shaking voice, Lexa replies, "I'm not scared of them—usually. I guess when they shoot out from under a bush right across my foot, they startle me."

"Well you're probably good to get off my back, yeah?" Landon asks, trying not to laugh.

"Oh. Right, right, yeah," Lexa says, extricating herself from Landon.

Once she's back on the ground, her eyes flick to mine. She smiles self-consciously before walking over to me.

I reach for her hand before pulling back at the last moment. I meet her eyes, trying to convey the questions I want to ask. Instead I say, "You looked like a monkey."

She fully laughs at that, reaching out and slapping me lightly on the shoulder.

We take a moment to decompress from that, everyone getting back into the mood for hiking. We still have a good hour to go before we end up at the beach where we'll be spending the day.

I look down at Lexa and ask quietly, "You okay? Heart rate back to normal?"

She places her first two fingers of her right hand under her chin, obviously feeling her pulse. "Feels alright to me, what about you?" She takes my hand laying it against her throat. As her eyes track up to meet mine, I feel the pulse under my fingers increase dramatically. I watch as her pupils dilate, and her tongue flicks out and licks at her bottom lip. *Oh shit,* I think. This is not going to end well if I don't take a step back.

I feel absolutely feral right now, almost caveman status, having to tell myself not to take Lexa behind a tree right now.

I suck in a breath of air to try to steady myself and smile down at her. "If I stand here any longer, everyone is going to get a show," I tell Lexa.

A blush rushes across her face but she takes a step back. I let my breath back out in a silent huff. I have never felt like this around another person. She smiles sheepishly back up at me before winking and turning back to where the rest of the group is still talking.

"Well then," I hear from behind me. I spin to see Ansley standing there, Landon behind her with his mouth dropped open.

"Oh shut up," I say, smacking her arm. I look back up to Landon who is still looking at me like I grew an extra head. "What? Some things happened while you were on your deathbed."

"I would think I was still there and hallucinating if it weren't for the bugs attacking me every two minutes," Landon says, finally shutting his mouth.

"You hadn't already told him?" I ask Ansley.

She just shakes her head, saying, "I figured that was for you to do. But what's telling when you can just show?" She smiles brightly at me before grabbing Landon's hand and returning to the front of the group.

"Okay everyone! Let's get this hike finished so we can drink something besides water!" Ansley says to our friends. A fair amount of "woos" ring out for that statement.

✿

The beaches on this island are gorgeous but this one is so different. There aren't very many people here, for one. But with the trees backing the sand, it feels like we're completely secluded. There aren't any big buildings here and it's nice.

The only tip off that we're still within the bounds of civilization is the small restaurant and bar about 100 yards from the trail head.

"Solid business plan," Patrick says, walking up to me. I laugh but can't disagree. Being the only place selling a cold drink after a two hour hike is a wonderful business model. "Maybe we should work on branching out to some… untapped locations," he continues, slapping me on the back.

"Hey no business talk, remember?" I say, glancing around to see who's close to us. No one is within ear shot, but I'm not taking that chance. My plans are still in the works.

Speaking of plans, I call out to Ansley, "Hey boss lady, any plans for now or are we free to grab a drink?"

"A drink in my hand is my only plan, dear brother. Anyone else?"

406

Grace and Amanda skip over, joining our group heading to the bar. Everyone else seems to be staking out the best real estate for laying out and lounging. We have several hours to spend here, just relaxing, before our next adventure.

Chapter 87

Lexa

I've just gotten situated, laying in a comfortable spot without too many bumps under me, when someone is standing over me, throwing a cool shadow across my skin.

"Can I help you?" I ask, shading my eyes from the sun streaming around Drew. He doesn't answer, just holds out a drink. The condensation drips off the cup, directly onto my chest. I yelp at the sudden cold contact but sit up to accept the drink.

I pat the towel beside me, asking him to sit with me. He sinks down onto the towel and I realize suddenly that he has completely changed clothes.

"Did you have those trunks underneath your shorts?" I ask, indicating the near skin tight swim trunks he's now sporting.

"Nope. Just changed in the bathroom while I was waiting on drinks. I came prepared. These shorts are not great for hiking," he replies, taking a pull of his strawberry colored cocktail.

"I can't imagine they'd be easy to walk in at all," I say, waggling my eyebrows suggestively at what the shorts aren't hiding.

"As long as I behave, there's still plenty of room for movement," he says, winking at me.

"Oh God, you are so corny." I fake gag but can't help my laugh. I take a sip of the drink he brought me, pineapple and rum immediately invading my senses. *Yum.*

"I was going to ask if you liked it, but the groan that just came from your mouth leads me to believe yes. Using past data to come to that conclusion, of course."

I feel my face flush, I hadn't even known that I made a noise. But knowing the noises I make around him, there's no doubt his thoughts are just as dirty as mine right now.

"You know, there's plenty of places off the trail that no one would find us for a bit," I say, lowering my voice and nipping at his shoulder with my teeth.

"Shit Lex. Behave. I really won't be able to hide anything in these shorts if you keep this up."

"Yes sir," I say, batting my eyelashes at him. "As long as you promise to make it up to me later."

"You can count on it, baby. Now, watch my drink. I have to get in that cold ass water for a minute to keep these shorts from ripping open." He gets up a little slower than he normally moves and saunters towards the water. Watching the sunlight play off of his tanned muscles causes a reaction lower in my stomach. Sometimes, I'm glad there's not as much physical evidence of attraction for females.

I laugh, looking around at the rest of our group. We're all sitting close enough together to talk and most of them are sitting up and hanging out. It looks like Weston is already asleep. I'm sure the ones recovering from that stomach bug are really feeling it today after that hike. I'm so glad we're taking a boat back for a sunset cruise. I sip on my drink some more, letting my mind wander.

My thoughts race ahead to the end of the trip. We only have one more full day after today and I'm not ready for this to end. As much as I tell myself to live in the moment and enjoy what I'm being given right now, I'm having a hard time actually doing so. I'm not ready to go back to real life, living so far away from Drew. The thought of having to live without him again after everything we've shared on this trip has me sinking into despair.

"Why the long face?" Ansley asks, plopping down beside me and wrestling me from my thoughts.

I try to shake my head and smile but it's not coming across very genuine. Like I could fool my sleuth of a best friend anyway. "I need to talk to you about some stuff. I wanted to wait until the end of the trip, but it's starting to get to me," I say, looking up and into her eyes.

She holds my gaze, looking slightly worried. "Go on, you know you can tell me anything," she prompts. She reaches over and grabs my hand in both of hers, giving me a physical rock to hold onto.

"Well," I start, my eyes dropping from her gaze. "I don't even know how to say this but, I hooked up with Drew." I glance up quickly as I finish the sentence, waiting for her shocked reaction. But it doesn't come. She just gives me a timid smile that tells me everything I need to know. "You already knew?"

"Girl, you left your sandals by his door. And not all of your clothes made it into the bathroom with you. Plus, you're glowing like I've never seen before and it's not from the sun. Are you upset that I knew and didn't say anything?"

I laugh, I should have known she would have pieced it together that morning. "No, I'm relieved. I've been nervous to tell you because I don't want to mess up our relationship for a guy."

"But he's not just any guy. That's why you're sitting over here looking like someone yelled at your puppy, right? Tell me where your head is at right now." Ansley lets go of my hand and puts her arm around my shoulder, pulling me into her.

I take in a deep shuddering breath. On the exhale I whisper, "I can't lose him again." A tear tracks down my cheek and Ansley wipes it away, smiling at me with so much warmth.

"Then don't."

Chapter 88

Lexa

After several hours of sun, sand and some stiff drinks, it's time to climb aboard our boat for the sunset cruise that takes us back around to the resort. We had lunch but that feels like forever ago. As we start getting dressed, we notice that several people are very badly burnt.

"Dude you look like a damn lobster," Landon says to Wes. And yeah, he does. He pulls the side of his trunks down to see the tan line and it's even more noticeable.

"I guess the two hour nap without reapplying sunscreen probably wasn't the smartest move," Wes says, wincing as he pulls his shirt over his head.

"We have aloe back at our place if you want me to rub some on you," Grace says. "I mean or you can just take it to your room and do it yourself of course," she babbles, blushing cutely.

It's probably a good thing we're spending most of our day fully clothed and in shade tomorrow. Sightseeing on the last day will definitely be for the best.

We're all laughing and ribbing those who fried a little too much today as we board the boat from the dock. I'm stepping up on the edge when my sandals betray me once again and cause me to slip sideways from the boat. I drop my towel on the dock but can't get a grip on the handle fast enough. I'm weightless, falling towards the water when I feel a strong calloused hand wrap around my bicep and pull me forward and away from the water. I collide with a strong chest and arms like steel wrap around my back. That same hand makes its way into my hair, pulling gently to force me to look up.

"You just can't stand not having my hands on you, huh?" Drew rasps into my ear.

I let out a breathless laugh and shake my head. "No, I'm just that lucky I guess," I say, smiling up at his dark and stormy eyes. They lighten slightly, now that he knows I'm safe. But seeing him look that scared, has me feeling the opposite. I do what I know we both need. I wrap my hand around the back of his neck and pull him down. I reach up on my tiptoes and press my mouth to his.

I hear cheers and clapping as soon as I'm able to think again. With my face as red as a tomato, I pull away and look at our friends.

"Finally!" Claire says, jumping and clapping.

"So we can stop pretending like we didn't already know now, right?" Patrick asks.

I scoff and then start laughing. I guess we weren't as good at hiding it as we thought we were.

"Let's just get on this damn boat and eat some food, I'm starving," I say, trying to act tough.

"I bet you are," Jackson says, suggestively. He throws me a wink that causes Claire to smack his arm. "Leave her alone, you toddler!" she says, laughing.

Once we've all finally made it onto the boat in one piece, we head to the front. There's a table big enough to fit us all and water already at each seat. We'll be eating dinner for the next hour before we move to the top deck for drinks and to watch the sunset. Thankfully the table is set under some shade. We still put Weston under the most shadowed part.

The waiter on board approaches us and takes our drink orders. As soon as he's gone, another one appears with two large charcuterie boards. We all ooh and ahh before digging in.

The boat begins to slowly move away from the dock, edging us out into the sea away from the island. We'll be heading out into the open water for a bit while we eat.

Our drinks come quickly, followed by salads. Both waiters come out to take our dinner orders. There are only a few options but they each sound tantalizing. I opt for the braised fish on a bed of jasmine rice set over a grilled plantain. Drew orders the steak meal and I can already see him salivating.

Dinner passes in a blur and then it's finally time to head up to the top deck to watch the sunset. With our newfound freedom, Drew settles in right behind me, bracketing my body with his arms. We sip champagne and watch the sky as the blue fades into pink and orange over the water.

"Almost as beautiful as you," Drew mutters, dropping a kiss onto my cheek. I blush instantly and turn to smile at him. He catches my mouth in a kiss that has me wanting to turn in his arms and deepen it. It takes all of my willpower to remember that we're not alone and that there's something else I'm supposed to be watching. It's hard to tear my eyes away from the way the setting sun is highlighting Drew's features and turning him into even more of a masterpiece.

"What are you doing when we get back on dry land?" Drew asks, letting his head rest on the top of mine.

"I don't have any plans. I think we're pretty clear until tomorrow for the tours."

"Then hang out with me. I want to take you somewhere," he says, placing a kiss to the top of my head.

"Of course, I'd love to." I smile to myself, trying to take the advice of my best friend. I don't have to give him up.

Chapter 89

Drew

"Come on, it's just a little further," I say, pulling Lexa's hand to help her keep up.

"Listen, if I would've known there would be more hiking involved, I might have said no."

"Yeah, I know. That's why I didn't tell you. How are you better at walking through here in the dark than you were in daylight?" I ask, genuinely curious.

"Because you're holding my hand and keeping my mind from wandering."

"So what you're saying is, as long as I'm around, you won't fall?"

She's silent for a moment and then I feel her pull my hand to stop me. I turn to face her and she reaches up, threading her hands through my hair. She kisses me hard, making me lose my breath. "I already did."

I scoop her up from the ground, cradling her in my arms and take off in our original direction. I wasn't lying when I said we weren't very far. Once we reach the edge of the water, I set her down and let her look around. There's enough moonlight filtering through the trees that you can make out the waterfall and the collecting pool beneath. The reflection of the light off the water makes it look ethereal. I pull her back against my chest and lean down to whisper into her ear. "Me too," I say, hugging her to me, afraid to let go. This is the first time we've really admitted our feelings to each other and I'm as nervous as I am elated.

"Want to go for a swim?" I ask, letting her turn and look at me. I brush a strand of hair from her face, tucking it behind her ear. I let my hand rest there, feeling her pulse drumming away beneath my fingers again.

"I didn't wear a swimsuit," Lexa says, looking around like there may be people anywhere.

I take a small step back, gathering the hem of my t-shirt and yanking it off. "I didn't either."

Lexa's eye follow my movements as I strip from my shorts and then my briefs. I back toward the water, beckoning her.

As my heel touches the water lapping up onto the ground, she grins and begins to undress. She slips off her sandals, then slides one strap of her dress off of her shoulder, then the other. She shimmies out of it, leaving only her lace underwear. She hooks her fingers into each side before slowly pulling them down her gorgeous legs. Lexa is all stealthy muscle and sexy curves in all the right places. I love it. I love her.

She steps toward me, reaching out for me like she's afraid I'm going to disappear on her. "Is it cold?" she asks.

"Come on in and find out," I reply, stepping back to submerge myself up to my waist. The warm water laps at my stomach. I see Lexa watch me for a moment, trying to assess my reaction to the temperature.

I give her another come-hither gesture, bringing out a laugh but finally drawing her into the water. She lets out a sigh as she wades in, the water wrapping around her like a blanket.

I continue to walk backwards, letting my feet slide across the bottom in case there's a drop off. Lexa follows me out deeper, her eyes never leaving mine.

When I reach chest level, I stop, knowing Lexa won't be able to touch much deeper. Not that I plan on letting her be on her feet much, anyway.

Lexa makes her way to me. As soon as she's close enough, I reach out and pull her up to my chest. She wraps her legs around me, pulling me even closer. I drop one hand down to cradle her ass and leave the other on her upper back, supporting her so she doesn't have to tread water. She wraps her arms around my neck, threading her fingers into my hair and starts kissing along my jawline. I instantly harden and I know she can feel it because she shifts over me ever so slightly, pulling a groan from my mouth.

The mixture of her mouth on my skin and her heat enveloping me has me ready to lose control. I don't want this to be fast though, so I pull my face away a few inches to look into her eyes. Once she's looking at me again, I lean in and place a tender kiss against her lips. She immediately tries to deepen it so I pull back again, teasing her. Another soft kiss, another breath. Teasing her is only teasing myself though and soon enough, I'm lost in the kiss again. She's stealing my breath along with my heart and I'm powerless to stop it. We have all night but I can't wait another minute, I move her back down into position and carefully push in. I hear her mumble my name along with "shit" and "damn" and I smile, knowing she's coming apart just as quickly as I am.

Her fingers are clutching at my hair, her teeth nipping at the sensitive spot on my neck. Both of my hands are on her ass, keeping her glued to me. Having my hands full of her like this drives me wild. She stops biting me and starts to buck against me. Her breasts are pressed right up against my chest and I can feel her pebbled nipples running over my skin. I groan again, unable to control it. She's moving wildly against me, searching for any friction she can find on my body.

Her movements become more and more stilted as she nears her edge. It's tough but I manage to hold on just long enough for her to come undone and start clenching around me.

We're both breathless and wild-eyed and we stare at each other. Her mouth is hanging open, adorably panting. "So um, you like waterfalls?" I ask.

She throws her head back in laughter before leaning back in and meeting my gaze once again, "I like you."

I rearrange our bodies until she's straddling my stomach again and she wraps her arms back around my neck. We soak in the moment for a while until I feel like the time is finally right.

"I have something I need to tell you," I say. Her eyes open a fraction of an inch wider and I hear her breath catch. "Nothing bad! Just news, I guess."

"Okay," she says, sounding unsure. "Go ahead, you pretty much have a captive audience right now."

I chuckle and then take a deep breath. "I took a new job," I say. "In a different city. I don't live in Dallas anymore. I actually moved several weeks ago."

She studies my face a moment before finally replying. "There's nursing jobs everywhere. I'm sure there's a hospital close by."

I'm shocked to silence. Is she saying that she's wanting to do this? She'd be willing to move to wherever I am and leave the family she found?

"I mean, of course, if you want me to. I don't want to intrude on your–" she starts, but it's hard to continue once I've crushed my mouth onto hers, stealing her words.

"I moved back to Savannah, Lex."

Now it's her turn to be shocked. But then another emotion flits across her face. Anger. *Shit.*

"Are you telling me that you've been back in the same city as me for almost a month and waited until now to tell me? Why?" She struggles to remove herself from my grasp, but I'm not letting her go. Not this time.

"I needed to make sure you were ready for life with me. I didn't want you to feel obligated to try things out with me just because it would be convenient now."

"Drew. I want to be with you. I want to be with you wherever you are. You had to know that."

"I wanted to believe that, but it was hard with how we left things in Atlanta last year." Lexa's eyes drop to my chest. I place a finger underneath to bring her face back up to mine, "Hey, that's all in the past now. This is our future. You are my future."

A tear rolls down her face and I reach up to swipe it away.

"I love you," she says, so quietly I almost miss it. My heart stutters in my chest before kicking back into double time. "Drew, I love you," she says again, louder this time.

"I love you more than you could ever know," I say. "From

the day you walked into my dorm room and told me your name, I have loved you. Through every awful Christmas party we had to attend with my parents and all of the wonderful summer days we spent on the beach, I have loved you. I never stopped loving you, not even once. I'll never stop loving you."

Chapter 90

Lexa

Sunday

Our last full day was yesterday. We spent it sightseeing and enjoying the island one last time before finishing the trip off with a beautiful dinner at the nicest restaurant on the resort. Drew stayed in my room again last night. We decided there was really no point in staying separate, one of us would have just ended up in the other's villa at some point in the night.

It's still dark out when we get up. Waking up next to Drew has quickly become something I want to do every day. We're both smiling softly, talking about the trip and mundane things like the weather. I just like to hear his voice, so I'll keep him talking with whatever I can.

Since his midnight declaration of love and the news that he is back in Savannah, our relationship has settled into something very comfortable. Without even really talking about it, we already decided he'd be moving in with me when we get back since I'm established there. He's excited to become a cat dad and Sneakers loves him.

Lost in my thoughts of the future again–but for entirely different reasons this time–I don't hear him walk up right behind me. "Well I'm all packed, what about you?" Drew asks, wrapping his arms around my stomach. I nod my head, looking around the room again, making sure to scan all the surfaces.

"And you're sure you double checked your room?" I ask, letting my hands fall to rest on top of his forearms.

"Yes ma'am," he says with a smile in his voice. "Remember, you inspected it thoroughly yesterday before we brought all my stuff over here."

"True enough," I say, spinning to look at him. "Well we still have like 30 minutes before we have to meet up with the group. Can you think of anything we could do to kill some time?"

In answer, Drew picks me up by my ass and tosses me onto the bed. He crawls over the top of me, undoing the buttons to my shirt as he goes. He pulls off my pants and underwear in one motion and tosses it all on the floor. Once I'm fully naked, he leans back and gazes down at me. I feel my cheeks heat and then the flush spreads down to my collarbones. Drew leans down, pressing hot kisses to the already heated skin.

"Are you going to join me or just stare at me?" I ask, giggling.

He growls, ripping off his shirt and divesting himself of his shorts and briefs quickly thereafter. "Better?" he asks, gruffly.

"Much," I say, still breathless at the sight of him. "Now

come here."

✿

It's a miracle we make it onto the little plane on time. "Couldn't just keep your hands to yourselves for five minutes?" Ansley asks once we're settled into our seats.

"You know how it is, I had to look for my hair brush three times before realizing I had already packed it," I answer with a shrug.

"Mhm, not buying that for one second."

I just smile at my best friend until she's grinning back at me. She blows me a kiss and turns to talk to Landon about the logistics once we get to the airport.

"That reminds me," Drew says, "I kinda already made plans for us once we land in Savannah." He threads his fingers through mine as I raise an eyebrow in question. "Sunday dinner with my parents. I thought maybe they'd like to hear the good news from us."

I reel back slightly in my seat. I hadn't even thought of their parents. Oh God, what are they going to think?

"Hey, Lex, come back to me," Drew says, turning my face to look him in the eyes. "My parents are going to be thrilled. Do you know how many times they've asked me when I'm going to ask you out over the years? They're going to be ecstatic."

"You're sure?" I ask nervously.

"I'm positive. They already love you, what's this going to change?"

I smile at him with some residual angst but try to push past it to see the positives. His parents do already know me and love me. This is going to be fine.

✿

I don't think a meal at the Parkers has ever filled me with so much nervous energy. We're standing outside the house, Drew on one side and Ansley on the other. When I found out Ansley was coming too, it made me feel a little less on edge. She'd at least be a buffer. Drew reaches down, taking my hand and we all walk towards the door. Landon and Anlsey step up and ring the doorbell. Mrs. Parker answers with a warm smile and says she's so glad we're all here. She hugs Ansley and then Landon, ushering them inside before turning back to me and Drew. Her eyes immediately track down to our entwined hands and her smile takes over her entire face.

"Finally," she says, placing her hand on her chest. "Come here, Lexa dear. Let me give you a proper hug."

Drew squeezes my hand before dropping it and letting his mom pull me in. Mr. Parker comes to the door after greeting his daughter and son-in-law. He pulls Drew in with a handshake. Once we're all inside the front door, Mrs. Parker turns to her husband and says, "It's finally happening. They were holding hands when I opened the door."

"About damn time son!" Mr. Parker bellows before wrapping Drew and I up into a bear hug. He lets Drew go, but keeps hold of me. "Now, little lady, I know he's my blood, but he steps outta line and you come find me okay?"

"Thanks Dad," Drew huffs. But he's smiling. And so am I. This is going to be just fine.

Epilogue

Lexa

April

Drew popped the question in September, saying he just didn't want to wait any longer. We had a gorgeous December wedding with all of our friends and family in attendance. Claire and Jackson have gotten engaged. Patrick and Connor have their brewery in town where Drew is the Director of Marketing. PaCo Brewery even provided the beer for our reception.

It's been a wonderful year since the anniversary trip. Our family is getting together for Easter today. *Our family*, I love that. Ansley and Landon are meeting us at the Parkers' house for dinner. We have some news we need to share and it feels right to do it today while everyone is together.

We have our round of hugs at the door, then another round once we're in the kitchen. I have found the most loving family and I wouldn't trade it for the world. Both Ansley and I have to work tomorrow night but we're off tonight and get to spend it here. The men all congregate in the living room to talk about sports and work. Us women head into the kitchen to talk about the men.

"He said what?" I say, almost spitting the water from my mouth.

"Yeah, he said that orange is not my color," Ansley says.

"Was he maybe referring to the prison jumpsuit you'd be wearing if you would have gone through with that?" I ask.

"Well maybe. But still. Everything is my color," she says, flipping her chestnut hair over her shoulder.

The three of us dissolve into snorting laughter, drawing the men into the kitchen to check on us.

Once we're all in the same room, I see my opportunity. I turn to Ansley and say, "So I've been meaning to let you know, if you're planning for any trips this summer, we might not be able to make it. We'll be saving up for the baby."

Gasps fly from the mouths around us and Drew scoops me up into his arms, kissing me on the cheek. I turn to find my best friend crying big happy tears. She wipes them from her face, resting her hand on her stomach before saying, "Well it looks like our little one is going to have a ready-made best friend." More gasping and crying. Landon picks me up as Drew picks up his little sister and we're both being spun around like kids. Once we're set down, we immediately find each other, crying and snotty but so happy. We'll be pregnant together, raising a little set of best friends and giving them the best family any could ever dream of.

I guess that old saying is true after all–good things come to those who wait.

About the Author

Our author, Leah Beach, originates from a small town in North Alabama. She attended the University of Alabama, where she fell in love with nursing. She moved to South Alabama where she works in the Emergency Room with her best friends.

Leah is married to Nick, who is a teacher. Together, they help coach the girls' soccer team at his school. They were high school sweethearts and stayed together through separate college careers.

Leah's main love in life is helping people, either through nursing or coaching, she lives to serve others. Coming in a very close second, is reading. You can catch Leah with a book in her bag whether it's on the beach or at dinner. You never know when you need an emergency book, or just to kill some time.

This is Leah's debut novel, but we hope to see many more from her in the years to come!

You can connect with me on:

🌐 https://www.amazon.com/author/leahbeach